WALKING 400 ALASKAN MILES TO HOME

CHARLES BROBST

Copyright © 2023 Charles Brobst.

All rights reserved. No part of this book may be reproduced, stored, or transmitted by any means—whether auditory, graphic, mechanical, or electronic—without written permission of both publisher and author, except in the case of brief excerpts used in critical articles and reviews. Unauthorized reproduction of any part of this work is illegal and is punishable by law.

ISBN: 979-8-89031-201-3 (sc)
ISBN: 979-8-89031-202-0 (hc)
ISBN: 979-8-89031-203-7 (e)

Because of the dynamic nature of the Internet, any web addresses or links contained in this book may have changed since publication and may no longer be valid. The views expressed in this work are solely those of the author and do not necessarily reflect the views of the publisher, and the publisher hereby disclaims any responsibility for them.

One Galleria Blvd., Suite 1900, Metairie, LA 70001
1-888-421-2397

CHAPTER 1

Harry Miller was sitting at the kitchen table drinking coffee while reading the Anchorage Daily News, this was his daily ritual when Samantha his wife came into the dining room.

Harry was always an early riser and had already eaten his breakfast of bacon and eggs a meal he had almost every morning. Sometimes he sliced a small Yukon Gold potato and fried it in the bacon fat before he fried his eggs. "Good morning, Sam, there's fresh coffee in the pot and if you want, I'll make you some bacon and eggs." Harry said.

"That sounds good," Samantha replied as she sat down. Harry got up, taking his coffee cup with him, he topped his off and poured her a cup of coffee, he started some bacon frying. Taking both cups into the dining room handing one to her he sat down to his paper.

Samantha took a sip, "This taste's different from our regular coffee what did you do?"

"I told you last week that I wanted to try some different coffee so I ordered some from Black Rifle Coffee Company, how do you like it?"

"It tastes richer more flavorful compared to Folgers, I like it."
"Adam's birthday is next week what should we get him for a present?" Samantha asked.

"I was thinking he will turn 14 and next month on August 20th Moose season starts. I know last year; he was disappointed that I didn't take him along when Michael and I went hunting." Michael was their oldest grandson who was 16 years old.

1

When Harry graduated from high school, he was 17 years old. He convinced his mother to sign the papers so he could enlist in the Army. While he was at AIT, he made some friends, or so Harry thought. One night there was a Sargent on Post trying to get people to sign up for Airborne training. He was in fresh starched fatigues with a crease in them so sharp it looked like you could cut butter with the crease. It started with his three friends, "I'll sign if you sign," "If you sign, I'll sign." So, Harry went over and signed up for Airborne training, he turned to give the pen to one of his buddies and saw that they were across the narrow street laughing. Harry laughed at being snookered but he took it good naturedly and became a paratrooper. Ever since then, even though he wasn't a Catholic, he had a St. Michael's medal around his neck along with his dog tags.

After jump school he was assigned to the 1st of the 504 with the 82nd Airborne Division. It was boring duty, KP, Guard Duty, Work Details and the incessant inspections on Friday for a weekend pass.

One day he was pulled out of the morning formation and told to go to the motor pool to get a duce-and-a-half truck and report to a Sargent Carmichael at Sicily Drop Zone. He liked going to the drop zones, it was easy duty and he liked driving that type of truck.

When Harry got there, he was surprised to only see a jeep parked in the vehicle area, when there was a jump, usually there were six or seven trucks parked there some with trailers for the used parachutes. He turned his truck off and got out to stretch his legs when a soldier wearing a Green Beret came over to him. Harry still remembers the conversation.

"You must be our ride." The Sargent said, "take it easy for a while they'll soon be here". Harry went to a picnic table and sat on the tabletop with his shoes on the bench seat. He soon heard an airplane overhead and looking up he saw a C-130 at an altitude higher than the normal drop altitude. Harry then saw black specks leave the plane and holy shit their chutes didn't open.

Then the chutes opened one by one. They weren't the standard T-10 but a different type of chute. The jumpers steered their chutes and landed gracefully on their feet three hundred feet in front of him.

Laughing they secured their chutes and walking to his truck putting on Green Berets. One of them dropped the tailgate on his truck and as they loaded their chutes, he saw what he thought was a familiar face.

"Hey Harry," the guy said, it was Josh from high school. He was on the basketball and baseball team with Harry but in class two years ahead of him. Josh took a note pad out of his shirt pocket and wrote down his unit and gave it to Harry telling him to come by. He said that there was no KP, Guard duty or any of the chicken shit he has in the Division.

When Harry dropped the team off on Smoke Bomb Hill a Master Sargent saw Harry talking with Josh and walked over to them. The Master Sargent talked to Josh a minute then asked Harry if he wanted to join them. Harry didn't know what to reply but what Josh said about no KP or Guard duty seemed to appeal to him so he said, "yes'. The next day after morning formation Harry was ordered to go to the Orderly room and report to the First Sargent.

Harry rapped on the door-jam of the orderly room and entered. A PFC company clerk looked up from a typewriter, "dam Harry what did you get yourself into, Top is pissed. Come with me."

The Clerk rapped on the First Sargent's door-jam and was ordered to enter. The PFC told Harry to enter and left.

On entering Harry stood in front of the First Sargent's desk at attention. "Stand easy Private Miller. I didn't know that Special Forces was recruiting Private's."

"I met a high school buddy the other day who is in Special Forces. I think he might have had something to do with this First Sargent," Harry said.

"Here are your orders, you have two days to clear the company, turn in your TA-50 to Supply and your weapon, gas mask and bayonet to the armorer and any other company property you might have. I hope you enjoy eating snakes now get the hell out of here."

At the suggestion of an uncle, before Harry left home for Basic Training, he started a savings account at the local bank in his home town. He had a small allotment from his pay going into it then when he was deployed to Vietnam, he had most of his pay sent to it.

He re-enlisted when he was in Vietnam and since he had a critical MOS, he got a very good re-enlistment bonus that money also went into his savings account.

While in the Special Forces on his first tour in Vietnam, Harry received a commission as a Second lieutenant. He eventually became a Captain and lead an A Team. On his last deployment to Vietnam, the team Harry was leading was ambushed by Vietcong. Harry laid down suppressive fire and though wounded he helped carry two of his wounded teammates to an LZ for pick up. For this he received a Purple Heart and the Distinguished Service Cross for Gallantry. His enlistment was soon up and after recovering from his wounds he was medically discharged with a 70% disability.

Harry went back to his parent's house and when he found out that his mother was planning a welcome home party against Harry's wishes.

Harry withdrew all of his money from the bank, closing the account and had his brother give him a ride to the Philadelphia airport where he bought a one-way ticket to Anchorage, Alaska. While in Special Forces Harry did some winter training at Black Rapids Glacier. Harry loved the remote area and vowed if he ever could he would return to Alaska.

Harry joined the Teamsters 959 Union; getting a job driving a truck three days a week from Anchorage to Seward or the town of Kenai hauling groceries.

The construction of the Alaskan Pipeline was starting and he got a job on the pipeline driving a dump truck, instead of a two week on and a two week off schedule like everyone had, since he lived in a small apartment in Anchorage and had no one to go home to, he put his few belongings into storage and gave up the apartment, he stayed on the job for four years. He thought it was just like being in the Army. He was put up in a camp, there was a 24-hour mess hall, showers and laundromat. All but one hundred dollars went into his Bank of Alaska savings account, after four years he had a very large six figure account.

With the end of the pipeline construction many people that helped construct it left Alaska, at the height of construction over 50,000 people worked on the pipeline. As a result of all the people leaving for other construction jobs in other parts of the country there was a recession in

Alaska. Anchorage was hit the hardest, there was a sell off of all sorts of property. He managed to buy three fourplexes outright at bankruptcy auctions and was able to get a fourth paying a good down payment.

At one of these auctions Harry met Samantha his future wife. During the pipeline construction she was a cook and later became a dump truck operator. She had bought two fourplexes and a duplex at these auctions. Although they were competitors at these auctions, they became friends. They both realized that they had a lot in common and enjoyed each other's company.

When dating Samantha, she once asked him if he was a Catholic because of his St. Michaels medallion around his neck and his reply was, "St. Michael is the patron saint of airborne and God's archangel. It is only fitting that I wear his medal. It kept me safe all of these years."

When they got married and their son was born, Harry insisted, much to the consternation of Harry's mother, who wanted a different name, that he be named Michael. Knowing how Harry felt Samantha agreed to it.

Michael was their only child. Michael grew up, served in the Army as a helicopter pilot. When he was in the Army, he married and had two sons named Michael Junior and Adam. Since Michael was a helicopter pilot in the Army with over one-thousand hours of flight time and experience, he easily got a pilot's job with a small bush airline in Anchorage.

Michael liked flying. He bought a Cessna 180 and took Harry up a few times, Harry enjoyed flying in small airplanes around the state, so Harry got his pilot's license and also bought a Cessna 180.

Michael along with his wife and several other pilots always helped the Iditarod Sled Dog race every winter hauling dog food and supplies to the check points for the mushers. On a trip back from a delivery to the town of Iditarod Michael and his wife never made it back to Merrill Field.

The search for them was one of the largest in Alaska at that time with the CAP, Army helicopters from the 120th. Aviation Company, Air Force rescue helicopters, National Guard helicopters, even the Coast Guard from Kodiak Air Station sent a rescue helicopter and an electronic C-130 to search for an ELT beacon, none was located. After two weeks the search was called off, but when everyone gave up Harry still flew looking for them. A large low pressure came in from the Bearing Sea and in the area where it was suspected it snowed heavily for three days. During that time Harry took his airplane to a friend's maintenance hangar and had a switch installed that when flopped made his landing lights flash alternately, this was so other pilots could see him easier. He also had another red strobe light mounted to the belly of his airplane. When it cleared Harry knew what he had to do. He flew low and slow over the area looking for evidence of carrion eaters. As goulash and horrific as it may be, a large group of Ravens or tracks of foxes or coyotes in the snow all going to the same place could lead him to the bodies of his son and his wife. He knew he was no longer on a rescue mission but a retrieval mission. After a month Harry had to finally accept that his son and daughter-in-law were dead somewhere in Alaska.

Harry and Samantha took their grandsons in and were raising them as their own. Over the years Harry and Samantha bought more rental properties and in the 80's when there was another recession in Alaska, they managed to purchase a small strip mall. They used one of the store fronts as an office for all of their rental properties. They had to hire two maintenance men to take care of the properties, mow the grass in the summer and plow the snow in winter plus repair all of the damage the tenants caused.

"So, I was thinking I would go to Sportsman's Warehouse and get him a .270 like Michael has."

"Do you think he is ready for such a big gun?" Sam asked. "Oh yeah, I take him to the Birchwood range with me, he can handle a 10/.22 quite well and I have allowed him shoot my 30.06 and M1A a few times, so I think he will be able to handle a .270."

Harry got up going into the kitchen he turned the bacon and cracked two eggs into the cast iron skillet, he then went back to the table.

"What are your plans for today," Samantha asked.

"Well, if you don't have anything planned, I would like to take the boys over to the garden and try to get the weeds under control."

"I'm sure they will love that," Sam said.

"Well, they better, since it will teach them how to grow food if the time ever comes when we need to do it, also, it's time I start teaching them how to can vegetables with the pressure canner."

"Why don't you come along, you can pick snails out of the garden then if you get enough tonight, I'll stir-fry them in garlic butter and put them on a bed of rice."

"No, you won't," Sam said.

Harry just chuckled took a sip of his coffee and got up to get Sam's bacon, eggs and toast.

"Well look who is finally awake," Harry said as Mike and Adam came into the dining room. "Do you guys want some bacon and eggs?" Harry asked.

"How about some French Toast," Adam asked.

"Yeah, I'll take some French Toast," Mike replied.

Harry took Samantha's breakfast to her and went back to the kitchen to make the boys some French Toast as Mike pulled the sports section from the paper Adam grabbed the comic section and Samantha took the rest of the paper. *Well, there goes my reading of the rest of the paper,* Harry thought.

"Do you guys have any plans for today?" Harry asked. "Who? You talking to us?" Mike said.

"Mike be careful what you say," Adam said, "when Granddad asks this question, he usually has some work for us to do."

"I was thinking of going to the Dimond mall and hang out with Jessica at Dave and Busters," Mike said.

"What about you Adam, what do you have planned?"

"I guess whatever you have planned for us," Adam replied.

"Good reply," Harry said. "We must weed the garden; the Chickweed, Horse Tail and Bird Vetch are starting to get out of control and the garden must be checked for slugs before those slimy bas.."

"HARRY!" Sam said loudly.

"I was going to say those slimy Gastropod's"

"Sure, you were" Sam said.

"Before those slimy Gastropod's eat all the vegetable plants." Harry said. "Mike tomorrow is the Fourth of July you can spend all day with Jessy down at the Park Strip but today I need you and Adam's help."

"What do you have there," Samantha asked? "A bottle of Alaskan Amber," Harry said. "And what are you going to do with that?"

"I read that slugs like fermented stuff and people make slug traps with beer and paper cups." "Well don't use good stuff like that get some Budweiser that stuff is cheaper and tastes like crap."

"Since when have you become a connoisseur of beer?" Harry said as he and the boys left.

CHAPTER 2

Harry was up early, he had breakfast and headed out the door before anyone was up. He was in one of his moods and didn't want to be around people, not even his own family. He liked the Fourth of July and parades but Anchorage was different.

There is an Air Force Base and an Army Post on the North side of the city but not even a color guard from either showed up, and the bands, well there was only one and it was a made-up ad-hock group.

With over six high schools in the area there were no marching bands in any of them. With all of the service organizations like VFW's, American Legions, Moose, Elks, Rotary and others not one drum and bugle corps, and when the few American flags that did go by, he was the only one who stood up and because he was a combat veteran, he saluted the flag to stares and an occasional snicker from the people around him.

At the picnic on the Park Strip there was a portable stage set up and the music that came from it was everything but the patriotic songs that he remembered as a boy. It also seemed the bands felt that the louder they played, the better they sounded. Harry soon had a headache from the volume and the music.

Harry was headed to the garden by himself, it had been 2 days since he was there and he wanted to see if the beer traps had caught any slugs. He unlocked the tool shed at the garden getting out a hoe he went to the first trap.

He had buried 8 Red Solo cups the first one was full of slugs. He went to all 8 cups and they were all full of slugs. Damn this really works Harry thought, well let's empty them and do it again as he went to the shed and got a small trash bag like you use in small trash cans and two cans of Budweiser beer from the six pack he bought. It didn't matter if the beer was warm, Harry felt that the slugs didn't care.

He emptied the Cups into the trash bag and put more beer into the cups and then placed them back into the holes they came out of. He had a little beer left in the can so he thought what the hell and dug a hole for it also. Harry was feeling a little better it was almost like his anger towards the Liberals on the fourth was consumed by killing slugs.

Harry checked his watch it was almost 9 AM he locked up his tools into the shed and headed to Sportsman's Warehouse to get a rifle for Adam's birthday which was tomorrow.

When Harry went into Sportsman's, he headed back to the firearm area and was looking around when he heard his name called. He turned and saw David Yoder behind him.

"What are you doing here," David asked?

"Tomorrow is my youngest's grandson's birthday and I'm here to see what kind of .270's you have that I can afford."

"Well let me show you a Remington they have a 15% mail in company rebate right now and they are good rifles." I know they have good rifles but the past three times I bought a Remington product and mailed in their rebate I received nothing back so I stopped buying Remington products unless they have an immediate in store savings." Harry said.

"I'm sorry to hear that but you aren't the only person who told me this. Here is a Savage they are good rifles and not too pricy." As David opened the bolt action, he handed Harry the rifle.

"These are fine rifles but my oldest son Michael has one of these, I guess we could do something with it so it is different from Michaels that they won't get them mixed up." "I guess I'll take it. I need a gun case and some ammo for it and my 30.06. I'll be back after I pick those items up and pay for it and then fill out the 4473."

"Fine it'll be here when you get back."

Adam's birthday party went fairly well. We had a store-bought cake and I grilled some hot dogs and hamburgers. A few neighbors came by to wish Adam a Happy Birthday but I suspected it was more for a burger and the beer that I had in a cooler. Tom with his ever-present cup of wine in his hand and his teenage son came by, Tom Samuels is my next-door neighbor who is an alcoholic, a mooch and a gossip, his son when growing up swiped a few of my grandkid's smaller toys. Now that he is a teenager there are a few things that happened in the neighborhood, a few minor things came up missing from the yards. Tom has a few people in the neighborhood believing it is my grandsons that are doing it but I know who is doing it.

My grandsons, Michael has classes at King Career Center and is studying Wildfire management hoping to get his Red Card next year to be able to fight forest fires in the state and Adam is taking courses there for automotive repair. They are out going boys and in winter help the neighbors shovel snow. Tommy Jr. sits at home and plays video games. So, many of the neighbors who are close to us really know what is going on and don't pay attention to Tom Senior.

Whenever a few of us neighbors get together the subject of food storage usually comes up. I once asked Tom about his food storage in case of an emergency, he replied he didn't have any, he would just come to my house for food. He would help himself to my lawnmower in the summer and my snowblower in the winter but when I caught him with my Stihl chainsaw that is when I laid the law down and locked my shed. Since then, things were cool between us. I tolerated him and his son just to keep peace in the neighborhood.

On Monday after Adam's birthday, we went to Birchwood Shooting Range to sight in all of our rifles for hunting season. I chose Monday because it was members only that day and the range wouldn't be crowded. The rest of July and into August the boys and I alternated between going to the range and working at the garden, we started to pick vegetables as they matured, I taught them how to pickle with a water bath canner and fresh can them with a pressure canner.

"When are you going to bring the motorhome to the house to pack it?" Samantha asked.

"I'm thinking on the 10th and leave on the 15th. The season opens on the 20th."

"Why so soon," Sam asked.

"Well after last summer I want some leeway if something happens." Remember last summer we were headed to Homer to go Halibut fishing when a spark plug blew out of the engine of the motorhome. Luckily, we were in Soldotna and were able to limp back to Riverside campground. We were lucky to find a mechanic to come to the campground to replace the plug. The mechanic said that on the Ford Triton engine they were notorious to blow a plug after 100,000 miles. Ford knows it and you can buy a self-threading plug replacement kit at most auto parts stores. When we got back to Anchorage, I took our motorhome to Rally Automotive and had them check the other plugs.

"I'm going to NAPA and getting 3 spark plug kits just in case and I'll also load a better tool set."

"You guy's better be coming home and not be broken down in the boonies," Sam said.

"I hope to be back by the 30th and we will still be able go to the fair in Palmer," I replied.

"Where are you going?" Sam asked.

"I'm thinking of going to the Taylor Highway near Chicken, I overheard two guys talking at the range, one was up there several weeks ago, he said he saw several bulls that looked legal."

I brought the motorhome a 29-foot 1997 Winnebago home and started loading it with food, clothing, rain gear, I drained the water holding tank, flushed it and refilled it, loaded a bunch of tools just in case and our back packs with frames. We would carry these while hunting they had homemade game bags made from un-bleached muslin cloth. The muslin was strong and durable and could be washed after its use, and re-used not like some of the other game bags sold in stores. Plus, we each had a small 1,000-pound metal block and tackle, a moose can weigh 1,000 pounds or more and these make it easier to move them around to gut them, a bunch of para-cord and all the other things we put into them over the years.

Samantha came out of the house to wish us luck.

"I told her to remember to feed the rabbits and chickens and to collect their eggs and when we get back, I'll clean their pens and butcher the rabbits that were ready to eat and not to allow Tom to borrow anything or give him anything and to watch out for Tommy."

She said she would, we had a goodbye kiss and the boys and I left.

AUGUST 16

"Well guys what do you think?" I asked.

"Let's go down the road a little more the map shows some lakes, swampy areas and a little rise about 2 or three miles ahead." Adam said.

We were using an Alaska Gazetteer map book to look for a likely area to hunt.

"You guys know that the rocks and stones on this road are rough on these old tires and I haven't replaced them in a few years."

"Yes, but in another few miles we should find some good moose areas to hunt," Michael said. As luck would have it, we came around a corner and saw the road dipped down and across a swampy area, there was a gravel cut alongside of the road where the state took gravel from the side of a hill to build and repair the road. It was a good place to back into and as I did so while the boys directed me so I wouldn't hit anything, but what I was worried about happened, a tire went flat. I couldn't get angry I expected this and had bought an extra tire and rim from Alaska Tire and Rim before we left Anchorage. I knew the owner and delt with him for over twenty years, he gave me a good deal saying he wanted some steaks if we were lucky.

I looked at Adam, "you're the mechanic you know what to do." He just grinned at me and got the jack, leveling boards a tire wrench and went to work. When we went through Glennallen I stopped and filled the gas tank, I had this thing about gas and traveling in Alaska, I also did it again at Tok so when we stopped, we had just over three-quarters tank of fuel. I thought this will be enough to run the generator and get back to Tok for more fuel on the way back home.

After the tire was changed, we leveled the motorhome, dropped the awning down and set up camp. The boys wanted to start a fire but I said no that I didn't want wood smoke to scare anything away. They grumbled but understood.

We had four more days before the season opened so we did a few walks around the area to get the lay of the land. We had binoculars and looked the lakes and swampy areas over. I didn't want to shoot a bull in this area but we all brought hip waders just in case. On these trips we took GMRS radios with ear buds to check them out since my plan was to split up and hunt different areas to increase our odds of getting a moose.

We were walking the road back to our camp and occasionally a motorhome that was pulling a trailer with 4 wheelers went past us.

"What's the bet that when we get back to camp there will be another camper there," Mike said.

"I hope not," I replied, "but the odds are that there will be one there." Sure, enough when we turned a corner, we saw another motorhome in the gravel cut we were in. *Oh well, it's a free country and I don't own this area so let's see what they are like I thought.*

As we came walking up, I gave a little cough, "I heard you" a chubby but solid bearded old man in bib overalls with a large wad of something in his right cheek said. He turned his head and sent a brown stream down range and stood up from the easy chair he was sitting in. As he stuck his hand out, "the name's Ken" he said. As I grabbed his hand, it was a strong callused hand a hand that did a lot of work, a firm but not a challenging shake.

"I'm Harry and these are my grandsons Michael and Adam," I replied.

Just then his camper door opened, "This is my oldest son Henry and his son Jerry is around here somewhere," Ken said. "You guys just get here," Ken asked.

"No, we've been here for a few days," I said. Ken looked around "No fire," he said.

"No sir, we didn't want to scare anything off with wood smoke." Mike said.

Ken launched another brown stream and nodded his head and muttered "good thinking, good".

"Which way are you guys going tomorrow, I don't want to step on any toes or get shot," Ken said.

"Well," I replied, "the swamp and small lakes down there have some hills on both sides of them so I was going to send Mike down the road and then turn right and go along that ridge and Adam and me will go straight out on the ridge on this side."

"That sounds like a good plan the road goes across the swampy area and behind us is another lake and swamp and We plan on doing something like that back there," Ken said.

"Sounds like a plan," I said and looked quizzically at his chair. Ken chuckled, "Just because you are outside it doesn't mean you cannot be comfortable." He looked at Adam and said, "your first hunt young man?"

Adam nodded and replied, "yes sir."

"Well remember, once you pull the trigger the fun ends and that's when the work begins," and laughed and sent another brown stream down range. I noticed Ken always spit in the same general area and not randomly around the area.

"Mike how about you and Adam go in and get some supper going while I stay out here and talk with Ken awhile." Both boys left and I got my camp chair and sat by Ken. "Where are you guys from?" I asked.

"We come down from Fairbanks every year for opening day. We always try to camp in this spot. There is a little hill behind us to block the wind if it blows and a lot of good moose country here. If we don't get something on the first day usually by the third day, we get lucky." Ken replied. "What's on the menu?" Ken asked.

"Just some fried smoked sausage, fried potatoes with onion and a can of corn. I like to keep it simple when camping," I replied. "And you?" I asked.

"We were lucky, coming down the Richardson Highway we saw some Ptarmigan we stopped and shot a few. So, we're having roasted Ptarmigan tonight." "By the way Harry, do you know how the town of Chicken got its name?" Ken asked.

"I sure do, back in the day the miners there ate Ptarmigan in winter to keep from starving. They wanted to name the town Ptarmigan but no one knew how to spell Ptarmigan so they named it Chicken instead because the Ptarmigan looked like chickens." Harry replied.

Ken slapped his knee, spit and laughed, "You have been up here for a while, haven't you?"

"Yep," Harry said "a little over 40 years. I got up here in 1970 worked on the pipeline then when the real estate crashed at the end of its construction, I used my savings and picked up some fourplexes in Anchorage and as money became available, I bought more then, in the 80's crash I was able to buy a small strip mall. Then I got wind of Crypto currency and when Bit Coin came out, I gambled and bought some of them. How about you."

"Well, I also worked on the pipeline and when that ended, I started a construction company with the equipment that I bought at their surplus auction. My company helped to build some of the roads up here, we worked on the oil spill. I also bought some rental properties in the 80's."

Harry stood up tapping his ear, "I have just been told supper is ready. It was nice chatting with you, we will be running our generator for a while to charge our coach battery for the night and our radios. I'll shut it off before we go to bed so as not to disturb you."

"Bon Apatite," Ken said as he stood up and shook Harry's hand he also went to his camper.

AUGUST 20
OPENING DAY OF MOOSE SEASON

Harry got a bow saw out of one of the rear storage compartments on the motorhome and went to cut some small Birch trees down. Adam had shot a moose and Harry wanted to build an "A" frame to hang the meat. The boys went back to the carcass to bring more meat back while he lashed the trees together. Ken, his son and grandson came back and saw what Harry was doing and had his son and grandson help him. "I heard the shot and hoped it was you guys," Ken said.

"Adam shot him; they are trying to get more meat in before dark. I sat by him rattling deer antlers and after about an hour of doing this off and on a legal bull showed up. It is his first bull." Harry said.

"Well good for him." Ken said. Both Ken and Harry turned as Mike and Adam came across the road. They both looked beat but were smiling. "Did you get it all," Harry asked?

"No, we have one more trip and then it will all be in," Mike said. Harry looked at Ken, "Could I ask if you and your boy hang this meat while I get a lantern and go with my boys to bring in the rest of the meat?"

"Sure, we would be glad to help, you guys better hurry it will be dark in less than an hour."

"I know that's why I'm getting a lantern," Harry said. After two round trips there was a fairly well trampled trail to what was left of the moose carcass. They hurriedly went to the kill site and tied the last two bags of meat to the two pack frames and by now it was really dark.

Harry lit the Coleman lantern and it cast a bright circle of light but their bodies made dark shadows in the area. "We must be careful walking out so we don't twist an ankle. I'll walk in between you guys so both of you will get some light from the lantern." Harry said.

It was slow going, taking care where we stepped and a trail that was visible in daylight but almost disappeared in the darkness. After about a half hour of walking I was starting to worry that we had gotten off of the trail. I was ready to call a break to see if we were going the correct way when in the distance, I saw a lantern swinging back and forth.

Good old Ken or I hoped it was Ken, he was showing us our destination. I raised and lowered my lantern showing him that I see his lantern and the swinging stopped so we headed in his direction. We were about one-hundred feet from the road when I heard a "Woof" and then "Ow". I looked behind me and saw Adam lying face down on the trail with his pack weighing him down. *"Shit, I thought so close and yet so far."* I set the lantern down and went to him grabbing his pack I lifted him up. "Are you alright, are you hurt?" I asked him.

"Granddad, I think I twisted my ankle I'm sorry." "Don't be," I said "things happen." I took his pack off of him and had him sit, I took Adams hiking shoe off and was holding his ankle when Ken asked, "how bad is it?"

He startled me I thought, *for a big old man he sure was quite getting here.* "Adam can you move your foot?" Ken was holding his lantern up and I could see Adam wince a little as he wiggled his foot but I didn't feel any bones grating. *Good I thought just a sprain. We can handle that.*

"What's the verdict," Ken asked. "It feels like it is just a sprain." I replied.

"Well while it's a bummer that it happened at least it's not broken." Ken replied. "Give me his pack and I'll take it back to camp and you can help Adam back to camp," Ken said. He reached down and effortlessly picked the pack up, slinging it over his shoulder he grabbed the handle on his lantern and saying. "I'll be right behind you."

I grabbed Adams right arm and pulled it over my shoulder grabbing my lantern, we slowly proceeded to camp.

"Here put him in my chair," Ken said. "Henry, would you go into the camper and get my first aid kit please," Ken asked.

Henry came out with a large pack, giving it to Ken his father. Ken gently took Adams sock off and manipulated his ankle. You could see it was starting to swell and turn black & blue. "Well Henry you are correct it is a sprain I'll wrap it with a compression bandage and don't let him use it for a day or two. He should be good as new in about a week." Ken said.

Harry looked at Ken, "That's a pretty well stocked bag you have there." Ken smiled, "Yup, in another life I was a medic in the Army, I spent 14 weeks at Fort Sam Huston for basic medic training then I received more intense training. I once removed a guy's appendix and yes, he survived and no I didn't put any marbles in his abdomen."

Harry chuckled at Making reference to the movie Ensign Pulver. "Are you guy's going to pull out," Henry asked.

"I was thinking about that but since Adam has no serious injury, I think we will stay here for a day or two that's if we aren't bothering you," Harry Replied.

"That's fine with me and besides Adam can keep the old man company here at the camp." Henry replied.

"Who are you calling an old man, I helped bring you into the world and I can sure as hell chase you out," Ken replied launching a brown stream at Henry's feet.

Henry just chuckled and turning said, "I'm going to get supper started."

"Henry, wait a minute," Harry said, "let me give you this," as he opened one of the muslin bags and pulled out a backstrap from the moose. "This is for helping us," Harry said.

"You don't need to do this but if you insist, we'll take it with thanks," Ken replied. "Mike will you help Adam to the motorhome while I hang these two bags and I'll bring the other backstrap in for our supper," Harry said.

"Sure Grandpop, no problem and backstrap for supper sounds good."

AUGUST 21

Harry woke up, he laid in bed for a minute, something was wrong. He listened was there a bear at the meat hanging outside or was an unlucky hunter trying to steal part of it? He listened but he didn't hear anything. Getting up and pulling the covers back, *damn it's cold in here* he thought. Putting his pants on he hit the bedroom light switch and nothing happened. *Damn the coach battery is dead* he thought that is why it's cold there is no power to the furnace blower. He went into the bathroom and relieved himself thinking *why do the motorhome companies make these rooms so small are they designed by anorexic people or midgets,* he thought.

He went to the kitchen area and found a flashlight in a drawer, turning it on he checked the idiot panel on the wall to see if there was any power in the battery, nothing. He took the vehicle ignition key from his pocket to start the vehicle, this would give power to start the generator, and turning the key, Nothing. Shit he thought now I'll have to get the dashboard solar panel and have it trickle charge the vehicle battery. This will probably take 2 or three days to do. Harry went outside for the Coleman lantern and brought it into the motorhome, lighting it he fished around the cabinets for coffee grounds and filling a pot with water, the pressure was weak so he got two bottles of drinking water and filled the pot. He lit a burner on the propane stove and put the pot on to brew.

Over the hiss of the lantern, he heard a light tapping on the camper door. Harry picked up a Ruger Blackhawk .44 magnum that was on the kitchen counter and realizing he had it loaded with bird shot shells in case they saw some Ptarmigan. *Well, they will still hurt* he thought. He stood off to the side in front of the refrigerator and in a low voice called out "who's there?"

"Harry it's me Ken, may I come in."

"Yes of course come in," Harry replied. Entering Ken looked around, "Either you like to work in the dark with a lantern or your power is also out." The coffee was done perking on the stove so Harry turned off the burner and grabbed two cups out of a cabinet pouring one for Ken and one for himself. Blowing on it to cool it Harry looked at Ken, "you don't have power on your rig, did you try your vehicle engine?"

"Yup," Ken replied.

Harry thought *we have no power and Ken doesn't have any power we're screwed.*

Ken replied taking a sip of coffee. "There are only two things that can do this and both aren't good."

Harry replied, "that's what I figure either way we're screwed."

"Michael, get up, Ken, swat his feet wake him up and get him off of the couch." "I'm awake," Mike said. "So am I," Adam chirped from the overhead bunk. Harry took the top off of the coffee pot and removed the grounds holder, he took the pot and topped off Kens and his cup, then he put more grounds on top of the used grounds and started another pot of coffee.

Ken looked at him and cocked his head.

"This will soon be worth its weight in gold so I'm recycling the old grounds with some fresh ones."

Picking up his cup taking another sip and looking at Harry, "yup we're screwed."

"You live in Fairbanks, that's what? About three hundred miles." Ken nodded his head, "more or less." "Let's see The Alaska Highway to Tok then Delta Junction, Ft. Greeley, Eielson Air Force Base, North

Pole then Fairbanks for you guys," Harry said, "and for us the Alaska Highway, Tok, Chistochina, Gakona, Gakona Junction, Gulkana, Glennallen, Tazlina, Eureka Lodge, Chickaloon, Sutton, Palmer, Eklutna, Eagle River then across Anchorage, a little over four hundred miles. We're not just screwed but royally screwed." Harry sighed.

"Yeah, and you have to get past those crazy natives at Chickaloon," Ken said "and Palmer Correctional, there is no telling what they will do with those prisoners with no electrical locks."

Harry turned the stove burner off and sat at the campers dining table, he took another large gulp of coffee, looking at Ken, "I have a tenant in Palmer that works there and I know what will happen and it will not be good for them. How much salt and pepper do you have in your rig," Harry asked.

Ken looked at him quizzically, "I put a new container in before we left home and about half of another of salt, and almost a full large can of pepper."

"We have two full ones and about half of another of table salt plus we have two five-pound bags of rock salt we use when camping to make ice cream and two large cans of pepper."

Ken took a big gulp of his coffee as Harry got up and refilled both cups. "Jerky." Ken said.

"Yes, we have about eight hundred pounds of meat and a long way to go but the meat even if we could carry it, would spoil in a few days, but if we make as much jerky as we can we should be alright for two or three weeks plus some other supplies I keep in here, maybe thirty days of food. I hope we can pick up some supplies in Tok or Glennallen but, I'll plan on not being able to and hope for rabbits, ptarmigan and maybe a caribou when we get past Glennallen."

"Don't forget, Sandhill Cranes will be migrating south, they are called prime rib in the sky by those who have eaten them and I must say they are right, they taste good." Ken said.

"We have a lot to do, it should take about a week to dry as much moose meat as we can before it spoils and this will allow Adam's ankle to heal." Harry said.

"The natives air-dry a lot of their salmon and meat so we will start a small smokey fire and hang strips of meat over it," Ken said. "And our stoves work so we soak strips of meat in a salt solution, dry it and put it on racks in the oven at 160 degrees. It should take about three or four hours to dry and then rub some pepper on them to keep flies off of them and we have zip lock bags to put them in." Harry said.

"What's going on?" Michael asked. I looked at Ken and nodded my head. "It seems someone turned the electricity off." Ken said.

Mike looked puzzled, "An EMP," Ken said. Mike's face looked serious then fearful, "what about Grand-mom?" he said.

"Well, we cannot do anything for her here and we surely cannot do anything for her if we lose our heads and go off half-cocked and die between here and there so we must have cool heads and plan what we are going to do," I said.

Ken drained his coffee; it looked like he had aged sitting there his shoulders were slumped. As he got up, "thanks for the coffee and when the sun comes up can you have Michael come to my trailer. I would like to send him and Henry to look for standing dead Birch trees for a fire." "I'll do that, there is a lot to do and really little time to do it because it's starting to get cold at night." Harry replied.

When Ken left, Harry said, "Boy's, it's time to get up we have a lot of work to do and not much time to do it. Get dressed and do what you have to do."

"Grandfather," Adam said with a quavering voice, "are we going to die?"

"Not if we work hard and work together, we have a long walk ahead of us and we must get ready. Now get dressed."

Harry went outside it was still dark but he could see with a half moon and stars, *dam he thought, it's pretty out here and he just stared at the sky for a minute,* Then, he softly said, "Lord watch over us and help us."

"Amen" he heard. He turned and saw Ken sitting in his chair with a cup of coffee. Ken turned his head and spit, "I wonder how fast this stuff will disappear," he said. "Well, the wife, always wanted me to stop. I guess she will soon get her wish."

"You said you had medical training at Ft. Sam, were you a medic in the army?" Harry asked.

"Well yes and no," I was with the teams for a few years." Ken said. "And your son Henry. Does he have any military time?" Harry asked.

"Yes, he was in three years and a deployment to the sand box," Ken replied. "How about you, do you have any military time?" Ken asked.

"De Oppresso Liber," Harry replied. "Dam it's a long time since I heard that," Ken said, "Hell, I now think we might have a chance to get out of this or at least to Tok."

"Yeah, I believe the first leg should be somewhat easy, it will give us a chance to get our legs back. I wish we could leave now but I would hate to see all of this meat go to waste and I have Adam's ankle to think about."

"In a week the boy should be ok if he stays off of it now," Ken replied.

"That's what I think also, so that gives us time to make as much jerky as we can." "I was thinking, if we get three poles about ten feet long and about two inches in diameter, I can build a tepee of sorts with some tarps I have. We could build Willow racks in it and a smokey fire with Alder chunks in it. This way we could dry more meat, because we won't be able to make enough in our ovens."

"Before I send Mike over to you, I'm going to want him to crawl under our motorhome with a few large bowls and I will open the drain cock and drain water out of our holding tank. Our pump doesn't work and this way I can make a salt brine and have Adam start cutting and brining meat while we construct what we have to do."

"Good idea," Ken said, "we have to keep everyone working to their ability." "We have room here for three or four tepees, but do we have enough to cover them?" Ken said. "I was hoping you saw this I think we can do five or more tepees, four for smoking and one to cut up the moose quarters. They won't fit in our camper whole so we have to make them smaller and there isn't enough room inside for all of us to work so some of this must be done outside." I spoke.

When it got a little lighter Harry had Michael crawl under the motorhome and every pot they had was filled with water. They washed both sides of the kitchen sink and drained more water filling the sinks with a brine solution so Adam could put the cut meat into them. They refilled the pots again and made a brine solution in them also.

Michael then went with Henry with a bow saw that was in a storage compartment in the camper and started cutting down Birch trees to build smoking tepees. Harry went down to the swampy area with a machete and cut Alder branches and Willow branches to make smoke and branch shelves in the tepees. Ken, with the help of his grandson drained water from his camper's water holding tank and also cleaned his sinks and was now cutting meat for smoking. Harry and Ken both agreed that the meat should soak about twelve hours before smoking.

As Mike and Henry came in with two-inch diameter Birch logs Harry would lash them with para-cord cut from the large reel that he had in the motorhome to make a tripod and as they raised the legs on the first one Harry brought out a large tarp. They unfolded it and tied one end to the top and as they raised it continued to bring the tarp around. It was a long wide tarp that Harry used every fall to cover the motorhome.

Harry left out a sigh, his shoulders sagging, grabbed his Buck 110 knife and cut the excess tarp off. There was enough for another tepee. Harry cut small slits down the two ends and used a piece of para-cord to lace them together.

They worked all day and by evening there were six tepees made, Harry cut the awning off of his motorhome to help make these, saying "I doubt that this won't run for several years and we need the awning for the tepee's." Harry also had collected a large pile of Willow and Alder.

Jerry and Ken were busy making Willow shelves for the Tepees, Kens 10-year-old Grandson Jerry was very adept at weaving the Willow twigs into shelves and before long they had three tepees ready for meat.

Fires were built in the smokers from some dead Birch, Harry didn't want to use Spruce since it would give off a bad taste.

Harry chopped some Alder into small pieces and put them into a bucket of water to soak. These would be pulled out of the bucket and let drain a little then be put on the fire bed to produce smoke. We cooked some moose meat for supper and continued to cut meat to marinate in the salt water and tend to the fires and meat in the motorhome ovens, these had to be checked at four hours, as well as the smoke tepees, here the meat had to be rotated from the bottom shelf to the top shelf every four hours so they would dry evenly. We also made more Willow shelves by lantern light.

Harry, Ken and Henry agreed to taking turns on guard duty through the night to maintain the smoke fires and to protect against bears.

The next day was a little easier in that we only had to get wood for the fires, make more shelves and of course cut more meat.

We now had all six tepees working along with the ovens in the campers. I found a bottle of teriyaki sauce and poured it into one of the brine tubs for something different and we put a light dusting of black pepper on most of the Jerky sticks before we put them into the smokers. This was to keep the flies off of the sticks.

Around one in the afternoon we had our first visitors. They caught us by surprise and fortunately they were friendly. It was two hunters stranded as we were. We invited them to our camp and talked a bit. They asked if we knew what happened and we said no we had no idea what happened. They were eyeing the moose meat hanging over the fire cooking. I looked at Ken, he got out of his chair and went into his trailer and came out with two plates and some forks, I noticed he now had a Colt 1911 on his hip. We told the new commers to lean their rifles against the front of Ken's camper and come sit and have some moose meat. As they were eating, they told us that they were from Anchorage but they were going to Chicken to see if they could spend the winter and then see what the situation was in the spring. They wanted to know if we knew how far they had to go to get to Chicken.

Ken told them that they had about 40 to 50 miles to hike down the road. They thanked us for the meal and before they left, I cut a large roast from the hind-quarter we were cutting up and told them to take it with them since they had two or three day walk ahead of them. Ken walked them to the road and stood there for a few minutes, I saw him wave and stand there.

When he came back, I had already gotten my sidearm in a leather holster on my belt and I also had Michael with a sidearm in a holster on his belt.

"That was close," Ken said "it could have gone either way and it wouldn't have been good for us." "I agree," I said. "We have the hill

25

behind us why don't we have someone with a rifle up there to provide overwatch for us." "Good idea," Ken said. "Where is Henry," I asked. "He's taking a nap for tonight," Ken said.

We went back to cutting meat and tending the fires. I went for more Alder and Willow, when I came back Henry was at our campfire eating a steak. Ken was sitting next to him talking and I saw Henry's head nodding. Henry stood up taking his plate into their camper and came out with a rifle and took off toward the back. Ken came up to me, "I asked Henry to provide overwatch and if there was any more dead Birch to toss them over the bank down to us."

The next day was more of the same but we had to get more water from the camper to make more brine. The way it was going I didn't think we would last seven days before we ran out of salt. We were on day three and we had already done one hind quarter and were almost done with the other. Tomorrow we will start on a front quarter they didn't have as much meat on them. I built a separate fire and went to the back of the motorhome and pulled a Dutch oven out. Taking it to the fire I just built setting it down I went into the camper and got three cans of sliced peaches, brown sugar, butter and mixed some Bisquick into a dough. I went outside and dumped the peaches into the Dutch oven, the brown sugar and butter on top then I put the Bisquick on top. I scraped some coals from the fire I built and leveled the rest of the coals. I put the Dutch oven on that bed and the coals on top of the lid. We cooked some moose meat over the fire and when we were finished eating, I went and got a pair of channel-lock pliers and removed the Dutch oven lid. The peach cobbler smelled good. I took it off the fire and we all got plates and spoons and dug in. I used to make this when we went camping with my son and later my grandsons. I thought, this will be the last time I use it since it was too heavy to take with us. I cleaned it and put it back where it belonged.

Adam up till now stayed in the camper and was getting stir crazy from cutting meat all day and not being outside.

Our camper door opened and Adam came walking out. Ken looked up. "Adam come over here and sit in my chair, let me look at your ankle." Ken unwrapped the bandage, we could see the swelling was way down, and moved Adam's foot asking from time to time if this or that hurt. "Harry, I think we can keep the bandage off and let him walk a little with it. It will do him good.

Day four was almost like the others, the only change was Ken and I decided we should start making up our packs to leave. I had my boys retrieve four-small eight-gallon Rubbermaid totes hidden in the space under my bed in the back of the motorhome. I had extra supplies in the old motorhome in case we ever had to leave our home in a hurry.

With my Foodsaver, I vacuum packed packages of Pinto beans, 15 bean packs with ham flavoring, Rice, Instant oatmeal, sugar, salt, ground coffee and instant cocoa mix in three of the totes and the fourth had a gun cleaning kit, two Beretta 92FS 9mm. pistols with 5 loaded 17 round magazines for each, four-50 round JHP boxes of 9MM ammo and two drop-leg holsters for them and four Balaclavas. We would take the Balaclavas with us since it will soon turn cold. I would take one drop-leg holster and a Beretta and Michael would get the other. My Ruger .44 and its ammo would go into my pack for now.

I took some zip lock bags out of a cabinet and filled them with supplies we had from the kitchen cabinets in the camper. We got our packs put back onto their frames and started making piles.

"Boy's" I said, "You must remember to pack some cold weather clothing and make sure you both have four pairs of wool socks."

I went over to Ken's camper and told him what we were doing, he agreed it was a good move. He said, "We have been here four days it could start getting dicey with any other hunters out here, they might be running low on food." "How are you guy's fixed for food to get heme", I asked. "I have some Mountain House meals, about ten days for us". "If you have a way to cook it, I can give you a bag of rice and a bag of Pinto beans that I packed in about one-pound bags and maybe some canned stuff if you want to carry them," I said.

We were as packed as we could be and still function cutting and drying meat. We were pushing, putting out as much as we could and then we would put the Jerky into zip lock bags. We divided the meat as equally as we could between Ken and his boys and us. It was getting to be a large amount and I thought maybe just maybe we could pull this off.

Adam's ankle seemed to be holding up around camp but I still made him take it easy.

Day five was like the other days when in the afternoon a rock landed close to the table where Ken and I were working. We looked up at the hill and Henry was pointing and showing he saw five people coming our way. I went into the camper and got my rifle. I told Michael to get his and follow me. I told Adam to get into the camper and stay there.

Michael and I went behind the camper, I whispered asking him if his rifle was loaded and a bullet in the chamber he nodded. I whispered for him to watch the right side of the camper and I was going to watch the left side.

I was watching the left side when three men appeared on the far side of the road and helloed the camp. Ken had his left side to the road shielding his pistol from the men. A pebble landed close to me and I looked at Henry, he signaled that he saw two were coming down the right side of the camper. I put my hand on Michael's shoulder and gently pulled him back. I gripped my rifle, I always liked Walnut stocks on rifles over the black plastic ones, and I got ready. They were quietly walking one behind the other trying to sneak around the motorhome. I gave the first one a vicious hard horizontal butt stroke to his chin and my rifle was perfectly positioned that with a step the butt went straight into the nose of the second one. The nose exploded like a ripe grape, I turned and hit the first one hard at the base of his skull with my rifle butt, spinning around I hit the other man a second time a hard stroke up beside his head. They both quietly went down while Michael watched this slack jawed. His grandfather just knocked out two men. I handed him my rifle and pulled a piece of parachute cord out of my pocket, rolling the first one onto his stomach I tied his hands to feet cross wise behind his back and then did the other one the same way. I grabbed my rifle from Michael and told him to get a stout stick and if they wake up to hit them with all of his might. I gave Henry a thumbs-up and crept to the front of my camper.

As I looked through the passenger and driver's windows, I saw that the three men had come across the road. I heard Sam say, "I told you, that you are welcome to part of that front quarter hanging back there."

"But that won't be enough to feed all of us through the winter, we want all of it, not just a front quarter. We are going to spend the winter here and we will need it."

"Well shoot a moose", Ken said.

I stepped around the front slightly on the road behind them

"But we need it also," I said.

One turned and lifted his rifle without thinking I pulled the trigger shooting from the hip, catching him in the chest. Henrys rifle barked from the top of the hill as Ken pulled his pistol and dropped the other one. A 180-grain soft-point hunting round from a 30-06 makes a hell of a hole coming out the back of a chest and I don't know what Henry was shooting but the other guy's head was missing half of it and Kens .45, well what can I say a .45 also makes a mess.

I was gathering their weapons when Ken asked me where the other two were. I said sleeping. We signaled Henry that we were alright and continued to gather their weapons and checked them for sidearms.

I heard Michael yell "GRANDPA" I spun and running around the front of the camper I saw that the two were awake and trying to get out of their bonds. I knew it was futile to try and they couldn't. A right hand was tied behind their back to their left foot and the left hand tied to the right foot. "Michael," I said "I told you to hit them if they woke up."

"But it would hurt them, I might kill them," Michael said. I looked around and saw a limb about two inches in diameter sticking out of a pile of dirt, I pulled it out of a dirt pile that was made by a dozer when they cleared this area for gravel for the road and walked over and hit one of them behind the head again. The other one started to cry asking not to hit him and he would behave. Michael looked at me with an expression like "What did I just see." Backing up, he thought, *his grandfather, who he always knew to be kind and gentle, who, he thought would never hurt a fly, just beat the shit out of two men with guns and one may be dead.* Harry grabbed their rifles and took them around to take to the other side of the camper to put with the other firearms, "Mike lets go around front," he said. Ken had picked up the firearms from the other men and they were laying on the cutting table. Adam came out of the camper and Jerry came out of the other camper. All three of them looked scared and were looking at Ken and me with a different look.

A look like they had just seen the Boogeyman. Jerry was the first to speak, "Grandfather what will the police do." "Son," Ken said softly, "There are no police anymore, no one to call if you are in trouble or someone is attacking you. Now we must take care of ourselves because there are no more police, firemen or paramedics to come to your aid when you dial 911, there is no more 911 it is all gone."

Michael and Aron looked at me, I nodded, "yes, all of those John Wayne movies you guys watched with me, well that is now." "We must take care of ourselves and do things the veneer of civilization we were wrapped in kept us from doing. It is no longer wrapped around us; it is now gone."

"Ken, what do you think? and how much Jerky do you estimate we have, and how is Adam's ankle?"

"The Jerky, I would guess both hind quarters weighed 150 or more pounds we got both done and part of a front quarter so I would guess we have about 200 or more pounds of meat dried, smoked and turned into jerky. Adam's ankle, well I would have liked to have it rest another day and your unspoken question, yes, tonight."

I had the boys unroll the sleeping bags we had and I had them put a wool Army blanket into each one and reroll them. They were summer bags and this would allow them to be good to temperatures around zero. I pulled winter jackets out of closets along with extra pants and shirts.

"Grandpop why do we need winter clothing," Adam asked.

"Because it will soon get cold and we will need it" Michael said. *Good I thought Michael is thinking.*

There was a lot I wanted to take but we were limited to what we could carry. I sat at the kitchen table and made a priority list: Food, Guns and ammo, Toilet paper, Water filter kit. matches, Ferro bar, clothing, first aid, cooking gear, sleeping bags a tarp for each of the boys from one of the tepees to sleep under, Para-cord, ax, saw, tools, there were more but I thought this will be a start. When I opened my tool box in the compartment in the back of the camper, I thought Channel locks, 6-inch Crescent wrench, Lineman's pliers, I then saw a one-pound roll of .032 stainless steel safety wire. That went into my bag.

Going through the outer compartments I found my Tackle Box, opening it a flood of memories came over me of taking Michael my son fishing and then his boys. The Fenwick rods made me stop. I saw a fish scale that went to 100 pounds and memories came to me. I thought of Mike's first King Salmon. He swore it was a hundred pounder and made me buy a scale at the Soldotna Sportsman's Warehouse to weigh it. I remember his dejection that it only weighed 35 pounds. I had to cheer him up saying it was a large King Salmon for the stream we were in. I heard a man's voice behind me softly say, *"Pop's it will be alright we will be with you, you'll make it,"* and a soft woman's voice say, *"and so will our boys."*

"I searched for you," I said. *"We know, we're fine, now go you don't have much time."* Tears were running down my cheeks, as I let out a sob. Michael always called me "Pop's" I turned away from the compartment and I swear I saw a wisp of smoke from one of the fires that looked like Michael and his wife holding hands swirl up into the sky and disappear. "I miss you guys" I said as the smoke vanished and two Steller Jays, a male and a female, flew by, side by side, past me.

I dried my eyes and as I grabbed the scale to use it to weigh the packs. I saw Ken by the cutting table we had made. "They were here, your son and daughter-in-law, weren't they?" he asked softly.

"Yes" was all I could muster still trying to wipe the tears from my eyes. "It's soon time to leave, are you guy's ready". "Yeah, I want to weigh the packs and close them up and we'll be ready" I replied.

We were in a group outside discussing what we were going to do. Ken made sure the boys knew that this was serious and to not talk to each other or anyone we might meet and to be as quiet as possible. We decided that Henry should take the lead followed by Ken then James, Adam, Michael and I would be rear guard.

Michael asked, "what about the guys at the back of the trailer?" "After you guy's leave, I'll give you about a half hour, I'll loosen their bonds so they can free themselves", I replied.

I saw Ken's head turn and I gave him a wink and tilted my head towards the boys. "Good Idea," he said smiling. Ken reached into a front pocket of his overalls and pulled a fresh pack of Redman chew out, opening it he took a large wad putting it into his mouth and working it to his right cheek, seeing Adam looking at him he held the pouch out to him. Adam smelled it and stepped back making a face and pinching his nose. Ken launched a brown stream towards the road, "let's get this show on the road," he said and away they went down the Taylor Highway towards the Alaska Highway and Tok, our first destination.

When they were out of sight I went to the back of the camper and Michael was correct one was dead, I guess I hit him pretty hard but the other one was still alive, but barely. He looked at me, "it's time isn't it" he said. "Yea", is all I could say. "You don't have to do this," he said. "No but I have to, you and your friends would have killed us for what we had and I don't want to keep looking over my shoulder" I replied as I took the tree limb I used on the other guy and hit him over the head. I hit him several more times to be sure he was dead and threw the limb as far as I could. I took no satisfaction on what I had just done but I knew it had to be done.

My pack was on Ken's easy chair, I looked at the chair and grinned, I saw Ken sitting in it chewing tobacco and sighed knowing that he would never sit in it again. We still had a small fire going, I checked the firearms we took from the men we just killed. I checked each one to make sure that it was unloaded and sadly laid each one on the fire. I hated to do it but I reasoned we didn't need to worry about anyone following us and using them on us. I went to the chair and put my arms through the straps. When I weighed it, the scale showed 80 pounds, I didn't like all of the weight but we had over 400 miles to walk and food would be important. As I straightened up, I fell backwards. Dam I thought, I carried heavier packs but that was over 40 years ago. I took a deep breath and tried it again.

Standing up I bounced listening for noise as I tightened the waist band. That helped to have my hips carry some of the load, looking around at our campsite and sighed, *A journey of a thousand miles starts with the first step*, ran through my mind as I started down the road.

THE WALK STARTS

THE NIGHT OF AUGUST 26

A waxing three-quarter moon was just coming over the trees and with the stars the dirt road shone in the night. The night sky was so clear it looked as if you could reach up and grab the moon or a star, it was beautiful. I thought how many people have seen the night sky like this? It was more beautiful than any church or cathedral I was in. This was truly God's church. I could see the road in front of me. I chuckled, now "a road less traveled" I thought.

When we started to use the oven to make Jerky, I looked at the microwave above the stove, I opened the door and pulled an ammo can out of it. I had forgotten that I put our radios into the can and then the can into the microwave oven like a poor man's faraday cage. I didn't expect them to work so I put the can to the side. When packing to leave I opened the can pulling a radio out, I turned it on and was surprised that it worked. I gave one to Henry, one to Ken and I had the third. We all had earbuds. I walked what I thought was half a mile, every now and then I would count my steps. Whenever there was a bend in the road, I walked to the far side of the road so I could better see around the bend. At this bend I saw a low campfire burning, just embers, almost out ahead on the left, I stopped. I keyed the mike, "Point, Trail, I see a campfire." "Tail, we passed it about ten minutes ago with no problem. Be quiet and you should be ok." I went to the far side of the road and carefully placing my feet to not make any noise I walked past the camp fire. I looked at it and saw a motorhome backed into the side of the road where someone cleared out some trees and brush on a level area. When I was about twenty feet past the vehicle, I took a deep breath and continued my pace.

It took me another twenty minutes to come up to the end of the group. I keyed the mic, "Trail on station" I heard squelch break twice. We walked for about another ten minutes when I heard break for ten. I took my pack off and it felt like I was floating.

I walked forward and told Michael that when we take a break to watch toward the right side and scan forty-five degrees on each side. Also, to have a pack of Jerky handy and eat one piece of it and take two swallows of water from his canteen at each break. Both boys had a two-liter plastic water bag in the top of their packs, two one-quart plastic military canteens with cups in a nylon case attached to the sides of their packs and a one-quart plastic military canteen attached to a pistol belt around their waist. I went up to Adam and told him that when we take breaks that he was to watch the left side of the road and to have a pack of Jerky handy and eat one stick and to also to take two swallows of water.

I went forward to James and met Ken there. I told Ken what I had the boys doing and he thought it was a good idea. He had James do the same thing. I soon heard "saddle up". I went down the line and told Adam to keep about ten feet behind James, going to Michael, I told him to also keep ten feet behind Adam and to come back and help me get my pack on. We continued on and as I had done when we came to a curve we went to the far side. I was paying attention as the moon moved across the sky, I soon heard take ten. I was pleased to see Michael turn to the right. I guessed from my step count that we went just a little over two miles in about two hours. Oh man I thought a mile an hour this will take forever. Then I thought of James and Adam and thought that was about as fast as they could go with their packs. I heard "saddle up" again, but this time I hadn't taken my pack off. We went like this all night and as the sun started to come up, which was around 6:30 this time of the year Henry said he was going to look for a place for us to camp and get some sleep. We had walked for about eleven hours and the boys were really dragging.

Henry found a place about thirty feet off of the road with large Spruce trees whose branches went to the ground. Good I thought the trees will shield us from anyone who is walking on the road. Henry, Ken and James took one tree and the boys and I took another tree. I took a small bow saw from Adams pack and cut a few dead branches from the tree and had Michael pick up the dead branches under the canopy and lay out a tarp to roll our sleeping bags on. I had the boys take their shoes and socks off and hang the socks on a tree branch. I told them to get undressed and hang their clothing on tree branches and get into their bags and get some sleep.

I went over to Henry and Ken's tree. "Well guy's, how do you think it went," I asked.

Ken said, "I think for a bunch of old men and young kids it went very well."

"What about the distance we covered", I asked.

"Well, we must realize we aren't as young as we once were and the boys aren't as strong as us. We did about eight or nine miles and I think that is good." Ken said.

"I agree," I said "so what is the game plan, do we need to put out guards?" "James is sound asleep, let's wait about two hours and make a decision then," Ken said. "Ok, I'm going to eat a little and wait to see what shakes out," I said. Then I left for our tree.

I was laying on my sleeping bag with my feet up on my pack and shoes and socks off when Ken came under the tree branches and kneeled. "Henry said he would find a hide and watch the road for a while, if you want you can get some sleep, I'll wake you in a few hours", Ken said.

"I don't think there will be many people if any, walking and if they do it will be around noon when that happens. If anyone is still back here, they either don't know the magnitude of the problem, they are headed to Chicken or they plan to stay until what ever happened gets fixed and we know that won't happen for years," I said.

Ken sighed, "I think you are right."

"What's your guess as to how far it is to the road", I asked. "We were in about twenty-five miles, last night we walked about nine miles, so we should have about fifteen miles or so to go to hit the Alaskan Highway about two more days of walking", Ken said.

"I agree, I just wanted some reassurance on my estimate", I said.

Getting up Ken said, "get some rest Henry or I will come for you if you're needed", and he left.

When I set up my bed, I always orient it North and South I carried a compass and that is how it was set up now. I did this incase I had to wake up in a hurry I would at least know what my directions were. I unzipped my sleeping bag and flipped the top part over me and was sound asleep. I was dreaming that I was at Deep Creek with Michael my son fishing. He had a large King Salmon on the line and it was a tug of war. He would get line in then it would run and strip the line back out. He was finally winning and the fish was close to shore when it jumped out. A giant mouth filled with large pointed teeth opened and swallowed him.

The gun shot woke me up at that point. The boys woke up and I hissed "BE QUIET, get dressed and roll up your sleeping bags and do mine also, in case we must leave in a hurry", as I put my socks and shoes on and staying low, I went to Ken's tree. Giving a low whistle I let Ken know I was there a responding low whistle let me know it was alright to come in.

He had a finger to his ear nodding to one, he turned, "Henry said someone shot a moose on the other side of the curve in the road behind us. It's nothing serious but he wants some sleep and for one us to relieve him." "Ok, I'll go relieve him but first let me tell my boys it's alright and what I'm doing. Right now, they are packing in case we had to leave."

I went and told the boys everything was alright and to unroll their bags and to go back to sleep and that I will be gone for a while on guard duty but that I would be back.

I went to where Henry had his observation post set up, he told me that it looked like there were four hunters that came from the camp that we passed last night and they had shot a moose just around the bend in the road behind us.

I told him I would keep an eye on the right side because hearing the shot people might come from that direction. He thought it was a wise thing to do. We discussed leaving early in case the gut pile from the moose brought bears or other scavengers. He handed me the radio and ear bud, wished me good luck and left.

Henry must have had a small shovel with him since there was a shallow depression dug the length of my body lined with cut grass. I settled in and looked at my fields of fire. A good hide and defensive position, "*defensive with a bolt action rifle with six rounds in it*" I thought, "*but everyone has a bolt hunting rifle, well almost everyone*".

I pulled out my Rite in rain pocket notebook, flipping thru I found a blank page and started jotting down what the area looked like. This way if a new bush, rock pile or tree showed up I would know. I laid there thinking of the night back at camp, when going through the motorhome I found some cans of peaches so I started a fire, then I got out our Dutch Oven. There was no way I knew that could carry it all the way back to Anchorage so I thought why not make a cobbler. I dumped the three cans of peaches into it, then about two cups of Brown Sugar, some butter and I mixed up some Bisquick and put that on top, put the lid on and went to the fire. With an entrenching tool I scraped some coals out of the fire and smoothed the remaining coals. I put the coals I scraped out onto the lid and put my shovel away. When I felt it was done, I lifted the lid with channel lock pliers and was pleased with what I saw. It was a big hit with everyone and the first time I saw Ken without a wad of chew in his cheek. We ate all of the cobbler, then I cleaned the Dutch oven and lovingly wiped it with cooking oil and put it away knowing that I would never see it or use it again. There were many memories of camping trips with that Dutch Oven.

After a while I saw a movement to my left. Your peripheral vision picks up movement quicker than staring straight at something. I slowly turned my head and saw a male Steller's Jay sitting on a branch of a small tree close by, then a female Steller's Jay landed next to it.

"You're here to watch over your children aren't you", I softly said. I continued to scan the road and sky. I saw "Mares Tails" a type of cloud formation the had wispy ends caused by high winds pushing a front they looked like Mares tails when they ran in a pasture and that is how the clouds got their name. There is an old saying "Mares Tails and Mackerel scales make sailors take in their sails". It looked like our good weather would soon end. Maybe a day but two at the most.

The male Steller's Jay flew away toward the way we came, I watched him and he circled over the area just past the bend we were on. He dived down a few times and came back and chattered a few times and took off again in the same direction.

I keyed my radio, "Base, OP," I said, nothing, I called again and a sleepy Ken replied Base.

"Base, OP something is going on around the bend in the road behind us, I'm going to take a look."

"Be careful out," was the reply I got.

I stretched my legs and arms and then got up. Staying in the brush and grass I slowly walked to the back side of the curve and stopped. Shit, a mama brown bear and two cubs were on the moose gut pile. She stood up looking around and sniffing. Luckily, I was down wind, I froze. She looked away and I squatted down. I slowly backed away being careful where I stepped, moving only when she wasn't looking in my direction.

I was far enough back where I couldn't see her and turned and quickly and as quietly as I could I headed towards the trees. I keyed the radio "Base, OP." It was answered immediately "OP, Base."

"Base get packed as quietly as you can we must leave", I said.

"What's up", I heard.

"Female Brown Bear and two cubs", I replied.

I went to our tree and found the boys already packing. My sleeping bag was still rolled up so all I had to do was tie it to my pack. I had Michael help me get into it and we met Ken, Henry and James coming out of their tree.

"How are we going to do this", James asked. I looked at Ken and said, "how about instead of going straight to the road we cut over land as quiet as we can in that direction. We should pick up the road hopefully about a mile from here".

Ken nodded, spit, "let's go, same order as last night," he said.

Henry led off and I hung a little farther back then last night. It was rough walking cross country, there were blowdowns to walk around and clumps of grass. After about two hours of hard walking, we picked up the road and headed toward the Alaska Highway.

We kept walking not taking any breaks but we had a stimulus behind us and no one complained, though the boys were starting to drag a bit. The sun was going down when I heard "Take fifteen", come over the radio. I was relieved to see the boys take positions like I showed them. We were tired, I took my pack off and went to the boys telling them to eat some Jerky and drink some water. I sat down on the dirt berm alongside of the road chewing on some Jerky. I scanned the sky, the sun was going down and I saw the clouds were coming, tomorrow I thought.

"Saddle Up" I heard on the radio. I took another swallow of water and motioned Michael back to help me with the pack.

The pace Henry set was a little slower, I guess he felt we had enough distance from the bear and cubs but I wasn't complaining I was feeling it also. Darkness came as the coming storm clouds started to block the moon and stars. Harry was concerned, this area in the summer had some of the warmest temperatures in the state and in the winter, it saw some of the coldest temperatures. One thing for certain about the weather here was at this time of the year it was unpredictable, with these storms it could either rain or snow or both. Harry and the group kept plodding down the road.

This was decidedly different from patrols in Vietnam. There you had to constantly be aware of your surroundings and threat potential. Here the threat was running into a bear or a bull moose in rut since it was still rutting season. Harry weighed the odd of this, while they were as quiet as possible there still was some noise. As for an ambush, well we would hopefully have some advance warning of it now. He didn't feel people have gone all Mad Max yet, but give it a month and as some see their food dwindling then there would be problems.

"Ten-minute break" shook Harry out of his reverie. Henry found another area where there was a dirt berm on the side of the road. Harry took his pack off and walked up to Ken and Henry. "It looks like we are going to get some weather soon", Harry said to no one in particular. Ken said, "yes I've been watching the clouds, I'm hoping it will hold off until tomorrow or blow past us".

"What's the estimate on distance covered?" I asked.

Henry said, "about five or more miles. I pushed hard to get away from that bear, they can be unpredictable, then I went slower so let's say five miles."

"How are the boys doing?" Ken asked.

"When I came up, I talked to each of them, their tired from the walk but they are alert and not sleepy", I said. I could see in the dark Ken nod. "Good, a storm is coming it'll be hard to set up a good camp in the dark, so let's push on and after a few more miles when Henry finds a good spot for a camp we'll stop. These night walks are getting old, I think we can start walking during the day", Ken said.

"Oh joy," I said, "I'm also tired of these nightly strolls". "Let's saddle up", Ken said. I worked my way back to my pack, when I came to James's pack, I didn't see him at first, I looked around and saw him just off the road peeing. I told him to finish up that we were heading out. I went to Adam and told him if he had to pee to do it now, I told Michael the same thing and to help me with my pack.

Henry started off and we followed, I was glad to see the boys were still keeping their intervals. I started to run a Jody cadence thru my head to kill the boredom of walking. I keyed my radio, "I don't know but I've been told, sergeant Ken is getting old", I said.

"Who's old, and that's sergeant major", came the reply.

I started to reminisce about hikes I had in the Uwharrie National Forrest. It was a popular training area for people from the Groups at Ft. Bragg and civilians also liked hiking and camping in it. I started to chuckle, we were on a timed compass exercise with maps and were going cross country, not using trails, there were three of us in our team, when we came to a grassy meadow in the woods. There were six tents set up and a small campfire, there were six men and six women and we could tell they were women since everyone was nude. It didn't faze them one bit that three men in camo with their faces painted in camo carrying huge packs and rifles came out of the woods. We walked around the edge of the meadow eyeing them. They nonchalantly waved to us as we waved back and then they went back to eating lunch. We melted back into the woods but Joey, our rear guard, was a little slower entering the woods. In the following years when a situation became dicey someone would bring it up to break the tension. It had become one of those legends circulated among the groups and more and more men swore they were there.

"Take ten," I heard. I thought wow that was quick, when I looked at my analog self-winding wrist watch, I saw that we were walking for over an hour.

I saw that Michael had grabbed a piece of Jerky and was gnawing on it, I also saw him shake his canteen. I thought we must find a stream or lake soon to replenish our water. Even though it was cool outside walking caused us to sweat and eating a piece of Jerky helped to replace the salt we were losing from sweating.

Not taking off my pack I eased myself down and sitting alongside of the dirt road leaning back against my pack I pulled my Buck 110 knife and continued to peal bark off a piece of Diamond Willow that I cut. It was a strong straight piece about two inches in diameter and about five feet long that I was using to help me walk. Diamond Willow happens when a fungus attacks the Willow plant. It caused irregular multi colored patterns in the wood that when the bark is removed and polished makes beautiful walking sticks. Since no two pieces are alike it is prized by carvers and people as works of art. Some larger diameter pieces are sanded then polished and turned into lamps. I was sitting pealing bark when I realized we were sitting for what I thought was longer than ten minutes. Putting my knife away I got up and went forward.

I saw Ken and Henry talking. I went up and Ken filled me in. Henry found a place where many trees, mostly Cottonwoods, were either uprooted or broken, we were discussing if we should take a long break there because of the upcoming storm. "We're far enough away from the Brown Bear and cubs and we could use a break, we've been pushing it hard a little rest wouldn't hurt", I said.

Henry and Ken went and looked for a place to get into the blowdowns while I went and told the boys what we were going to do. I then went forward and waited for Ken or Henry to come back. I waited for what seemed a long time when I saw them coming down the road. "It's a real mess in there", Henry said. "It looks like a tornado went through there, everything is jumbled and twisted together." "Williwaws will do that", I said.

"Well, it must have been one hell of a Williwaw", Ken said. We all put our packs on and followed Henry into the maize of twisted fallen tree trunks. I saw that they laid every which way like the old game of pick-up sticks. We came to an area where the trees fell in such a way to form a natural shelter and wind break.

We dropped our packs and pulled out our sleeping bags and got ready to sleep. Looking up I asked, "who is on guard duty first"? "No one" Ken said, "we are well off of the road and no one will be able to see in here and if they do come in, we will hear the noise they will make". I cleared the dead branches from the area I was going to sleep in and used a branch to rake more leaves together to try to soften where I was going to sleep. I looked over and saw both my grandson's doing the same thing.

When they had their sleeping bags out, I had them take off their shoes and socks. I checked their feet and Adam's ankle. Sam came over and also looked at Adams ankle. He said that it looked fine and the walk didn't harm it. I told the boys to hang these socks up to dry and to dig a fresh set from their bags. I saw Ken and Henry were setting up and that James was already in his sleeping bag. I unzipped mine and took my pants and shirt off and keeping it unzipped I pulled the top over me.

AUGUST 28

Waking up, I looked up through the branches of the downed Cottonwood trees to a slate grey sky. "Good morning sleepyhead", I looked and Ken was awake sitting on the trunk of a downed tree.

"Morning neighbor', I said. I got up, stretching I put my pants on and slipped my bare feet into my shoes and grabbing my entrenching tool and a zip lock bag with toilet paper in it went for a walk.

When I came back, I kicked the feet of my boy's telling them to get up. I finished getting dressed and went to a side pocket of my pack and pulled out a Ziploc bag holding a can of Sno-Proof boot dressing and a piece of towel. I sat cross-legged on my sleeping bag, taking my hiking boots off and started to rub them working the water proofing compound into them.

The boys came back and I had them take their hiking shoes off and I also rubbed their shoes with waterproofing. We put on clean dry socks and our shoes, I then told them to shake out their sleeping bags and to roll them up tight. I did the same and then rummaged in my pack and brought out three large black plastic garbage bags. I gave one to each boy and told them to put their sleeping bags in them. I saw that Ken watched what was going on so I asked him if he wanted to waterproof his leather boots also. He said "It might be a good idea to do so". I held up my plastic bag and he nodded. I pulled nine more bags out of the roll of 25 that I had in my pack, I gave Ken six and the boys another one each telling them to untie the small tarp on their packs and then to put the plastic bag over their packs because we were going to soon get rain. I took my tarp off of my pack, we all had 8-foot by 10-foot blue nylon tarps. I took these off of the tepee smokers we built knowing we would need them if it would rain. I matched the sides of two and did a slight overlap then I cut little slits down the side of them and taking some paracord I sewed them together. We now had an 8-foot by 20-foot tarp to hang over the trees. Ken and I tied the tarp to the trees. We hung the other tarp on one of the sides. It was somewhat cozy and just in time as the first drops started hitting the tarp.

All this time Henry and his son James were missing, I asked Ken where they were, he said they went looking for water. "Well, we'll soon have a lot of water, I said as I wrapped my pack in a garbage bag.

"They'll come in soaked, boy's go gather some firewood before it gets too wet, we'll build a fire against that root ball from the overturned tree. You know what we need get going." I said.

The boys took off and started dragging in dead Spruce and Birch trees. The Spruce trees were not large diameter trees but Black Spruce a scrub type tree that grows all over Alaska is plentiful and easy to get. The cold climate is such that these trees might be fifteen or twenty years old but are no larger in diameter than four or six inches. The ones brought in were dead from the Spruce Bark Beetle. There are large areas of these dead trees throughout the state. We broke the branches off the Spruce trees and piled it by the root ball. I found two trunks close together and started breaking the trees into smaller fire sized pieces. We had a good stack so I told the boys to start the fire.

I didn't have to tell them twice. I don't know what it is with kids and fire but we had a fire going in no time. While this was going on Ken watched and said "you guys worked as a team, everyone seemed to know what to do". "Yeah", I said "this isn't the first fire these boys had to make".

With the roof and one side up, while not real warm the fire took a chill out of the area. Henry and James came in looking like drowned rats. Ken told them to take their clothing off and put dry clothing on and get next to the fire. I had put a pot of water on earlier and got out two canteen cups. I put cocoa powder into them and poured hot water into the cups, stirring them with a clean stick. I handed a cup to each of them and they gratefully accepted the cups and I refilled the pot with rain water and put it on the fire. Ken told James to get into his sleeping bag and get warm.

I got another pot out of my pack, I had a set of three stacking pots with lids that I brought along knowing we couldn't live on Jerky alone, and holding it under the edge of the tarp filled it half full with rain water and dumped some beans into it and put it by the fire. I went back to my pack and rummaging around I pulled a coffee pot out and some coffee. Filling the pot with rain water and put it on some coals to perk.

"Damn", Ken said, "what don't you have in that bag".

"A pickup truck to get us home", I said. "A few years ago, we set our motorhome up with a lot of supplies in case something happened to our home. This way we would have a place to live in case of an emergency. I had to leave a lot behind like almost all of our canned food, my cast iron Dutch oven and pans, a lot of hand tools, clothing and other things. I only have a few pounds of coffee so when that runs out and if I cannot find any more than the coffee pot will be left where ever that happens. In the boy's packs are beans, rice, Bisquick, flour all in vacuumed packed pouches with oxygen absorbers and desiccant to keep it dry, Jerky and clothing. Also, one has a Bow Saw, the other an ax, each has a tarp and sleeping bag. Their packs run around 40 pounds for Aron and 50 pounds for Michael and 80 pounds for me".

"That's quite a bit you guys are carrying," Henry said.

I sighed, "yes but we have around 400 miles to walk and knowing that there are many miles of desolate stretches of road on the way to Anchorage I figured to bring as much as we could carry. Who knows if we can find food along the way?" "The way I figure it at 400 miles we must do ten miles or more a day and not counting lay-overs for weather, like we are doing now, that's 40 days to get home to my wife". "There is a saying, the rule of three."

"Three minutes without air, three days without water and three weeks without food", Ken said.

"That's right", I said, "and the big kicker is our neighbor's kid. He cannot be trusted so it is important that we get home as quickly as we can."

I saw Michael and Adam filling their canteens with rainwater from the tarp, I asked them to fill mine also. The coffee was perking so I set the pot off of the fire to settle down. I asked Ken if he wanted some coffee and he magically produced a cup. I got my canteen cup and several packets of Nestle cocoa mix. I told the boys to come with a canteen cup and get some hot cocoa, I then put some cocoa mix into my cup and looking at Ken he shook his head no. I put hot water in the boy's cups and coffee into Ken's and my cup. When I was in the Army, I would always take the instant coffee pack, creamer pack and cocoa pack from our C-Rats and pour them into my canteen cup with hot water. It made a stimulating drink.

The bean pot started to form bubbles so I put the pot on some coals and got the other pot out, filling it with some rainwater I put it on the fire also. Ken sitting by the fire asked me what I was making. I told him, "When the Pinto beans are cooked, I plan to mash them and the other pot I'll put rice into it". "Mashed Pinto beans, rice and Jerky, That's a good meal". Ken said. "There's enough for you guy's", I said.

"No, we just need some hot water, we have Mountain House meals", Ken said. I nodded my head, "water we have". I replied.

Henry had James wake up, he felt his forehead and shrugged, "I don't think he has a fever" he said. They got food packs out of their bags and poured hot water into them and set them aside. I filled the pot back up with water and putting it back on the fire the tarp started to flop. "The winds starting to pick up," Ken said.

Looking around "Yeah, I hope it means the rain will blow thru tonight and we get nice weather for tomorrow", I said.

"Four weeks of sun would be nice", Henry said. "I'll second that", I said as I poured another cup of coffee.

I went to my pack and pulled out an Alaska Gazetteer, it's a book of topographic maps of Alaska showing roads, trails and terrain. I kept this book in the camper for when we went camping. I put it in my pack to keep track of the miles covered since all the roads in Alaska have mile posts showing how far it was to or from a major town. I wanted it to keep track of where we were on the desolate roads. There is a lot of open space between towns or houses on the roads of Alaska if anything happened to us, we would be on our own there would be no help coming. I opened the book to the area we were in, looking it over I asked Henry if he and James went down the road and how far they went. He replied about a mile when it started to rain. I looked at the map and its key and found the distance for a mile. I cut a twig and marked a mile on the twig with the pen I had in my pocket. I asked Henry if they saw a powerline cut on their walk. He said no. Sam came over and I showed him where the map showed a powerline and about a mile up the powerline a short dirt road or trail led to the Alaska Highway.

Sam looked at it, "If that powerline isn't overgrown and it probably isn't, we could cut about four miles off of our walk". I used my twig and measured how far the road was from the powerline and how the highway curved back to the trail. "It looks like four or five miles of walking we could save and it doesn't show any swampy areas," I said.

"OK," Sam said, "as soon as it stops raining tomorrow, we will look for this powerline and take the road to Tok". I stowed the map back into my pack where I could easily get to it and took out a gun cleaning kit wrapped in plastic. I cleaned and oiled my rifle and pistol and had the boys do the same to their guns.

I woke up early, it was still dark and poked what was left of our fire to life. There was a bulge in the tarp where water collected so I pushed up on it and got some water into a pot. I put that on the fire I went and got the coffee pot out and filled it from another water bulge in the tarp and put that on the fire. I then put water in another pot and put it on the fire also. I got the boys up and my moving around caused Ken and Henry to wake up and they got James up.

The coffee was perking so I set it to the side and the other pots had hot water in them. I put some rice in one pot for our breakfast and got some packs of cocoa ready for the boys. I told the boys to shake out their sleeping bags and to roll them up and put them into a garbage bag to keep them dry. They wanted to take the tarps down, but I told them to wait that would be the last thing we did before we left. There were two more water bulges in the tarp, I told the boys that we needed the water that was in them and not to spill them.

I poured cups of coffee for me, Sam and Henry and for the boys there was hot water for cocoa. The pot of rice was boiling so I took it off of the fire and set it aside. I heated more water for Ken, James and Henry for their Mountain House meals.

I packed my sleeping bag and after we were finished eating the boiled rice, I used the last water bulge to wash the pot. I dried everything with a towel and stowed them in my pack covering it with a garbage bag. I looked at Ken, "are you guys ready?"

"Yup", Ken said. We got the tarp down and tied to our packs and were ready to go.

AUGUST 30

Under a broken cloudy sky, James led off and we all fell into line out to the road and turned towards the Alaska Highway that was somewhere in front of us. I was glad we were on the paved section of the highway after the rain we had that meant we didn't have any mud puddles to contend with. It was nice to walk in the daylight, I was able to watch the line and everyone kind of kept a distance from each other, Henry knew to look for the powerline cut. We walked slowly at first to get the stiffness out of our muscles after spending a day resting. I noticed the pace slowly picking up and I felt we were making better time than we were when we were walking at night. To break the boredom of walking

I would count steps or count cadence in my head. It helped me to carry my load. James signaled for a break and I was pleased that my boys automatically went to defensive positions when they sat down. I used my walking stick and eased down to the pavement and rested against my pack. I watched the clouds as they scurried across the sky.

I saw Henry get up so I struggled to my feet and away we went towards Tetlin Junction on the Alaska Highway. We walked for a long time and surprisingly the boys were keeping up. Henry signaled a stop, I looked at my watch and it showed noon. I dropped my pack and went forward telling the boys to eat some Jerky to keep their energy up. I went up to Henry and Ken.

Henry had a shit eating grin and next to him was a mile marker. It showed 10. Ten miles to Tetlin Junction that means we will soon hit the powerline right of way. I walked back to my pack and smiling I got some Jerky out. This means we are 22 miles from Tok. If we take the powerline cutoff that means we have 17 or 18 miles to Tok. One more night then Tok.

With long journeys I always broke them down into segments or way points, that way the journey didn't seem to be as formable or to take as long. It helped with my moral. I struggled into my pack and we started out. My steps were lighter a major waypoint was coming up, we're making progress.

We walked for about two hours and took another break, up ahead I could see the powerline. Henry turned right onto the easement and I was glad to see that the brush was knocked down. This easement was used every winter by the Yukon Quest 1000 sled dog race from Fairbanks to Whitehorse in Canada then the following year it is from Whitehorse to Fairbanks. This long distance 1,000-mile race is a qualifier for the Iditarod race held later in the year. There was a trail used by the local people with their 4-wheelers. We had to navigate several mudholes from the recent rain as we walked along the trail. It was getting late in the day when we came to the cutoff to the Alaska Highway.

What we thought was an uninhabited area turned out to have someone's homestead. Henry saw it as we came out of the woods and dogs started barking. Henry was committed to continue walking so he went as far to the left as he could.

A man came around the house trailer carrying a rifle he could see all of us and shouted what did we want. Ken raised his hand and put the butt of his rifle on the ground and said, "we're just passing thru trying to get home, we mean no harm to anyone."

The man came forward looking us over, "I thought by now that everyone going home would have passed," he said. Ken our spokesman told him that we had shot a moose on opening day and one of the boys sprained their ankle packing it out and we didn't want the meat to spoil so we set up some makeshift smokers and made Jerky out of as much of the moose as we could.

"How much of the moose did you guys leave behind?" the man accusingly asked. I thought this could go South real fast. A local thinking that we shot a moose and left it to rot. I dropped my pack and took out a Ziploc bag with a few pieces of Jerky left in it and rested my rifle against my pack. I still had my pistol on a drop leg rig with me. I walked up to the man and taking a piece of Jerky out I offered him some Jerky. I took a bite out of mine while he sniffed the inside of the bag and took a piece out and bit and ripped a piece off of the piece he had in his hand. "Not bad", he said, "a little salty and peppery but edible." he replied. "This is what we did to the moose we shot," I replied.

As Ken and him talked I looked his place over, several raised bed gardens still full of vegetables and a Hi Tunnel greenhouse. The dogs settled down and I heard chickens and a rooster from behind the house. I also saw some goats in a pen. I thought this guy and his wife standing on the porch with a rifle had their act together and were not someone to mess with.

I heard "Granddad" from Michael, turning toward him my hand went to my pistol.

"Easy there", the man said "that is my son." "We didn't know what you folks would do so I sent him around a trail in back in case there was trouble". The man waved at his son to come forward and as he passed Henry and my grandboy's he gave them the stink eye, like he was better than us. I didn't care for his attitude but I kept it to myself.

The man identified himself only as Lester, he asked us where we were headed. Ken told him that for now Tok but he and his boys were headed to Fairbanks and we were headed to Anchorage. "You folks have a long hard walk ahead of you," Lester said.

"Yes, we sure do but if you break it into segments it doesn't seem so daunting", I replied. Lester stuck his hand out shaking both Ken's and my hand saying, "good luck to you folks", and went back to the house. I walked back with Ken to our packs, Henry stayed back with the boys. I said, "I didn't like the way Lester's boy looked at our boys and gear as he walked up."

Henry replied that he also got a bad feeling about the boy. "Let's make tracks and move on. I was hoping to camp near here but the chances of conflict are too great," Henry said. Ken nodded and I said, "there is still about an hour of daylight so we should be able to make it to the bridge over the Tanana river before it gets too dark. We can camp under it and be out of sight from people."

"Good idea", Sam said. We got into our packs and headed out.

We hit the bridge just as it was getting dark, it was decided to cross the bridge. On the other side there was a State maintained boat launch ramp with pickup trucks and motorhomes with empty and full boat trailers and there were boats tied to shore.

Henry signaled a stop. I went forward to him and Ken, we had a discussion about what we were seeing. "There is a large stack of firewood by the camper on the end there." Henry said and "I think there are a few guards here."

"I agree", I said, "let's stay on the far side of the road and move on until we pass this."

We walked just past the entrance to the boat launch parking lot and went into the woods. I took a bow saw and with Michael we cut some skinny Birch trees. I lashed two together to make two X's and a pole between them. We put a tarp across it. We didn't want to make a fire for security reasons so, we ate Jerky and drank water then after a discussion decided that we wouldn't need security for the night.

My eyes popped open, what's wrong I asked myself. I slowly turned my head and saw Ken and Henry were also awake. I sat up and quickly put my shoes on. I slipped out the back of the sleeping area and made a hard right going deeper into the woods. Ken and Henry came out and went left towards the road.

When we passed the parking area, we went into the woods on the opposite side of the boat ramp. I went behind a scrub Spruce and took a knee. I could see part of the road above us as two men went by. I was just barely able to hear them talking to someone on the other side of the road asking if they saw any signs. I heard a "NO, they either kept going or didn't make a fire." I heard.

I watched them walk past and I held my position. I saw movement and recognized Ken in the dark coming silently towards me. I moved slightly and he stopped, I moved again and he came to me. "Henry and I were talking, if these guys are hunting us, how many other people have they waylaid over the past few days," Ken said.

"I know these people should be taken out, but it's not our job to do this. We are close to Tok and if one or more of their friends come out here and find them dead or missing and we are the new people coming in from this direction we will be lynched."

I could see Ken's teeth as he smiled, "that is almost exactly what I told Henry a minute ago. We'll sit tight until sunup and see if they are still looking for us. If we can we should try to get into Tok without any confrontations," Ken said.

I agreed with him. I told him, "I would like to put a jacket on and then I would be able to stay up the rest of the night." I quietly got a jacket and went to where I was. The men came back down the road talking among themselves, I thought no military experience or they were POG's.

I slipped up to Ken, "do you see any of them on the road?" I asked.

He replied, "No but that doesn't mean they aren't up there listening." "I found a trail behind us if we can get the tarp down and folded without making any noise, we might be able to get away from them."

"Try folding that tarp without making a noise, good luck," Ken said.

"That's why you and Henry should have your packs ready so we can bug out," I said. "Go get Henry and get your packs made up and wake the boys. I'll stand guard until you're finished then I'll go and get my pack made and my boys and I will try to get the tarp down and folded without making noise."

Things were going great everyone was packed and we had the tarp down and were folding it as quietly as you could with one of those kind tarps. I was hurrying because the sky was starting to turn from black to grey the sun was coming and we had to be gone.

I froze as a whistle was being blown up on the road. They had left a guard on the road to watch for us and with the coming light we were found. I finished tying the tarp to my pack as Ken and Henry came to me. Henry said, "We cannot outrun those guys with the boys and these packs, we will have to fight them somehow."

"Listen up," I said, "I'll find a position and you guy's hit the trail behind us and get as far as you can, if they start to shoot, I'll lay down covering fire. Then when they come to me Henry you lay down fire while Ken continues to lead the boys toward town. I feel if we can hit one or two of them, they will lose their will to fight."

Ken piped up, "Harry, you must get back to your wife you lead the boys and I'll stay behind and Henry can engage them from the front if the shooting starts. There is no further discussion."

Henry and I took off with the boy's as Ken dropped his pack and looked for a good hide where he could cover the road without being seen.

We had gotten maybe 200 feet when a voice called out, "you folks in the woods come on out." We kept going as Henry dropped his pack and looked for cover. "I won't ask again the voice said." I told Michael, "no matter what happens keep going to Tok."

I was about 20 or so feet past Henry, I whistled at him so he could see me dropping my pack and maneuvering on his left. I figured with Ken back there, me up here and Henry in the middle we would have a good killing zone set up. I moved to Henry's left toward the road when a shot rang out from the road, "That's a warning, if you don't come out there will be more."

I heard Ken's 45-70 go off I guess that caught them by surprise. One fell screaming, while they were confused by the shot from behind them Henry and I opened up and two more fell. I knew that last night that there were four of them, a shot came into the trees. It was wild and didn't come anywhere close to us. I moved a little and saw him lying on the road as he saw me. I dropped behind a small Birch as Henry's rifle barked again.

We waited a few minutes; I didn't see any movement but there was a lot of moaning. Henry came to me, "What do you think?" he asked. "I don't see any movement just some moaning, let's get our gear and Dee Dee the area and let them suffer. After all they wanted to kill us," I said. "Go get your dad while I catch up with the boy's and let them know we are alright", I said.

I put on my pack and went after the boys. I caught them waiting at a side trail that led to the highway. Ken and Henry were right behind me puffing out of breath. You could see the relief in their faces but this gave me a concern. When we split from Ken and his boys, if we run into a situation, I would need at least Michael to step up as a shooter.

Ken, Henry and I decided it would be safe once again to use the road. We passed a few houses set far back from the road. They all had the same thing in common, raised bed gardens, log caches high off the ground, dogs and a variety of small farm animals but always there were chickens. They were far enough back that us walking on the road posed no threat to the occupants.

We continued walking all day taking the occasional break. Up ahead was another small bridge the sign next to it read the Tok River, that meant we had about a mile to the town of Tok. There was no road block at the bridge, I wondered if there would be one when we enter Tok. As it turned out there was a welcoming group of sorts at the edge of the town. It was more like a custom's check point. There was a table set up, they had an Igloo water cooler on the edge of the table for people to use. There were four people there, two looked like bored security people wearing ballistic vests and carrying AR style rifles and two had tablets and pens in front of them.

The security men perked up a bit as we came towards the table. As we came to the table one of the security men told us this could take a few minutes so go ahead and take your packs off. One of the people sitting at the table asked if we had our driver's license or other identification and if we did, they wanted to see it. Ken and Henry pulled their license's out of their wallets, I got mine and so did Michael. He got his license as soon as he was 16. As Ken and Henry's licenses were checked I talked to one of the guards. I asked if there were any problems in town, he told me at first there were some issues with alcoholics and drug dealers, but those were handled quickly and a few people tried to help themselves to what other people had but they were also dealt with. He said some headed down the road saying they were going to Chicken to live. What helped was there is a State Trooper detachment and a Fish and Game detachment here."

"So, what's the word here?" I asked.

I was told that most of the people here had gardens and a supply of food and most of the people were hunters and were waiting for the temperatures to drop so they could go hunting.

I heard Michael's and my name called to talk to a person at the table. "Is this your name and address?" I was asked. "Yes," I replied, "we are planning to walk home if we can," I said.

"That was my other question." "You have a long walk, is Michael your son?" I was asked. "No, Michael and Adam are my grandsons, we were hunting up the Taylor highway," I said.

"You said your group was planning to walk home, is Anchorage your home?" "Yes, I replied."

"Good because we are not letting anyone stay here."

"All I am hoping for is maybe a soft bed for the night and if possible, a hot shower and a meal," I said.

"Well, there are arrangements for the hunters coming in from the bush go down the road to Fast Eddy's restaurant and behind that is Youngs Motel. They are open and have solar power, a generator and gas so you can still get a room and a meal but we don't know how much longer they can do it."

We walked down the road to the Restaurant and Motel, no longer in trail formation but walked as a group. There were few people about but the ones that were, were walking as we were or riding bicycles. The incident that we thought was an EMP happened at night so as a result there were very few vehicles abandoned on the road. As we approached the Restaurant and Motel, I mentioned to Ken that I could use a shower right now and then a meal. He agreed that we were a bit gamey so we walked past the Restaurant to the motel in the back. As we did so, I saw several tractor-trailer trucks pulling doubles siting in the parking lot of the Restaurant and none of them had their engines running.

As we entered the office the manager came out from a back room, oriental looking "Young's Motel," probably Korean I thought.

"Ahh some more wayward souls," he said in very good English. "How many rooms will you be needing". I replied, "one for my grandsons and me," and Ken said, "we will take one, also."

"How much is the room and how many beds", I asked. "For two night's it is 100 dollars a night and we have two Queen beds in each room, BUT you can only stay two nights, town rules," he said. "Are there laundry facilities available?" I asked.

"We don't have enough electricity to run our washing and drying machines, but we have an antique manual washing contraption that was brought to Alaska in the 1900's. There is a place to heat water outside and you put your laundry in a tub and spin a handle that washes the clothing. You must drain it and refill it for a rinse but there are no cloths driers just rope strung in the back to dry your wash in the sun." the clerk said.

"How about showers?" Ken asked.

"Yes, we still have hot water for showers," the clerk replied.

I got my wallet out and put ten twenty-dollar bills and my driver's license on the counter as Ken did the same. After we were registered the clerk gave us keys and pointed down a hallway to our rooms. We had rooms across the hall from each other.

I put my pack onto my bed and took my shoes, socks and shirt off, rummaging in my pack I brought out a shaving kit with a toothbrush and toothpaste in it along with a razor and shaving cream, I was always clean shaven and I wanted to get this beard off my face. I told the boys to get their dirty clothing out of their bag and when I'm finished with my shower, they can take turns in the shower.

We had a small pile of dirty clothing on the floor as we left our room. I knocked on Ken's door and Henry answered. I asked if they were going to the restaurant and he said they would be there a little later and not to wait for them.

Walking to the restaurant I noticed two 1,000-gallon propane tanks behind it, several solar panels and a large generator running in a shed, entering I saw a hand written sign saying that they are now accepting silver coins and gold for payment and no credit cards. *Going back to old standards* I thought.

A waitress seated us and gave us menus, "We still have everything on the menu," she said. "Do you know what you want to drink?" she asked.

Both boys almost in unison said, "Coke," I smiled and said, "Sweet tea for me if you have it." Looking around there were several men seated at two tables pushed together drinking coffee, *the drivers of the trucks parked out front* I thought. I wondered if the truck drivers also had a two-night stay imposed on them. Then I realized that the trucks were all pointed North in the parking lot.

I saw the companies name on the side of the tractors, "Lynden", that meant they had come up the Alaska Highway and they were probably loaded with mixed cargo which could contain anything from food to other things. This is why they were allowed to stay it was what they might have in their trailers.

It felt strange after days of walking to be sitting here in a restaurant eating a hamburger and fries, it was like nothing happened. The boys when asked both ordered an Alaskan Burger and Fries, I thought why not and ordered one also and a double order of onion rings. The boys and I loved onion rings.

Harry asked the waitress how was it possible that they still had gas to operate the stoves. She replied that every year just before moose season they would have their tanks topped off for when the moose hunters would come, but this year because of the incident not many were coming. *The incident is that what they are calling this,* Harry thought.

The waitress asked Harry where they were from and Harry replied Anchorage and that they were going to try to walk home before the snows came.

As we were walking back to the motel Ken and his boys came walking toward us. "How was the chow?" Ken asked.

"It was very good, we had the Alaskan Burger and fries," Michael replied.

"Tomorrow, while we have the opportunity, I would like to wash our dirty clothing for our next leg of our walk," I said.

Harry said. "I think we will do the same, I thought of doing it tonight but I'm concerned that if we left our clothing on the line overnight that it might not be there in the morning," Sam said.

"I thought the same thing," Harry replied. "I'm going to have a good night's sleep tonight, it may be the last one for a while, then get up early and do the laundry," Harry said.

"Well good night and we'll see you in the morning", Ken replied.

Harry and the boys went to their room, Adam tried to turn the TV on but it didn't work. "What did you expect", Michael said. I went to my pack and pulled out the gun cleaning gear, "here you go boy's if you are bored you can clean and oil all of our firearms."

The boys went right to it and I watched to make sure they unloaded them first. They finished and put the gear away, we all were ready for bed. I slept fitfully dreaming all night. I dreamt of bears and wolves chasing us, of me flying looking for my son and his wife after their crash, I finally gave up trying to sleep. I quietly got dressed and left the room. On an off chance that the restaurant was open I walked over to it. The generator wasn't running, but I continued to the front door and surprisingly found it open. Going in I saw the only light came from oil lamps. There were three others inside beside the waitress, he went to a stool at the counter. The waitress came over, "can't sleep either," she said. I just nodded, "coffee black," I said.

She brought me a cup of coffee and a menu just in case I was hungry. I was looking at it when Ken and Henry walked in. "Can't sleep either?" Ken said.

Sighing "no," I replied. "Since I can't sleep, I figured I'd get breakfast and then get an early start on the washing."

The waitress came down with two cups of black coffee and put them in front of Ken and Henry along with two menus. Harry held up his menu, "I'll have a Denver omelet, home fried potatoes and sourdough toast," Harry said.

"That sounds good, I'll have the same," Ken said.

"So, will I," Henry said.

Ken looked at Harry, "You worried?" he asked.

Harry took a large sip of his coffee and looked down at the counter, he paused and looked up, taking another drink of his coffee, "Yes," he whispered. "I'm worried about the safety of my wife while I'm gone, I'm worried that we won't be able to make the trek that lies ahead of us, I'm worried that something may become of me and my boys would be stranded on some desolate stretch of road, so, yes, I am worried." Harry took another large drink of his coffee draining the cup.

Ken took a long pull of coffee from his cup. "There is a lot of issues you have to be concerned about, to get thru this exercise, and you must treat it as an exercise, you will have to put more trust in your boys. You must make them ready for the journey, not only must they be fit for the walk, which I think they are from the way they handled themselves so far, BUT you must make them, or at least Michael, ready to take a life it ever comes to it. This will be your hardest task to accomplish, no one knows how they will react when that time comes, even the most trained soldier doesn't know how he will act when that time comes. This is why we, as soldiers, have traditionally de-humanized our foe's, we called them "Gooks, Dinks, VC, Hineys, Krauts, Japs, Slopes' and other names just so we didn't feel we were killing humans. Next it is good you have concerns for your wife BUT, you must not let her situation consume you to the point that you get careless and forget that your mission is to get you and your boy's home to her, and not trying to rush home to her. You must focus on your mission, its strategy and its execution. By doing this you and your boys will make it. End of sermon." Ken said.

"Here comes our food, let's eat." The waitress placed their food in front of them and refilled their coffee cups. They didn't talk while eating. Some people say you can always tell a military person by how he eats. They are usually finished before anyone else. Some think it is because they don't like being in a large group in case of incoming shell fire. That they want to be finished and be away from a large target.

The waitress came by and placed their check in front of them, Ken picked them all up saying, "Breakfast was on him."

I got up and thanked Ken for breakfast and his pep talk then said, "I must now be a laundry maid," and headed towards the motel as the sun was rising.

Harry quietly entered the room only to find Michael in the bathroom and Adam wrapped in blankets sleeping. Michael came out of the bathroom, "get Adam awake and I'll give you guy's some money so you can eat breakfast. I'm going to start doing the wash so when you guys are finished eating come behind the motel and help me, and remember to take your pistol with you when you leave." I said.

"Why do I need my pistol, are there any animals here?" Michael asked.

"Yes, the two-legged kind," I said.

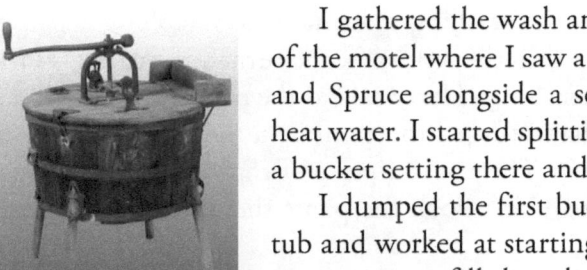

I gathered the wash and headed to the back of the motel where I saw a stack of unsplit Birch and Spruce alongside a scorched metal tub to heat water. I started splitting some wood. I took a bucket setting there and looked for water.

I dumped the first bucket of water into the tub and worked at starting a fire, then went for more water to fill the tub.

While the water heated, I went and looked the washing machine over. It was sturdily built with wooden legs and a wooden tub. There was a crank attached on top to a series of gears to make the agitator work. Harry found a bottle of liquid Tide sitting on a cement block by the washer. The water was starting to steam so Harry put the laundry into the washer, some detergent and started to scoop hot water out of the tub with the bucket. After filling the washer, he went and refilled the water tub so there would be hot water to rinse the clothing.

Harry looked at his watch as he grabbed to agitator handle, He tried to remember how long his wife Samantha set their washing machine for. Thirty minutes kept popping into his mind. After ten minutes in he had to take off his outer shirt and was in a tee shirt, his arms, shoulders and back were starting to hurt. Damn he thought, those pioneer women that used these had to be strong women, but he thought it beat using the old wash boards. As Harry spun the crank to operate the agitator, he looked around the area, that's when he saw the two Steller's Jays sitting on a nearby tree limb. "Still watching over us", he said to the birds and the male bird started to bob its head as if it understood.

Looking at his watch, 20 minutes that's enough. There was a hose attached to the washer tub so Henry opened the spigot and drained the dirty wash water onto the grass. He refilled the washer tub with hot water and refilled the water tub again.

Once again, he grabbed the handle but only agitated it about five minutes. Draining the washer tub, he refilled it once again. Harry wanted to get all the soap out of the clothing.

There was an old hand crank wringer setting on another cement block. It slipped onto the washing machine tub. Grabbing a pair of pants-legs he fed them into the wringer as he turned the crank. Harry wasn't paying attention, "shit", Harry said as the pants started to touch the ground. So, one hand turned the crank and the other he kept the wash off of the ground. There was a piece of rope stretched between two trees close by and Harry took the pants there and draped them over the rope.

He saw the boys coming so he had them hold the clothing as it came from the wringer and put it on the wash line.

Harry saw Ken, Henry and James coming their way with laundry in their arms.

"You guys timed it right, we're almost finished and there is hot water ready for you guys," Harry said.

"Well thank you", Ken said, "and I take back everything I told the nice waitress about you." Ken, James and Henry put their clothing into the washer and while Henry got some hot water. Ken pulled Harry off to the side. "Harry, why don't you take James and Adam and look around town a bit, leave Michael here to help us," Ken said.

"The Man Talk," Harry said.

Ken just grinned. "He needs it, you cannot do this alone and it will mean more coming from me."

I rounded up Adam and James and we went for a walk toward town. Tok is spread out so we didn't go far when we turned around and headed to the Diner. I told the boys that I would buy them some cocoa and if they had any, some ice cream, I would get them a cone. I really didn't think there would be ice cream but who knows maybe.

Going into the diner, on the left, I saw two tables pushed together and the truck drivers and an Alaskan State Trooper sitting at them drinking coffee. I thought this cannot be good as the boys and me took a table on the right side of the diner. The State Trooper got up from the truck drivers, he must have told them some bad news because they were talking and shaking their heads. The Trooper headed to our table.

As he approached, I stood up, "keep your seat" he said as he sat on the other empty chair. "I'm officer Cole," he said.

"It looks like you stirred the pot over there," I said. "Yes," he sighed, "I just told them the realities of life as we now know it," "They have been waiting for replacement tractors for their broke-down trucks and I just told them what I just learned." "Let me guess," I said, "They have no idea about EMP's."

Officer Cole looked at me, "enlighten me, what do you know about EMP's?" he asked.

"Well, the short answer is, everyone when you say Atom Bomb, freaks out thinking of Hiroshima, well that is not what is being developed. Today the countries are developing high energy bombs to be detonated 200 to 300 miles in the sky. These bombs put out an energy burst that fries almost all electronic circuitry. Anything electronic or electrical stops working as you have found out since you walked here." Officer Cole looked at me, "I didn't see any cars out front. Getting back to EMP's, by detonating an EMP bomb you don't destroy infrastructure, building's, bridges, airports are still there what won't be there in about nine months to a year will be 80-90 percent of your population. Since your truck drivers are upset and it's been what, ten days since everything turned off and no cars or trucks have come up the highway, that means Canada and the lower 48 got an EMP also."

Officer Cole just looked at me, "where did you get this information?"

"It's not hard to deduce if you know anything about EMP's or CME's and what to look for," I said.

Officer Cole took a sip of coffee the waitress had brought, it looked like he was thinking. "We have plenty of people here who consider themselves as Survivalists, sometimes they can be a real pain but they almost immediately knew what happened. A few years ago, they formed what they called a Community Watch group it is basically a cover name for a Militia. We didn't bother them since they patrolled the area helping to keep crime down. We had to step in when they got too aggressive with some drug dealers, but with the constant surveillance they put on them, the druggies finally left. So, when this incident happened, they already had a plan in place. Before the sun was up, they had a security, force guarding the Three Bear's grocery store and the other grocery and convenience stores. There were a few tense moments but there was no looting or stealing, we soon realized what had happened here and now almost everyone in town is working together. Today one of the local Ham radio operators got his rig working, he came to our headquarters with some information he thought we should know. That's when he told us about what happened in Canada and the lower 48. It made sense, and your observation about no traffic coming North, well we noticed this also."

"What was that commotion you had with the truck drivers?" I asked.

"I just notified them that tomorrow they will have to take their truck manifests and go with me before the Magistrate for us to confiscate what they have in their trucks."

Ken, Henry and Michael came into the restaurant, we pulled a table to the one we were sitting at and they sat down. I introduced them to officer Cole.

"I'm glad you are all here so I don't have to hunt you down". Officer Cole said. "Tonight, is your second night so you all must be leaving tomorrow," he said.

Ken looked at him, "we are well aware of that and are planning to leave after we had breakfast."

"I wish you well on your journey home," Officer Cole said and left.

"What was that all about?" Ken asked after Officer Cole left.

"He was full of information, the EMP affected Canada and the lower 48 so there will be no help coming from them to help us and tomorrow they plan on confiscating the cargo in the trucks and telling the drivers that they must also leave." Harry said.

"I wonder what problems that will pose for us. I bet those drivers don't have enough stuff in their trucks to get them home." Ken said.

The waitress came by and asked them if they wanted to order anything to eat. After eating they all went back to their rooms. Harry had his boys pack everything up so they would be ready to leave early in the morning.

Harry was looking at his Alaska Gazetteer Atlas going over the route ahead when there was a knock on the room door. Getting up Harry looked at the boys and shrugged his shoulders. Opening the door Harry saw that two of the truck drivers he saw in the restaurant were standing there.

"May we come in and talk to you?" one of them said.

Harry had an idea what they wanted, but he allowed them into their room.

"We heard that you folks were headed to Anchorage, well there are two of us that live there and the other two live in Fairbanks. We were wondering if we could walk with you folks, after all there is strength in numbers." One of the drivers asked.

Harry thought a moment, "Several things come to my mind, first we don't know you guys, second we only have enough food, supplies and equipment for us and our food may not last us all the way to Anchorage."

"Officer Cole told us that after the meeting with the Magistrate we will have to leave since there will be no one coming to replace our trucks and since we probably won't have the food and equipment to go home that it was decided to take us to the Three Bears store and try to get us outfitted with packs, food and equipment." The spokesman said.

Harry thought a minute, "we are leaving right after we eat breakfast early tomorrow morning and it will take you people several hours to have your meeting and then get outfitted. I estimate at the speed we can walk it will take us between 12 to 14 days to get to Glennallen, weather permitting. I don't know what we will have to negotiate there, then another 20 to 25 days to our home in Anchorage. It will be no problem for you to catch up with us but if you want to walk at our slower pace well that is on you and we don't have enough food to share I'm guessing we will run out of food somewhere on our walk. Also, we will probably have to get past the natives in Chickaloon. Do any of you have military experience, real shooting experience?"

They just looked at each other.

"Do any of you have a firearm?" They looked at each other, "No, we drive through Canada and they take a dim view on guns," one of them said.

"OK, you guys want to walk with us but you have no food, sleeping bags, guns or any other gear is that it?" I asked.

"Well, they said they are going to outfit us tomorrow," one of them said.

I sighed, "they are going to try to pawn off junk to you guys. Look at our packs, they are earth tone Camo packs, we don't have tents but 8 X 10 tarps, you will need to be able to carry at least 3 quarts or more of water, a water filter, Mountain House dehydrated food in a quantity enough for at least 30 days, a way to make fire, pots to heat water, a sleeping bag rated to zero and a rifle with 200 rounds of ammo, and the most important thing, Toilet Paper. If you don't have at least that for each of you then when you catch up to us you just keep walking," I said.

I ushered them to the door and said, "remember what I said, don't let them give you junk and make sure they give you plenty of food." I watched them as they walked down the hall toward the exit, when the door to Ken's room opened and two people exited Ken's room. I walked over to Ken, "let me guess, truck drivers who want to walk with you to Fairbanks."

"Yup," he said, "I told them it would be a long walk and to have the equipment they needed for it and that they would have to pull their own weight."

"I basically told the ones who visited us the same thing. Do you think we can trust them?" I asked.

"Yeah," he replied "the trucking companies don't hire or allow Jack Shits to drive their trucks."

"We're planning on leaving early and eating breakfast," I said.

"Under the circumstances so are we," Ken said.

Going into our room "boys make sure you are ready to leave early tomorrow. Get a shower because it will be a long time before we get another one.

SEPTEMBER 2

My grandsons and I, Ken and his sons were at the diner just finishing our breakfasts. Our packs were on the floor behind us with our rifles leaning against them.

"Well, I guess it's time to put leather to the pavement," Ken said. We were a solemn group knowing that soon we would be going different directions into the new unknown.

We shouldered our packs and I swear mine got heavier during our two-day break. Grabbing our rifles, we filed out of the restaurant to the "Good-bye's and good luck," from our waitress and the cook.

The sun hadn't come up yet and the morning air had a winter coming chill to it. We headed toward town and the cut off for the Glenn Highway where our group would split up. We were walking in a group when we came to a sign post. One arrow pointed to the left and showed Anchorage 316 miles and another arrow pointed straight and showed Fairbanks 202 miles.

Ken and Henry stopped and turned to me and my boys, "Good luck," Ken said and He and Henry shook my hand.

"Luck to you guys," I said and then Ken surprised me by coming to attention and saluting me. I returned the salute and turning, my grandsons and I started for Anchorage.

The population of Tok wasn't great, only about 1,300 people live here in the winter and slightly more for the summer tourist season. While the population is small the area that Tok encompasses is large. We were walking down the highway and passed several RV campgrounds. The sun was starting to rise and I could see the few RV's that were parked in them were empty. I wondered what became of these people. Many of the RV's were from tourists, where did these people go? Did they try to head down the Alaska Highway to Whitehorse in Canada? Were they stopped at the border by Canadian customs, or did they head to

Anchorage? What supplies did they have, will we meet them along the road, if so, will they be desperate for food? Did they band together and try to take what they needed from the isolated homesteads along the highway.

All of this and more was going through my mind when I saw a movement to my right in a camp ground. A Beagle came trotting out of the campground. I had my rifle up expecting the worst but the dog stopped and sat with a paw up like he wanted to shake. Adam took a piece of jerky out and held it out. The dog sniffed the air and timidly took it and ran off. I told the boys to be careful with stray dogs and not to feed them since we didn't have enough food for them and us. I felt it odd that the dog didn't immediately wolf it down but carried it off into the RV park.

The Beagle came back and sat down in front of Adam with his paw up again. Adam gave him another piece of jerky and the dog took off into the campground again. I told the boys to stay where they were while I took off my pack and went into the park.

There were only a few motorhomes in it, they all had out of state license plates and they all seemed to be empty. I heard some whimpering behind one motorhome, I approached it from two spaces to its side. What I saw made me angry, there was a dog, a Rottweiler, tied to a trailer hitch in back of the RV, it was laying on its side and the two pieces of jerky were laying on the ground by his nose. He was too weak to even lift his head to eat the jerky by his nose. I banged on the side of the RV but there was no answer. I saw two empty bowls with no food or water, taking the canteen from my belt I poured water into the bowl. The dog didn't raise its head it just laid there. Going over to it I knelt down and cupped its nose in my hand and poured a little water into it. The dog licked the moisture from my cupped palm. Pouring more the dog continued to lap. After about ten minutes of this the dog shakily got to his feet and greedily lapped the water in the bowl. I unhooked his leash from his collar and he came to my feet and rolled over for a belly rub. I looked for the hot water tank to drain it for more water but the drain plug was too tight. I went back to my pack and got my channel locks and going back I removed the plug and refilled the dogs water bowl. The dog lapped this water up, again emptying the bowl.

I refilled it a third time but he sat off to the side and the Beagle came and drank from the bowl.

"It looks like you guys are buddies and your little buddy saved your life," I said to the Rottweiler. I went back to the boys and told them to get their packs on and let's get moving. I didn't think about the dogs. The houses started to diminish so I called a break. I looked at my watch and was surprised we had walked almost two hours. I had the boys take their packs off and eat a piece of jerky. I took my pack off and pulled out the radios. "Guy's we are on the edge of town I want Michael to walk lead, Adam you are in the center and I'll be trail. I want everyone to keep twenty or more feet between them but Adam don't let Michael get out of your sight. Be careful, be observant and most of all be quiet. Michael, keep your eyes open, look for campfires or the remains of campfires. There are a few homesites along the road so be careful when you approach them, go across the road from them. It is up to you to set our pace so let's keep it a steady one." I said. "Any questions?" Both boys shook their head,

Adam looked at me, "Grandpop, what did you do in the Army?" he asked. This took me by surprise, "Why do you ask?"

"Well, Michael told me what happened at the campsite when those men came and walking to Tok you sent Michael, James and me ahead and then there was shooting and you and Mr. Ken and Mr. Henry seemed to always know what to do." Adam said.

"Yes, I was in the Army," this was all I said for now. "Let's get going, I would like our goal to be twenty or more miles each day. We now have mile markers to track our progress."

We put on our packs and I held Adam's shoulder as Michael started walking, at about 25 feet I told Adam to keep this distance unless there was a sharp curve ahead. Adam started walking and I kept about 25 feet behind him. I could easily see Michael in case there was trouble.

We had been walking for a while when I passed the eight-mile marker, looking at my watch I saw we had been walking for three hours since we left the RV park. I got on the radio and called a break. I was pleased to see the boys look to the sides. After ten minutes I called again to saddle up and start moving.

We were moving down the road at what I felt was a good pace, the twelve-mile marker passed so I made note of the time and when the thirteen-mile marker passed I checked the time, it took thirty-five minutes to cover this distance. This was good I thought if we can keep up with two-miles per hour when walking we should be able to do twenty miles per day.

The radio crackled in my ear and Michael's voice came over it, "house on the right," was all he said. "stay far left," I said. I saw the top of the house, if I can see it, they can see us I thought. Michael kept walking, the radio crackled, "I'm past it," Michael said.

"Keep going and do not look back," I said. I saw Adam pass the driveway to the house and look at it but kept walking. As I approached, I heard a four-wheeler start and come our way. Oh, shit I thought. I could see Michael, he heard it and went to the side of the road, dropping his pack he got behind it with his rifle. Adam saw what Michael did and did the same.

Where did they learn this, I thought? The four-wheeler stopped at the end of the driveway and the motor was turned off. "Where are you folks headed?" the rider asked.

"We're hoping to make it to Anchorage before the snows come," I replied.

"Do you have any information on what happened?" the rider asked.

"From what I was told and saw in Tok, there were three EMP's detonated, one in Alaska, one over Canada and one in the lower 48, and what I was told we are on our own, no help will be coming" I replied.

"Who or why would someone do this?" the driver asked.

"Anything I say would be a guess, but think of what is happening in the world. You have a petulant spoiled brat of a kid running North Korea who has nukes capable of doing this, you have religious Muslim fanatics that would love to see the United States humiliated and conquered and then you have China, Russia, Cuba and Venezuela. Pick one or all." I replied. The guy just frowned.

"How many people have passed by here in the past days?" I asked.

He looked up, and thought for about a minute, "about a week ago a large group of people went by here. They wanted me to help them but my sons and I persuaded them to move on." The man replied.

"How were they dressed, what weapons did they have and what was their food situation?" I asked.

"They were not dressed for what is coming, I didn't see any firearms and they only had a little food, that I could see," the man said.

"There will be two men coming behind us, they were truck drivers stuck in Tok when this hit, I do not know their disposition, but I feel they just want to get home to Anchorage like we do," I informed him.

"Well thanks for the information and good luck" the man said and started his four-wheeler and went back to his home.

I went back to my pack and told the boys to get up and let's get going. We went at a good pace for a while, I think Michael wanted to get away from the house. The sun was getting low in the sky as we passed mile post 21. I called for a stop and group gathering on the radio.

"What's up Granddad," Michael asked.

"Well, several things, about 7 days ago a large group of people went by here, there are 2 men behind us and I want to stop and cook some rice for supper and then if we feel up to it, I would like to walk about an hour or two away from our fire before we settle in for the night."

The boys went for wood as I got my pots and rice out. They came back and I poured water from my 2-quart bladder into the pots. The boys had a fire going and I put the two-pots of water on to cook.

In a short time, the water pot was boiling. I put about two cups of rice into the boiling water and set it off to the side. The other pot I used for hot cocoa for the boys and coffee for me to drink while the rice cooked. I got the Gazetteer out of my pack and tried to determine where we were. It showed a stream about a mile or two ahead, I told the boys that after we were finished eating, I thought we should go there for the night.

The rice was ready so I told the boys to get their mess kits out and some jerky, I gave them both a heaping pile of rice while I ate what was in the pot, this would be our supper.

We loaded up and started down the road once more. I wasn't too worried about security since we had over seventy miles or more of desolate country to walk through to get to the next settlement and it had been thirteen days since the event. I felt that anyone who was not from the area who was up here hunting had left for Glennallen by now.

Most hunters take a week off from work for Moose season so at thirteen days, hunger would have pushed them out by now.

We went around a sweeping curve and in the waning moonlight I saw a sign identifying the stream as the Tok River. "This is where we'll spend the night," I said to the boys. "We'll try to find a spot to camp down by the river," I said as Michael started to leave the roadway.

All of a sudden, a Steller's Jay flew by squawking and flew down toward the river. Remembering how it acted with the brown bear when we were on the Taylor highway I yelled, "Michael! Get back here," as I unslung my rifle and brought it to play down the bank toward the stream. I heard a low guttural growl behind me, swinging around I saw a black blur go past me growling and barking as it went over the edge of the road toward the river.

There was barking, growling and the bawling of a bear, the brush thrashing from what sounded as a battle royal going on down there. The noise moved away from us and soon the only sound was barking and that soon stopped. I was startled by a bump on my right leg, looking down a beagle was sitting there with his right paw up ready to shake. I turned my head and a rottweiler was sitting on the road in front of me. Panting with his tongue hanging out of the side of his mouth and I swear he was grinning, like that was fun let's do it again. I scratched the Rottweilers head looking him over for wounds on him but saw none, I got a piece of jerky out of my pack and gave a piece to both dogs.

"Boys, I know you are tired but we must move on to get away from this area."

We walked for about an hour to get away from the stream where the bear was. We looked for and found an area off of the road to set up camp for the night. It was a slight hill that was on our right that the construction of the road had cut into. If we camped on top of the hill it would give us a commanding view of the road in both directions.

We cleared an area and strung a length of 550 cord between two trees about four feet off of the ground, we hung a tarp over it and anchored the four corners to the ground. We laid a tarp on the ground and unrolled our sleeping bags and as we settled in the dogs came in and laid between the boys and me. I had my rifle next to me but I felt secure knowing that the Rottweiler would wake me if any animal approached us.

SEPTEMBER 3

I awoke with a start as the rottweiler was licking my face. The sun was just starting to come up as I got out of my sleeping bag, putting my pants and shoes on I went away from the camp to take care of business. There were a lot of Alder bushes that were about five feet high. Since all the bushes were the same height it meant that there were a lot of moose in the area. A bull moose can be as dangerous as a bear, since there was a rut going on also, a cow moose with a calf can be very protective.

I found some dead wood on the ground and brought an arm load back to camp for a fire to cook some oatmeal for breakfast. The noise of cutting and splitting the wood woke the boys and after they came back from the brush, I told them to break camp and we would leave after eating. Our water supply was getting low so sometime today we would have to stop by a stream to refill our canteens and water bladder.

We passed the pot of cooked oatmeal around and chewed on some moose jerky, when there was still a little oatmeal left in the pot, I poured a little water in it and rubbed the sides. I then set it on the ground for the dogs to lick the pot clean. I was surprised as the Rottweiler allowed the Beagle to eat first and watched as the Beagle left some oatmeal for his buddy the Rottweiler. I gave each dog a piece of jerky to eat as we finished packing.

When we got back onto the road, I held my right arm straight out and bent my hand in. I held it that way and put my little finger on what I was using as a horizon which was a mountain range and put the sun on top of my stacked fingers. It took five fingers from my horizon to the bottom of the sun. That meant it was about an hour and a half since sunrise. Each finger meant fifteen to twenty minutes of time. This can also be used in the afternoon to tell you about how much day light you have left to set up camp before it gets dark.

As we headed down the road toward Glennallen the next large town on our way. We walked together since I didn't think out in the wilderness like we were we would need to be tactical. We were talking and the conversation came around as to what we should name the dogs. We tried calling them different names to see if they would react to them but with no luck. I finally said, "we will call the Rottweiler Buck,"

Adam looked at me, "why Buck," he asked?

"He reminds me of the dog Buck in the book Call of the Wild by Jack London," I said.

"Let's call the Beagle Snoopy," Adam chirped.

"What do you think Michael, are those names ok?" I asked.

Turning around he said, "if they will understand their names, OH, SHIT," he said as he unslung his rifle.

I turned around and saw two men coming down the road toward us. Unslinging my rifle, I held it at a low ready and out of my peripheral I saw the boys spread apart to either side of the two-lane road. They dropped their packs and laid behind them. There was a bump on my right leg and looking down I saw Buck sitting beside me just looking at the approaching strangers, a low growl was coming from him.

As they approached, I observed that they both had a pack with a sleeping bag tied on top and they had a rifle of some sort which one was carrying his slung over his shoulder.

I dropped my pack, keeping my rifle I took a few steps toward them with Buck staying beside me and softly growling. I reached down and rubbed his head and ear telling him it was alright.

At about two hundred feet they stopped and one called, "Hello, may we approach?"

I replied for them to sling your rifle's and come forward. When they got closer, I recognized them as two of the truck drivers I saw in Tok.

One of them stuck his hand out and I shook it, "I'm Rick Davis and this is Matthew Barns," he said.

"I'm Harry Miller," I replied. "I see you got out of Tok alright."

"Yeah, the good citizens confiscated our trucks and their loads for the good of the community. The Magistrate gave all of us letters to give to our dispatchers explaining this and we have our manifests for our loads to prove we didn't sell them."

I looked at their packs, "did they give you anything for the trip?"

"Yeah, we went into 3 Bears and did some shopping. They had cases of MRE's but we only took 6 packs each since they took up a lot of room. I went and grabbed two boxes of gallon zip-loc bags and a box of quart bags. I filled the gallon bags with rice and pinto beans. I'm guessing I have about 20 pounds of each. Then I grabbed two large containers of quick oatmeal, some sugar, salt, pepper, two bottles of Soy Sauce, some beef and chicken bouillon, two jars of instant coffee plus a water filter and two Life Straws, canteens, a metal cup, stacking camping pot's, a 4X8 tarp, a sleeping bag good to 0 degrees and a wool blanket, a box of contractor trash bags, a box of strike anywhere matches and a ferro-magnesium bar. They gave Matt and me a Mossberg 30-06 rifle, Matt has a scope on his and 4 boxes each of ammo and a Buck 110 knife. I asked for a side arm but they said no so I then added several bags of Jerky and a box of Snickers bars. Matt has pretty much of what I have but instead of cooking pots he grabbed a little more rice and beans, some more jerky, matches, a ferro stick, first aid supplies and he also grabbed a box of Snickers bars. We have our clothing we kept in our trucks so we feel we have a chance of getting to Anchorage. Our big question is may we walk with you and your grandsons? By the way where are your grandsons?" Rick asked.

I looked at them and asked, "do either of you have military time?"

"Yeah," Matt said "I was a Ranger in the Army."

"I was a paratrooper in the Army and have Sand Box time," Rick replied.

Buck was at my side the whole time not moving but eyeing the new commers while the whole time I was rubbing his head and ears.

Buck stood up and walked to the men and started to sniff them and when he stuck his nose into Rick's crouch Rick jumped back saying, "Yes, I'm a boy be careful there."

I just chuckled as did Matt.

"You had two grandchildren back in Tok are they still with you?" Rick asked again.

I turned and went to my pack where I left it in the road and raised my right hand and made a circling motion. The boys stood up one was on each side of the road laying behind their packs just off the edge of the road.

"Your boys are trained?" Rick asked.

"Only some OJT since this started," I replied.

"Well, they looked good for the situation. I didn't see them where they were." Rick said.

The boys put their packs on and grabbed their rifles holding them at a low ready position with the muzzles down and waited for us to catch up.

As we walked to the boy's I looked at Rick and Matt, "I think I should tell you that we try to average twenty miles a day since Adam sprained his ankle on the first day of Moose season packing out a moose he shot. I don't want to push his ankle too hard," I said.

"That's fine by us," Rick said, "that is also what we hoped to average each day."

As we went to where the boys were Buck stayed close to me and continued to observe the two new strangers. I introduced the boys to Matthew and Rick and we once again started down the road only this time Matt was in the lead as we hung back a bit.

After a bit Rick asked about the dogs so I told him how we came to acquire them. After I was finished Rick said, "that was a shitty thing to do to them."

"Yes, I replied but now they are with people who appreciate them. I just hope we don't encounter their former owners going to Anchorage."

Matt set a good pace, not fast but not leisurely either. After about two hours of walking, I saw a mile post and realized we had gone four miles. I called for a break to check feet and chew on a piece of jerky and have a drink of water. I then remembered that we needed more water and decided the next clear stream we came to I would rectify this.

I tried to keep our breaks to around ten minutes so our muscles wouldn't cramp up.

We continued down the road with Matt about fifty feet in front of us. This part of the road was desolate, no houses next to the highway only an occasional dirt road or track leading off to who knew where.

The mile markers seemed to pass silently by reminding us of the distance we still had to travel. With no vehicles on the road, it was eerily quiet. We were on a plain between distant mountain ranges, I could envision prehistoric humans traveling thru here in search of game. There were many signs that game was plentiful if you knew what to look for. The Alders were almost all the same height from moose browsing on them in winter, the bases of them occasionally showed where rabbits in the winter gnawed on their bark. In some of the marshy areas there were Blueberry plants. If it wasn't for the thought of the upcoming winter it would have been really enjoyable. The thought of being caught out here in winter weighed heavily on my mind. I was lost in my thoughts as we walked which could be dangerous when there was an explosion of wings and birds to our right in front of us. Everyone grabbed their rifles and formed a circle then Matt started to chuckle and we all started to laugh.

"Let's take a break for lunch and clean our drawers," I said.

It didn't take much convincing and we were on the side of the road, packs off, airing our feet and chewing on jerky. I rummaged in my pack and pulled out my Ruger .44 magnum revolver.

Rick looked at me, "what are you going to do with that hand cannon?" he asked.

"It's loaded with shot shells so the next time we come across a flock of Ptarmigan maybe I can shoot one or two," I replied.

Matthew dug into his pack and pulled out five Snickers bars and passed them around.

We put our packs back on and continued down the road. The caramel, nuts and chocolate provided an energy sugar rush as we ate them while we walked.

We passed three more mile markers and were on a sweeping turn to the left, I was ready to call a break, when Matt put his left arm up with a clenched fist. The boys went to a knee, spread apart and faced opposite directions on the side of the road their rifles ready. Rick looked at me and raised an eyebrow.

"Some OJT," I replied.

Rick just smiled and nodded.

Matt backed up and Rick and I joined him.

"I saw a mailbox," Matt said.

We had a small conversation and decided that with my age, I was the least imposing among them and I should go forward and make contact. Rick and Matt would drop their packs and cross the road going into the brush to provide cover for me if things went South.

When they were in position I walked forward toward the mailbox. There was a homestead set about 100 yards from the road. A house, barn like structure, some outbuildings one being a chicken coop, several raised bed gardens, a large flat ground garden, some rusting vehicles off to the side. A typical Alaskan homestead. There was an older man and women and three children, two teenagers and a late in life what looked like a ten-year-old working in the gardens getting the last vegetables up before winter.

I called out, "HELLO THE HOUSE."

They stopped and looked my direction. I had my rifle slung over my shoulder trying to look like I wasn't a threat. Standing up I saw all but the ten-year-old had pistols on their hips. I raised my hands palm out to show I wasn't a threat. The man walked toward me with his hand on his revolver. He stopped about fifty feet from me.

"We don't have any food to spare for you if that is what you are looking for," he said.

"No," I replied, "I didn't want to startle you folks and thought it best to call out. My name is Harry Miller and we are headed for Anchorage."

"You said We?" the man said.

"Yes, there are five of us, my two grandsons and two truck drivers who were stuck in Tok when this happened. We want to let you know we pose no threat to you or your family," I said.

He seemed to relax a little until Buck and Snoopy came up behind me. I looked down, "don't worry about them they were left behind in a campground in Tok by their owners. Buck, the Rottweiler was tied up to a camper with no food or water almost dead. I gave him some water and a few pieces of moose jerky and untied him and he just kind of adopted us."

"What kind of Scum Buzzard would do something like that," the man said.

"The worst kind, someone who is a real asshole," I replied.

The man came forward, "I'm Alex Jones," he said.

"Good to meet you Alex," I said.

"Go ahead and have your people come on by and I'll tell the wife that you people are ok," Alex said.

"Mr. Jones, there is one thing, could I ask you if you have water may we can fill our canteens," I asked.

"Sure, but just one of you come up and leave a weapon behind," Alex said.

I raised my arm and made a circular motion with it and the boys and men came toward me. "Get your canteens out and Michael leave your rifle here and go with Mr. Jones and fill them up," I said.

We dropped our packs and gave all of our canteens to Michael who followed Mr. Jones to the side of the house where there was a garden hose bib. While he was doing this Rick dug into his pack and brought out five Snickers bars. When they came back Rick handed them to Alex saying, "This isn't much but we appreciate the water."

"Well thank you," Alex said, "the other group that came by about a week ago weren't as nice as you folks. They demanded food and water. I gave them water and told them to move on that we didn't have any food to spare. They didn't move but when my wife shot a round over their head's they got the message and left."

"How many were in this group?" I asked.

"About a dozen or so," Alex said "and they weren't really dressed for the walk they had before them."

This concerned me but I didn't ask any more questions as we put our canteens away and put our packs back on.

"Thank you, Mr. Jones," I said, "we will leave you to your work." We shook hands and with Matt leading the way we headed back down the road.

As we walked Rick and I talked, "a dozen or so people in front of us, even with about a week head start with their attitude they could be a problem for us," he said.

I agreed with him, "and, with their attitude we must be careful as we approach any more people living along the road," I said.

We passed two more mile markers and I called for another break to rest and check our feet.

Matt looked at me, "Harry, do you have a foot fetish," he asked.

"Yes, I learned a long time ago that if your feet get a blister you will be of no use for anyone," I replied.

Grinning he agreed with me.

During the break we discussed the people in front of us. It was agreed that they were probably people in the campers in Tok and were also trying to get to Anchorage. I figured that we would catch up to them in or around Glennallen and they agreed.

We saddled up and continued on down the road.

We were making good time walking and every 2 miles were taking breaks. After the second break I started to watch the sun. We came up to another mile marker which would have been another two miles from the last break when I said, "let's do one more mile."

This surprised everyone until I said, "one more mile and we will then stop for the night."

We took off and it seemed with a goal announced we all were walking a little faster. Up ahead I saw what looked like another Blue Berry area so I got my .44 out and walked with it in my hand and I was soon rewarded when I saw some ptarmigan eating the berries. I raised my revolver and shot one when three more took flight. I quickly fired twice and got two more. Wow I thought three birds for supper tonight. Michael dropped his pack and retrieved the birds.

We continued on for about an hour when we found a small hill off of the road to camp in for the night.

The boys were getting good at setting up camp, they stretched some Para-cord and had a tarp up quickly while I cleared the area of sticks and debris and put one down for a ground cloth.

While the boys were gathering firewood, I got out two pots, in one I put Pinto beans and water and the other about two cups of water. Rick and Matt were watching all of this as the boys came back and started a fire and while I dry plucked the birds. Michael took a small camp saw and took off coming back with two forked branches and a long straight Willow stick.

I left the camp area and cut the birds heads and feet off and cleaned their insides out. The dogs made short work of this.

When I got back to the campsite, I saw that Rick and Matt had their area set up. I stuck the birds on the spit and put it on the two forked sticks stuck in the ground. I put the pot of beans on the fire and the pot of water to boil for rice.

There was probably more there then what we could eat, but the dogs could eat the left-overs.

As I put more wood on the fire Rick looked up, "It looks like you guys did this once or twice," he said.

"Yup, once or twice," I said.

The pot of water was boiling so I put some rice into it and put a lid on it. I shook some salt and pepper onto the birds and rotated them so they would cook evenly.

After about an hour the birds looked done as well as the rice and beans. I told Matt and Rick to eat one of the birds while the boys and I went to work on the other two and passed the beans and rice around.

As expected, with our belly's full there were left-overs for the dogs. They polished off everything we didn't eat. Matt sat back, "now if only we had a little JD this would be perfect."

I smiled and went to my pack rummaging around I came up with a pint Elderberry Brandy. "Will this do," I asked?

Rick sat up, "oh yea, that'll do," he said.

They poured the water out of their cups and I gave both of them a little from the bottle as I took a sip and put the bottle away.

SEPTEMBER 3

I awoke feeling rested but I had a feeling there was something watching me. Looking around I saw two Steller's Jays perched on a branch watching me. I got last night's fire going and put some water on to get hot, then I went into the brush to take care of nature.

When I got back to camp the boys were getting up and I kicked the foot of Rick to wake him up.

"I'm awake," he said, "How can anyone sleep with the racket you make."

The water was hot so I put in a generous amount of oatmeal and stirred it with a clean stick.

Rick and Matt were making oatmeal also for breakfast. As we finished, I rinsed the pot and set it down for the dogs. Rick seeing this did the same thing.

As we tore down the camp and got ready to leave, I said, "Guys, I'm concerned about what we were told yesterday. I fear the group of people in front of us might have caused trouble ahead and people might not be so trusting of us."

"If they are looking for food, I'm sure they caused trouble," Matt replied, "and, we don't know how fast they are traveling so we must be careful we don't come up on them by accident."

"I'll take lead and you guys stay about fifty or a hundred feet behind me," Matt said.

"I think I should be behind Matt and Harry you and the boys be a few yards behind me, that way if we have problems we aren't bunched together and you guys can flank any trouble we might get from them," Rick said.

"I feel we should walk on the opposite side of the road when we come upon any houses, who knows what their disposition will be," I added, "also Matt, the first clear stream we come to I need more water."

With that we all saddled up and started down the road. Counting the mile markers as they went by, I figured we were walking about two miles an hour. I guess with our packs getting a little lighter and our leg muscles were getting stronger.

Matt had gotten into the routine I had to stop for breaks but he did them at three-mile intervals. At each break the boys and I would eat a piece of moose jerky and take a few swallows of water. Matt signaled us forward and we saw that he came across a clear stream so I got out my water filter system and filled all the canteens. We all took a good drink and I refilled the canteens.

We continued down the road and I saw Matt go to the other side of the road and waved us to do the same thing. We passed a house that looked empty but I saw movement behind a window. I waved as I went by and continued down the road.

A few more mile markers went by and Matt waved us forward again. We took a little longer break for lunch.

The day went on like this and by evening I figured we had walked another twenty miles. I felt if we could keep this pace up in another twenty days we should be in Anchorage.

The next day September 4th. was more like the previous day but we passed two more houses and things were like the last house, they looked deserted and no one was in the yard. We had a routine established and things were going smoothly.

The next day September 5th. soon after we broke camp and were headed down the road Matt gave the halt sign and put his rifle to his shoulder in the ready position and started scanning the side of the road. Buck, who was walking in front of me started a low rumbling growl. I told Michael and Adam to cover each side of the road and watch our rear as I went forward rifle ready. Rick had already caught up to Matt and as I approached, I could smell what was bothering Matt. We had a discussion and it was decided that Matt and Rick would go forward and search for the smell as I stayed here watching them and providing cover. All I could think was we stumbled on an old bear kill and it may still be around.

I saw Rick turn around and start to throw up. He rinsed his mouth out and stood up and waved me forward. I turned and waved the boys forward and pointed to where I was standing making sure they knew to stop here. I then went forward to Matt and Rick.

"What's up? "I asked.

Rick was the first to speak, "We might have a serious problem in front of us, go forward and look over the side of the road" he said.

I went forward and saw a small clearing next to a small stream. Then I saw the remains of a large fire and the bones. They were not moose, caribou or bear, they were human.

All kinds of thoughts went through my mind, *what would possess someone to do this? How desperate did you have to be to do this? But lastly, we are now following some very dangerous people and must keep our guard up.*

I walked back to Rick and Matt. Rick beat me to my thoughts.

"We have some serious problem in front of us boss," Rick said.

"I'm not your boss," I replied. "But yes, there is a serious problem in front of us. Now that we know this the question is, do we tell my grandson's or keep them in the dark?'

"They must grow up some time," Matt said.

I looked at the boys and waved them forward. As they came up, I saw them looking back and forth at each other like two conspirators were caught in the act of doing something. I slowly walked toward them and stopped them.

"Do you two smell anything I asked?"

"Yes," Michael said. It smells like something is rotting. Is it a dead moose?"

"No," I replied, "something worse, go take a look."

I stepped aside as they went forward and looked. Adam started to retch while Michael just stared at the scene.

I walked up and put my hand on Michaels shoulder, He turned and I saw a hardness in his eyes. A hardness I saw in my men's eyes when we were in combat.

I went to Adam he was on his knees heaving but nothing was coming out. I pulled him to his feet and handed him my canteen. "Rinse your mouth," I said.

"Now do you two realize this is not a game but a serious situation. Things have changed from just a long hike home. The stakes have just been raised and we must conduct ourselves as such." I said to both boys.

Matt and Rick came up.

"Harry, I wasn't on the teams but you're right, we must now be careful and on guard at all times. Their fire is long out but from the looks of the remains they aren't weeks or even a week in front of us. I'm guessing five days, six days at the most." Rick said.

Harry listened to all of the information it just reinforced the conclusion he had already came to.

It seemed by default Rick and Matt looked to him as the leader of this group.

"Ok guys, from now on we must treat this as a combat patrol. We don't know what if any weapons the group in front of us have so we will continue with the spacing we had. We will also have the added task of looking for possible sites where they camped for the night and possible ambush sites." Harry said.

They left the gory site and headed down the road.

Rick led off and we all fell in in our designated position. After a while I started to puff a bit from the pace Rick was setting. I wondered if he wanted to catch up to the cannibal group or just make up lost time for the short delay.

Finally, Rick signaled a break. I saw the boys drop their packs and take up positions like they were instructed. I saw Rick coming down the line so I got up and met him where the boys were.

"Boss, there is a straight away up ahead and I saw a mail box in the distance. Do you think it is wise for us to try to make contact if anyone is there?" Rick asked.

Harry mulled this over in his mind, "what is the layout," he asked?

"Well, we will be coming around a bend to the left, then go down a slight hill. The farmstead is on the right with some small fields behind it on both sides of it." Rick said.

"So, if anyone is there, they will be able to see us before we get close?" Harry asked.

"Yes, we will have about half a mile of being in the open before we get to their mail box. The house sits about two hundred yards off the road." Rick said.

"Two hundred yards?" Harry said. "That's a fair piece," he said as he mulled the information over in his mind.

"What we will do is tighten up our intervals and when we get to their driveway, we drop our packs and rest our rifles on them and then step in front of our packs," Harry said. "This way, if we don't get shot, we will show them that we mean them no harm."

We put our packs on and started out down the road but this time there was only five feet separating us. We walked in the middle of the road trying to be as visible as possible hoping this would show anyone in the house that we weren't a threat.

Well so far so good I thought. We came abreast of the driveway and stopped. I took my pack off and placed my rifle against it as did everyone else. I walked to the edge of the road where the driveway met it.

I waited about a minute and looked behind me, everyone had their packs off and rifles leaning against them. I turned and cupped my hands to my mouth and called out, "Hello the house," and waited.

Buck was sitting next to me and I scratched behind his ear, I cupped my hands again and called out, "hello the house."

Buck stood up and turned around to face our back and started a low growl.

"I heard you the first time," a gravelly voice said behind me.

Surprised we all turned to see three men with rifles behind us. One was an older thin man with a thin white beard down to his chest, the other man looked to be about forty with a full black beard and the third man looked to be in his twenty's.

"What do you people want?" the old man asked. "If it's food you want, we have none to spare." He said.

"I'm Harry Miller," Harry said. "and we are not looking for food or trouble." "All we want is some information."

The old man relaxed a little. "What kind of information," he asked?

"About three days ago we came across a homestead up the road. They left us fill our canteens and then told us of a group of about a dozen people were about a week in front of us. Yesterday we came across an old campsite of theirs and it was rather grisly. So, what we would like to know if you saw them pass, if you did see them pass how long ago did they pass, how many were there, what condition they were in, did they have any firearms, how fast were they walking and any other information about them you could give us," Harry replied.

Scratching his chin through his beard the old man asked, "You don't want any food just information?"

"That's right," Harry said.

The old man eased his rifle down and nodded to his two companions and they also relaxed.

"About five days ago a group came down the road. We were working in one of our fields putting up hay. By the time we got to our house they were at our house. Our women folk were holding them back with their rifles and shotguns. They were a rough looking group just carrying what they had in their arms. They asked us for food but we told them we didn't have any to spare and to move on. One of them pointed to our cattle in the pasture and asked about them. I told them again that we did not have anything for them and to move on. About then Becky, Gabriel's wife let loose a round from her shotgun. That and all of us had weapons leveled at them. They got the message and left."

"Gabriel and Micha followed them for a way's until they pulled off the road and set up camp. When they came back the women and I had started to move the cattle to the barn. We put the chickens in their pen for the night and then we waited."

"Micha went behind the barn and Gabriel went to the road here. It didn't take them long once the sun went down to come. Three of them came down the road and the rest came through the pasture. Micha shot one and so did Gabriel. The rest turned and ran." "We spent the rest of the night guarding our place but they never came back."

"So, to answer your questions, no they do not have weapons, they are a rough looking group as far as the condition they are in, there about ten of them women and men, they weren't walking fast more of a shuffle and I guess they are about three days in front of you."

"Are those your dogs," the old man asked?

"Well, no and yes," Harry replied. He then went to tell them about the dogs and how we came to get them.

"What kind of person would do that to their dogs?" the old man said. "It just isn't right."

"You said you came upon a gristly sight. Do you want to tell us what it was? Do we have to be careful?" the old man asked.

Harry told them what they had seen. You could see this upset the old man and those that were with him.

"You will catch up with that group in a day or two, what will you folks do then?" the old man asked.

"Well, we will just have to play it by ear, I would like to get by them without any trouble but if we have to, we will have to take them out." Harry said.

"We're about Twenty-five miles from Chistochina, there are about twenty homes there. I don't know how many people are still there though. If you can get past them to Chistochina maybe you could warn those people and set up a greeting for them." The old man said.

"Like I said we will have to play it by ear but I hope we can pass them."

"I have a question for you," the old man said. "Do you know what happened?"

"From what we could figure out is either a Coronal Mass Ejection," Harry saw a quizzical look on the old man's face. "A large solar flare from the sun that hits earth, or an EMP. An Electrical magnetic Pulse from a nuclear device detonated 50 to 200 miles in our atmosphere." Harry replied.

"Do you mean we were nuked, what about fallout?" the old mand said.

"This is a different type of bomb. Not the Hiroshima type bomb but an air blast designed to send an electrical pulse out to destroy or damage electrical and electronic devices. This has no fallout and leaves all of the infrastructure in place." Harry said. "From what little information we could get in Tok is it has knocked out everything in the lower 48, Canada and Alaska. Anything with a computer chip in it is dead and this includes the trucks and ships that bring our food and supplies up here." Harry said.

"Yeah," Rick chimed in. "Matt and I are drivers and our trucks are stuck in Tok. The good people of Tok have confiscated our loads for the good of the people of Tok."

"Well, that explains why some of our vehicles don't work," the old man said.

"With your permission then may we take our leave and get going. It was nice talking to you." Harry replied.

The old man put his rifle into his left hand and walked toward Harry sticking his right hand out. Harry walked toward him and stuck his right hand out but the old man grabbed the middle of Harrys forearm with a powerful grip. Harry grabbed the old man's forearm in a like manner.

"Tell the people in Chistochina that Dale McCain sends them his good wishes, god speed and luck to you and yours." He said and with that he and the other two went towards the house.

"Guys, gather round," Harry said. "We have a difficult position ahead of us. I do not want to meet up with or engage the group in front of us but, I don't want to slow our pace to get home. So, Rick, you take lead and keep a close lookout for these scumbags. Michael, I want you up front with Rick. Both of you your job will be to not allow us to bump into this group watch each side of the road for foot prints.

Matt, you and Adam will be about fifty feet behind them on either side of the road and I will be about fifty feet behind you guys watching our rear."

We grabbed our rifles and helped each other with their packs and took off down the road.

After about three miles Rick stopped for a break. I took out some jerky and chewed on it thinking about what was in front of us. I noticed Adam doing the same. After about ten minutes Rick and Michael got up and we followed suit.

Rick was setting a good pace, I hoped he wouldn't bump into the people by accident by going too fast.

I was puffing a little when Rick signaled another break. I could see there was another curve in the road. We had passed three more mile-markers. I thought Rick was pushing too fast. We traveled six miles this was I figured what these people traveled in one day if they were shuffling down the road.

Rick was headed back toward me so I grabbed my canteen and took a good swallow and headed toward him hoping to meet him at Matt and Adam's location.

"Boss," Rick said, "There are two things ahead, we came upon one of their camp sites and there is a long sweeping curve that I cannot see around. I would like to take a closer look at their site and then go around the curve and see what is in front of us."

"Ok, let's all go up there," Harry said.

While matt and the boys formed a security perimeter on both sides of the road, Rick and Harry went to the campsite of the people who were in front of them.

Rick took a stick and moved the ashes around then squatting down he felt around the ashes of the remains of what looked like was a large fire.

"Boss, the ground is still warm from this fire." Rick said.

"Look around, it doesn't look like they tried to make sleeping areas but just huddled around the fire to keep warm. If they don't get to

Glennallen soon and get warm clothing when we start getting cold weather some of them will die from hypothermia." Harry said.

"We have another fifteen miles, more or less, to Chistochina and then another thirty-five miles to Glennallen. At the pace they are going they might not make it. I'm surprised we haven't gotten any freezing temperatures at night yet." Rick said.

"Let's get back to the road and see what is around the corner in front of us," Harry replied.

It was decided that Rick and Harry would go forward and see what was in front of them while Matt and the boys would stay about a hundred yards behind them as a support force if they needed one.

"I don't like the looks of this road," Rick said.

He and Harry were in a position to see what was beyond the sweeping curve in the road. What they saw was another sweeping curve to the left about a mile in front of them.

"I don't like this either," Harry said. "Let's bring Matt and the boys up and wait here for about an hour. We saw the group in front of us on the straight-away before the next curve but, they could be just out of sight in the curve."

Matt and the boys came forward and were briefed on the situation. They all spread out and Harry told them to take off their shoes to air their feet and prop their legs over their packs and try to get a nap.

Rick nodded his head, "good idea boss, if they are just ahead of us, we could pass them tonight in the dark,"

I pulled out a pack of jerky and tossed a piece to Snoopy and Buck, then I took a piece for me to chew on. I felt one of us should stay awake on guard. It didn't take long for the others to fall asleep. I found out when I was in the Army that a short power nap was almost as good as a night's sleep. There were two tall trees on the side of the road and I watched as the sun slowly went from behind one tree to the other.

During this time, I wondered what Samantha my wife was doing. I had a container garden of vegetables beside our home and I hoped Sam was able to harvest what was planted there and that Tommy the neighbor's kid didn't get into it. There also were the chickens to protect. A year ago, I had to put a lock on the chicken coop when I found our neighbor in there helping himself to a few eggs. I figured that this was about an hour so I got the guys up and ready to go.

Before we left, I had everyone jump up and down with their pack on. Any rattles were taken care of.

Rick and Michael led off and we followed keeping our distance.

As we approached the next curve, I saw Rick and Michael come together and then Rick started walking again as Michael stayed a few yards behind him with his rifle in a more ready position. Michael dropped to a knee and brought his rifle up to his shoulder. This got my attention so I started to jog a bit and as I passed Matt and Adam, I told them to keep watch behind us but to slowly keep coming forward.

I got to Michael out of breath, damn it was a long time since I had to do something like this. I had my rifle up and asked what was happening.

Michael said, "Rick told him to stay here and to provide covering fire if he needed it. That he was going to ease up and have a look see what was around the corner."

Rick was gone for what seemed a long time when he came walking backwards toward us.

"They are about a mile in front of us on a long flat stretch of highway." He replied.

"How long is this flat stretch," I asked.

"If my memory is accurate and from what I saw it is about five miles long with a hill and curve at the end. Maybe Matt will recognize this stretch," Rick said.

We waved Matt and Adam forward and then explained to them that the mob was in front of us and not to make any noise since sound will now travel far. Matt was briefed on what we wanted him to do. I told Rick and him to leave their packs here and to go forward. After what seemed an exceptionally long time they came back.

"Yes, I remember this area," Rick said. "Winter two years ago I was headed south with a car riding my ass. It passed me on the flat stretch and took off. I caught up to it where the road makes a sharp turn to the left at the top of the hill. He slid off the road and rolled a few times. I called it in to the Troopers and waited for them. When the Trooper showed up, I told him that I went down there and the driver was the only one in the vehicle and he was dead."

"It is a straight flat stretch with a hill and sharp turn to the left then about two-hundred yards it turns slightly to the right and goes down and flat again for about a mile then another small hill and a set of turns before it levels off, a bridge over the Chistochina River then Chistochina."

"How far to Chistochina?" I asked.

"Well, I'm guessing but we should have about twenty miles to go from where we are." Matt said and Rick agreed with him.

"Ok," Harry said. "Stay here or monitor the group and when they round the curve, we give them an hour and move forward. Then tonight, if we can, we pass them and make a push for Chistochina."

"We move forward, rest and then push for Chistochina," Rick said.

Matt nodded his head in agreement.

"Okay, that is what we will do," I said. "Rick, you and Matt go up and monitor the group. Get some rest if you can."

I told Michael to stay awake while I took a nap and started feeling the asphalt road with my hand.

"Grandfather what are you doing?" Adam asked.

"I'm looking for a soft spot to lay down on for my nap." I replied.

Michael snickered at my comet as I laid down and went immediately to sleep.

I woke up to a light kick to my foot and Rick looking down at me.

"Boss it's time to wake up," Rick said.

Getting up I saw the sun was well past its zenith. Holding my hand up it required both hands to determine we had about two or more hours of daylight.

"About how many hours ahead of us are they?" I asked.

"We watched them as they crested the next hill and went around the curve. We gave them an hour so at their speed and our speed I guess they are about two and a half hours in front of us." Rick replied.

Harry got up and stretched his back out, "Damn that asphalt is hard," he said.

"I don't want to bump into them by accident so Rick, you and Michael take the lead and watch both sides of the road, at the base of the hill find a place where we can get together and set up a defensive position. We will then plan our next move." Harry said.

Putting on their packs and with rifles in hand they started out down the road spacing themselves out once again.

Rick set a blistering pace and we covered the five miles in just over two hours. The road we were on was built up about five feet. Michael and Rick disappeared on the right side of the road just where the road met the hill. The curve started about two hundred feet from where they went missing.

When we got there, I was surprised to see two packs on the ground in a small clearing, a low whistle got my attention as Michael came out of a Willow thicket.

"Rick went ahead in the woods to see if he can spot the group. He wants us to wait here for him," Michael said.

We set up a perimeter with us being about five yards apart and waited. I got out some jerky and watched as Mike and Adam did the same. As I laid resting against my pack Buck came up behind me so quietly that I didn't know he was there until his cold nose was in my neck scaring the hell out of me thinking it was a bear. It was eerily quiet. I heard some geese flying high overhead then some fluttering as two birds landed on a nearby branch, they were Steller's Jays, a male and female. I watched them as their heads were looking around. *Helping us to keep watch,* I thought.

They suddenly took off and Bucks ears perked up. I heard a low whistle as Rick came in.

He sat down by his pack and pulled out a pack of the jerky he got from Three Bears Outpost when they left Tok.

"You were gone for a while," Harry said.

"Yeah, I went past the second curve and watched the group. They were Eleven of them, they are about a mile ahead and they went about a hundred yards into a wooded area. I saw some smoke come up from their area so it looks like they are in for the night." Rick reported.

"So, Rick, what do you think? Build a small fire and make some hot oatmeal, then use the burnt wood to blacken our faces and take off when it gets dark?" Harry asked.

Rick looked at Matt who shrugged his shoulders.

"That sounds like a plan. We should be able to get past them without too much trouble and if we push through the night, we should be several miles ahead of them by morning. I'm guessing we are about seventeen miles from Chistochina and a good push we should get there after sunrise." Rick said.

"Boys, you know what to do, get at it." Harry said.

While they were eating a pot of oatmeal Harry raked some coals to the side in order for them to extinguish themselves. After they were finished eating the dogs got what was left. Rick cleaned the pot putting it away and then they used the charcoal from the now extinguished fire to blacken their faces and hands. Once again one at a time they jumped up and down to listen for rattles.

When they got to the road Harry was pleased to see that they could follow the road with the lights from the stars and a waning fingernail of a moon.

Because of the darkness they walked single file keeping about five feet separation.

Rick signaled a halt and came down the line telling everyone that the groups camp was about a half of a mile in front of us on the right and to be especially careful with our noise.

Harry could see the light from the groups fire as they came closer. With no other light for miles around it stood out. *I hope the bastards don't start a forest fire,* Harry thought as he walked past and then turning around and walking backwards for a few yards. He turned forward but stopped and looked back often. The light from the fire was now in the distance and Harry hurried to catch up with the rest. He was puffing when he caught up, he didn't realize that he was that far behind the rest.

He saw his breath was showing in the cold night air. *We gotta be careful that we don't overheat ourselves in this cold air,* Harry thought.

Rick stopped walking and in a low voice said breaktime. The packs came off and everyone sat down tired from the push to get past the group.

Harry went up to Rick and told him at the next clear stream to stop so they could fill the canteens.

"Ok boss," was all he said.

They took off again but the pace was a little slower now that they were past the group.

In the dark Harry had lost track of the mile markers but he felt that they were about five miles past the group so maybe ten more miles to Chistochina.

Rick called a break next to a fast-moving stream where they all washed the black charcoal from their hands and faces in the cold water. Then Harry re-filled all of the canteens with the filter he had.

After the break they started off once again. Harry noticed that the air was getting colder and he could see his breath every time he exhaled. They plodded along under a clear starry night sky that was accented with a display of the Northern Lights. Buck was walking at his side and occasionally would leave and go into the brush alongside the road.

SEPTEMBER 6
Sixteen days into the event.

The sky was starting to turn grey with the upcoming sunrise when Rick called for a halt.

"Let's rest here for a while," Rick said. "Harry, do you think your boys could start a small fire to warm us up a bit? Nothing too big just to heat water for coffee and cocoa," he said.

"Okay boys, you know what to do. Let's build it on the side of the road here," Harry said.

"No," Rick said. "Build it here in the middle of the road. We don't have anyone close behind us." He replied.

The fire with coffee and cocoa was a great warming break from their walk in the frosty air. Rick had his shoes off with his feet towards the fire resting his back against his pack. Harry picked up on Rick's casualness and he and the boys did the same as did Matt.

Harry pulled a bag of jerky out of his pack and passed it to Rick, Matt and the boys. They all took a piece and were chewing on it.

Matt commented, "this jerky tastes different from store bought jerky."

"It isn't store bought, we made it from the moose Adam shot on opening day," Harry said. He then told them how Adam sprained his ankle and the next day nothing worked and how with the help of Ken and his son they used tarps to build tepees to smoke the meat. Buck and Snoopy came up and sat next to Harry. Harry took a piece of jerky from the bag for both dogs.

The sky started to lighten and Harry saw that about a mile ahead was a bridge with a river of some size running under it.

"Okay," Rick said "Break's over, let's go."

It didn't take them long to come to the edge of the bridge the sign beside it showed it was the Chistochina River.

Rick stopped the group saying, "sling your rifles and let's go meet the people on the other end."

Rick was about twenty feet in front of the group when he stopped a few feet short of the far end of the bridge.

"Good morning folks, Dale McCain sends you folks his good wishes," Rick said.

A man came from behind a position just off the side of the road.

"We saw your fire this morning so we knew you were coming," the guard said.

Rick replied, "I knew if someone was here, they would see it, I didn't want to walk into an ambush that's why I had the fire built."

"Did you say Dale McCain?" the man said.

"Yup," Rick said.

"How do you folks know him," the man asked.

"We stopped by his homestead on our way here to ask him for some information and tell him what we found on our way to him," Harry said.

The man was looking past Harry when he suddenly brought is rifle up. Harry turned to see Buck trotting across the bridge towards him.

Grabbing the barrel of the rifle Harry said, "take it easy, he's with us."

"You said you stopped at the McCain place? Were you looking for food?" the guard asked.

"No, we wanted some information if he had any about the group in front of us. He told us they came by about three days before we got there. He then told us that they tried to steel one of their steers but they had already brought them to the barn." Harry said.

"Why are you concerned about the people that were front of you," the man asked.

Harry told them what they found a few days ago. The guards face went white over this information.

"Are the dogs yours," the man asked?

Harry then told him how they came to have the dogs. This really affected the man.

"Are you the only person guarding the bridge?" Harry asked.

"No, there are two more behind you, come on out guys," the man said.

The men came from another defensive position from the other side of the road.

"I'm Eric the first guard said and that is Jacob and Peter there.

"Did you guys hear what we were talking about?" the guard asked the two men. They both nodded.

This group you called them, where are they now?" Eric asked.

"We passed them last night, they should be about a day behind us," Rick said.

"Mr. McCain said they were in rough condition and were just shuffling down the road," Harry said, "But, the issue is we don't know how the person that they ate died. Did one of them kill the person or did it die from exposure? We don't know. I don't know how many people you have in town but, I wouldn't want any people who were cannibals, for whatever reason, in my town."

"What should we do?" Eric asked.

"That is for you and your community to decide, but for us, we don't need anything yet and all we ask for is a safe place to get some sleep since we pushed hard all night and fresh water in our canteens. Then we will keep going to our homes in Anchorage." Harry said. "But with many lone homes along this road that group should be delt with, with extreme prejudice."

Eric looked at Jacob, "take one of the horses and go to town and get Walter and a few other men and meet these folks as they head your way. Peter and I will stay here. If they show up, we will keep them here.

Eric looked at Harry, "you guys are free to head down to town. Good luck in your travels."

As they left Eric and Peter shook their hands.

"God speed to you folks," Peter said.

As they headed down the road Harry saw Rick and Michael were walking side by side as were Matt and Adam. Harry stayed about ten feet behind them. Old habits were hard to break.

They walked for about an hour and started to see some houses off into the woods and a red building with a parking area in front of it. There was a sign on it showing that it was Posty's Native Gift Shop Chistochina, Alaska.

There were about a dozen men and a few women gathered there.

"It looks like we have a welcoming committee," Rick said over his shoulder.

Snoopy was walking beside Adam and Buck was next to me as we turned off of the road into the parking area.

"Mr. McCain sends you folks his greetings," Rick said as we approached the crowd.

A bearded man about six feet or more tall came forward, he had a large chest and looked like he was all muscle. "I'm Walter." He said in a deep voice "I'm kind of the unofficial mayor of this small town. You folks are welcome here."

The rest of the people formed a semi-circle behind him.

"Jacob tells me you have some disturbing information for us."

We took our packs off and rested our rifles on them. Buck sat next to them watching the people.

"I'm Rick, that guy over there is Matthew, we were truck drivers who were in Tok when this started. The good folks of Tok took control of the freight that was in our trucks then they invited us to leave. But they did give us a few supplies for our trip to Anchorage. We saw Harry and his grandsons there in Tok and met up with them on the road. We're trying to walk home to Anchorage when two day no now three days ago we came upon a gristly scene alongside of the road. It looked like some people who were in front of us cooked and ate someone who was in their group.

We met the McCain's at their homestead soon afterward and talked to them and told them what we saw.

They in turn told us of their run-in with this group which he told us is now two less. We caught up with them and were able to observe them from a distance yesterday. There are about eleven people, men and women, in the group and looked like they were in rough shape. They aren't walking very fast and it didn't seem like they had the clothing or supplies for the situation they are in.

We decided to get in front of them and warn anyone we came across of them. We passed them last night and I would guess they are a day's walk behind us." Rick said.

"Are you sure they ate one of their own," Walter asked?

"Yeah, we all saw the remains," Michael said.

Walter looked at Michael and Adam and frowned, then he gave an accusing look at me. "I felt they must know what the situation is and that we are not in a game of sorts," I replied.

Walter pursed his lips. "You say they are about a day's walk behind you?"

"Yes," I replied, "so this gives you people some time to discuss what you will do when they come here. Remember they ate one of their own. I don't know if all of them partook in eating the person or if just a few did but, to have a desperate group like that coming at you I would not like it."

"Are these your dogs," Walter asked? "They look a little thin."

Harry explained to Walter how he came about acquiring the dogs.

"What kind of people would do that? That's just terrible." Walter said. "What are you feeding them," he asked?

"Well, what we have, some moose jerky and a little rice, pinto beans and oatmeal, which is taking a toll on our supplies," Harry replied.

"Why don't you people take your packs over by Posty's store and rest a bit. I want to talk to the town folks, I might have some questions for you later," Walter said.

Walter walked off a bit and the crowd followed him. I saw him talk to some people and they went behind Posty's store. Then I heard engines start and three Polaris side by side four wheelers took off into the town area. Walter waved another person over and talked to him and he also took off toward town.

It was a long night so I and the rest of us sat down and rested against our packs. It didn't take long for all of us to fall asleep.

I woke up instantly to something tapping my foot to see Walter standing there.

Getting up I saw a few other townsfolks there.

"Did you have a good nap?" Walter asked as the rest of our group started to get up.

"Yes," I said "I'm getting too old to hump all night."

"But you did," Walter said. "Army?"

"Yeah," is all I said.

I saw both of the dogs had a small bowl of food that they were eating and a bowl of water next to it.

"Well, we had a town meeting and we all agreed to take care of the situation coming our way. We also feel we should give your group a little help. What we will do is load you all up in a few four wheelers we have and take you about ten miles down the road. It isn't far but we must conserve our gas. Also, we have a few Ziploc bags of rice, beans, oatmeal and dog food for you. It also isn't much but we all feel the dogs need it."

They gave us each a gallon size bag of rice, beans, oatmeal and dry dog food to put into our packs. Then three Polaris side by side four wheelers came.

"Your chariots await you," Walter said.

We loaded up and I thanked Walter for their generosity and shook his hand.

He leaned towards me and softly said, "De Oppresso Libra."

I smiled and replied, "To free the oppressed."

"I thought so," Walter said. "Harry Miller?" Walter asked.

This caught me off guard "Guilty," I warily replied.

"Is it true, what Joey Bowman said about a walk in the Uwharrie forest?" Walter asked.

I grinned and nodded, "You know Joey," I asked?

"Have a nice trip," Walter said and walked off.

We took off down the road. We would cover in a few hours what would have taken us about a half of a day or more to cover o foot.

I watched as the mile markers went by and enjoyed the colors of fall on the trees and bushes. I tapped the driver on the arm and pointed to some Caribou not too far off of the road. He grinned and nodded and then patted his rifle.

These people lived mostly a subsistence lifestyle around here. Many of them raise and can their own vegetables, pick berries, hunt and fish for meat. They only buy what they cannot grow like coffee, tea, sugar, salt and such. Many now have solar panels to power their homes that in the winter are supplemented by generators.

The Polaris started to slow down and came to a gradual stop.

The driver turned to me, "Walter told me to take you folks about ten miles down the road, Gakona is about twenty-two miles further down the road. I'm going to let you off here. You have about two more hours of daylight so if you can get about five miles in yet today then tomorrow you should hit Gakona. I don't envy your walk. Now we're going back and see if those Caribou are still there."

We got out and thanked the drivers and as they took off, we put our packs on and once again started down the road.

We no longer walked in tactical trail formation but walked as a group. I noticed that even with the sun out we could see our breaths as we walked. *Winter is coming*, I thought. This time of the year down in Anchorage it usually is rainy but here in the interior away from the ocean it was cold and dry. This walk would be miserable in the rain, I'm sure we all would have colds.

Rick said, "let's set up camp on that little hill up ahead."

It didn't take much convincing for us.

The hill was about twenty-five or Thirty feet tall. The top was about one hundred yards wide and dropped off the back to a brushy area.

The boys got firewood as Rick, Matt and I set up a tarp shelter. I started some water boiling for rice as did Rick for him and Matt.

We sat with our backs against our packs passing the pot of rice among our groups and watched the dogs eat the little bit of food I placed on the ground for them. When we were finished, I put some water in the pot for the dogs.

We laid our sleeping bags out as Matt dug through his pack. He pulled five Snickers bars out and gave each of us one. After the day we had, it felt like a celebration. Just two more days to Glennallen.

SEPTEMBER 7

Waking up I realized the sky was just starting to turn grey. Getting dressed I pulled a jacket from my pack as it was chilly, I could see my breath and from experience I knew it would get colder before the sun came up.

I woke the boys then Matt and Rick. I then got the fire going for hot water to make some oat meal and for coffee and cocoa. As usual there was some oatmeal in the pot to which I added water to make a thin gruel for the dogs and gave each a piece of moose jerky for their breakfast.

Breaking camp I hated to put water on our fire but I knew the last thing we needed was a forest fire and besides there were plenty of streams and small rivers along our way to get more water.

We hit the road and walked as a loose group somewhat in a trail formation but close together. It seemed everyone had a spring in their step as the mile markers seemed to go by quicker. I guessed this was because we were at most only two days walk from Glennallen a major waypoint in our trek.

I started wondering what we would find in Glennallen. Would the people be as hospitable as the ones in Chistochina? Oh well, we'll find out soon enough and the saying, "do not take counsel of your fears" once again came to mind.

Rick stopped us by a clear stream and we took a break to fill our canteens and get some jerky to chew on. Rick and Matt had gone through the jerky they had gotten in Tok so we gave them some bags of ours. Buck and Snoopy went to the stream for a drink, then came to beg a piece of jerky from me. I gave each of them a piece and watched as Snoopy laid down with the jerky between his paws gnawing on it.

Buck chewed his piece a few times and swallowed it looking around for more.

Gakona was the next small village in front of us and I thought if we can get close to it or past it then tomorrow, we can go past Gulkana and hit Glennallen.

As we walked, I would occasionally see a mail box next to the road but the houses were usually out of sight. The sun had gone past its zenith and showed it was halfway to sundown when another mailbox came into view. Some of the mailboxes I had seen had names on them and numbers, usually mile numbers, and some just had their mile number on them. This one had both a name and mile number on it. As we passed it, I read J. Bowman on its side. Could it be I thought. How did Walter know about Joey Bowman and the incident in the Uwharrie forest years ago?

"Let's stop here for a break," I called out.

Rick looked at me, "Boss you want to stop by a house," he asked?

"Yes, I have a feeling about this place," I replied.

There was a house set back about one-hundred yards with a shed and a barn next to it. There were chickens and several raised bed gardens. It looked just like many of the homesteads that we have passed since we started our walk.

"You guys stay here, I want to see if anyone is home," I said.

"Boss that doesn't sound like a good idea, you should take some backup with you" Rick said.

"I think I'll be okay, but if you are worried, then set up a defensive position." I replied as I started down the lane leading to the house with Buck and Snoopy at my side.

I kept my pack on and had my rifle slung on my shoulder as I walked toward the house. At about thirty yards from the house, I saw some movement in a window and stopped.

I cupped my hands over my mouth and called "HELLO THE HOUSE."

I saw some movement and soon the front door cracked open.

"What do you want? We have no food to give out," a voice called from behind the door.

"We don't need any food I wonder does a Mr. Joey Bowman live here?" I called back.

"Who wants to know," the voice said.

"If it is the Joey Bowman I know, does a walk in the Uwharrie forest many years ago mean anything? If not, I will leave and continue my walk to Glennallen." I replied.

A bearded stout muscular man of about five feet eight inches came out the door holding what looked like an old M-16 rifle.

"Who the hell are you," the man asked.

"Just a man who went for a walk with two other assholes in the Uwharrie forest many years ago. Were you one of them," I asked?

He stared at me for what seemed a long minute, then relaxed just a little but he kept his rifle at the ready and just stared at me.

"Are you that prick Captain Harry Miller?" the man said, but the tone of his voice had changed.

"Yeah, I'm Harry Miller," I replied.

The man turned, sticking his head in the door opening saying something I couldn't hear he turned and came toward me slinging his rifle. Stopping about five feet from me he came to the position of attention and saluted saying, "Master Sargent Joey Bishop reporting sir."

I returned his salute saying, "at ease."

Buck was growling and the hairs on his back were raised.

"Easy Buck," I said and stroked his head.

He then wrapped his arms around me almost crushing me in a bear hug.

"How the hell are you doing," Joey asked.

"Well, I'm no longer a Captain," I replied, "and under the current circumstances we're doing pretty good."

"It can be dangerous out here, are you by yourself?" Joey asked.

"No, I'm with my two grandsons and two other men and these two dogs. Snoopy was sitting with a paw in the air to shake but Buck still eyed Joey with suspicion, we're trying to get home to Anchorage." I replied.

"Damn, you are a sight for these old eyes, wave your group in." Joey said as he turned and started toward his house.

I waved our group forward and waited for them.

"What's the story boss?" Rick asked.

"I found an old army friend, he wants us to come to his home," Harry replied.

As we walked the short distance to Joey's home, Joey and slim women in shirt and jeans, who I assumed was his wife, were waiting for us on the porch of his home. Joey introduced the woman as Susan his wife and as introductions were being made two teenagers an older boy around 12 and younger boy around 10 years old came out of the house along with another mid-aged woman who we found out was Joey's daughter Mary and the teenagers were her children named Ted and William and that their father was killed in the war in Iraq.

Joey looked at his two grandsons and asked them to do their nightly chores then to come in for supper.

I told my grandsons to drop their packs and rifles on the porch and go see if they can help them.

Susan and Mary excused themselves saying that they were going to get supper going while we men stayed on the porch out of their way.

We went up onto the porch, dropping our packs out of the way. There were four rocking chairs and a porch swing. We were all sitting on rocking chairs when Susan came out with four bottles of Alaskan Amber beer handing a bottle to each of us.

"Wow, cold beer," Rick said, "how do you do it."

"Living out here sometimes the electricity isn't reliable so years ago we set up a solar system for the house and a smaller one for our barn and equipment shed. All of our outside lights are individual motion activated solar powered lights. We also have some solar perimeter sensors with cameras and alarms at different parts of the property. These let us know if anyone is snooping around," Joey said.

"Why motion sensors?" I asked.

"Soon after we got here and set up with our animals, we had some problems. We lost some cows but that was corrected," Joey said.

"Harry, when did you get up here?" Joey asked.

"I got up here just before the pipeline. I worked full-time on it and then moved to Anchorage. When the real estate crash hit after the pipeline, I bought a bunch of land and rental properties at bankruptcy auctions. I met Samantha my wife at one of these auctions, she was doing the same thing I was doing so we dated and got married."

"I know you have children since you have grandsons, how many children do you have,"

Joey saw Harry stop rocking and look down to the porch floor. In a soft voice he said, "I had a son, named Michael. He went into the Army and flew helicopters. When he got out, he flew helicopters here in Alaska. He bought a Cessna 180 and every Iditarod he and his wife helped ferry food out to the checkpoints. One day they went out and never came back."

"I read about it in the paper, there was quite a search for them," Joey said, "I'm sorry to hear that."

"Yeah, when everyone stopped searching, I kept on for a month whenever weather allowed but we never found them."

As Harry was saying this a male and female Steller's Jay flew in and landed on the porch railing and started to preen themselves. Harry looked up and seeing the birds and smiled.

Joey saw the birds, "that's unusual, to see a male and female Steller's Jay together," he said.

"They have been following us since we started this walk," Harry said.

Joey just looked at Harry and then the birds, "do you think," he said.

"Yeah," Harry said.

The boys came around the house, one of them was carrying a pail of milk and the other had a double handful of eggs. All four went into the house.

Joey asked, "Harry what is your take on why the power is off."

"I think from the ways things are we were hit with an EMP. These guy's trucks don't run and neither do any other vehicles that rely on a computer."

"That's what I thought," Joey said. "You guys are truck drivers?" Joey asked.

"I'm Rick and that is Mathew. We drive for Carlyle running from the port of Tacoma or Bellingham to Anchorage."

The sun was starting to set as Susan came out of the house and sat on Joey's lap.

"How did you guys meet," Harry asked.

Harry saw Susan blush.

"Do you remember that walk in the Uwharrie forest when we met those people? Well, every time I had some time off, I went back there camping and after about a month one warm sunny day they came back and Susan was with them. I asked if they minded if I camped with them and once the ice was broken and we got to know one and another well, I got one hell of a sunburn that weekend." He had his arm around Susan and gave her a good hug. You could see they were still very much in love.

Mary came out, "supper is ready."

We filed in to see a table set with two beef roasts, potatoes, carrots and onions that were cooked with the roasts, gravy, fresh string beans and a bowl of salad.

There wasn't room for all of us at the table so the boys each got a plate and found seats in the living room while we adults sat at the table.

"We grew all of what we are eating," Susan said.

"This food tastes great," Rick said.

"It sure beats Mountain House food and rice," Mathew said.

"Is that what you are eating?" Joey asked.

"Well for the long walk, weight and space was critical so we have pinto beans, rice, oatmeal and jerky we made from a moose Adam shot," Harry replied.

"That sounds boring," Mary said.

"Yea, boring but easy, and we can carry a lot of jerky, beans and rice and it will keep us alive until we get home," Harry said.

"Susan you said you grew everything we are eating tonight?" Mathew asked.

"Yes," Susan said, "we have two sow's and a boar in the barn that we usually get ten piglets from each. When they get to weigh around two-hundred pounds all but two we usually sell or trade. Moose and Caribou meat gets boring after a while and not everyone kills a moose. We also have ten beef cows, a milk cow and a bull, we usually get calves that we sell or trade when they get to size. We have some chickens for eggs and meat. The garden usually produces enough vegetables to last a year and if not, we go into Glenallen and buy canned vegetables until our garden starts to produce again. We also get coffee, tea, sugar, flour and other staples that we cannot grow there."

"We also grow hay, wheat, barley and oats for cattle feed. We are pretty much self-sufficient," Joey said.

"But now," Mary said, "we must keep an eye out for people who want to steal our animals."

"What do you do when you catch someone?" I asked.

"We have a back-ho on the back of one of our tractors," Joey said. "It beats using a shovel."

As we finished our meals, Susan came out with a large sheet cake for dessert.

Joey went to the kitchen and came out with glasses and a bottle of Hiram Walker Blackberry Brandy. He poured about two fingers into each glass and passed it around. We sat at the table and talked while we sipped on the brandy. Joey said that there was a shower upstairs if anyone wanted a shower. One by one we all took him up on the offer.

When it was time for bed the boys and dogs went to the barn to sleep in the hay with their sleeping bags, I got the couch and Rick and Mat got the beds in the boy's room. It was nice to sleep indoors in a warm building. I and the rest of our group knew winter was coming and it will soon get really cold.

I was sleeping soundly when a buzzing noise woke me. Joey came down the steps saying, "don't turn on any lights."

"What's up?" I asked as Susan and Mary came down the stairs dressed in cammo each with a rifle.

Rick and Mat came out of their room, "what's happening?" Rick asked.

"We have someone or something outside of the cow pasture," Joey said.

"What's that you have there," I asked Joey.

"It's an ATN BINOX 4T 640 1-10X Thermal binocular. I can see heat signatures in the dark as if it was daylight. Susan, Mary and I each have one and we all have ATN THOR HD 640 thermal scopes on our rifles. They are all Remington 700's in .308. With this setup anything within 800 meters will be taken care of."

"What do you want us to do?" I asked.

"Harry, you go to the barn and let the boys know what we are doing and secure the barn, Rick, you and Mat one of you watch the front and the other the back of the house. Here are radios with earbuds. Remember, no lights. Let's go," Joey said.

I went to the barn as the others went to their positions. Joey, Susan and Mary melted into the darkness. I went into the barn and whispered loudly for the boys. I told them not to turn any lights on and to get up. As they were dressing, I told them that a motion sensor went off and we were to secure the barn.

"Probably another bear," Ted said.

As we were exiting the barn, I heard three shots that were very close together and then the howling of what sounded a dog in pain, then there was another three shots and more dogs howling in pain. Two more shots and the howling stopped.

"It sounds like they got some of the wolves that were sneaking around here," William said.

We stayed around the barn until Susan came by.

"Let's go and see how many wolves we got," she said. "At night these scopes make any fight unfair to our advantage. It shows the heat signature and shape of whatever is out there whether animal or human. Even if they are hiding behind a tree or bush."

I told Adam to find Rick or Mat and let them know what happened and that we were going out into one of the fields and to keep watch around the house.

Michael and I followed Susan across the field aided by the stars and Starfire flashlights she and her boys had.

Coming up on Joey I saw he had a large stick and with Mary covering him, he was poking a wolf to make sure it was dead.

"Well Joey, what do you have here," I asked.

"We got four on the first volley, a bullet passed through one wolf and wounded the wolf behind it. Then the others went to him and we got two more. That's six wolves, at a hundred dollars each that's not a bad night, Joey replied.

Susan handed me her flashlight and Ted handed his flashlight to Michael. While we held the lights Joey, Susan, Mary and Ted went to work skinning the wolves. As fast as they worked, I'm sure these weren't the first wolves that they skinned out. It was getting cold out and steam rose from the skinned carcasses.

Ted took a flashlight and took off at a trot towards the barn. After a while he came back with a large Adirondack style

Trapper's wicker pack on his back. Joey pulled out a roll of 550 cord, cutting a piece off of it he tied a wolf hide into a bundle and put it into the pack, Susan and Mary were doing the same.

By now the sky was starting to lighten with the coming sunrise turning it into brilliant pink hues. Mary and Susan got on each side of the pack, lifting it up as Joey slipped his arms into its straps, we all headed back to the barn marveling at the sunrise.

SEPTEMBER 8

We were sitting around the table finishing a breakfast of Bacon, eggs, home-fried Yukon Gold potatoes and coffee when Joey asked, "what's the plan for you guys?"

"My wife is home alone and my neighbor and his son are trouble maker's so I would like to get home as quickly as I can," I said.

"So are our wives," Rick added.

"I understand," Joey said. "With winter coming, I was going to offer you folks a place to stay. I feel that when the snows come it will be harder to protect this place and a few more bodies would be helpful," Joey said.

"I know winter is coming that is why we are anxious to be going. I, we appreciate what you have done for us and we don't want to be ungrateful but our wives need us," I replied. I feel that we have at least two but more than likely three weeks of walking and I want to get through Chickaloon Pass before it snows."

"I understand but before you go let us give you some more supplies for the road," Joey said. "Go get your packs awhile and Susan and I will get some things for you guys."

When we had our packs ready Joey and Susan had a small pile on the table.

"Here are four Ziploc bags they each have about three pounds of sliced bacon that I cured and smoked and two bags for each of you filled with cured and smoked salmon. These are cured and smoked into squaw candy so you don't need refrigeration. Also, a gallon bag of homemade beef jerky for each of you and another bag of rice for each of you. I would like to give you more but I know weight and space are a premium for you guys," Joey said.

"If things get better or you have to leave your place you will always have a bed here," Susan said.

"Captain, here is something that can help you on your walk," Joey said as he handed Harry an ATN BINOX 4T 640 1-10X Thermal binocular.

"Joey, I can't take this," Harry said.

"No, take it I have another one and you folks will more than likely need this on your walk," joey replied.

Thanking Joey and his wife we put our packs on and slung our rifles, I looked at Joey and gave him a slight nod.

"I'll walk you guys out to the road," Joey said and grabbed his rifle and followed us down the lane to the road.

"What's up, Captain."

"Joey, a few days ago on the other side of Chistochina we passed a group that were in very rough shape that we think ate one of their group. The people of Chistochina said they would take care of the problem, but, if any got past, in a day or two, they will be coming down the road. You guys be careful," I said.

"Shit, that is some shitty news. I'll have to find a way to tell the rest and set up an observation post," Joey replied. Shaking our hands again and giving me another hug "I wish you guys well and safe travels."

We continued down the highway toward the small town of Gakona which I guessed was about ten miles in front of us.

In Alaska you could usually tell when you were nearing a town. The sight of houses closer to the road with junk cars in the yard became more frequent. We soon saw a sign announcing Gakona when Rick called a halt.

"Guy's we are about to hit Gakona, we don't know what their attitude will be towards strangers so let's stay on the right side of the road and keep about two or three yards apart. I'll lead just as before and Harry you be trail. Carry our rifles slung over our shoulders. We don't want to look threatening to these people," Rick said.

We moved out. There wasn't much to Gakona, about two dozen houses and a lodge with a trading post. We were coming up to the bridge over the Gakona River. There was a car parked sideways on the road and a few people behind it. We were out in the open for a long way so they had plenty of notice that we were coming.

A man stepped out from behind the car and asked us to stop. Another came out and asked us what our intentions were.

We told them that we came from Tok and were headed home to Anchorage and hoped to get there before it got too cold and the snow flew. About this time Buck and Snoopy showed up.

"What's with the dogs? Do they belong to one of you," The man asked?

I explained the situation on how we got the dogs and how buck saved us from a bear early in our trek. About then Snoopy came up and sat down with a paw up to shake. The man looked down and just chuckled.

"They look a little thin," the man said.

"Well like I said we weren't expecting them and they were eating what we were which is beans, rice and jerky. That is until we reached Chistochina where we were given a little dog food for them," I said.

"We got word from a ham operator in Chistochina about three men, two teenagers and two dogs, to watch for them and to take care of them and to thank them for the warning. We were told to pass a message to you folks. The problem was taken care of," he said. "Can you elaborate on what the problem was or is it better not to ask?"

I looked at him, "let's just say the people between there and here are now safe," is all he said.

"What are your plans," the man asked.

"We would like to pass through and find a place to camp for the night and then tomorrow get to Glennallen if we can," Rick said. "Will we run into any trouble along the way?" Rick asked.

"No, things are quiet now," the man said. "The first week there were a few incidents but they were delt with. About two or three miles down the road you will hit the Richardson Highway, on the left you will see a cutout. There are places to camp there. Have a safe trip," the guy said and left us through.

As we crossed the bridge, Matt said, "that went better then I first expected when I saw the roadblock."

"I was also worried when I saw the roadblock," Harry replied.

It wasn't long before we saw the cutoff on our left and crossing the road, I looked both ways for traffic. Old habits are hard to break. We found a campsite just into the woods and set up camp, getting our tarps up and a fire started to cook some rice. We had a little dog food left from Chistochina so we gave the last to Buck and Snoopy, hoping to be able to find some more in Glennallen tomorrow.

I had trouble sleeping knowing that tomorrow we would hit our first major goal in our trip. I was worried about what might befall us tomorrow. When I finally did fall asleep, the face of my wife came to me in a dream about problems she was having with the piece of shit neighbor Tom and his son Tom Junior.

SEPTEMBER 9

I suddenly came awake it was still dark but the dream of my wife was still fresh in my mind. Was this a premonition of what was happening at home? We, must get home for the sake of my wife. As was now the custom we stretch a rope between two trees and then put a tarp over it and then tie the four corners down. The tarp doesn't reach to the ground so we can see what is around us. Getting out of my sleeping bag and putting my clothing on while looking around, I saw that Snoopy was curled up next to Adam but Buck was nowhere to be seen. That's when I spotted the two Steller's Jays. They were flitting from branch to branch as if something was agitating them. A knot formed in my stomach we must get going.

I made some noise and woke Rick and Matt up but I had to kick the feet of Mike and Adam to wake them.

Rick popped awake, "what's up boss?"

I explained my dream and our relationship with our next-door neighbor and the agitated birds that were following us and show up just when something was going to happen.

Matthew was rolling out of bed getting dressed, "we had a guy in our unit when we were in Iraq that had dreams like that just before we would get hit."

I got the boys moving as I built up the remains of last night's fire so we could make our breakfast of oatmeal and hot chocolate and coffee.

After eating we broke camp and were on the road to Glennallen. On this leg of their journey, we started to pass more houses and businesses. Many of these houses were stereotypical for this area in that they looked like Goodyear houses. A Goodyear house had an addition added to it when the family had a good financial year and of course there were at least one or two nonrunning cars in the yard but now almost all vehicles were nonrunning.

Harry new they were close to Glennallen when they passed a lumber yard/hardware store on their right. We were walking in a loose trail formation as we approached a makeshift road block just before the Tesoro gas station at the Glenn Highway cutoff to Anchorage.

The roadblock was staffed by an Alaskan State Trooper and two other people. It was set up much like the one they had stopped at in Tok with a table and chairs under a canopy.

When they approached, they were asked for ID's, why they were on the road where they came from and where they were headed.

Harry said that he and his grandsons were moose hunting on the Taylor Highway when the event happened and they were trying to get to Anchorage before the snow flew.

Rick and Matthew both said they were truck drivers who were in Tok when the event happened and the good towns people confiscated their loads for the good of the town and then asked them to leave. They explained that they hooked up with Harry and his boys for mutual support and that they too were trying to get to Anchorage.

While this took place Snoopy sat with the boys while Buck roamed around sniffing and marking territory. The trooper asked if the dogs were theirs and Harry told him the story about how they came about getting them. The trooper frowned when he heard this.

"You folks will be allowed to pass thru town but you must do it as quickly as you can. We are not allowing anyone to stay in town. It is getting late and you can stay at the Northern Nights campground in town, but tomorrow you must leave," the trooper said.

"Are there any place to buy supplies?" Harry asked the trooper.

"Across from Northern Nights Campground is Sparks General Store but I don't know what they have if anything left to sell." The trooper replied.

We left the check point and headed to Northern Nights Campground which was about a mile down the road. I felt like we had turned a corner and were starting the home stretch. I saw a sign showing it was 180 miles to Anchorage. I started doing the math in my head, if we can walk 20 miles a day that would be 9 days to home and if we did 30 miles a day that would be 6 days of walking.

"Hey boss, we're here," Rick called out. Breaking me from my thoughts.

Walking into the campground I couldn't help but notice several motorhomes parked in camping spots but no one was around them. We headed towards what looked like an office and were greeted by a man standing on a porch.

"What can I do for you folks?" he asked.

"The State trooper at the road block said that we might be able to spend the night," Harry replied.

"Where are you folks coming from and where are you headed?" the man asked.

"We are walking from Tok and are headed to Anchorage. All we need is a place to set up a place to sleep and refill our canteens," Matt replied.

"Just find an empty place and don't mind the motorhomes, they are all empty," the man said.

"Do you know if the store across the street has any supplies for sale?" Rick asked.

"They were busy when this first happened so I don't know if they have anything to sell," the man replied.

"Thanks," Harry said. And they went into the campground looking for a place to set up camp for the night.

Setting their packs down Rick looked at Harry, while these guys set up camp why don't you and me go across the street the store and see if they have anything we could use?"

As Harry and Rick approached the store, they could see two men with rifles standing outside.

"What do you men want?" one of them asked.

"Well, we were wondering if there was anything to be had in the store," Harry said.

One of them turned and stuck his head in the door and said something they couldn't hear. Turning around he said, "okay, I'll escort you in."

As we went in, I looked around, while there were gaps in the merchandise on the shelves there seemed to still be many items to be had.

"What are you folks looking for?" the lady behind the checkout counter asked.

"Well, we just came from Tok and are headed to Anchorage so we cannot carry too much. We are just curious what is here and maybe get any news on what is in front of us." Harry replied.

As Harry and Rick walked around the store, they agreed that the cans of food would add too much weight for what they were getting. As harry walked around the end of a row holding detergents, he saw shelves on the wall holding work and hiking shoes. Harry looked down at his footwear and wondered if they would last another 200 miles. He made a mental note to check the boy's shoes when he got back to the camp site.

While Harry was looking at the shoes Rick came up. "Boss it's going to snow before we get home Maybe we should get some Sorrels if they have any."

I was thinking the same thing. Let's get some soup or something for supper and I'm getting low on TP and Oatmeal."

As they were checking out Harry asked if they had any Sorrels for sale. The clerk said they had some in the back room and to follow him. Following the clerk back, harry saw several shelves of different size

Sorrels. Looking at the clerk, I will be back with my boys to see if you have their sizes as Rick pulled one off of the shelf for him. As Harry turned to leave, he looked around a corner of the stock room and that's when Harry saw a pallet of fifty-pound bags of dog food.

"I'll take a bag of dog food now," Harry said.

"You must be desperate to be eating dog food," the clerk said.

That's when Harry told him about the dogs that were accompanying them and how he rescued them.

Harry was surprised when the clerk accepted paper money for the purchases.

When they got back to the campsite with their purchases Harry asked Rick if he would stay there while he, Matt and the boys went back to the store.

Back at the store Harry got the boys Sorrels and then grabbed three tubes of Quick Oats, more TP, the last box of gallon zip-loc bags, three one-pound bags of rice and two jars each of beef and chicken bouillon cubes. He paid for it with almost the last of his paper money. Matt also got himself a pair of Sorrels and had a pile of items for him and Rick.

After eating they divided their purchases among them with everyone carrying about ten pounds of dog food, they tied their Sorrels to their pack for use later.

SEPTEMBER 10

They all were up early in anticipation of being on the last long stretch of road. After eating breakfast, they were on their way before the sun rose. Their packs were a little heavier but they were walking at a good pace. Well, they should, Harry thought he and the boys have been at it now for over two weeks. Rick was in the lead and it seemed they were passing the mile posts a little quicker. Everyone was in good spirits as they headed down the road to their next major waypoint which was Eureka Lodge.

They stopped for a little longer break of Jerky, water and a Snickers bar then pushed on. They were walking in a loose trail formation when

Rick suddenly stopped, holding his hand up with a fist. Matt and the boys went down on a knee as Rick motioned Harry front.

Going front Harry saw what Rick saw, an abandoned car in the North bound lane with its doors open.

"What do you think boss?" Rick asked.

"It looks like someone was headed north when this happened," Harry replied. "Let me look through these," as Harry pulled the thermal binoculars out and scanned the car and the sides of the road. "I don't see any heat signatures, "drop your pack and I'll cover you as you check the car," Harry replied.

Harry dropped his pack next to Ricks and scanned the area again with the binoculars, he then brought his rifle up to the ready as Rick went forward to check the car.

Coming back Rick said, "Boss we might be seeing more stalled cars and if we do this at every car it will take us longer to get home. We must develop a quicker way to clear the cars so we can keep up our pace."

"I agree, let's get everyone together and come up with an SOP for when we come upon these cars," Harry replied.

Harry waved everyone front. "Guys, we will more than likely come upon more abandoned cars as we get closer to Palmer, so this is what I think we should do. When Rick sees an abandoned vehicle, he will have the thermal binoculars to check it out, if he sees no heat signature, we will give it a wide berth and keep moving. If he sees a heat signature, we will set up a defensive perimeter until we can determine if it is safe to pass by. Matt you and I will cover Rick while you boys cover our rear and sides. Are there any questions? Okay, Rick lead off and we will keep fifty-foot distances."

We continued down the road passing two more stalled cars before they passed the cut-off for Lake Louise.

As they passed Lake Louise road and Harry wondered to himself how many hunters might be stranded back there. He called a break and had a meeting.

"Guys, Lake Louise is back there, I'm wondering how many stranded hunters are back there and how many are trying to walk out. I'm wondering what their supplies are and what condition they are in."

"You're thinking about that group back at Chistochina aren't you," Rick replied.

"Yeah, and they may be in front of us desperate for food," Harry said.

With the sun just past its zenith, they made it to the small town of Mendeltna. This was about a dozen homes scattered in about a mile area with a Roadhouse that served meals and alcohol. Not wanting to take the chance to be around people who might be desperate they went past the lodge and about five miles down the road they started looking for a place to camp for the night.

SEPTEMBER 11

They woke up just as the sun was rising, Michael got the fire going and put the pot of beans that were soaking overnight on it. Harry had chopped up some bacon and put it in the bean pot. Rick looked at the pot of beans, "I'm glad you guys will be behind me today."

Adam made two small piles of dog food for the dogs which they sniffed then ate.

Taking off again even though they were strung out Rick continued the blistering pace he had yesterday.

They passed Nelchina, another small town with a roadhouse for meals and alcohol. They crossed the stream and camped in a pull out for the night.

SEPTEMBER 12

While we were eating breakfast, I mentioned that today we will probably pass Eureka Lodge and that this area usually had a heavy presence of hunters, I don't know what we might run into. Hopefully they all left for their homes and all we will see will be abandoned campers.

We took off and Rick set a medium fast pace.

I could see we were approaching Eureka so I called for a break. I wanted to be somewhat rested so we could pass by without stopping.

I wanted to be able to get several miles past Eureka if the situation there warranted that we had to. There were gravel cutouts where the contractor that built the road mined gravel for the road. In these cutouts I was seeing motorhomes, camp trailers, pickup campers and trailers for small ATV's. some of the RV's were burnt out hulks causing me to wonder what caused the fire. As we walked, I kept an eye on these vehicles looking for any sign of life. I was doing the math in my head of when this EMP happened and today's date. I came up with 22 days. By now any animals harvested their meat would be spoiled from the heat during the day and unless they smoked and dried it like we did they would be awfully hungry by now and thirsty since there is no water around to drink.

I called a break and had everyone gather. I told them what I was thinking.

Rick and Matt looked around.

Rick said, "Harry you're right, this looks like a place that had very desperate people. We need to be very cautious from now on."

Adam looked at me, "Grandpop, I'm scared."

"I know but do you know what being brave is? It's being scared but saddling up and doing the mission at hand. We must now be extra vigilant in our travel. You scan one side of the road and Michael you must scan the other side. Matt and Rick will be doing it also. They will be looking for ambush sites and I will be watching our rear so no one sneaks up behind us. But we have extra help with Buck and Snoopy and this" as I pointed to the thermal binocular that Rick

"This will give us an edge," Rick said.

We rounded a bend in the road and saw Eureka Lodge and a tractor-trailer truck That was pulling double trailers in the left lane in front of us.

Rick signaled for a stop and as he looked the truck and Lodge over, I moved up.

"What do you see?" I asked.

"The truck looks deserted but I saw some heat signatures by the Lodge." Rick replied.

"Let's keep an eye on the Lodge and hurry past it," I said.

As we were looking the situation over two Stellers Jays landed on the hood of the truck. Buck went forward and put his front paws on the front tire of the truck and "Woofed" twice. The Jays bobbed their heads and chattered back at him and then Buck turned his head and looked at us. He put his front paws back onto the pavement and started sniffing the tires and lifted his leg and watered one of the tires.

"Let's go I don't think we will have any problems here," I said.

Rick looked at me with a quizzical look, as a lump formed in my throat. "We'll be okay," is all I managed to say.

Going forward in our file formation I saw the truck was a Sourdough trucking truck pulling two Matson trailers, as we came abreast of the Lodge someone "Helloed" us and came walking toward us. He wasn't carrying any weapons that we could see.

"I'm John Roberts, my wife Ella & I run Eureka Lodge how far are you folks going?" he asked.

Rick looked at me, "We are going to try to make it to Anchorage before the snow flies," I replied.

Would you folks be willing to allow a family to accompany you as far as Palmer?" the John asked.

Rick looked at me, "It's your call boss but we are making good time and snow is coming soon."

"We don't have any supplies to spare for extra people, in fact we may run out of food before we get to our homes in Anchorage. Also, we are walking about thirty miles a day could they keep up and do they have any firearms?" I replied to the man.

John lowered his head, "No, they have no firearms. They came here two days after the problem happened and we were hoping that whatever caused it would be fixed. Well after a week and nothing happened all of the hunters who came here and the driver of that truck left. None of them wanted to take these people with them. With all of the people gone I went with them and we went through all of the motorhomes and camper trailers that were abandoned in the gravel cuts. We found a small mountain of supplies that were left behind. Also, that trailer truck was loaded with groceries and other items headed to Valdez which we unloaded into the Lodge so we have food, warm clothing, shoes, sleeping bags and packs for them but no firearms." John replied.

"Well, if you have all of this food and supplies why don't they stay here with you?" Rick asked.

"They also want to get home to Palmer," John replied.

While we were talking to John a young couple in their twenties with a young girl of about six years old came out of the Lodge. Buck and Snoopy went to them sniffing them and the little girl hugged Buck. Then the two Stellers Jays flew over them and landed close to them squawking and bobbing their heads.

I looked at Rick as he looked at me, "well Boss, I guess the decision has been made for us," is all he said.

"We are trying to walk thirty miles a day, if you can keep up and have your own food and water you can come with us but, we will not slow our pace for you and if you cannot keep up, we will leave you behind." I said to the couple.

"Sir, we will make every effort to keep up and promise not to be a hinderance if you take us with you," the young woman said.

I looked at the man from the Lodge, "okay, we will take them with us, can we fill our water containers while they get ready?" I asked.

"Of course, come up and come inside we will fill your water containers and we will even cook all of you a burger while they get ready." the man said.

Going into the Lodge I was amazed at all of the food stacked around. "You guys must have found a lot of groceries in those campers," I said.

"Yes, but most of it came from the trailer truck outside. It was headed to Valdez with a mixed load of groceries and other items." The man said.

True to his word we all were given huge hamburgers and fries, even Buck and Snoopy received one. Looking around I saw several new Radio-Flyer wagons and a large stack of bags of dog food.

"What would one of those wagons, a bag of dog food and one of those cans of Folgers Coffee cost me?" I asked John.

"Tell you what, since you are allowing Chris, Jennet and Meghan to go with you, you can have a wagon, a bag of dog food, the coffee and you said you were low on food each of you can have a case of Beef Stew." John said.

Rick looked at Harry, "that's a good deal Boss, eating rice and beans is getting old. Mixing a can or two into the rice would be a good change for a while."

Chris and Jennet came into the dining area, each one had a pack, "Chris," John called out, "grab a wagon, two cases of beef stew and open that box of bagged rice and grab five of those two pound bags of rice, two of those tubes of oatmeal, a jar of peanut butter and a box of Ritz Crackers to take with you. Ella, do we have a small pot we can spare for Chris and Jennet to cook in?"

"We have all of those pots and pans we got in the campers'
they can have their choice of them and forks, spoons and bowls."

It was around two in the afternoon and with handshakes and good byes our group with three additional folks and pulling two loaded wagons left Eureka Lodge headed back down the road to Anchorage.

Rick was back at the head of our column and as Rick and I had discussed, he was setting a fast pace. We put Chris, Jennet and Meghan in the back but in front of me in our file of march.

As I expected at first little Meghan was barely keeping up, Buck and Snoopy were at her side but finally, she was put onto the wagon with the supplies that Chris was pulling but Chris and Jennet were barely keeping up with the pace we were doing.

After about two hours and five, mile markers, Rick signaled for a planned break. Going forward I told Chris and Jennet to take their shoes off and check their feet. Going forward I was pleased to see Michael and Adam had their shoes off and each had a piece of jerky that they were chewing on. I continued up to Matt and Rick.

"Well boss was that fast enough?" Rick asked.

"Yeah, if you hadn't stopped when you did, I would have called a stop." I replied.

"How did our new folks hold up?"

"As I expected, it didn't take long for little Meghan to tire and be put into their wagon." I replied.

"Do you want me to slow down?" Rick asked.

"Not quite yet, we have about an hour or two before we should break for the night and we are going to soon hit some up and down hills as we start going thru the pass, so let's see how that shakes out." I replied.

"Okay another two hours and then decide if we want to continue or look for a campsite for the night," Rick replied.

I dropped my pack, why should I carry it to the back of the line only to carry it back here. I grabbed some jerky from the pack and headed to the back telling everyone to get ready. I was pleased to see the boys were facing outwards with their shoes off airing their feet and chewing on a piece of Jerky. When I got to Chris and Jennet, I gave each of them a piece of jerky telling them to chew on it to give them energy and to get ready we were about to head out.

I walked with them until we reached my pack which Chris helped me to put on. This was easier now as we were using some of the supplies from it.

We came to our first very steep down grade as we entered the pass. At first going downhill was a relief but soon my knees were screaming from the change. At the bottom of the grade Rick stopped early and came back to Michael and Adam as I went forward.

"We are going to hit some longer and steeper hills soon. Why don't you tie a short piece of 550 cord to the back axel of the wagons with a stick tied to the other end for a person to hold onto to help slow it down when you go down-hill and a piece of 550 cord to the handle with a stick tied to it to help pull it up-hill."

We continued on, with Rick still setting a blistering pace as the Mile Posts went by. The flat stretches of the Glenn Highway were now welcome compared to going up or down the hills. We were in the pass with the mountain on our right side and on occasion a steep drop-off on our left. We didn't see any more houses but occasionally we passed an abandoned car or pickup truck. Although we were strung out farther than normal, we were still walking at a faster than our normal pace.

Being in the mountains I started to notice that it was getting darker sooner when Rick called a halt. Walking front I had everyone come forward with me.

"I thought we should stop for a break and start looking for a campsite for tonight," Rick said.

"Yeah, it gets dark early in the mountains," I said. "Let's take a little slower pace as we search for a place for tonight. I still don't want to camp on the road, I would feel safer a hundred yards or more off of the road." I replied.

We walked for another half hour going down a long hill with a sweeping turn to the left. At the bottom we found a bridge with a small stream going under it.

While the others took a break, Rick and I followed a slight trail along the creek to find an area to set up our camp.

It wasn't much of a stream only about three yards wide and as we walked along the trail, I was able to scan both banks. I was looking for salmon carcasses a sure sign of bears in the area. I was feeling somewhat at ease as Buck was with us and he would give a warning of bears.

We soon came to a small clearing that held a small rustic cabin in disrepair. It looked like a trapper's cabin that had been abandoned for years. I covered Rick as he did a quick search of the area.

"Well boss, it looks like the cabin has been abandoned for several years. There are a few old campfires but none recent. I think his would be a good place for tonight." Rick said.

"Okay, let's go back and get the others," I said.

As we turned to go to get the others, two Stellers Jays came squawking up the trail and Bucks hackles came up and started a low growl. Rick looked at me saying, "we have trouble."

We slowly and stealthily made our way down the trail. We stopped just inside of the wood line and saw four men holding guns pointed at our people.

"There are two packs on the ground, where did those people go?" A man that looked and sounded like the leader asked Matt.

Matt didn't say anything as he and the rest sat on the far side of the road with their hands on their heads.

The man kicked Matt in his back, "I asked where are the two people that these packs belong to, I won't ask again."

All four of them were standing facing our group with their backs toward us. Matt had his head down. He raised his head looking toward the trail we took.

"The trail to Pete's old cabin. Kerry, you and Alex sneak up that trail and take care of those two and when you get back, we'll take care of these people." The guy that was the leader said.

Rick looked at me as he raised his rifle, but I shook my head no. I motioned that we should go back up the trail. We quickly but quietly went about thirty feet up the trail and I whispered to Rick to stop.

"I want to take these two guys alive if we can, are you up to do a snatch ambush." I asked.

"You bet boss, do you want the lead or trail?"

"I'll take lead, remember I want them alive to question them."

The good thing was the trail was overgrown that would provide good hides for us, the bad thing was the trail was overgrown and the two guys would be on us without too much warning. The trail made a sharp turn to the right and Rick and I thought this would be a good place for our ambush. As Rick picked a spot just before the trail turned and settled in, I went around the turn about ten feet up the trail and found a good spot.

It wasn't long before I heard them coming up the trail.

"That damn Bob, just because his father declared himself chief of the tribe, he thinks he can boss everyone around."

"Well one day maybe that will change, my parents are not happy how things are going and think Bob's father is keeping more food than he says he has. They were never good hunters and his mother Bessy can only grow weeds in her garden. My dad says that if it wasn't for the fact that they own the village store, they would starve."

The snatch went easier than I expected. Kerry and Alex had their heads down watching the trail and not their surroundings, Rick and I just stepped out with our rifles pointed at them. We quickly disarmed them and tied their hands behind their backs taking them to the old cabin.

"What are you going to do with us?" The one called Alex asked.

"Nothing if you honestly answer our questions," I replied.

"What are your groups intentions with our group?" I asked.

Alex looked at Kerry who just shrugged his shoulders.

"Every day Bobs dad sends patrols out a few miles up and down the road to look for travelers. We're supposed to tell them that we are there to help them."

"Then what happens?" I asked

"If they have any weapons, we take them from them and escort them to Chickaloon." Alex replied

"Then what happens?" Harry asked.

"Bob goes through their packs and takes half of their food as a toll to travel through Chickaloon." Kerry replied.

"Are there any check points or guard points before we enter Chickaloon?" Rick asked.

"Yes, at both ends of town is a check point." Kerry replied.

"How is it maned?" Rick asked.

"One of Bobs sons and a villager at each end." Alex said.

"How often and when are they changed?" Rick asked.

"Every four hours, 3 AM, 7 AM, 11 AM, 3 PM, 7 PM, 11 PM." Alex said.

"How many children does Bob have?" Harry asked.

"There are eight kids, six boys and two girls." Kerry replied.

"The girls, are they part of the guard group?" Rick asked.

"The girls are just as bad as the boys; some townsfolks say they are want-to-be-boys. They can be mean, meaner than their brothers." Kerry replied.

"Your rifles, how much ammo do you have for them?" Rick asked.

"Kerry and Alex looked at each other and shrugged their shoulders once again, "None, Bob and his kids keep control of it." Alex said.

"So, no one in the village has any ammo?" Rick asked.

"No." Kerry replied.

"Okay guys, we don't want you to go anywhere or do something stupid so I'm going to tie your legs together for a few minutes while Harry and I talk." Rick said.

He and Harry went a little way away from them out of hearing distance.

"Harry, I have a plan. We grab the other two and if what Rick and Alex said is true, we walk up to the guard post and capture it around 2:30 in the morning. When they come to change the guard, we snatch them also. That will give us three of Bob's kids and if we can grab the one at the other end that would be four. Half of his kids."

"Then what?" Harry said.

"Then if what Kerry and Alex said, they have arms but no ammo. They will now have ammo from Bob's kids and if any of them have weapons that use the ammo, we have we give them just five rounds each. We ask them to give us a three-hour head start, then it's up to them to take care of Bob, his wife, and kids. While we hustle down the road.

Going back to Alex and Kerry Harry asked, "what is the name of Bob's son down there and the other person?"

"Bob's son's name is Jimmy and the other guy goes by the name Little John," Kerry replied.

"Kerry you and Alex have been no trouble for us and answered our questions without any problems so we are going to tell you guys our plan and you let us know what you think." Harry said.

"Yes, I think it will work. There is bound to be one or two who like Bob's family but most of the town and area hate them." Kerry said.

"Okay, lets' get this show on the road." Harry said.

Kerry and Alex led the way as Harry and Rick followed. Just before they reached the road Rick went left while Harry stayed with Kerry and Alex.

After waiting the agreed upon time, Alex and Kerry followed by Harry stepped out onto the road. Little John saw them first and raised his rifle, Harry just ignored him as Jimmy turned around. Harry in his best parade ground, I shall be obeyed voice yelled, "Jimmy, put your rifle on the ground or you will die."

Jimmy just laughed bringing his rifle up, "who's going to do it, you?"

"No, me." Rick said as he stood fifty feet away with his rifle aimed at Jimmy.

"Little John, put your rifle down I know you have no ammunition for it." Harry said.

Harry's comment shook Little John and he lowered his rifle but Jimmy turned to now face Harry who had his rifle up to his shoulder, "Put your rifle down." Harry commanded once again.

On reflection Harry couldn't put his finger on what it was, a look in Jimmy's eye's, a flinch, a tensing of mussels in his body but Harry's rifle fired and Jimmy's head exploded with a pink mist.

Jennet let out a short scream and turned her head away while shielding Meghan from the gore.

"Well, now that we got that out of the way, what next boss," Matthew said.

Michael looked like he was about to puke while Adam was off to the side of the road retching.

Harry went over to the boys, "are you guy's, okay?" he asked.

Michael just nodded while Adam was still on his knees trying to vomit.

Harry gave them another minute, while he got a flask out of his pack and going over to Adam holding it out said, "take a little sip, it might help."

The Blackberry Brandy seemed to calm Adam a bit while Michael looked at his grandfather, "okay, just a sip." He said to Michael.

"All right everyone, gather around, you too you three you're in this too." Harry went on to explain what they planned to do. After he was finished, he asked for questions.

Little John raised his hand, "what are we going to do with Jimmy?" he asked.

"We're going to remove what gear we can use the rifle and ammunition will go to you guys for the village to use and the body will feed the Ravens."

"How will we explain him not being with us when we hit the check point?" Alex asked.

"Simple, you three will be escorting me and my sons to the check point, Rick and Matthew will be off into the woods covering us in case of trouble BUT, I don't want trouble. Alex and Kerry will go to any villagers at the check point. That way Matthew and Rick will know who Bob's kid is and can zero in on him. If anyone asks about Jimmy, say he is escorting a husband and wife with a small child who are walking slower. Chris you, Jennet and Meghan, with the wagon stay about 300-feet behind us. Just enough for them to see you but not be able to count how many you are. Alex and Kerry will separate any villagers from Bob's kid and I will do the rest. We want to get to the check point as close to two-thirty as possible but not later."

"Let's get what we can use off of the body and get closer to the check point then we will rest for a while." Harry said.

They found a pullout about a half a mile from the check point and stopped there until the time to go. Harry said he would take first watch and for everyone to get some sleep.

Harry rummaged in his pack and found a small container that held Folgers ground coffee. He put a pinch of it between his cheek and gum like someone would do with a pinch of Copenhagen. The caffeine rush started slowly then it hit him. This was something he did when he was on patrol in Vietnam. Harry looked at his watch and sighed. He ran his tongue thru his mouth and spit out the coffee grounds, reaching into his pack he got the Folgers ad put another pinch into his mouth and then went to wake the group by nudging each one on the foot with his foot.

1 AM THE MORNING OF SEPTEMBER 13

The group started out but this time with three extra people from the native village of Chickaloon to the town of Chickaloon.

They were spread out, Harry was in the lead with the three men from Chickaloon with Harry's grandsons next, then Rick and Matthew, and Chris, Jennet, and Meghan with both wagons starting to trail behind with Snoopy and Buck alongside. It was dark with just the stars and no moon to illuminate the way but it was still easy to follow the asphalt road. There was a steep drop-off on the left to the Matanuska Glacier and its river.

They were coming to a bend in the road when Alex told Harry to stop.

"Around this bend is the check point." Alex said.

"Rick, Matthew do you guys think you can get to the top of that hill on our right and look down onto the check point without making too much noise?" Harry asked.

"This shouldn't be too hard to do boss. Give us about forty-five minutes and we'll be in place. Let's go Mat." Rick said.

Harry looked at Alex, Kerry, and Little John, "are you guys ready for this. You must convince whichever one of Bob's kids that Jimmy is following behind with the family and any villagers there, make sure that they will go along with our plan."

"Chris, you and Jennet stay here with the dogs, I'll send one of my boys for you when we have control of the situation. Any questions? If not. Let's get this show on the road. Boys, stay a few feet behind us and no one get between Bob's kid and Rick and Mat."

They took off walking with Alex in the lead and Harry behind him. As they turned the corner the check point came into view. There was a fifty-five-gallon metal drum with it's top cut out with a warming fire burning in it. Three men were standing around it when Little John called out.

"Hey Billy, what's the good news?"

"Hey Alex, same shit different day. What's up with you guys? Where's my brother, Jimmy?"

"Jimmy is escorting a young family with a little girl. They cannot walk as fast as us. This is Harry and his two grandsons. They have been walking since the Taylor Highway almost at Chicken." Alex said.

While Alex was talking to Billy, Harry was slowly walking to Billy's side as Little John and Kerry went to the other two villagers.

"Alex what gives, these people still have their weapons?" Billy said.

"Yeah, I forgot to mention."

Harry moved quickly, he had slowly gotten close to Billy and while Billy had his rifle slung over his shoulder, Harry was carrying his cradled in his arm. He now swiftly brought it up with the muzzle pointed between Billy's eyes.

"Now be a smart man Billy and allow Alex to secure your rifle and then get onto your knees." Harry said in an even but forceful voice.

Billy moved to unsling his rifle and faster than can be imagined for an old man Harry pivoted bringing the butt of his stock up and caught Billy alongside of his head. Harry then hit him squarely in the forehead with a horizontal butt stroke knocking Billy out.

As Harry was doing this the two villagers moved to help Billy but Alex, Little John, and Kerry stepped in front of them stopping them.

129

"Okay guys let's get him trussed up and you two explain what is happening to the two villagers here." Harry said.

Once the villagers were explained what was going on they also were on board with the plan.

They now had less than thirty minutes before shift change to get ready to capture another of Bob's kids.

The capture of the other of Bob's kid went easier then the first. Harry was by the warming fire as the relief came towards them. Alex walked up to Bob's boy and stuck a pistol in his ear and pulled the hammer back saying. "Yes, it's loaded. Now get on your knees," as Kerry took his rifle and revolver from him.

Harry sent Michael to get Chris and Jennet. He then stood in front of the warming fire and raised his arms up and down like a bird flapping its wings. This was the signal for Rick and Mat to come in.

It didn't take long for everyone to make it to the check point.

"Alex, how far is it to the other check point?" Harry asked.

"Its about a mile-and-a-half down the road," Alex replied.

"Do you guys think you can take that check point without our help?" Harry asked.

"It'll be easy, they won't expect us to be coming so it will be a surprise." Little John said.

"Someone has to stay here to guard these guys. You should have a central point to keep these prisoners and once you recapture the town the whole town must decide what to do with them. If you keep them as prisoners you will have to feed them forever. If you turn them loose, they could come back with a large force and attack the town. So, you folks have to weigh what is the safest situation for the town in the future." Rick said.

"We'll give you guys about ten minutes then we will be coming toward you headed to Sutton and then Palmer. Remember stealth is paramount." Harry said.

As we passed the Southern check point, we saw Bob's son tied up and his face sported many bruises and cuts. I guess one of the townsfolks got a little revenge.

We shook hands with the people there and wished them well.

"Remember stealth is your only hope to carry this off. Pass out any ammo you got from their guns to town folks. You can do this and you must do what must be done no matter how distasteful it may be." Harry said.

With that they took off down the Glenn Highway towards Sutton. Rick was back on point with Mat behind him, then Adam and Michael, the Wilsons and their daughter who was sleeping in one of the wagons and Harry was in trail.

Rick was pushing the pace to get as much distance from Chickaloon as he could when they all heard it. The hairs on the back of Harry's neck stood on end, two Stellers Jays came flying by squawking.

"Jog," he said as he caught up with the Wilsons. Chris had a short piece of 550 cord tied to the wagons handle and the other end tied to a long stick so two people could pull the wagon at once like a team of horses. He just took off on a shuffling jog with Jennet right beside him. We caught up to Michael and he started jogging as did Adam. Mat and Rick were already in their airborne shuffle. I noticed that we were not in a disorganized panic mob but still in our normal places in line but now moving much faster. There were several more shots but a little fainter since we were putting more distance from Chickaloon.

Mat and Rick started to chant a "Jodie" cadence to keep our minds off of what we were doing and to keep us going. I was starting to puff and gasp for air. I thought *Hell Harry you ran further and with heavier packs than this, what's wrong with you?* I answered, *I'm no longer a thirty-year-old Green Beret paratrooper.*

I was relieved to see Rick and Mat starting to puff a bit and slow down. Two of the mile markers along the highway passed before we stopped for a break. Well, we slowed to a walk for a while to cool down before we stopped.

The boys took some moose jerky out of their packs and I went forward with pieces for Chris, Janet, Rick, and Matthew. When I did this, I noted that this bag of moose jerky was almost gone and when that happened, I would only have one more bag to get me home.

I was up front talking to Rick and Mat when we heard several small engines coming down the road. The two Stellers Jays were in a tree close by squawking.

Looking around I saw two sturdy trees almost opposite from each other across the road. Dropping my pack I pulled a large hank of 550 cord, tossing it to Mat I said, "You and Rick stretch this across the road using those two trees Then get ready to take care of any survivors. Michael, you and Adam get into that ditch there Adam use that culvert for cover. Don't shoot unless Mat, Rick or I start shooting. Chris, you, Janet and Meghan hustle down the road and find a place to hide off the road where no one can see you. I want all of you to know we don't know who is coming, it could be friendlies and if so, we don't want to harm them but, if it is someone who wants to hurt us then we will bring the hurt to them. Any questions? Then let's get ready." Harry said.

It was still dark since it takes a while for the sun the reach the pass through the mountains that they were in. The sounds of the engines was getting louder but Harry couldn't determine how many there were yet since they were in a small valley with a hill between them.

Suddenly the lights of one crested the hill and stopped, then three more pulled up beside it. It looked like they were talking among themselves when one took off and headed toward them. The other three were not so quick to follow but follow they did.

"Okay guys, it's show time," Harry said for all to hear as he went to be with his grandsons firing position.

The lead ATV looked like a Honda Foreman; it sported a gun boot in the front. The rider was traveling as fast as the machine would go. The other three ATVs were about one hundred feet behind him trying their best to keep up with the bigger machine when he hit the 550 cord and was pulled off of the machine landing on his back while the machine continued on and veered to the left going over the embankment three-hundred feet into the Matanuska River. The driver skidded twenty feet on his back, when he stopped, he got shakenly up reaching for his pistol. As soon as it cleared its holster a single shot rang out and he collapsed without a sound. The other ATVs skidded to a stop running into each other as they tried to turn around. Harry yelled, "SHOOT," to his grandsons as he started to fire his bolt action Winchester 30-06. He knew he hit one hard, a 180-grain soft-point hunting round is designed to mushroom on contact and make a terrible wound channel causing excessive bleeding. Harry heard one of his grandson's rifles bark close by feeling the heat from the muzzle blast.

Somehow, the three ATVs got tangle with each other in the effort to turn around, a stray bullet must have hit a fuel tank, the fuel must have gotten onto a hot exhaust because there was a whoosh and the dark morning sky lit up. One of the riders was caught in the tangled mess when the ATV's erupted in flames, his screams were horrifying.

Ten-year-old Adam never saw or dreamed of such a horror. He dropped his gun, putting his hands over his ears to stop the screams. Then the sickening stench of burning flesh reached his nose and he started to vomit uncontrollably what little he had in his stomach.

Harry took aim and the screams stopped.

As the ATV's burned there were pops as the tires exploded, then the ammo in the rifles that were in the gun boots started to go off and everyone took cover incase a stray round or ricochet would hit them.

There was one rider on the asphalt moaning, Harry, Rick, and Mat went to him and asked what happened back in Chickaloon.

He replied that the townsfolks had taken over the town and he, his brother and two friends were leaving before the townsfolks could arrest them. Harry asked him what the villagers were doing to his family, but he didn't answer, he had passed away.

"Michael, if Adam is finished, you and him gather what weapons and ammunition you can find then get ready to move out," Harry said.

"Boss, here is the 550 cord, it's too bad none of the ATVs survived," Rick said.

"Yeah, it would have been nice to ride for a while, at least until the gas ran out. The boys are policing up the firearms and ammo, when their done let's get going." Harry replied.

The rising sun was starting to turn the morning sky grey, when they saddled up and started out down the road to join up with the Wilsons.

Their walk normally was quiet but something was in the air now, it seemed more somber, even the Stellers Jays were quietly sitting in a tree on a branch just watching them. Snoopy and Buck just walked beside Adam and Buck would occasionally lick Adams hand. They walked slowly down the road each one lost in their own thoughts, a dangerous state of mind to be in.

Harry was the first to come out of the stupor, calling out to Rick to hold up for a break.

Going front he told the boys to come with him. When he got to Mat and Rick Harry said, "look I know it's hard to take a life, but if they could they would have killed us. This is the world we live in now. We must be ever vigilant for danger, trust no one until they prove themselves and then never really trust them. You two get your heads on and get over it. Michael, Adam, how are you guys feeling?"

"Everything happened so fast, how do you know which one to shoot," Michael said.

"You don't, instinct takes over. Ninety percent of the time men don't remember accurately what they did in a firefight. The best thing you can do is shoot the one closest to you then the next one and the next one until they are all dead." Harry said.

"It was so awful, that man burning alive, his screams, I don't know if I'll ever forget them and the smell as he burned, it was the worst thing I ever saw or imagined." Adam said.

Harry went over to Adam, putting his hand on his shoulder, "it is something that will stay with you forever. Oh, it will fade in time, but later in life when you aren't busy earning a living it will come back from the farthest recess of your brain to once again give you nightmares. This is the PTSD our fighting men in the military face every day. Some can handle it and some, well some cannot. You mustn't dwell on it. It happened, we're alive and that's all that counts, it's over, life goes on, we go on. Now let's go find the Wilsons and get on the way to Sutton." Harry said.

They started walking and before long Chris Wilson called to them from the side of the road.

They stopped as the Wilsons came out of the woods pulling the two wagons with food and Meghan.

"What happened back there, we heard shooting and a blood curdling scream like I have never heard before?" Meghan asked.

"Four people from Chickaloon were trying to escape village justice and they chose to fight instead of talk. Let's head to Sutton" Is all Harry said.

Ricks pace was slowing, they were a tired bunch as they headed to Sutton. The adrenalin from the ambush was wearing off.

Rick called for a break and everyone almost collapsed where they stopped.

Seeing this, Harry went forward to Rick, saying "let's find a camping spot off of the road as soon as we can. I figure we have about another ten miles before Sutton and I don't want to get there in the dark not knowing what we will find there."

I agree boss, I'm tired as hell, it's been a long time since I had to do anything like this." Rick replied.

About a mile later Rick saw an ATV trail leading off to the right and they all followed it finding a campsite about two hundred yards in. There were blackened stones from campfires and a small stack of cut wood close by.

"What do you think boss, a fire tonight?" Rick asked.

"Yeah, a warm meal and a fire might raise every one's spirits." Harry replied.

Harry went and talked to Chris and got two pots and a lid for one from him. He put water in one and got it boiling he then measured out some rice and put it into the pot, putting the lid on it and set it to the side of the fire. Chris came over with several cans of beef stew and emptied them into the other pot. By the time the stew was warm the rice was ready and everyone had a scoop of rice and of beef stew on top of it. It made for a hearty meal. Even Snoopy and Buck got a bowl of it.

After their meal they sat around the campfire but not for long. By the time it burned down to just embers they all were in their sleeping bags fast asleep.

MORNING SEPTEMBER 15

Harry was the first to arise. He rebuilt the now dead fire in order to brew some coffee. While that was happening, taking a firearm with him he went into the woods to relieve himself. When finished force of habit caused him to take a walk around their campsite. There was the usual things beer cans, broken bottles and jars and of course used toilet paper. Harry thought, *why can't people learn to dig a cat hole to bury their shit instead of letting it lay where it fell.* Harry was about to return to camp when he thought he saw something in his peripheral vision. He froze where he was. There it was, a huge bull moose bedded down. This is serious since it is the rut and the bulls are unpredictable during the rut.

Harry watched the bull chew its cud as he slowly left the area. As long as the bull was chewing his cud Harry knew he was not agitated. Getting back to the camp he quietly woke the rest of the group telling them about the bull and that they must quietly and quickly break camp and leave. Harry didn't want to kill it if he didn't have to, killing it meant either wasting the meat which was unacceptable, staying where they were and making jerky, which was also unacceptable with the approaching winter so that left carrying it to Sutton.

Harry was standing guard with his rifle as the rest broke camp and packed their gear. Harry had already packed his gear and was ready to leave.

The bull started to stir, he must have sensed or heard them. Harry was ready, standing up, the bull was a massive muscled specimen with a huge rack of over 50 inches. He was definitely master of his breed. A cow that Harry didn't see also stood up. The bull looked directly at Harry, lowered his head, pawed the ground when two Stellers Jays flew past him squawking. Shaking his massive rack, he turned and quietly melted into the forest. Harry was impressed, something so massive moving silently through the forest.

Getting on the Glenn Highway they headed south to Sutton.

The meal last night and a full night's sleep did wonders for them. As the their muscles started to warm from walking, walking became easier and the pace picked up. The anticipation and uncertainty of what awaited them at Sutton drew them like a magnet. Sutton was the last town before the farming town of Palmer.

Harry was worried that the pace they were going would burn them out and they would hit a wall of exhaustion. He thought that he would talk to Rick about the pace at the next break.

But he didn't have to, the pace slowed a bit and we started seeing houses meaning we were close to Sutton. Before I knew it, we saw a road block ahead. The ground had leveled out and several cars were pushed to each side of the road making a funnel that narrowed so a vehicle could not get through. There were two cars parked side-by-side making it more difficult to push them out of the way. This led to a road block maned by two men but I saw two maned firing positions on either side a safe distance from the road block but covering it. We were walking in our normal trail formation with Rick in the lead so he reached them first and everyone stopped where they were. I walked up to Rick and while doing this I quietly told everyone to be ready if anything happens.

When I arrived at the road block, Rick had his rifle off of his shoulder with the stock on the ground and he was resting on the muzzle in order to take some of the weight of his pack from his back.

"Charlie, this is Harry Miller, he and his two grandsons have been walking since the Taylor Highway up by Chicken, he's kind of our leader."

"Rick here says your group is just passing through and you don't need anything. Is that true?" Charlie asked.

"Well, we could use some fresh water if some is available, otherwise we are good." I replied.

"It's nice to see people who don't need anything but water." Charlie replied.

"Did you folks have any problems, is this why there is a barricade and guards with overlooks?" Harry asked.

The look on Charlie's face was all Harry needed to confirm what he speculated.

"When this first happened many of the people didn't think much of it, except for their vehicles not working it was just another outage and MEA would have it fixed soon. Only a few people recognized it for what it was and they took it upon themselves to secure our general store. There were a few tense moments but the community soon realized when the first hunters started walking in that this was not just another power outage but some sort of major event. A quick meeting of most of the town folks was held. Several of them, mostly women, wanted the food in the General Store distributed to the people but cooler heads took over. Guards were put on the store and we set up road blocks at each end of town. No one stays we have younger people who escort strangers thru town to make sure no one tries to stay." Charlie said.

"Well, we don't want to stay but if we could top off our water supply, we would appreciate it. Also, do you have any information on what we can expect between here and Palmer?" Harry said.

"We sent some men to Palmer about two weeks ago to see if they could get any supplies. Where the Glenn goes down a hill, then makes a hard left turn over a stream and then up a hill, there is a campground on the right there at the bottom by the stream. They said that going down the hill they could see tome activity there so they waited until dark to go past there and they did the same on the way back. You might want to do the same," Charlie said.

"Thanks, that is good to know since I thought of spending a night there. So, if you can get us our guide, and some water, well be on our way." Harry said.

The guide took them to a café at the intersection of the Jonesville Mine Road where they were able to fill their canteens and water jugs. He then took them to the other end of town where they parted ways.

They started out again in their trail formation with Rick in the lead but at a much slower pace. Harry was looking at the sky and the clouds when he called to Rick to hold up. Going forward as he passed a person; he told them to come forward with him for a meeting.

"Rick, Matt, you guys drive this a lot. How far is it to the place where we have to be careful of the campers?" Harry asked.

Matt looked at Rick and said, "it's about ten miles to Palmer from Sutton and that place is about four or five miles out of Palmer. I've been watching the mile markers and we're about seven miles from Palmer so we should be about two or three miles from that campsite."

"I've been watching the sky and the clouds. It's starting to look overcast and it's starting to feel like snow. I don't think we should go past that campground in daylight but at night but it's looking and feeling like snow so I'm open for suggestions. Do we stay here and put up a tarp, eat some food, get a little sleep and dig out any snow gear we might have or do we chance a confrontation and someone getting hurt or killed at the campground." Harry said.

Rick was the first to speak, "As much as I want to get home, I feel it's prudent we lagger here until about midnight and then head to Palmer. If it does start to snow besides the cover of night, we will have the snow to help us get by. No one wants to be out in the snow, especially at night."

Matthew spoke next, " I agree with Rick, but lets get a little closer but not to close that they would see any fire we build or hear us."

Harry looked at Chris and Jennet, they had their heads together and were whispering and nodding. "What say you guys?"

"We're under you guy's protection. We don't have any military experience like you guys do, you know better what to do in a situation like this than we do. We will go along with what you decide, but it does seem safer to wait until later to pass them."

"Okay, then it's decided. We will walk a little more, look for a good campsite and then try to gauge how long it will take to get to the campground and plan accordingly. Rick lead on." Harry said.

They walked for another hour when Rick stopped and looked into the forest on his right. Harry went up front.

"I feel this should be about as far as we go right now. I know there isn't much for a camping area but I feel we will have to make do." Rick said to Harry. Matt had come forward also and he agreed with Rick.

"Alright let's look for an easy place to get off of the road with the wagons and an area to set up a tarp for all of us in case it does snow." Harry said.

Harry sent his boys to quietly find some firewood while he and Matt joined two tarps the same size together by tying them at their grommets, then running some 550-cord down that seam and tying those ends off at two trees and tying the four corners off.

"It's not the Captain Cook but it will keep any snow we might get off of us." Matt said.

Harry looked around, "Where's Rick?" he asked Matt.

"He said he was going to see how far we were from the campground and how long it would take us to get there." Matt replied.

The boys got a fire started so the group could start cooking their meal. Rice has been on the menu every night. Even Snoopy and Buck got a bowl of rice to go with the little dog food they got. There was still a case of twelve cans of beef stew, so they opened six cans of that. They were trying to use up the items that weighed the most because they knew that they soon wouldn't have the wagons to carry their items, soon they would be back to carrying everything on their back but that was okay since Palmer would be about a five day walk to home if nothing went wrong.

Rick came back to the campsite just as the meal was being served, grabbing a bowl he sat down.

"Guy's, we made the correct decision to bypass them at night. I saw a warming barrel and three men standing around it all heavily armed. I worked my way down through the forest as close as I dared. I had to use binoculars but what I saw was troubling. It looked like I was looking at the walking dead. These people are either starving or they are druggies. Either way they will be desperate. We must be dam careful and quiet as we go past them. I think Matt and I should go past them first and set up an overwatch. When we are set up Harry, you and your boys set up an overwatch on this side while Chris, Jennet, and Meghan go by and keep going towards Palmer. Once they are past then Harry, you and your boys come by. With a little luck and stealth, we can pull this off."

After eating everyone but Harry bedded down for a little sleep. He told them he would stand guard since they were so close. He didn't want to be surprised again.

Snoopy curled up with the boys while Buck stayed with Harry. Once everyone was asleep, Harry got up and went a short way into the woods where he could still keep an eye on the camp and the way they came into their campsite.

"Wayne, are you sure you saw someone watching us from this side?" Alvin asked.

"Yes Al, I saw him plain as day. Stop your talking a minute and sniff the air."

"Why should I sniff the air? I'm not a dog."

"Sniff, there is wood smoke in the air. Somewhere close by there is a camp fire and that means people and people means supplies. Let's see if we can find them and steal their supplies."

"What if they have a guard?" Alvin said.

"Then we kill the guard and everyone in the camp. Besides they may have some food." Wayne replied.

"Okay I could use something to eat. Let's look for a trail." Alvin said.

Harry was sitting on a downed tree lost in thought thinking about his wife Samantha. He was wondering how she was doing. He knew that she had plenty of supplies, that wasn't the problem. The problem was his neighbor Tom and his son Tom Junior. Tom Senior often said if anything happened, he would come over for supplies. Harry told him the only supplies he would get was a load of double ought buck shot. But Tom Junior, he was a little sneak thief. Well, he wasn't little, he was seventeen years old and he was a trouble maker.

Harry's thinking was interrupted by a low rumbling from Buck and a male Stellers Jay was on a branch squawking.

"I hear them." Harry said.

Here I go again Harry thought. *Where are you bastards? How many are you?* As Harry quietly moved through the forest like a ghost. Slowly, quietly, step by quiet step he moved toward the trail they made. The Stellers Jay flittered from branch to branch leading the way. Buck stayed close to Harry.

Harry picked up the trail they made coming into their camp. He slowly squatted down to silhouette whoever was coming. He looked to his right and saw nothing, then looking to his left he saw the silhouette of two persons. He put his hand down to Buck to hold him back as he slowly crept up to the two persons.

He could hear them talking now. He was only a few feet behind them.

"You start shooting the ones on the right and I'll start on the left on the count of three." Wayne said

Harry took three hurried steps and cold-cocked the one on the left and he fell like a windblown tree, he stuck the rifle barrel into the ear of the person on the right and told him not to move and to slowly put his firearm down and step away from it.

Buck went to the other one that was out cold and laid down facing him so he would be the first thing the person saw when he woke up.

Harry told the other one to get onto his knees, and when he did Harry made a set of "Rope handcuffs" and slipped them over his hands and pulled them tight. These are impossible to get out of. He made another set and put them around the ankles on his legs. Now that this person was immovable, he went to the other one and was surprised to see that he was awake but not moving. Harry thought *I guess waking up and seeing buck staring at you has this kind of effect.*

"Slowly put your weapon away from you and put your hands behind your back. Harry made two more sets of rope handcuffs.

By now Rick and Matt were awake and at Harry's side asking all kinds of questions of Harry.

"Okay guys, simmer down. I overheard these guys discussing killing all of us and taking our food and supplies. Matt, would you be so kind as to police up these turds firearms and take them to the tent site. Rick, give me a hand dragging these turds to the tent area so we can question them. As we were doing this it started to snow.

By now everyone was awake and the boys had the fire going while Chris started getting items ready for a quick breakfast so we could leave. Jennet was taking care of Meghan who didn't want to get out of her sleeping bag this early.

We set the men outside but not too close to the fire, I didn't want them to get too comfortable. The snow was falling harder now and I could see out guests were getting uncomfortable so it was time to go to work.

"Gentlemen, may I have your attention, my name is Harry and I have some questions for you."

"Fuck you, you asshole, my head hurts. Why did you have to hit me so hard?"

"Well, it was to get your attention. I'm not fooling around. We all want to get home to our families so we need to know what awaits us at your camp down the road." Harry said.

"My head hurts, I'm not going to tell you anything until you give me something for my headache."

Harry went to his pack and rummaged thru it making a big production of it until he finally came back to the two prisoners. He had a six inch sharpening stone in his left hand and was stroking a wicked looking knife along it.

"Gentlemen, do you know what hurts like hell but isn't life threatening?" Harry asked.

"Why should we care," headache man said.

"Well a paper cut really hurts but your life isn't in jeopardy from it, that is unless it is just one cut."

Harry reached down and easily cut the jacket and shirt from headache man.

"What the fuck are you doing, it's cold and snowing." Headache man screamed.

His friend just sat there not saying anything.

Harry reached down and grabbed headache mans feet and took his knife and easily sliced up the sides of each leg pant to the waist taking the top half of the pant and tossed it into the fire.

Headache man tried to kick Harry but both his legs were secured at the ankles and he couldn't do anything.

"Like I said earlier I want some information and I don't have much time so let's get this on. Something easy, what is your name." Harry asked.

"You all are dead people, when Bruce realizes we aren't back he will come with a group looking for us and when he finds you, he will kill all of you and have fun with that nice piece by the fire."

Headache man howled in pain as Harry's knife made three quick slashes across his back.

"When I was in the Army I was with the Special Forces in Vietnam. We all had a pact with each other that if any one saw any of us being captured, they were supposed to kill us because if they didn't this is what was waiting for us." As Harry's knife made three more slashes across headache man's back.

"I can do this all night." Harry said as his knife slashed again and headache man howled in pain.

"Now let's try this again, how many people are in your group?"

"More than one but less than a thousand." Headache man said.

Harry made a cut around the thigh and then down the leg to the ankle and made a cut around it. All the while headache man was

143

screaming the whole time. When Harry stopped, he just laid there whimpering. Harry looked over at his buddy and winked as he lifted a leg and found a corner of skin and started to skin the leg of headache man. The screams were blood curdling. Rick came up to Harry, boss maybe we should set up an ambush in case someone heard the screams. Good idea because it might get much louder once I start in earnest.

"When you start in earnest?" Rick asked.

"Yes, this is just a little foreplay, I'm just getting his attention, I'm letting him know what is coming his way. It makes them talk quicker. When you go to set the ambush take the boys. Watch Adam he is a little green but Michael should be okay. This snow should cover our trail in here from the Glenn so stay back from it a bit." Harry said.

"Okay gentlemen back to business. How many people are in the camp you are from?" Harry asked as he picked up the leg he started to skin.

"65" the man cried.

"See that was easy, now what is your name?" Harry asked as he laid his knife on the leg.

"Wayne," the man croaked.

Harry dropped his leg as a scream came from Wayne. He looked at the other one and started stroking his knife on the sharpening stone as he walked over to him.

The man's eyes got wide and his bladder emptied as he started to cry.

"Don't hurt me, I'll tell you anything you want. My name is Alvin, there are 65 people in our camp, 24 men, 23 women, and 18 children." Alvin cried.

"What kind of firearms do the people in the camp have?" Harry asked.

No one said anything so Harry picked up Alvin's legs and started cutting his pants off.

"Hunting rifles, shotguns, some hand guns." Alvin cried don't hurt me.

"Too late, you didn't answer fast enough." Harry said. As he continued to cut away Alvin's pants and shirt.

"Next question, do you have a guard at the entrance to your camp on the Glenn Highway?" Harry asked.

"NNNNNot always," Alvin stuttered.

"Why not always?" Harry asked.

"People go hunting for food so we don't have enough to man a guard post. Besides there hasn't been anyone come by in a few weeks and when locals come by they are better armed then we are and we leave them alone." Alvin said.

"Will anyone come looking for you two?" Harry asked.

With the snow everyone will stay in their campers or tents." Alvin replied.

Alvin didn't notice Harry was pacing around while he asked his questions. He was behind Alvin for the last question and calmly reached around his neck and a quick pull and twist and Alvin went to a permanent sleep. Harry just laid him on his side. He went to Wayne who was in shock and did the same thing.

Harry went to Chris who was cooking breakfast by the fire, "I'm going to get Rick, Matt and the boys. After breakfast we're going to head out."

Harry followed the tacks in the snow but they were starting to disappear because it was snowing that hard, but fortunately there was now wind with the snow storm. A wind, even a little one will make their trek miserable.

Harry came up on the ambush site, "have you seen or heard anything?" Harry asked of Matt.

"No, the snow blankets all sound, it is scary quiet. Nothing is moving. I haven't heard anymore screams; you must have gotten all the information you needed." Matt replied.

"Yes, the other one, Alvin, was quite talkative. I cleaned the blood off of my knife and started sharpening it and looking at him. He wet his pants and wouldn't stop talking. He answered every question I asked of him with no snide remarks. I almost felt bad about putting him to sleep. Now his buddy putting him to sleep was a pleasure. Chris has breakfast ready then we will break camp and try to get past their encampment without any trouble. From what Alvin said everyone should be holed up because of the weather so that should be helpful for us then it should be about five miles to Palmer. Maybe we can find a place to weather the storm there." Harry replied.

2 AM THE MORNING OF SEPTEMBER 16

Breakfast was a simple affair of cooked rice with a little sugar on top. It wasn't fancy but it was hot and filling for a snowy day. The snow was coming down in big flakes and was starting to really accumulate in the mountain pass that they were in.

They decided that because of the snow and the reduced visibility to forgo the long spread-out trail formation that they normally were in and adopted a group formation. This helped with pulling the wagons of supplies that were starting to get bogged in the snow.

Little Meghan was riding in a wagon since she didn't have adequate shoes for the snow the rest of us were fine. Except for Chris and Jennet, the rest of us were able to get shoes for snow when we passed through Glennallen.

It was a little slower going with the snow but we soon came to the hill going down to the curve to the left and the stream where the campsite was. It was still snowing so hard that we couldn't see more than fifty feet. Rick picked up his pace to scout ahead as did Matthew. If need be we were going to neutralize any guards that might be out but I didn't believe there would be any especially at this time of the morning. I wanted to get here by three AM but it was almost four AM. I felt with the snow it would be still early enough to get by without any problems.

Before I knew it we were at the bottom of the hill and going left over the bridge that crosses the mountain stream. I didn't see Rick or Matt nor did I hear any gun shots so we kept going.

Suddenly there was a wide spot on our right signaling the entrance to the campground. There was a metal drum with the top cut out that was used for a warming fire but there was no fire or even smoke coming from it. We hurried past it and on the other side we had a hill to go up and at the top of this long hill the Glenn made a right turn. I wouldn't feel comfortable until we were past that turn.

After that turn the road levels out and the mountain angles away and the area opens up. Several houses are built along this stretch. The snow was still coming down and was about six inches deep and getting deeper. It was starting to be fatiguing walking and we reverted back to a trail formation with Rick and Matt walking side-by-side breaking trail. The boys were pulling one wagon and I was helping Chris pull the wagon Meghan was on And Jennet was walking beside it to keep Meghan quiet and from falling off. We had to be careful not to get overheated and start to sweat. Sweating would make us cold. We started making frequent stops to rest and cool off.

The heavy wet snow stuck to us and we soon looked like walking snow people. I lost track of the mile markers and soon we were going down a grade and on the right was the Palmer water tank. I was relieved to see this since earlier I had to help the boys by looping a piece of 550 cord around my pack and tying it off to the handle of the wagon and help them pull the wagon. With the water tower in sight, I knew it wouldn't be long before we would be going through the edge of town. I was sure since we were on the Glenn Highway and this was the Northern Avenue of approach that we would soon come across a check point.

We shuffled along, we stopped walking for a while, we were fatigued and in this condition in this kind of weather this was very dangerous. Hypothermia could set in bad decisions could be made that could cost a life.

We were passing a national chain gas station on our left, I was thinking how long will it be before there will be vehicles there to buy gasoline when we came upon one of those construction office trailers parked in the middle of an intersection of the Glenn and a side street leading into Palmer proper.

Rick and Matt stopped in front of the trailer, and so did Chris and Jennet. When the boys and I came up I saw two men with guns standing there but they were not in a menacing manner. There were two more men off to a side watching us. I noticed that there wasn't much snow on any of them so that meant there was shelter for them. Probably this office trailer and it probably had some sort of heat like a Mr. Buddy heater.

"Good morning, folks, I'm officer Jennings. Is there a leader of your group?"

Everyone looked at me, "I guess I am. What do you want to know?"

"What are your intentions?"

"Well in the short run, find a warm place where we can dry out until this storm is over. Then head on our different ways to our homes. Chris, Jennet and their daughter live here in Palmer. We were escorting them from Eureka Lodge. My boys and me live on the South side of Anchorage down by Dimond Boulevard, Rick and Matt also live somewhere in Anchorage. So, once we warm up, dry out, and the storm is over, with the exception of Chris and Jennet, we will be heading on to Anchorage." I replied.

The one that identified himself as Officer Jennings looked at the other officer who nodded. "Okay, go the gas station over there. We have been using it as a rest area for the hunters coming in but you folks are the only ones we have seen for a week. I guess they are all in from the hunting grounds or are holed up somewhere waiting for spring to come out."

"Go ahead and head over there now, Officer Baker will guide you. I'll be over in a little while for what information you folks can give us on how the conditions are up the Glenn."

He turned to the other officer, "Take them to the gas station and let them settle in, stay with them I'll be over soon."

He then went into the office trailer. I couldn't help but notice that there were several antenna's on and around the trailer, one I recognized as an antenna for a Ham radio.

We followed the other Officer to the gas station. In normal times it would have been an easy two-hundred-yard walk but the wind had picked up and the snow that was on the ground was blowing and it was still falling from the steel grey sky. This made for almost white-out conditions. This was the longest two-hundred yards that I ever walked. We were tired, cold and wet.

When we reached the building, the officer took a key from the ring he was carrying, unlocking the door he said, "I'll get some heaters going. We no longer keep all of them running continuously, just one to keep the pipes from freezing.

We filed into the building pulling our wagons in with us and the dogs following I noticed three Mr. Buddy heaters in a corner and a fourth that was running.

The gas station was like many others, a two-bay repair area attached by a door to the store area. Harry could see marks where shelving once stood holding chips, candy, donuts, bread, a a sundry of other products. The shelves which were now empty were relocated to the shop area and in their place were a dozen cots and more stacked in a corner. Where the counter where people paid for their purchases the cash register was gone and in its place were two, two burner Coleman propane cook stoves with some pots and pans, and a few spices on the shelves underneath.

A cozy efficient setup to handle refugees coming in from the hunting grounds north of here I thought.

The officer quickly had all three heaters going. I made a questioning comment, "Mr. Buddy heaters?"

"Yes, when things went south, several men knew immediately something serious was wrong. One of them contacted us while the others went to secure the grocery/department store across the street, while others went to restaurants, convenience stores, bars, liquor stores and secured those locations. It kept looters from running wild. We at the police department knew that there was a Militia or as they call themselves a Volunteer Alaska Guard of sorts here in Palmer. They were a close-knit group and we didn't know how many were in it. Horses with armed riders appeared who patrolled the community especially the downtown area they acted as a reactionary force to go to areas where trouble was brewing. Mayor Ed, declared Martial Law and a curfew. These people kept the peace and helped with the refugee hunters coming in from the hunting grounds. It seems your little group is the last to arrive." Officer Baker said.

"When the power went off were there any problems?" Harry asked.

"There were a few at first but the militia or guard stopped it before it got out of hand." Officer Baker replied.

"They stopped it?" Harry asked.

"We didn't get too involved; a few lawyers, the ACLU, and a few liberal citizens made some accusations to us about civil rights and abuse of power but then even they became quiet and minded their own business. I guess they realized or were shown the futility of complaining of civil rights and stopped complaining. Maybe they are taking notes of what is happening for when the power comes on but by then who knows how we will be when we come out of this." Officer Baker replied.

Everyone was claiming a cot and getting squared away when Officer Jennings and another Officer carrying a grocery bag came in the door shaking the snow off of themselves.

"This is Chief Ross," Officer Jennings said, "He has a few questions for you folks." Then he stepped aside.

"Good afternoon, folks I have a few questions. First where did you folks start from?"

Rick was sitting on his cot, standing up he said, "Matt and I are truck drivers for Lynden if it still exists. We joined this merry band of miscreants in Tok when the good townsfolks confiscated the loads in our trucks for the good of the town and sent us on our way South."

Harry chimed in, "us miscreants started on the Taylor Highway close to Chicken. We and another family group spent a week there smoking the moose meat that my grandson Adam shot and waiting for his sprained ankle that he got carrying part of it out to heal. We live in South Anchorage down by Arctic and Dimond Boulevard. That's where we are headed."

"Chris stood up, this group was good enough to allow my wife Jennet, daughter Meghan and I to join them at Eureka Lodge and tag along. We live here in Palmer and tomorrow hope to go to our home if it is still habitable."

"Fair enough, I'll talk with all of you again tomorrow. I brought all of you breakfast, don't get used to it this is the only food we will give you." Chief Ross said. Turning he put his collar up and with Officer Jennings following he went out into the snow storm.

Chris went to see what was in the paper bag. "We have breakfast here, eighteen eggs, a half-pound of bacon and a few potatoes." He spoke.

"Put them in the maintenance bay, it's cooler in there, that way they'll keep until morning," Rick replied.

"They, said they keep a heater going to keep the pipes from freezing, I'm going to heat some water up and take a sitz bath. I stink. I hope the men's room isn't destroyed." Harry replied.

After Harry came back everyone else heated water and washed themselves as best as they could.

Everyone was tired and after that they all crashed onto their cot. Harry lay on his awake wondering, how Samantha his wife is faring as he fell into a troubled sleep.

AUGUST 21, IN ANCHORAGE

Samantha woke up in bed with a feeling something was wrong. There was a slight chill in the bedroom. Rolling over to look at the alarm clock she noticed the light on the clock wasn't on. *"Oh shit, she thought another power failure. When will Chugach Electric get their act together."* She thought.

Throwing the covers off the chill hit her, she thought of putting her bathrobe on but thought the hell with it, the boys aren't here so she just slipped into her slippers and walked to the archway to the kitchen, there was a key caddy attached to the archway. Picking up a key fob and hit the remote start button. She waited but didn't hear the engine start. She hit it again and again the engine didn't start. Throwing on her rob, she went out to their Dodge Longhorn pickup and tried opening the driver's door. It wouldn't open with the key fob so she took the emergency key out of the fob and unlocked the door. Opening the driver's door, she noticed the curtesy light didn't come on. Trying the key in the ignition there was nothing.

"Shit," she said to no-one in particular. Going back to the house she went up-stairs, since it was a raised ranch house, and dug out a battery powered transistor radio. Turning it on and nothing, not even static.

"Shit, shit, shit, Harry, why do you have to be gone," Samantha said to no-one.

Taking a quick shower, she went to the emergency closet filled with emergency gear, and retrieved a Water Bob and four five-gallon collapsible water jugs. Going to the bathtub she filled the jugs and then unfolding the Water Bob and attached it to the tub spigot, filling it. This gave her one-hundred-twenty gallons of drinking water. She raced downstairs to the garage and found two more five-gallon water jugs that they used for camping with spigots on them. She was about to rush outdoors to fill them at the spigot beside the house but stopped just before opening the door. She then realized that she was still naked and ran upstairs to throw on some sweat pants and a pullover sweater. Running outside she filled those two jugs. Going around the side of the house she grabbed a stack of five-gallon plastic buckets and filled them also. Then she went back into the house and filled anything that would hold water. When she was finished, she had drinking and cooking water and water to flush her toilet.

Samantha tried her radio again twisting the dial thru all of the FM and AM stations and there still wasn't anything.

Samantha then went to their back yard where she fed the rabbits and chickens and gathered their eggs. She wished they had a rooster to be able to keep the flock going but the city codes prevented this.

Samantha then went into the house, after putting the eggs into the refrigerator, she went into the laundry room tripping all but the very necessary circuit brakers. They had a solar system to run the forced air natural gas heating system for the house, two freezers that were full of meat and other food, and the refrigerator. They had bought three sets of solar operated yard-lights at a local hardware store that she put on the back sundeck to charge. These would provide light in the house at night.

Samantha then went into the garage and retrieved a DeWalt drill with a number 2 Philips head in the chuck a spare battery, and a box of three-inch self-tapping screws. Going back outside she retrieved several boards that Harry had cut ahead of time incase this ever happened. She fixed the side gate that it could not be easily opened from the outside.

By now Sam was hungry so she opened a can of vegetable soup and set up one of the propane camp cook stoves from the emergency closet on top of her glass top stove.

When the soup was hot, she broke some crackers into it and carried it to the kitchen table to eat. She ate straight out of the pot it was warmed in to save washing dishes.

"Harry be careful but hurry home. Things are going to get bad very soon." Sam said to the four walls of the house. Tears started down her cheeks when there was a knock at the front door.

Drying her eyes, she went into the bedroom where one of their gun cabinets was located. Opening the door, she pulled out a Taurus Judge that was loaded with .410 number 4 shot alternating with .45 long colt rounds. Going downstairs she stood off to the side of the door and told whoever was there to come in the door was unlocked.

"Samantha, it's me Gary from across the street may I come in?"

"Gary of course you may come in. What brings you here?" Samantha asked.

"Well Phillis and I woke up and the electricity was off, then I tried to start our car to go to work and it won't even start. Then we saw you filling all the buckets and jugs with water. Do you know what is happening?" Gary asked.

"Well, Harry, the boys, and I have had this discussion several times and we have read books like "Lights Out", "One Second After", and read about the effects of a solar flare and what one did in 1859. Back then the most advanced electronics we had was the Telegraph. A solar flare hit earth so strong that the induced electricity caused sparks to fly from telegraph key boards, wires caught fire, poles burned and random fires were started. This later was called "The Carrington Effect (1). The other cause, it could be the results of an EMP." Samantha replied.

Gary looked at Samantha and asked, "EMP?"

Samantha looked at Gary, "let's go into the family room to talk."

Gary followed Samantha down a short hallway and turning left entered the family room. There he saw an 86-inch TV on the wall and four Las Vegas style IGT slot machines sitting on small tables. There was a couch and recliner's facing the TV. A small apartment size refrigerator sat in a corner.

"Have a seat would you like something to drink, a soft drink, water, sweet tea, or a beer?" Samantha asked as she retrieved a gallon jug of sweet tea and pouring herself a glass of tea from a plastic jug from Raising Cane's.

"A sweet tea would be fine," Gary replied

Handing Gary his tea, Samantha sat in a recliner chair and moved a lever on the side and the chair pivoted to face Gary.

"You are curious about EMP's. EMP stands for Electromagnetic Pulse. It comes from the detonation of an atomic type bomb at a high altitude over a country to disrupt and disable it's electronic and electrical abilities. Because it is detonated at a high altitude no infrastructure on the ground is damaged and there is minimal radiation involved." Samantha said.

"So, in other words, someone turned off the electricity and electronics on us. How soon will the power come back?" Gary asked.

Depending on the strength a few weeks to a few years. We now are back in the 1800's as far as electronics and electricity are involved." Samantha replied.

"What can I do now to survive?" Gary asked with a hint of panic in his voice.

"Do you have any firearms in your home, a propane camp stove, oil lamps, firewood for your fireplace, a stock pile of freeze-dried food or rice and pinto beans?" Samantha asked as she looked over her glass and took a sip of her tea. She could see the look of panic starting on Gary's face.

"I'm going to ask you some questions, you must answer them truthfully. Will you do that." Samantha stated.

Gary nodded his head.

"How much food do you have in your house, in your pantry, and refrigerator?" Samantha asked.

"I think we could stretch it to two weeks." Gary replied.

"In other words, maybe a week of groceries. How much cash on hand do you have at home?" Samantha asked.

"Two maybe three hundred bucks." Gary replied.

"Firearms, how many, what type, and what caliber are they?" Samantha asked.

Gary looked at Samantha sheepishly, "I don't have any firearms in my house." He replied.

Samantha took another sip of her sweet tea thinking, *"do I want to get involved and help them? He is a neighbor who lives across the street from us, he can help me by keeping an eye on our place, and he is the only one to make contact with me so far since this happened.*

Samantha let out a long sigh, "Okay Gary this is what we, you, your wife, and I are going to do. You're going back home and tell your wife to fill the bathtub as high as she can with water. You won't be able to drink it but there will be a time when the water system will stop working and it will give you a few more flushes for your toilet. Then she is to fill everything that will hold drinking water and put that to the side for the same reason. YOU, will gather all of the money you have in the house and come immediately back here. I'm going to rig two bicycles up with trailers Harry built, I will give you a pistol and quickly show you how to use it, and we are going to ride the bikes to the grocery store and try to get you folks as much long-term food as we can before the riots and looting start. It will take me about thirty minutes to get ready so be back here in thirty minutes. Tell her not to talk to anyone until we get back and if she asks what is happening, just tell her that you are going to help me with an errand. Can you do this?"

"Yes, I can." Gary replied.

"Good, finish your drink and let's get moving. I suspect we have only a few hours before the people will start to panic," Samantha said.

As soon as Gary left Samantha changed out of the sweater and sweat pants into durable pants with cargo pockets into which she put six seventeen round Glock 19 magazines. She slipped a black T-shirt over her head. It was a birthday gift from Harry. It was special in that there was a holster incorporated under each arm which she put her Glock into the left holster. She then put a Western style shirt with snap buttons on. Next, she put on a sturdy pair of well-worn hiking shoes.

Once dressed she went out the back door, down the stairs to a large 16 X 24 locked shed with a Gambrel roof that gave the second floor seven feet of headroom. Harry built it several summers ago with the help of several friends and many cases of Alaskan Amber.

Once inside Samantha unlocked two of the four multi-speed mountain bikes. Taking them outside she went back in and one at a time she removed two of the four homemade trailers about twelve feet long designed to haul freight.

Her next task was to reverse what she did to the side gate so she could open it. Just as she got the second bike and trailer out, she saw Gary come across the street.

"Gary, do you still know how to ride a bicycle?" Samantha asked.

"Yeah, but what are those contraptions behind them?" Gary asked.

"Harry built these from salvaged material. They are cargo trailers. We've had as much as one thousand pounds on each one, but I'll admit it was a bit tiring to pull it. We're going to the grocery store and get you guy's some long-term food that doesn't need refrigeration. Instead of the bike trail, we'll take the streets since no vehicles are operating. Let's get going."

The streets were almost devoid of vehicles since the EMP happened at night but there were a few that they had to navigate around. It took them about twenty-minutes to get to the grocery store, all the way Samantha kept wondering how many people would be there and will the manager allow them to go shopping.

Pulling into the vast parking lot Samantha saw about ten people arguing with a man at the main entrance. Riding up she could hear what was going on. The man was the night manager and with no communication he locked the store so no one could get in.

Samantha got off of her bike and strode up to the manager she recognized him as a deacon at the church she and Harry attend.

Samantha could see he was very stressed with the power being out, and people yelling at him didn't help.

"Excuse me David, do you have any employees working in the store right now?" She asked.

Looking at her he gave her a scowl until he recognized that she and her husband attended the church he did., "Hello Samantha why do you want to know?" He asked.

"Let me explain something if you don't know this already. It's obvious the power is out, but have you or anyone tried to start their vehicle? If they haven't, they will find that their vehicle won't start. What happened is one of two things. First earth might have been hit with a huge solar flare of a Carrington level or greater. This I doubt because there are enough people who monitor such things and they would have broadcast something.

The other thing that can do what happened is an EMP, an Electrical magnetic Pulse. Whatever caused this the electricity may not come on for a year or more. You now have a decision to make. Your freezers are full of food as well as your coolers. This food will soon spoil and you and the company will lose that revenue. Without electricity your cash registers won't work. So, if you have any employees in the store have them, go to the stationary section and get some tablets and pens. Have one employee escort one customer at a time and write down what the customer bought and price. You have mechanical scales to weigh items that need weighing, jot down the weight and multiply the cost per pound and jot that number down. Unless you have some old manual adding machines the employee will have to add the cost column and that is what the customer owes.

You won't be able to accept a credit card, snap card or any other plastic card. The customers will have to pay in cash and only in cash. When you make that announcement most of these people will leave since they more than likely won't have but a few dollars in their wallets, but they will be back with lots of money.

In the mean time you can get your employees briefed and you will be ready."

David looked at Samantha and she could see it was like a large weight had been lifted from his shoulders.

"Samantha, that just might work. I felt bad about all the frozen Food, meat, and produce spoiling. This way the people will have it."

David turned to address the crowd, "Folks, since the power is Out and we cannot use the cash registers, we can only take cash for your purchases. We will pair you with an employee and they will write down your purchases, then add them up. This is the only way this will work. So, form a line and as soon as I brief my few employees will get started. Those of you who must go home for cash, tell your neighbors about this."

"Samantha, do you and your friend want to come in?" David asked.

"I would like to but we cannot let our bikes and trailers outside unguarded," Samantha replied.

"Go around to the back of the store, there is a loading dock with a ramp to the back of the store," David said.

Gary followed Samantha to the back of the store complex where they saw three trailers with refrigeration units on the front of them but they were no longer running. Going into the back area they saw narrow carts with high racks on each end filled with cases of groceries to go out onto the shelves. These are called "U BOATS".

While Samantha and Gary waited until David the store manager got the program going in the front of the store to come back to them they looked at what was already on the U-boats. Samantha and Gary restacked the U-boats setting off to the side boxes of groceries, they wanted.

"Samantha, your suggestion saved me from having to make a big decision. What can I do for you?" David said.

"We would like to make at least three trips with groceries to our homes. What I would like to do is buy eighteen-gallon Rubber Maid totes and fill them with non-perishable food. I'd like to use one of the U-Boats to use for shopping and then stage the totes back here until we can move them." Samantha replied.

"I know I can trust you so I'll get you a tablet and pen to log your purchases." David said.

Samantha found an empty U-boat and with Gary following she loaded it with all of the Rubber Maid eighteen-gallon totes she could find. Taking them into the back room she then loaded it with the next size smaller tote. She dropped these off in the back room also.

Then putting twelve of the smaller totes with lids onto the U-Boat, with Gary following they headed to the rice and bean section of the store. Sam was surprised that there was no one in this section. With Gary writing down item, quantity, and price, Samantha started to load the totes.

When they were finished, having loaded all of the white rice and beans into totes, they went to the canned meat section loading up with all of the cans of Spam, beef, chicken, pork, tuna and turkey, they went to the back room to unload.

Going back out with larger totes, Samantha went to the dried milk section and loaded three totes with boxes of dried milk, she then filled a small tote with cans of Evaporated Milk. She learned years ago, when reconstituting powdered milk, a can or two of Evaporated milk will make it taste better.

Swinging by dehydrated mashed potatoes, she filled three totes with boxes of instant mashed potatoes. Next Samantha went to the shelves that held boxes of Au Gratin and Scalloped potatoes.

They filled four totes and had to go back and empty the U-boat.

Going back out Samantha filled four little totes with ten-pound Bags of sugar. Next Samantha filled a small tote with bags of All Purpose flour, she then filled two large totes with boxes of Bisquick. Then off to the Pasta aisle she loaded all of the spaghetti, boxes of macaroni, and other pasta she could find. Going to the spice isle she got six boxes of canning salt then filled the tote the rest of the way with Iodized salt, and pepper.

After unloading they went back to the spice aisle again and grabbed a small tote full of Garlic powder, Johnny's seasoning, several containers of dehydrated onions, several celery seed and mustard seed containers, dried mustard powder, coriander, and any other spice she could think of that they might need. She grabbed several bottles of Soy Sauce and Worcestershire sauce.

She went to the cereal section and filled two large totes with containers of instant oat meal. She filled two small containers with creamy and chunky peanut butter then grabbed six cans of cocoa powder and several bags of shredded coconut. Going to the meat section, Samantha grabbed six frozen turkeys. She filled a large tote with bacon and two large totes with spiral sliced hams.

Leaving the loading dock area after their last drop off, Samantha surprised Gary and made a left turn and headed towards the camping and sporting goods area of the store. There she grabbed four Blue Enamel coffee pots, cast iron pans in different sizes, two Dutch ovens, 2 griddles, four multi-fuel two burner Coleman camp stoves, she filled five large totes with the small green propane bottles, she set four Mr. Buddy heaters still in their boxes onto the cart, several Space blankets, all of the Mountain House meals on the rack, and the fifteen 72-hour food buckets, four five-gallon water jugs, all of the Life Straws, four Magnesium fire starters, two back packs with hip straps, and anything else she thought Gary and his wife could use.

On the way back to the stock room Samantha filled the side pockets of the packs with as many vegetable seed packets as she could. There still were many to be had. Then she filled the back packs with bath towels, hand towels, and face cloths packing it as tight as she could.

In the stock room Samantha started loading their bike trailers with cases of canned vegetables and fruit making sure to have room for some of the totes of meat, rice, and beans.

While they were doing this David came to the stock room.

Samantha could see he was stressed and tired.

"How is it going out front?" Samantha asked.

"It started out fine, people were understanding and courteous but a man and wife came and started to rile the people waiting in line. I went out and talked to the people and for now they are understanding but I don't know how long that will last." David stated.

"Do you have any firearms here." Sam asked.

David's face registered shock at Samantha's question.

"No, the company forbids firearms in the store unless you are a police officer or a security guard." David replied.

"We're getting ready to make our first trip, but we will be back. When I come back, I'll bring you some firearms and ammunition for them." Samantha said.

David looked at her, "I don't want to shoot anyone." He replied.

"You won't have to. Just the sight of what I will bring you should keep people in line and if things do start to get out of control a shot over their heads will get their attention and if I'm here when it happens, send someone to get me and I will back you up. Here is the list of what we have either on our trailers or stacked in the corner over there. We'll be back as soon as we can." Samantha replied.

"May God and Jesus protect you and your neighbor on your trip." David intoned.

The trailers were heavy. Harry built them with bicycle parts, using the front forks and bike wheels in the back and making a pivoting front axle for steering thus making them like long four wheeled wagons that were ten feet long.

Sam made sure to load the heavy items first on the bottom then placing lighter items on the second row. The load was heavy but they could manage it. Just before they left Sam realized the contents of the trailers would be a tempting target so she ran to the bedding section grabbing two comforters and some 550 cord from the tool area she covered the loads and tied the comforters in place.

"Out of sight, out of mind." She said to Gary.

Sam told Gary to take the lead and she would be behind him to provide security if they needed it.

As they rounded the back of the store and headed towards Dimond Boulevard Sam could see the line of people. Many of them were pulling wagons of some sort, she saw several wheelbarrows, and a few push type garden carts.

"Gary, me must hurry as fast as we can to get back here," Sam said.

"It does look ugly out front here. Well, the good thing is we won't have to worry about traffic or red lights." Gary replied.

Heading East on Dimond after they crossed the bridge over Minnesota Drive, there was a slight downhill grade. Samantha thought, *when you downhill, eventually you will have to go uphill.*

Turning East on Arctic Boulevard there was a short steep hill they had to go up. The load they were towing necessitated them to get off of their bikes and push them and their load up the hill.

Sam was anxious to get their load's back to their homes without drawing attention to them or their load by curious people.

As they crested the hill at the seventy-sixth street light, Samantha could see a crowd of people at the gas station/convenience store and it didn't look good.

Sam had Gary turn down seventy-sixth to take the back road to their home. She wanted to put distance between them and the mob.

Fortunately, no one was following them to their home.

"Gary, is your car in your garage?" Samantha asked as they turned onto the street that they live on.

"Yes," is all Gary could muster through his heavy breathing from the exertion of getting home.

As they were turning the corner to the street they lived on, Samantha said, "When we get to your home, run into the garage and release the latch to your door opener. We'll need your wife to help push your car out onto your driveway and then we'll pull the bikes into your garage and close the door behind us. We cannot let Big or Little Tom see us or what we have. If he does, he'll come begging or his son will try to steal it at night."

Pulling into the driveway Gary got off of the bicycle he was riding and on very shaky, rubbery legs hurried to the front door. Samantha noticed that Gary was very out of shape from the three-mile trip they had just made. *Gee I hope Gary can hold up, we have at least three more trips to make,* Samantha thought.

Getting off of her bike, Sam turned to look across the street to her home and was surprised to see Big Tom and his teenage son Little Tom coming out of the gate she locked beside their house, both were carrying totes of something.

Sam knew when she and Gary left, she secured the gate from the inside of their yard and went thru the house locking the doors to the house as she went thru them. So, the only way they could use the gate to get into their back yard was to either go thru their home or someone climbed over the fence. Big Tom was too fat to do that so it meant that his teenage son, Little Tom climbed the fence. The last time they replaced the raised sun deck they had the contractor put a rubberized membrane down on top of the joists before they laid the decking boards down. This caught the rain water and snow melt, channeling it to a gutter going to their back yard. This made the underside of the deck dry for storage. There were several totes and coolers stacked on pallets to keep them off of the ground full of extra survival food that wouldn't spoil from the cold of winter and in the summer, it was always cool under there since the sun didn't shine directly in there. As Sam raced across the street, she popped the snap buttons on her shirt getting ready to use the Glock 19 resting in the T-shirt holster.

"WHAT THE HELL ARE YOU TWO DOING IN MY BACK YARD AND WHAT'S IN THOSE TOTES," Samantha said forcefully, almost at a shout.

"Your husband, Harry, said if anything went wrong, we could have some of the supplies you have back there." Tom replied in a forceful challenging tone.

"THE HELL HE DID, YOU FUCKERS ARE STEALING FROM US. PUT THOSE TOTES BACK NOW! Samantha replied.

Having worked on the Trans-Alaskan Pipeline Samantha had a very colorful language to use when she had to and now was the time to use it.

"Or WHAT? Little Tom replied.

"OR THIS," as Sam pulled the handgun from inside her shirt where it was resting and aiming it at Little Tom's forehead.

"What, are you going to shoot me, we'll get the police." Little Tom said with a sneer on his face.

"IF you two assholes don't realize it, there are NO police things have changed. Sam emphasized. "NOW PUT THOSE TOTES BACK." She said as she thumbed the safety off.

"N N Now Sam, let's not do something that you'll regret." Big Tom stammered.

"The only thing I regret is not shooting you two sooner. NOW put those totes back!"

At gunpoint Big and Little Tom turned around and carried the totes back as Sam followed. Getting to where they were stored Sam could see that there were four other totes missing.

"Where the HELL are the four totes that were here? Did you fucking thieves take these already?" Samantha accused with venom in her voice.

"But, but, you guys have so much and we don't have anything," Big Tom stammered.

"I heard Harry tell you over the past few years to get ready for trouble and start buying extra supplies and each time you just chuckled and said that you would come to us if there was a problem. If you weren't such a fucking drunkard and leach you would have bought extra supplies. Now it's too late. I want the four totes you two took returned." Sam said.

"What if we don't" Little Tommy sneered.

The gunshot's surprised both of them. Big Tom wet his pants as dirt kicked up between his feet.

"The next ones will be in your guts. It's a very painful way to die and could take days of being in agony. You will put these totes back and go home and put the other four totes in front of our gate and if I catch either of you two in our yard without permission I WILL kill you. Do you two understand? DO YOU." Sam said.

Both of them just nodded.

Samantha kept her pistol on them as she followed them out of the yard, resecuring the gate behind her. She noticed how both of them eyed her bicycles and the two loaded covered trailers.

I'm eventually going to have to kill them, Samantha thought.

She helped Gary and his wife push their car out of the garage and pushed her bike and trailer into it. Closing the overhead garage door, she and Gary uncovered their trailers and hurriedly unloaded them onto the garage floor.

"Phyllis, you'll have to take all of this into your house while Gary and I go back for another load. Be ready for when we come back. We have at least three more trips to make. I must run over to my house to put some meat into one of our freezers and to get some things but I'll be back then Gary and I'll be gone."

Going into her garage Samantha put the turkeys, hams, and bacon into a chest freezer then went to the gun safe. She was surprised that the electronic combination worked on their gun safe.

Reaching inside she removed four-magazine fed 12 gage semi-automatic shotguns and four bandoliers holding six ten round magazines loaded with double ought buck shot. She had custom made these and other bandoliers.

Slinging this over her shoulder she relocked the safe and went over to Gary's house.

"Phyllis, with all of the commotion and Big Tom's mouth your house may become a target for people in the neighborhood who don't have much food. Do you know how to use one of these?" Samantha asked.

Phyllis shook her head no.

"Alright, I'll get it ready for you. The magazine holds ten rounds of double 0 buckshot. This is the safety switch, move it this way to fire it and to fire it just bull this trigger. Every time you pull the trigger it will reload itself and you just have to release and repull the trigger to shoot again. Hold it here tight against your hip and just two or three rounds and anyone trying to take your food will leave you alone." Same said.

Putting two others into one of the trailers and slinging the third over her back muzzle down so she could swing it up if she had to use it, she and Gary took off for another load.

Instead of using Arctic Blvd. they went down Rovena then crossed Seventy Sixth street and continued down to the Campbell Creek bicycle trail. They were going fast with their eighteen speed bikes even with the trailers behind them. Rounding a curve, they sped through a homeless encampment before they could react. These camps are populated by petty thieves who panhandle on the streets or steal things to sell so they can buy the next bottle of liquor or hit of drugs. They live a rather spartan life going to one of the several free meal kitchens set up by people who feel sorry for these bums when they want a meal. Otherwise, they roam the streets night and day looking for something that is not secured to steal or hang out on street corners panhandling for money and sharing a bottle in a paper bag. They still had no idea what happened since they had no electricity or any electronic devise.

They crossed a bike bridge over Campbell Creek and onto Dimond Blvd. just a short trip to the grocery store.

As they turned into the parking lot Samantha could see a larger crowd at the entrance so they went straight to the back loading dock door. Surprisingly there were no people in the back and when Sam tried the door it was unlocked and opened when she twisted the handle.

Hurrying inside they quickly closed the door and turned their bikes and trailers around.

Sam had Gary load the trailers while she took an empty U-boat and went out onto the sales floor and started gathering more supplies. This time she gathered personal care items, tooth brushes, tooth paste, shaving cream, bath soap, shampoo, she took all of the first aid items, rubbing alcohol, Tylenol, Neosporin, Cloverine salve, Vaseline, and other medications. She then went back to sporting goods. She grabbed two more back packs, sleeping bags, several of the blue tarps, knife sharpening stones, and 550 cord. Going thru the garden section she saw the seeds were still out so she grabbed hands full of flower seeds and vegetable seeds. Going thru the tool section she grabbed several cans of WD-40, several rolls of Duct Tape, in the kitchen wares she grabbed all of the vegetable peelers and church keys. She then looked for the largest stainless-steel pots she could find and grabbed three of those. Then she went back into the grocery store and grabbed all of the large black garbage bags that were left which was six. She grabbed rolls of aluminum foil and waxed paper. In the caning section she took all of the lids, cases of quart and pint canning jars, canning kits, two pressure cookers and two water bath cookers. She saw a display of Red Solo cups and grabbed several large sleeves of them.

Sam saw thru the front door that the crowed was getting unruly so she went to the storeroom and grabbed her shotgun and one of the spares she brought with her. Slinging two bandoleers of magazines crosswise over her shoulder she went front to find David.

She found him outside trying to calm the crowd and reason with a very large burly man who was talking and waving his arms around. It looked like the situation was almost at the boiling point. Samantha slipped out the door and walked up beside David and fired a round into the air. She then leveled her firearm and in a very loud authoritative voice commanded everyone to calm down and get back in line. The people slowly got back into some semblance of a line, all but the man who was arguing with David.

Samantha calmly turned and asked the man in a low voice, "Where should I shoot? Your elbow and take an arm off, your knee and remove a leg, or your Dick and remove your Dick and Balls," as Sam lowered the shotgun barrel to his crouch.

The man stopped talking as his eyes grew wide.

"You wouldn't shoot," the man said.

"Are you willing to find out," Sam replied

The man's face turned red as he backed away and got into line.

Samantha turned to David, "do you know how to operate one of these?" as she handed her shotgun to David.

"Ten round, magazine fed, semi-automatic 12-gage," David said as he took the gun and a bandoleer of ammunition.

"Tell me Samantha, would you really have shot his ahh Dick and balls off?"

Looking David in the eyes, Sam simply said," yes." As she turned and walked back into the store.

When she got into the stock room, she saw that Gary had both trailers packed and bed comforters over them hiding what was on them and tied down. There were shovels, rakes, garden hoes and other garden tools shoved under the 550 cord.

Gary looked at Sam saying, "I thought it would help stabilize the load and make us look like some homeless bums."

"Good idea Gary, put your pack on and let's get going. We're going to take Dimond again to Arctic but at eighty-first Street we are going to turn left and take the side streets back to your house." Sam replied.

Samantha remembered something Harry once said, "If possible, in a bad situation, never take the same route twice and if you can change up your schedule."

For some reason Samantha's watch still worked. She looked at it and realized the first trip she was gone from her house for over three hours but this time it would be just under two hours that she would be gone.

They cut down eighty-first street, this way if anyone was at the convenience store, they wouldn't be seen. Once again Gary was in the lead with Sam following. As they turned onto the street that they lived on Samantha could see the garage door at Gary's house was up and at that instant Big and Little Tom came out carrying a tote between them. Sam stood up on her bike's pedals and started to pump furiously. She was able to close the distance between them and cut them off from getting into their driveway with her bike and trailer. Stopping, Sam leaped off swinging her shotgun up and pointing it at them she stopped both of them but little Tommy reached behind his back. Realizing what was about to happen as Tommy brought his right hand from his back Sam saw his gun and fired point blank at Tommy. From ten feet the double-ought buckshot didn't have very much distance to spread out and ripped through Tommy's left side ripping it open. The

167

shot spun him around and knocked him off of his feet. The massive wound caused Tommy to bleed out in less than a minute. Big Tom started to curse Samantha while he went and picked up the pistol Tommy had. As he raised it Samantha fired again point blank into Big Toms large belly. A typical 3-inch 12 gage double-ought buckshot shell holds twelve 0.33-inch pellets, The #00 Buck pellet weighs 53.8 grains. This made a huge mess of Tom's stomach. Big Tom bled out in seconds. There were two large pools of blood in the street. Tom's garage door was open and Susan, Tom's wife saw what happened. She came running down the driveway screaming like a banshee picking up the pistol in Big Tom's hand. Turning she raised the pistol pointing it at Samantha. The twelve-gage roared again striking Susan in the chest. She fell backwards over Big Tom.

By now there was a small group of people coming to see what happened. Sam could see several were carrying rifles. She lowered her shotgun slightly so not to look threatening.

Sam recognized a few of them but she and Harry didn't have much interaction with them even though they lived in the neighborhood for over thirty years the demographics of the neighborhood changed dramatically, many of the first owners of homes in the neighborhood had raised their children and retired, moving out of state. The new home owners, even though Samantha and Harry tried to be sociable and welcoming the new neighbors they were younger and had interests different from Harry and Sam.

The first to arrive was Terry another longtime neighbor.

"Sam, what happened?"

"Hi Terry, it was bound to happen sooner or later. Earlier I caught Big Tom and his son stealing from our back yard. I made them put the items back and warned them that I would kill them if I ever caught them stealing again. Well Gary and I went to the grocery store and when we came back, I caught Tom and his son carrying a tote from Gary's garage over to their garage. Tom's garage door is open and I saw several totes that were in Gary's garage stacked in there. I confronted them and Little Tom pulled a pistol he had hidden and was about to shoot me when I shot him. Then Big Tom went and grabbed the pistol and tried to shoot me so I shot him. Tom's wife Susan saw all of this from their garage and came running and screaming. She went to Big Tom and grabbed the pistol that was in his hand and turned, pointing it at me so I defended myself again and shot her." Sam replied.

While Sam was explaining to Terry what happened the rest of the neighbors had arrived and heard most of what happened.

Gary came down his driveway going to Sam.

"Samantha, little Tom beat up Phyllis my wife. When she wouldn't open the door he broke in somehow and beat Phyllis then him and big Tom started going through the things we brought back, taking what they wanted to their garage.

Earl, the other original owner of a home in the neighborhood spoke up. "I caught Tom's kid in my back yard several times over the years trying to steal things. One time he was in my chicken coop stealing eggs. When he saw me, he dropped six fresh laid eggs on the ground breaking them and was over my six-foot wooden fence like a shot. I told Tom if I ever caught his thieving son in my coop or back yard again that I would beat the crap out of him. Tom got all huffy saying it wasn't his kid."

"What do we do now? Call the police?" a new comer asked.

"I'm sorry I haven't meet you yet, I'm Earl and my wife's name is Kathy, we live two doors up from Harry and Samantha, what's your name?"

"I'm Peter, Sally, my wife and I moved into this neighborhood about five years ago."

"Are you new to Anchorage or have you lived in Alaska for a while?" Earl asked.

"We're fairly new to Alaska. I work for the Caterpillar dealership on Arctic as a mechanic." Peter replied.

"I'm Tim, I too would like to know do we call the police and does anyone know why we don't have electricity and why our vehicles won't start?"

"No, we can't call the police, if any of you haven't noticed the phones both the land lines and cell phones don't work so we cannot call the police. Many of you may have already found out that your vehicles won't start. Only two things can cause this and neither one of these is a good thing. A CME or an EMP." Earl replied.

"What's a CME or EMP." Tim asked.

"A CME stands for Coronal Mass Ejection or Solar Flare. It had to be a very large one to kill all of our electricity and electronics so, I don't think that is what happened last night. The other EMP stands for Electrical Magnetic Pulse. Those are caused but a high altitude detonation of a nuclear detonation high in the atmosphere. This is what I think happened. Some country hit us with a high-altitude nuke." Earl replied.

"Does this mean we are all going to die from radiation?" Tim asked.

"Well, no and yes maybe. An emp is designed to knock out the electrical power and for those that aren't prepared they will eventually either die of thirst for lack of water, starve to death, or die from freezing this winter, or disease. Whoever did this want's the infrastructure in place and the people dead." Earl replied.

"My name is Terry, raise your hand's, who here has six months or more of supplies?"

Looking around Terry saw only a few hands go up.

"Folks, for those of you who do not know me I'm Samantha. What I was doing was helping Gary here to get supplies from the grocery store. As you all can see, I have two bicycles with trailers. I have two more a little smaller that my husband Harry put together for our grandsons to use if we ever had to leave. If we are going to survive as a neighborhood, we all must work together as a group." Sam looked at Gary, "Are you up to a few more trips?" Gary just nodded yes.

"As I said I have two more bikes with trailers. This will give us four bikes to haul supplies. We'll need at least two more bikes for people to provide security. If any of you have child trailers for your bikes, we can use you also. What I want you all to do is go home, have your wives fill everything that will hold water to drink and your bathtubs to flush your toilets when the water runs out, Then, come down here with your bikes and firearms. By then Gary and I will have this unloaded and we'll be ready for another trip. I want to warn all of you that things are starting to get sporty on the trip to the store so all of you must be ready and willing to use your weapons to protect us. Now go!" Sam said.

Terry, Peter and Earl stayed after the crowed left.

"We'll see who shows back up. Then Terry and me will move all of the stuff that is in Tom's garage back into Gary's and provide some sort of security for the neighborhood." Earl said.

"We can't leave the bodies lying here," Peter said.

"I'll get some shovels, Peter if you want to help we'll dig some graves and burry them while the rest go for more food.

Sam and Gary had emptied their trailers and retrieved the two bikes and trailers from behind Sam's house that Harry made for the boys and were waiting in the street when they saw Four bicycles coming down the street at seventieth street two more bikes pulling child trailers joined them.

One of the new riders said, "My name is Sue, don't ask my father was a Johnny Cash fan. We saw you guys make two trips and saw what went down. We live in those two houses over on the other street. Do you mind if we tag along?" Sue asked.

"Are there any others over there that are willing to help?" Sam asked.

"Yes, but they were afraid to ask thinking you guys wouldn't want them." Sue replied.

Sam looked at the four that came down the street, "Are any more coming?" She asked.

"No, they are staying back to help our wives and to tell the other neighbors to store water." Tim replied.

"Sue, are there any neighbors you can get to pedal these two bikes?" Sam asked.

"Yes, there were more but they didn't know if they would be welcome."

"Go get them, we will need some guards also. We are going to take Rovena down to seventy-sixth. Street, then follow it to the bike trail. There is a homeless camp along the trail, a group our size will get their attention so we must be armed, ready and willing to shoot our way past them. Also, I can foresee problems from them in a few days either with us or other neighbors so maybe we should clean out the camp when we go by there." Samantha said.

"Do you mean we just kill all of them?" Sue asked.

171

"YES, they will be a huge problem in a day or two when they can no longer get their alcohol or drugs. They will come through at night or team up with others and we will have to deal with them then. It's best to do what eventually will have to be done now." Samantha said.

"I agree, as distasteful as it seems we are now living in a different world and we will have to make difficult decisions. It will be best to do it now on our terms then later to be ambushed by them." Earl replied.

Sue and the other rider took off as Sam, Gary and the four other neighbors, two of which swapped their bikes for the two bikes with trailers left for the store.

They had crossed seventy-sixth St. and were half way to the Campbell bike trail when the others caught up with them. They had eight bikes with child carriers and four people riding as guards. All of them were wearing a backpack. Sam had Gary speed up as they continued to the encampment.

As they approached the place where the encampment was Sam was surprised to see all of the tents were gone, there were no people to be seen, just a pile of stripped stolen bicycle frames, busted shopping carts and mounds of trash and debris. Sam sighed in relief she really didn't want to shoot up the camp.

As they turned into the store's parking lot it looked like a riot was happening. They went to the back of the store and saw two bodies lying on the ground in a pool of blood. She was relieved to see none of them were David the store manager. Going to the personal door she found it locked. She beat on it and called out for David, letting him know it was her. The door swung open and David was standing there wild eyed with the shotgun she left him pointed at the door.

"DAVID IT'S ME SAMANTHA, DON'T SHOOT," she screamed. She saw a flicker of recognition in his eyes and his shoulders sag as he lowered the weapon.

"David, what happened?" she asked.

"It got to the point where there were too many of them and they rushed the doors. We managed to barricade and lock the inside doors but a few managed to get by. They then broke the windows down by the Deli area and they came in thru there. They are running amok out there destroying almost as much as they are taking." David replied.

Samantha turned to the people who came with her. "Guy's we're going to take back the store. We will form up in a column of twos. One will go right the other left. Keep about two arm width's apart and on my signal fire two shots into the ceiling."

Forming up Sam said, "Let's go."

When they came storming out the people in the back of the store saw the heavily armed people and started to run towards the front of the store yelling.

Sam saw that everyone who was with her was out and yelled, "FIRE."

The noise of eighteen rifles, shotguns and pistols going off at once was deafening inside the store and the falling debris from the ceiling further confused and frightened the looters.

In her best command voice Sam called out, "WE'RE COMING FORWARD, ANYONE WE SEE WILL BE KILLED ON THE SPOT GET OUT NOW WHILE YOU ARE STILL ALIVE!" she then fired of another shot.

She then told her people one person per isle and two on the far-right isle then they split up and moved forward.

The isle Sam was in had two elderly people in it a man and a woman she was in a wheel chair and he was slowly pushing it. Sam came up to them and the woman started crying.

"Get behind me and go to the back of the store and stay there. Don't move from the back." Sam commanded.

Sam heard an occasional shot both on her left and right. She came to the mid isle break and doing a quick peak around she saw several of her group forming for the final push front to the produce and check-out area. Several of them fired another round into the ceiling trying to hurry the people along. A mother with a baby and small child in an overloaded basket with baby formula came out of an isle next to her. The man behind her grabbed her at the break and seeing Sam gave her a questioning look. Sam shook her head and pointing to the rear of the store nodding her head. The man turned the mother around and told her to go to the back of the store. They continued front with an occasional shot and cleared the store of all but the people they told to go to the back.

Sam went out to the front doors. "This store is closed until tomorrow. We have enough manpower, guns, and ammunition to kill anyone trying to come in here. We are going to clean the mess you people made and tomorrow you people will act like humans and not animals. I, WE will kill you now go home."

They pushed shopping carts across the entrance and just inside where they broke the window at the deli section.

Sam had one person stand guard while the rest went and loaded U-boats to take back to the stock room.

The store was a mess with broken glass and cans all over the floor. Sam went to the sporting goods section and got several more back packs and went to the game section and put all of the decks of playing cards into one, she then went to the magazine section and grabbed crossword puzzle books. She worked her way towards the stock room. The store shelves were nearly empty of food so when she went into the stock room, she looked into the trailers parked there. One was empty but the other two had pallet loads of cases of canned goods, coffee, and other groceries. Sam told her people to use the pallet jacks to unload the trailers. As they came off the truck's they loaded what they wanted onto the four trailers. The people with child trailers pulled what they wanted. A pallet with boxes of bagged rice and another of bagged beans came off. Sam made everyone grab some bags of each until they were all gone. Sam went to the toy section of the store and lo-and-behold there were Radio Flyer Red Wagons there. She got some 550 cord from the camping area and tied them together in a long train and pulled it to the back room. They loaded the wagons with all that they could carry but there still was more pallets to unload.

Going over to David, Sam said, "This might be our last load. It will be dark soon and I don't want to be outdoors at night. How much do you want for all of the supplies we got?"

"Sam, you saved my life here several times you and your people don't owe me anything. The looters took it all is all I will tell my bosses if they even ask."

"Thank you, David. There are back packs and some wagons still out there. How close do you live from here?" Sam asked.

"I live close by," David said.

"Well David I and my neighbors thank you for the food. Why don't you get some wagons and tie them together, get a pack and load it and tie the wagons to the pack, and push a U-boat full of groceries home." Sam replied.

"I will, Sam. Good luck and I hope to see you when things get straightened out."

Sam and her group left with the guards pulling wagons mixed in with the people pulling trailers and wagons. Everyone had a backpack on filled with all manner of items.

It was dark by the time they got back to their homes. It was a tight fit but all four of her bikes with their trailers were put inside Gary's garage. Sam told Gary she would be over tomorrow to help sort what they got from the store. The trip home was interesting seeing which houses had candles or oil lights. Before the first trip Sam set out six solar powered garden lights for light inside of their home.

Going into their garage Sam removed several pistols from the gun safe, her Bushmaster AR-15 and two semi-automatic magazine, fed twelve gage shotguns. Going to a double steel wall locker she removed two cans of ammunition, a bandoleer's she made to hold six, thirty round magazines of 5.56 ammo for the Bushmaster, and two bandoleers holding five-ten round magazines for the shotguns loaded in double-aught three inch shells. She then staged the pistols around the house so she wouldn't be more than four feet from a loaded pistol. The AR-15 was staged upstairs beside the magazine fed semi-automatic twelve-gage shot gun with a ten-round magazine loaded with double-aught buckshot.

The day was very busy and exhausting for her when this was finished Samantha sat down in a recliner and started to cry with worry for her husband and two grandchildren. She eventually got herself under control and went down stairs to their second bathroom and took a hot shower. The day had been unseasonably warm and she sweated a lot, she thought she smelled like a horse from the sweat. Tomorrow she will go over to Gary's house and split up some of the food they had gotten from the store.

AUGUST 22 ANCHORAGE

Samantha woke with a start, was that a gunshot?

Getting out of bed she went to the bedroom window to peek out. What she saw made her angry. Throwing on a pair of pants and a shirt she hurried out of the bedroom, grabbing the shotgun and Bushmaster she raced down the stairs.

There was a crowed in front of Gary's house and shouts of, "we know you have food in your garage, we saw you take it in yesterday."

"Go away there is no food here for you." Gary said.

No one saw Samantha, she pointed the shotgun into the air and fired a shot. The sound of a gunshot behind them startled the crowed and they all turned and looked at Sam leveling her shotgun at them.

"You folks must leave. There is nothing here for you." She said.

She saw a movement on her right and saw Earl and Terry coming down the street. They were about twenty feet apart carrying shotguns.

"YOU FOLKS MUST LEAVE; I WON'T SAY IT AGAIN." Samantha yelled.

"Or what?" a man with a matted black beard who looked like he hadn't washed in weeks, pushed through the crowd walking towards Samantha.

"We WILL shoot, now go away and leave us alone." Sam replied.

The man kept coming, crossing the street and approached Sam's driveway.

"STOP RIGHT THERE," Sam shouted.

"Or what?" the man said again as he continued onto and up the driveway.

He was about fifteen feet from Sam when the shotgun fired. A woman in the crowd yelled, "she killed my boyfriend, get her."

The crowd turned and almost in unison yelled, "Let's get her." And started for her.

She lowered the shotgun holding the stock tight to the side of her right hip and started to pull the trigger moving the gun barrel from her right to left. No one saw that Earl and Terry were coming, spreading further apart they joined in with the shooting and with their backs now to Gary who overcame his shock also started firing.

It was over in less than a minute. With four shotguns firing double-aught buckshot rounds there were dead and dying along with blood and body parts laying in the street and on Samantha's driveway.

Samantha dropped the magazine from her gun and replaced it with a fresh one as Earl and Terry came to her. Gary went beside his garage and started to puke.

"Damn what a freaking mess," Terry said.

Peter Boyd came out of his home wondering what all the shouting was all about just as Samantha shot the first potential looter and watched in awe and horror as the people were cut down. He just stood there rooted in the horror he just witnessed. *What is happening*, he thought.

People along with Peter came from their homes and gravitated towards the shooting. Many were shocked and repulsed at what they saw. They started to talk among themselves and pointing to Samantha, Gary, Earl and Terry.

Earl spoke up, "Folks, all of you are wondering what happened here. Well, I'll tell you if you will listen. Samantha over there yesterday helped Gary to get some supplies and then when asked she helped other people to also get supplies. These people here were camped down by the Campbell Creek. It was a homeless camp or it really was a camp of thieves, drunks, and druggies. They came early this morning to steal from Gary what we worked hard to get. They were asked several times to leave but they chose to try to attack Gary and Samantha. What we just did was protect our neighborhood from an unorganized gang determined to take what they wanted. Yes, it's an ugly tragic mess. Look at it, LOOK. This is what will start to happen as people run out of food. We must band together as a neighborhood and become one. We must set up a defensive force and start to do security patrols. I will contact the people on the street behind us and tell them of our actions and invite them to a neighborhood meeting."

"I'll let them know," Sue said.

"Folks, it's not too late to grow some food. We need five-gallon buckets, plastic totes, lots of them, anything that will hold enough ground to grow potatoes, carrots, parsnips, and a few other calorie dense vegetables." Samantha said.

"Let's set up for either tonight or tomorrow around noon for the meeting. Another thing, I feel we can still get more supplies. Early tomorrow morning I would like to take a trip back to the grocery store as soon as we can with as many people we can safely remove from the neighborhood. Sue, could you go talk to the other neighbors behind us and see if they would like to accompany us?" Terry said.

"Let's do it, give me about an hour and let's meet back here and decide who will stay behind as a security force and who will go shopping. Everyone here pass the word to those that aren't here. This must be a community project if we are to survive." Earl said.

AUGUST 23 ANCHORAGE

Samantha woke early to feed and water the rabbits and chickens and gather their eggs. She unlocked the shed and removed four bikes and their trailers taking them to the front of the house. Then she relocked the side gate and shed door.

She saw Sue coming down the street with close to fifteen people on bicycles many were pulling child trailers and wagons. Every person was carrying a large empty back pack.

Earl and Kathy, his wife along with eight other neighbors from the street Sam lived on came riding down the street with trailers of some sort. There were over twenty of us in the bicycle convoy, and everyone was armed. Terry and Sally were standing close by.

"Would you guys like to come with us?" Sam asked.

"Yes, but we don't have any bicycles," Terry replied.

"I would like to too, we just moved here a few months ago and don't have much in our home." Sally replied.

"Sally, where's your husband?" Sam asked.

"He went to where he works to see if anyone is there and if not to see if he can get a backhoe and some other equipment into the neighborhood before someone either takes them or damages them."

"Okay, we have two bikes with trailers that need riders, I guess you two can handle them."

"Okay folks let's get going, single file. If someone cannot keep up call out and we will put that person in the front to set our pace." Samantha said.

Sam was apprehensive about what she would find when they got to the grocery store.

Turning the corner into the parking lot she saw about six people in the parking lot milling around.

Going around to the back of the store she saw no one around. Telling the people who came with her to stay back while she checked if anyone was around.

Checking the personal door, she found it unlocked. Knocking she called out for David. Not hearing anything Sam slowly opened the door. Calling out, "David it's me Samantha. I'm coming in don't shoot."

To Sam's surprise there was no one in the loading dock area. She had her shotgun at a low ready and peeked out onto the sales floor and saw no one, not even looters. Calling out again in a louder voice she got no reply.

Going to the back she called the people in telling them to also bring their bicycle's.

She had her four bikes with trailers taken out onto the sales floor and lining them up.

Addressing the group Samantha told them, "People with packs, put small light items into them like garden seeds, first aid items, small camping items, matches, magnesium/flint fire starters, wash cloths and hand towels, Mountain House dehydrated food packs. Save your trailers and wagons for heavier items. Pinto Beans or any beans, White Rice, Pasta, Potatoes or canned potatoes, beans, sauerkraut, corn. The frozen meat might be thawed out but it's only been three days so the meat should still be good if eaten in a day or two. Remember to get several face cloths, and cloth hand towels ten of each would be good and several gallons of unscented bleach if you can find it, if not any bleach.

One man asked, "Why do we need cloth face cloths, towels and bleach?"

Sam looked at him, "what will you do when your toilet paper runs out or, if your wife still has her period, grab even more. They can be washed in water with bleach. Be thoughtful in what you get but get seeds all of the vegetable seeds you can get. If there are any back packs left have one person fill it with the seeds and we will pass them out when we get back"

Sam, Gary, Sally, and Terry checked the trailer trucks that were backed up to the loading dock. Gary grabbed a pallet jack and started to unload while Sam went to the toy section of the store to look for more wagons. She didn't see any and as she was ready to leave the area was surprised to find four still in their boxes on top of a display shelf. She ran back to the loading dock and grabbing Terry they managed to get the last four wagons in the store.

They were careful opening the boxes and went to the camping section and were able to put two sleeping bags into each of the three boxes. They filled the gapes with packages of Pixie and Vibrex fishing lures, fishing line and reels. They then taped them shut with some duct tape. They roamed the sporting section and found four three-day boxes of mountain House food at the back of a top shelf.

Going thru the boating section she spotted a display with Olin flare guns and ammo for them. She grabbed all four of the guns and all of the packs of flare shells. Terry pointed to the air horns and their cartridges.

"Good find Terry," Sam said. They filled the last box with them and packages of whistles.

Back at the loading dock Sally under the directions of Gary were loading cases of canned food. Gary thought that this would be their last chance to get supplies here so he had Sally stack the trailers higher than they had in the past.

Sam and terry got back as Gary was finishing unloading the trailer and the others also started to arrive. Sam had everyone load as much as they could into and onto their packs and child trailers.

Everyone was back so Sam told them to form up outside with the four large trailers in the front. The wagons were tied to four bikes with child trailers.

"Folks, the route we will take is Dimond to Arctic then at eighty-first street we will turn in and head to Rovena and home." Samantha instructed.

The trip back was grueling with the loads that they had. At Arctic and Dimond Sam had two guards who weren't pulling anything to go further up Dimond and scout on the Costco warehouse store.

The two scouts returned out of breath, as they were pushing the last trailer up the hill to eighty-first and went to Sam.

"Tony, what did you guy's see?" Sam asked.

Still gasping, "Damn, I'm out of shape. Sam, at first, we didn't see anything in the parking lot but as we got closer, we saw several bodies close to the building and there were some men on the roof with guns. There were hand lettered signs warning people to keep away. We went down King Street to their distribution building and there were men on the roof there.

We tried to talk with them about what was going on but they shouted something that we couldn't understand. It was quite evident English isn't their mother tongue. I believe it is possible to take this store if done correctly and with patience."

"Let's get this back to the neighborhood and then we will have a meeting." Sam replied

As Sam turned onto her street, she was greeted with a street lined with yellow equipment. While they were gone Sally's husband Peter was busy. There was a Cat 420E backhoe loader, Cat 988H loader, Cat 313 TH Excavator, and a Cat D9 dozer.

The convoy of bicycles pulled in front of Gary and Sam's home.

"Folks, gather around. Tony and Troy went to scout the Costco store to see what its conditions are. We all know that if it hasn't been looted yet there are pallets of long-term food there. Enough to last all of us a year or more. I'll let Tony and Troy tell you what they saw." Samantha announced.

"Folks, Tony and I broke off and scouted the Costco warehouse store and the distribution center. When we were able to get a good look, we saw several bodies in the parking lot close to the entrance to the store. There were at least four-armed people on the roof of Costco and hand lettered signs warning people not to come onto the parking lot.

We went to King Street and scouted the distribution building. What we saw were three-armed people on the roof. We tried to talk to them but their responses were very garbled from another language.

The questions that must be asked is do we want to take the risk of injury or death taking one or both buildings. If we do take the buildings, what do we do with all of the food inside.

If we do decide to take one or both buildings, we will need more information on the people there. That should not be too hard to do since there is a hill at the King Street exit that has a wooden fence on the top. A perfect place to observe both buildings. Also, there is a car repair shop with several vehicles in a fenced yard where we could hide and observe them. Then the back side has a storage yard and Industrial yard that would give lots of concealment to observe them.

We don't know how many are inside the buildings so that is why a few days of observation by four or five three-man teams we should be able to get a good idea of their force."

Samantha came forward. "Thank you, Tony. So, do we try to take Costco and the distribution building or allow a gang of people who could eventually come into our neighborhood at night and attack us. Think about it talk it over among yourselves and then tomorrow at noon lets meet here.

The people who were pulling the four wagons, please leave them here. They have gear in them to share with the neighborhood."

AUGUST 24

Samantha woke up suddenly, something was wrong. She slept with her bedroom window open slightly and something was different. Lying still she strained her ears to hear, she smelled the fresh air almost as soon as she heard it. RAIN, it was almost two weeks since the last rainfall and the gardens needed it.

This will help us with the surveillance of Costco, Sam thought. She rolled over and went back to sleep.

Bells ringing, why are bells ringing" Time to wake up. This is all a dream and everything will be normal when I wake up.

Getting out of bed she turned off her windup alarm clock. Going to the kitchen she started their gas stove, *well at least the gas still works, I wonder for how long.* She thought. As she put a coffee pot on the burner. Going back to the bedroom she dressed for the day. The animals need to be fed and watered and egg collected.

Entering the house by the back door she realized with the eggs she just collected there are more eggs in the refrigerator than she can eat. She thought about sharing some of them with the neighbors.

Going back outside behind the house she brought several armloads of firewood into the house stacking it in a rack beside the fireplace.

Forty-five years ago, soon after they bought their house the house behind them burned. The investigation said the reason was the fire in the fireplace was too hot.

Harry said that these fireplaces were not made to heat the house but were made as mood fireplaces. Because of that Harry bought a FHK Hearth Heater. It has several tubes connected and a blower. They found out that even on the coldest winter night this would heat the upstairs of their home.

Going into the kitchen she started making herself an egg sandwich with a slice of ham and onion on it. While it was cooking, she took a snow apple from the fridge slicing it and salting the slices she ate that with her sandwich.

There was quite a crowed in front of Gary's garage for the meeting on what if anything they could do to secure the Costco store.

During the meeting it was discovered that there were two former Green Berets, three former Rangers, and six former Army Paratroopers, and two former Marines. It was decided that they would form four surveillance teams to scout the defenses of the Costco store. Samantha had Keven and Mac who were former Green Berets of come to her garage and she gave them four cases of MRE's, one for each group. She then loaned them two Bushnell thermal monoculars. They were very grateful for the MRE's and especially for the thermal optics. They then went to the volunteer's and broke them up into teams. Keven took two of the former paratroopers as did Mac, Peter a former Ranger said he would team up with the two Marines, Paul and Chris the other two former Rangers said they would team up with two of the former paratroopers and could be used as a reactionary force if any of the other teams got into trouble.

They then went off to Keven's garage to plan their mission.

Samantha went to Gary's home to help him break down the supplies they gotten.

There was quite a pile to go through. Sam pulled a few things out for her family but most of it was for Gary and his wife.

Once Sam felt that Gary and Phillis had an adequate supply to last at least a year, she started to make up "care" boxes for neighbors who might need help based on the help they supplied in the neighborhood. All of the supplies that Sally Parker brought back from the store Sam set off to the side and added some items to it.

While they were in the middle of doing this there was a knock on the side door of the garage. Sam's hand went immediately to the handgun on her hip.

"Who's there?" Sam called out.

"It's me, Earl," Earl called out.

Sam opened the door holstering her pistol.

"What can we do for you," Sam asked.

"My wife and I have a problem. We have been buying meat whenever there was a BOGO and have a freezer full of beef, pork and chicken and it's starting to thaw." Earl replied.

Sam thought for a minute, "Earl, we have several ways to preserve your meats. Canning, smoking, drying, and making Biltong."

"What's this Biltong thing?" Earl asked.

"It's one of the oldest forms of preserving meat. If done properly meat will never spoil and it won't need refrigeration." Sam replied.

"Well, I have a Big Chief smoker but no electricity to use it." Earl said.

"If you have a small cast iron pan you can put some charcoal in it and another pan of damp wood chips and you have a smoker. You can also take a vertical file cabinet and do the same," Gary stated.

"I can show you how to make Biltong, it's easy but a long process. I was planning on starting some later today as soon as I finish here." Sam said.

AUGUST 27

Samantha had finished with her outside chores and was sitting at the dining room table eating her omelet breakfast when there was a knock on her front door.

Answering it she saw one of the paratroopers that went with Keven standing there.

"Hi, my name is James Upton, is that bacon I smell?" James asked.

"Why yes. Would you like some and an omelet?" Sam replied.

"Real eggs?" the man asked.

"Yes, we have several chickens in the back," Sam replied.

"Ask no more, lead the way," the man said.

"What brings you here," Sam asked as they went up the stairs.

"Keven and Mac want to know what are we to do with the buildings now that we control them."

Stopping midway up the stairs, Sam top and turned around, "You guys have control of one of Costco's buildings?" Sam asked.

"No, both buildings and we will need more support to hold them."

"Don't let the bacon burn, I'll be right back." Sam said as she raced down the steps, grabbing the shotgun by the door and out the door to earl's house.

Banging on the door Phyllis opened it with a revolver in her hand.

"Samantha, what brings you here," she asked.

"It's important I need to talk to Earl now, is he around?"

"He's in the back with the chickens."

Racing around the back of the house, "Earl where are you?" Sam called out.

Coming out of the chicken coop with a small basket of eggs, "what's up?" Earl asked.

"One of the men we sent to surveille Costco came back saying they need more men. They captured both buildings and now we must hold them. Can you go to the next street and see if you can get as many shooters as you can. If they don't have a firearm or need ammunition have them come see me."

Sam headed to Gary's house, beating on the door and calling his name, Gary came out.

"Gary, can you keep an eye on my place for a few days. I'll have the side gate unlocked; the feed for the animals is in the metal drums in the coop. You're welcome to any eggs you collect." Sam said.

"Sure, what's up?" Gary asked.

"We control both of the Costco buildings and they need help to hold them."

"I'll come with you," Gary replied.

"No, we will need people here to watch the neighborhood. Get with Peter now and if he needs a firearm both of you come see me." Sam said.

Sam went home to question her guest.

"How were the eggs?" Sam asked.

"Ma'am, I hope you don't mind but I had four of your eggs. I haven't had a fresh egg in a few days."

"You can eat as many as you want, I get more every day. How desperate is it over at Costco?" Sam asked.

"Well right now it's not too bad but when we decided to take both places one got away. We took five of them alive and have them tied to pallet racking. They didn't know Mac spoke Spanish, they spoke of the coalition coming to rescue them and what they will do to us when they are free. Mac feels at the most we have two days to come up with a plan."

"I have a man rounding up some shooters but I don't know how many he will find. Harry, my husband was in the Special Forces many years ago. He didn't speak much of what he did. But; I helped him to make some things he called "force multipliers". While the men are being rounded up, help me load one of the big trailers with some of those.

We were in the shed when he pointed at a box labeled "field phones". "What's in that box?" He asked.

"It's marked field phones, whatever those are." Sam said.

"If they are what I think they are they will be a big help. Is there any wire on a green metal spool here?" James asked.

"Look behind the box." Sam said.

The box was large and heavy when James removed it from the shelf. Opening it he found six TA-1 PT field phones in a canvas zippered bag(2) and behind the box was eight DR-8 reels of WD-1 wire for them.

"We'll four of the phones and three reels of wire with us. What other goodies do you have in here?" James asked.

"Well, we have some of these twenty-pound propane tanks, boxes of new empty sand bags in different colors, how about some rolls of barbed wire, and behind the shed on pallets covered by tarps are twenty coils of fifty-foot razor concertina wire." Sam replied.

"Damn, what don't you have?" James replied.

"A pickup truck that runs." Samantha said.

They both chuckled over that.

"Let's load some of this up. We won't take all of it in case we need it here but some of this would be great to have at Costco."

As they were loading Earl showed up with twenty-five people. Some were husbands and wives, father and sons and one fifteen-year-old daughter.

"Who here needs a firearm?" Samantha asked.

"It depends, do we get to keep it and what it is you will give us." The girl said.

"Young Lady, that depends on you. If your parents will allow it, if you know how to handle firearms, if you are willing to follow orders and directions, and will you to become part of the neighborhood defense force or if this is just a one time gig for you to get a firearm. This also applies to everyone here. Times have changed, there are no police, par-medics, or fire department to call upon. We have just been put back to the eighteen-hundreds where we must take care of ourselves." Samantha replied.

"I'm Robert Samuels, Malissa's father. Malissa does have training and experience with firearms."

"Malissa will be put in harm's way are you and her mother comfortable with that?" Samantha asked.

"Malissa's mother passed away when she was six, I have been raising her ever since and yes, we both are aware of the situation and it's pearls and if called upon to defend our home and neighborhood."

"Okay everybody, your choices are, AR-15, AK-47, or a twelve-gauge semi-automatic magazine fed shotgun and for a side arm a M-9 pistol." Samantha said.

A grizzled old man who needed a shave raised his hand, "Missy, now that you have Costco what are your plans for it?"

"Our goal is to help everyone who takes part in this operation and who helps protect the neighborhood gets enough food and other supplies to last at least a year. That includes the people on the streets around us. If there is enough to provide for them and we have any supplies left over we will set up a distribution system for people for as long as the supplies last. But we will come first." Samantha said.

"That's what I wanted to hear. I may be old and look like a bum but in my youth, I was full of piss and vinegar. I guess I have one more rodeo in me. Sign me up." The old man said.

"Sir, what's your name?" Sam asked.

"Franklin Davis, I live just around the curve down the street" the old man said.

"Well Mr. Davis, we need someone to organize the neighborhood defense force with the people who stay behind. Do you think that is something you would like to do?" Sam asked.

"I can do that and we could be held in reserve as a reaction force if you need help at Costco. Do you have any comms?" Franklin asked.

"Yes, CB Radios but I don't want to use them because I don't know who else is listening." Sam said.

"Smart move Peaches. I have some BAOFENG radios all tuned ready to go I'll bring you three." Franklin said.

"Folks it's a long walk to Costco so if you have bicycles, especially bikes with child trailers, go get them. I need two people who can drive these two bikes with trailers and if anyone doesn't have a bike you can sit on one of the empty trailers. I want to leave in ten minutes. We must get there as soon as we can." Sam said.

There was a flurry of activity as people went for their bikes and to Sam for a better firearm. Two of Sam's bike trailers were loaded with supplies and ammunition. The other two were empty and were sitting out in the street ready to go.

The street started to fill with people on bicycles. Sam realized there were more people here now than earlier.

"Folks, where did you all come from?" Sam asked the crowd.

"I'm John Blaylock, I guess the unofficial leader of this group. Most of us live two streets behind you folks. Several of us have been prepping for a long time but most of the group are fairly new to the group. We formed a mutual aid and defense group mostly because of the crime especially from bums living in the pine forest behind our homes. When this happened, we formed a small defense group and when we heard what you folks were planning, we are hoping to join with you folks if you will allow it."

"Do you folks know what the understanding of the group will be?" Sam asked.

"Yes, you are the General in charge I'm comfortable to be the captain of our group answering to you." John replied.

About this time Franklin came to Sam. "It looks like word got out. I brought extra radios, I figured there would be more heads when I came back." He spoke.

"Okay give one to Mr. Blaylock there, one to James, I'll take one, and the rest tuck them in a box marked commo on the trailer." Sam replied.

"John, this is a large group. What are your thoughts on splitting into two groups. My group will go to Arctic and cut over seventy-sixth street to C street and your goes down Rovena to seventy-sixth and then down Arctic. This way if either one of us runs into trouble the other can come and help." Sam said.

"Sounds like a plan." John said.

"Bugler, sound boots and saddles." John commanded.

A teenage boy brought a trumpet to his lips and sounded a perfect "Boots and Saddles" as everyone mounted their bikes.

"I'll see you at Costco, safe trip," John said as he saluted Sam, and with a wave of his arm they were off.

"Let's go," is all Sam said to her group.

Keven and Mac were on the main Costco roof eating an MRE when Peter James came to them.

"Major, are we expecting company?" Peter asked.

"Which direction are they coming from?"

"I counted a group of armed men and a few women on bicycles coming up Dimond from Arctic. They joined a group that came down C Street on bicycles, many of them pulling trailers of some sort." Peter replied.

"That must be our reinforcements. Notify the men friendlies are coming."

"Roger that sir."

When Samantha pulled closer to the building Peter called down for them to go to the East side and a door will be opened.

Sam saw a man pulling on a chain opening a loading door while another kept guard. Leading the group in she saw stacks of blue pallets forming a funnel directing them onto the sales floor re they were met by Major Peterson.

"Samantha, what did you bring me?" Keven asked.

"Christmas presents. Ammo, Radios, Concertina wire, sand bags, but they need filling, force multipliers, and about fifty troops."

"Great, why don't you folks take a break and unload the supplies while Mac and I figure out how we will use your people."

"What I would like to do, if possible, is to use about eight people to start making trips with supplies." Samantha said.

"That's an admirable endeavor Sam but, we don't know where or when the gangs will show up. It's too dangerous. We don't want any of our people captured by them. The plan is to lure as many as we can into the funnel you guys came in and kill them in it. We have another funnel at the front door. The distribution center across the parking lot is also set up.

If you would, have everyone move their bikes back in the paper section out of sight." Keven said.

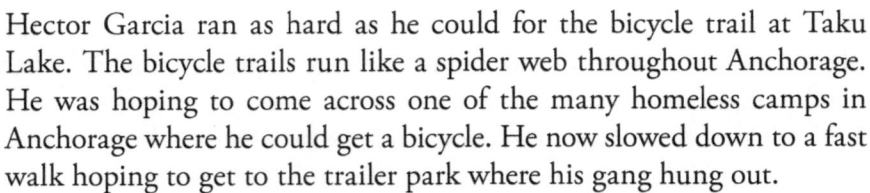

Hector Garcia ran as hard as he could for the bicycle trail at Taku Lake. The bicycle trails run like a spider web throughout Anchorage. He was hoping to come across one of the many homeless camps in Anchorage where he could get a bicycle. He now slowed down to a fast walk hoping to get to the trailer park where his gang hung out.

They had often had what if talks and one was the takeover of Costco if the power went out. They spent many hours sitting in the parking lot watching. Hector even got a job as a shopping cart wrangler. With the power going off at night it only made it easier for them to take over the store. The only people in the store were the night stockers.

Hector was the first one to realize the power went off He woke up to go to the toilet and none of the lights worked. After he finished peeing, he went outside to his car for a cigarette. He kept them in his car since his wife wouldn't let him smoke in the trailer. Opening the car door, the curtesy light didn't come on. Hector thought the bulb had burned out so he tried to start the car but it wouldn't turn over. He went to the trailer next to his and beat on the side of the trailer at the bedroom. "Longoria wake up." He called out.

The back door opened, "what do you want this late at night?".

"Do your lights work?" Hector asked.

"No, why do you wake me up for that?"

"Put your pants on and try to start your car." Hector told him.

Longoria's car also wouldn't start.

"What's wrong? This car always starts." Longoria lamented.

"This is something we always discussed. Something happened to disable the electricity and vehicles. It's time to put into action one of the planes we always discussed." Hector said.

"What plan is that?" Longoria asked.

"The taking over of Costco." Hector replied.

"I'm tired and going back to bed." Longoria replied.

"No, no, If this is one of those EMP things than we will need all of the food, water and other supplies we can get from Costco before any other people get there. Get dressed and get your guns, I'm going to wake the others. Just thing when people realize what happened they will panic and will pay any price for the food at Costco. They will have to pay our price." Hector said.

Hector could see in his eyes that Longoria now realized the opportunity they had.

It took Hector an hour to round up twelve of his gang members. They were assembled at his trailer.

"It's a long walk to Costco so get your bicycles and if you don't have one steal one. We must hurry." Hector commanded.

As Hector knew, there was only a few people working unloading trucks and restocking the store. The distribution center was unmanned. These people only worked during the day. One of the night stockers recognized Hector as an employee and opened the door to let him in and when that happened the rest of his armed gang rushed the door gaining entrance.

The plan was not to harm anyone and if they wanted to leave they could take a flatbed load of food and water with them. All but two took him up on his offer seeing the situation wasn't in their favor. Two went to their cars and Hector saw that they retrieved pistols from them. Two of Hectors men shot them dead in the parking lot before they could harm any of the gang. This was also something discussed in their "what if" talks.

After the rest of the employees left with overloaded flatbeds Hector called on Rodrigues one of his trusted lieutenants to get two other members and go to the Distribution building and secure and guard it.

They found the ladder to go to the roof and Hector had four of his men go there to keep watch of the area.

When the men left the neighborhood under the command of the Green Berets they chose to do it at night. By one-o'clock all of the teams were in position.

It didn't take Major Peterson long to realize that there wasn't much discipline among the gang members. He could see the roof guards smoking and was able to smell what they were smoking.

He had one of his men go to the other observation posts to instruct the men there to assemble at his location.

By two-thirty everyone was at major Petersons fall back location.

"Mac, what is your observation of our target in the short time we have been here?" Keven asked.

"Well sir, they are an undisciplined group with little or no military training. The guards on the roof are openly smoking what smells like Marijuana."

"That's my observation also. It will be easy to take them with what we have here. We'll take the Distribution Center first then concentrate on the main store." Major Peterson said.

"How will we do this without asking noise and alerting the others?" Paul asked.

"I brought with me my Winchester .338 Lapua. I have a suppressor on it and an ATN THOR 4 384 1.25-5X thermal scope. At the distance we are at they shouldn't hear the shot. I'll take out the three on the Distribution Centers roof then we'll send four men under Peter James to secure the building and defend it for now.

When that is done, I'll take out the ones on the store roof.

When that is done, I have a rope with a grapple on the end. We'll have two people climb the outside to the roof. When they come to change the guards we'll capture them for intel on who is left in the store. They will be expecting the guards that were on duty to come into the store so we will have an assault team quickly enter the store and kill anyone alive in there." Major Peterson replied.

The plan went off without any casualties to the group from the neighborhood. They managed to capture five gang members who were sleeping but they missed one.

Hector was in the restroom when they were attacked. He realized what was happening and left the building to get the rest of his gang and help from other gangs. There seldom were any turf wars among the gangs in town. They usually kept to their areas. It took him two days to contact the gangs closest to him managing to get forty-two men from the other gangs.

Their plan was to attack under the cover of darkness that night.

AUGUST 30 20:30 HOURS

"Major, outpost one is reporting, a large force of approximately forty men is assembling in the vacant lot on the South corner of Arctic and Dimond." Chris Holloway reported.

Keven looked at his hastily drawn map of the area.

"First Sargant Holloway, get on the land lines to the other outposts and alert them that where the OPFOR is staging for a possible attack tonight and to plan on an attack tonight. Then send three men over to the Distribution center to inform and reinforce them. Make sure they have adequate ammo." Major Peterson commanded.

Now it was a waiting game. Several of the men had pulled mattresses from the racking and were sacked out on them. The store had sheets, blankets and pillows that they used.

23:30 HOURS

"First Sargent, time to wake the troops and have them get ready. Use the Lateran if they have to and to eat something if they so desire. I want everyone in their assigned places by 23:30. Also, have the outposts go to full alert." Major Peterson instructed.

"On it, sir," First Sargent Holloway replied.

AUGUST 31, 00:30

"Outpost one reporting sir. There is movement." First Sargent Holloway reported.

"Okay inform the men. Was a direction given?" Major Peterson asked.

"No sir, just movement at their staging site." First Sargent Holloway reported.

00:100

"Sir, we have movement."

"Notify the men, full alert, an get ready to implement the plan." Major Holloway ordered.

"The roof guards report movement up Dimond and a group of approximately ten split off and are going South on C Street." The First Sargent reported.

"It looks like they are going to try to use that force to come in around the back while we watch the main force in our front. Order everyone to hold their fire, bring outpost one to their position two. That will cover our South and West area. Also tell them as soon as the break off force goes behind the building to go to their position three. That will provide flanking cover for the west side of outpost two. Have outpost three go to their position two so they can bring fire on this small group from the East and flanking cover for outpost two." Major Peterson thought, *this is like a giant game of RISK. Only instead of plastic pieces and dice, I'm using live people who some of them could lose their life.*

"Sir, roof reports main group maneuvering to rush the front doors and position three reports the break off group is about fifty feet from the east side of the building."

"First Sargent, have outpost one, two, and three on my command engage no survivors. When the shooting starts have group five come around the Credit union and engage the main body with maximum fire power. Let's push the main group to the front doors. All outposts, Engage."

The noise and rifle fire were loud and intense. The ten-man group behind the building was cut down in less than a minute. While not ordered to do so the small force on the Distribution center's roof also took the main force under fire. The survivors ran into the roofed cart area and hid behind the cement block wall and the main doors as glass rained down onto them.

"Groups one and five report what's left of the main force is in the cart area." The First Sargent reported.

"First Sargent, have them stand by with fire extinguishers if needed for the building and unleash hell NOW." The major commanded.

The force multipliers that Samantha brought had a mix of items. Some were four-foot-long six-inch diameter pipes whose ends were painted red. Four of them were four-foot long and also painted red but also had a yellow stripe painted on the end. These were all capped at one end with a small hole for two electrical wires connected to a blasting cap. The red with yellow stripe contained a home-made four-pound black powder charge, a gallon Zip-Lock plastic bag full of buck shot and a glass quart jar of home-made napalm and one of Magnesium shavings. There were fifty-pound bags of ice melt stacked behind and around it aiming and holding it in place. There were four of these. Two at the West end pointed East and two at the East end pointed West. There were also two, two-foot-long black iron pipes about four inches in diameter capped at both ends. They were spaced along the wall with bags of ice melt behind and on top of them. They were filled with home-made-black-powder. They had brought some batteries in from the battery and tire sales area. Harry made a switch board from phenolic and toggle switches. There were ten switches but only six had wires attached. They used a piece of commo wire to attach everything together. Samantha was inside the store behind a pallet of ice melt when she got the order to release HELL, she looked at Malissa, smiled, and said cover your ears.

The noise, even inside was deafening, she felt the concussion blast, and dust fell from the ceiling. Picking up her shotgun with Malissa following she rushed out the front doors along with the men with fire extinguishers.

The building was fine but there were screaming men rolling on the floor. The dry powder fire extinguishers were no good for magnesium fires that were burning inside almost all of the men.

Samantha pulled her pistol and started shooting the writhing, screaming men in the head silencing their screams and ending the hell they were feeling. Sam looked for Malissa and saw her on her knees against the wall puking. The screaming had stopped but the magnesium stilled burned, a sickly-sweet burnt smell over took Sam as she quickly pulled a small container of Vicks Vapor Rub out and put a large dab under her nose. Going over to Malissa she did the same. Sam was relieved to see men going through the carnage making sure everyone was dead and starting to police the serviceable weapons, ammunition and equipment, taking them into the store for their use later.

Sam took Malissa by the arm leading her thru the pile of carnage caused by the homemade bombs. Sam wanted her to be exposed to this kind of carnage because if there was a next time she wouldn't freeze up.

Malissa's eyes were closed and tears were running down her cheeks.

"MALISSA," Sam shouted and shaking her, "open your eyes, look around you. This is something you must see. As gory and distasteful as it may be, you must become immune to this if you want to be useful in case it ever happens again and you are called upon to help."

"This is horrible"

"Yes, this is horrible, many politicians in DC are fat and immune to sights like this and how they are created. They and their offspring never see the bad results of war but they have no problem sending other people's children to war. This is horrible, carnage at its worst but I'm afraid this will not be the last time we will have to do this." Major Peterson said.

"What are we going to do, are we going to burry them?" Malissa asked.

"We should because if not it could cause disease to spread. We'll send Peter over here with some security and the back-ho-loader to load up and bury the bodies but until then the Ravens will have a feast." Samantha replied.

"Well Samantha, you're up," Keven said.

"We'll still need security on the roof but anyone not being used in security let's get them together."

While Samantha was getting ready for the next phase which was the movement of tons of supplies Major Peterson had the First Sargent order outpost one back to it's original location and outpost five back to it's original location and to decrease their size to a two man outpost. He also pulled two, three, and four to return to the main building.

"Folks we have a huge task ahead of us if we want to be alive by this time next year or the year after. I have had a while to think of what we need to move first. The four trailers we have can hold up to one thousand pounds. So, with that lets put a layer of pinto beans and layer of rice on the bottom two courses, a mixed two layers of canned beef, chicken, pork and turkey. A layer of bottled water and Two layers of pasta. We'll do that with the four big trailers. The little child trailers we will load with fruits and vegetables. We have a daunting task ahead of us. Also, people will soon be coming here we must be ready to deal with that. Instead of sending them away we should have some boxes made up of supplies for them. So, lets get the bikes and get loading.

Using the flatbeds, the trailers were loaded and ready to depart when word came from outpost one that a tractor was coming up from Arctic pulling two pickup trucks.

Samantha and the Major went to the front of the store only to see Peter Baker and his back-ho loader come chugging up Dimond and turned into the parking lot pulling two pick-up trucks. Earl was behind the wheel of one and Gary behind the other.

Peter shut the tractor off, getting out he walked up to Samantha and Major Peterson. "We heard the shooting and figured you could use some help. Earl disconnected the drive shafts from the pick-up's so I could tow them and I can start digging a hole to bury all of these corpses.

"Major Peterson, have you thought of a place to burry all of these bodies?" Sam asked.

"I was thinking of the vacant lot over there," he said pointing to a large vacant parcel across King Street.

"The sun is coming up and we have tons of supplies to move. How about loading the pick-ups with all the Pinto Beans and white rice. If there is still room put canned meats, beef, chicken, pork, turkey, corned beef, tuna fish, and chopped clams. Get white sheets to cover what's on the trucks and tie-down straps to strap the load to help keep it on." Samantha asked.

Samantha rounded up all of the bicycle riders and with four riders as guards took off for the neighborhood.

They made quite a spectacle as they headed back home. The sun was now up and people were outside staring at them as they went by. It took a while to get to the neighborhood because they had to push the bikes up a short but steep hill.

Pulling into the neighborhood they had a problem, where to put all of the items. Someone said Tom and his family won't be back let's use his house as a store house for now.

They quickly unloaded the trailers and used the bathroom as needed and headed back for another load. When they got back, they found out the trucks were still being loaded. The people there used the time to bury the dead.

As they were loading for a second trip a person came running from the Distribution building. Major, Samantha, we were looking around the building and found four pallets of 100-Watt solar panels with load controllers.

"That's fantastic, we want every one of them. When they come back after unloading the pick-ups the solar panels will be the first thing they will load on the trucks." Sam said.

They took a different route home with the bikes. The tractor with the pick-ups left earlier. When they got into the neighborhood it was a bee hive of activity. People were still unloading the trucks and Peter was coming down the street with the large 988H loader pulling three pick-up's, a one-ton flatbed truck with a four-place twenty-foot toy hauler trailer used to transport four snowmachines or four-place off road vehicles attached to it. There were people sitting behind the steering wheel of each vehicle. Shutting down the loader Peter opened the door.

"Sam, look what I found, by the time they are finished unloading my first trip I should be back with this load and then take that train back for another load." Peter called down.

"Good idea, plus you can use the bucket on this to haul goods in. Listen, when you get there have two or three people make up care boxes. Use gallon zip lock bags and put rice and pinto beans in them and some cans of beef, chicken, or turkey, a few bottles of water and some snacks. We will give them out to people along our routes we take as a good will gesture. They are probably starting to hurt for food about now and some food might go a long way for us." Sam said.

"Peter, another thing, they found four pallets of 100-watt solar panels with load controllers. You're going to get them this trip. Cover them with several white sheets. I don't want anyone but those in our neighborhood and group to know we have them, and be careful if you strap them down so you don't break them. Now head out." Sam said.

Samantha went back to Tom's place thinking, *we have to think of a better name for our warehouse than Toms Place.*

Phillis Parker, Gary's wife was busy logging items on a yellow legal tablet.

"Phillis, how are things going?" Sam asked.

"We are using every room in the house and soon must find another place or stop bringing things here." Phillis replied.

"I figured it would come to this. I wonder if we can use the school to store some of our items," Sam replied.

"There is no one to ask but I would be careful. If the government ever gets their shit together, Schools would be the first place they will open for shelters and we would lose everything we have. I'm surprised they haven't come yet to secure Costco. There are a lot of food supplies and other things that can be used for the good of the people still in the buildings." Phillis replied.

"We'll have to store temperature sensitive items in peoples garages and the things that can freeze outdoors under tarps. Or we have the equipment maybe underground storage facility." Sam mused.

"We'll have to pass as much out as we can afford to, the people, especially the elderly and the ones along the routes we take. It will generate good will among the people that we might need some day." Phillis replied.

"Phillis your correct and the sooner we do this the better. I just had an idea. The beans and rice won't hurt to be outside as long as they are protected from moisture. I'll bring back several Food Saver machines and all of the food saver bags that I can find. You'll have to round up people to make up bags of rice and beans and vacuum seal them" Sam replied.

"What about electricity to operate the food saver machines?" Phillis asked.

"Don't worry, we have a 3K generator and extension cords to run them in our shed. When I come back, I'll get it for you to use." Sam replied.

The bikes were unloaded so it was time for another trip. On the way back to Costco, Sam started to count the days since the incident. She came up with the answer, it was ten days. *Thinking, a lot of food in the coolers and freezers might still be good. We can also pass those items out along our route.*

When Sam and her group turned into the Costco parking lot she saw a group of about twenty people at the front doors.

She directed her group to go around the side as she rode her bike to the group. Major Peterson was there talking to a person as Sam pulled up.

"We're trying to salvage and secure as much of the food and supplies as we can before we are attacked again or the government comes and takes it for their use. We are planning on making boxes of food and supplies to hand out to the people as our time permits." Sam heard Keven say.

Coming up beside Keven Sam put a hand on his shoulder and whispered into his ear. He nodded his head and Sam stood in front of him.

"Folks, we are shorthanded. As major Peterson hear said we plan on handing out food and supplies but right now we don't have the manpower to do so. What I want from all of you is to decide on ten people to come forward. Those people we will allow into the store and they will be responsible for gathering food and requested other items to distribute to the people here in front of the store. Some items are in large bulk like forty-and fifty-pound bags of beans and rice. We'll gather up all of the zip lock bags as we can find and some of you will have to break those bags down into smaller gallon size bags. Also, some of the products in the coolers and freezers may still be good to eat and we will bring those out to you. You people are the first here but we expect more to show up so you folks being here first it will be up to you folks to keep control of the people coming here and to fairly distribute the food and other supplies. Do we have a deal?"

The people looked at each other, talking among themselves when two men came front. "We'll do it." One of them said.

"Okay, here are the rules, no panic running around, ten people get flatbeds and I'll go with you to show what items are better to have. You will park the flatbeds at a central area and some of you oversee the distribution so there is no panic and a fair distribution. The ten shoppers can then go in for more food and special requests if any. You folks will have to do this for the rest of the day and at night we will stop it until sunrise tomorrow. You folks will have to come back then and continue to distribute food and supplies. IS THAT CLEAR." Sam said.

They nodded in agreement a few said "yes".

"Okay pick out who does what and let's get started." Sam said.

"We're going to the back to the cooler and freezer section to see what can be salvaged there first." Sam said.

Going to the egg section Sam opened the door and was surprised to feel it was still somewhat cool in there. She pulled a two-dozen carton of eggs out feeling the eggs and they were still cool.

"These eggs should be good for another week so someone load a flatbed with several cartons of eggs. You can come back for more if needed, let's keep them cool as long as we can. Let's check the bacon."

The bacon cooler was also still cool so she had someone load some of the bacon.

This went on through out the cooler and frozen food section. She instructed the people that when their flatbeds were full to take them out to the front and come back with an empty one. This went on throughout the entire food section of the store. Surprisingly for Sam the operation was running smoothly and as people went back to their homes more people showed up. People were pushing shopping carts loaded with food and other necessities back to their neighborhoods and their neighbors were bringing them back to get refilled.

Someone came front, telling Sam the bike people were ready to go so she left for her bike and trailer to get it loaded.

She had the loaders in the back load her trailer with two cases of two-dozen eggs and a case of five-dozen eggs and two cases of bacon along with a case of spaghetti and three cases of sauce. She also had them put thirty bags of ten-pound russet potatoes, a case of bananas, toilet paper, paper towels, 5 cases of water and any other thing she thought people would be glad to get. She told Terry to make up another load for her to distribute to people on her next trip.

Once loaded she told the others that she would follow them and stop when she saw people and hand out items from her trailer and also tell them if they can to go to Costco tomorrow morning for more and to also tell their neighbors to do it.

Sam went up C Street and then down 76th. Street. By the time she got back to the neighborhood she was almost empty and had told over twenty people about Costco. She felt that they could do one more trip before it got too dark so they went back to Costco for another load.

At Costco there was a larger crowd but everyone was behaving themselves so she immediately went to the loading area.

By now the people had a system set up and everyone was loaded quickly. Sam told Paul Roberts that they needed ten Food Savers and all of the Food Savor bags to be loaded also.

Sam's trailer was set up again to distribute food. She was surprised to see a box filled with Virginia style hams.

Taking off Sam went up C Street again but went into the Fox Ridge condominiums complex.

Word spread rapidly that someone was handing out food and she emptied her trailer in no time. As she handed out food, she told people to go to Costco in the morning and that they should also set up a guard post at the entrance to the complex.

Wen Samantha got home she parked her bike and trailer at the bottom of her driveway telling the people that there were Food Savers and Bags under the sheets on her trailer.

On wobbly legs she went to the back yard to feed and water the rabbits and chickens and gather their eggs.

Going into the house she put the eggs on the steps and locked the door. Putting her firearms by the door she went into the downstairs bathroom for a hot shower to ease her sore muscles.

She left her sweaty clothing downstairs and went upstairs with the fresh eggs in her hands to the kitchen to eat something before going to bed.

SEPTEMBER 1 IN ANCHORAGE

Samantha woke up to a pounding on her front door and her name being called. It was still dark outside. Throwing a robe on and grabbing a pistol she went downstairs to see who it was beating on her door in the dark.

"John, what's wrong," Samantha asked.

"There's a house on fire up the street," John replied.

"I'll be right out. Round up some men and meet me at my side gate." Sam replied.

As she took the stairs two at a time Samantha shed her bathrobe, going into the bedroom she pulled on a pair of pants, tossing her bra onto the bed she put a shirt on, buttoning it up as she raced to the back door, grabbing a ring of keys and a flashlight on the way, she raced down the stairs of the sun deck to unsecure the side gate from the inside of the yard.

There were four men there.

"Come quickly," Sam said as she turned and ran to their large shed.

Unlocking it "come here," she said as she entered and started handing out a fire hydrant adapter that they could attach to the 4 ½ inch discharge and had two nipples with gate valves that they could hook two 2 ½ inch hoses to, a hydrant wrench, passing out rolls of fire hose. There was a stack of twelve fifty-foot 2 ½ inch hoses. Sam came out carrying two nozzles, heading to the side of the shed there was a wheelbarrow into which Sam put the nozzles and four fifty-foot hose sections.

"Where is the closest hydrant to the house fire?" Sam asked.

Taking off toward the hydrant and fire. Passing two men with garden hoses over their shoulders, she told them to go to her back yard and grab some fire hoses.

Samantha saw that the house was fully involved and the houses on both sides were starting to burn. Getting to the hydrant Sam supervised the attachment of the hose coupler. Seeing more men coming she sent them back to her yard for all of the hoses left.

The coupler attached they started to roll the hose out and attach them together. Sam had them work on one hose line at once. When all the sections were connected and a nozzle attached, making sure both ball valves were closed she slowly, using the special hydrant wrench, turned the stem valve clockwise filling the hydrant pipe. Yelling ready she slowly opened the ball valve to the first completed hose while they were franticly assembling the other hose.

They used both hose lines on one of the houses beside the house that was on fire and got that under control then they hit the other house to the point where each line could protect each house.

Even though the house that caught fire was a total loss, they did manage to save and protect the houses on each side of it with minimal damage.

As the fire burned down and it was safe to do so, they turned the two hoses onto what was left of the house and extinguished that fire.

By now the sun was over the Chugach Mountains and more people came out to see the damage. Samantha went out to address the onlookers. When Earl saw where she was going, he gave the hose line he had to the person behind him and went to join up with Samantha.

"WHERE THE HELL WERE YOU PEOPLE LAST NIGHT," she screamed.

"When we have a problem in the neighborhood, we will need everyone to pitch in and help. There are no more police or fire department, we must now rely on each other to protect this neighborhood." Sam said.

A man came forward, "Ms. Miller, I didn't know that there was a fire or I would have been here, I used to be a volunteer fireman years ago. We need a way to summon everyone if there is an emergency." He replied.

Now, we can use some help rolling this hose up and taking it down to my house." Samantha replied.

With the fire-fighting gear put away, the rabbits and chickens fed and watered and eggs collected and put away, Samantha went downstairs to the bathroom shower and washed the stink of the fire off of her. She wondered how long the water would last. She could tell by the pressure that the pumps weren't working and they were relying on the million-gallon water tank on East Tudor and Patterson Street and gravity to supply water for the city.

She and Harry discussed that when the water stops running, they will have to go to Campbell Creek for water. They discussed what the possible dangers of that would be, would a gang take over a section of the stream and charge a fee to get water or rob people. Would a group take over the stream and deny people access to it. We'll just have to wait and see she thought as she stepped out of the shower.

She left her smelly clothing downstairs with those she wore the previous day and headed upstairs to eat breakfast and get ready to do more Costco runs. She was beat from getting up early and helping to

205

put the house fire out, which they couldn't do but, they saved the two houses on either side of it.

Samantha made herself a huge breakfast of eggs, home fried potatoes, and a large slice of Virginia ham. Even though she was tired she knew she had to do her part in hauling supplies from Costco.

She heard Peter and the 988H loader go by. It now was quite a sight. They chained two more pick-up trucks to it making it five pick-ups and a flatbed truck with a twenty-foot trailer. Putting her dishes in the sink she went to get the 3K generator for the people who were going to vacuum seal the rice and beans so they could be stored outdoors.

There still was a lot to move from Costco. Besides what was displayed on the floor the racking also held literally tons of items that had to be brought down by hand.

They still kept lookouts posted away from the store that were rotated out every two hours. Now they mostly directed people looking for food to the store or on occasion help an elderly couple to push their goods to their home and letting them know they could continue moving supplies as long as the supplies lasted. Many of these guards in their off time helped these older or handicapped folks move their supplies. This brought a lot of good will toward the group in control of Costco.

On one trip Sam searched for Keven Peterson finding him in the meat section of the store.

"Keven, during the attack we used a large quantity of force multipliers. I think we should send an armed group to a Lowes store to get more supplies." Samantha said.

"What supplies do you need?" Keven asked.

"Spectracide stump remover, visqueen, small nuts, nails, rolls of insulation, garden hoses and sprinklers, totes to hold items, and other things." Sam replied.

"The way things are going; in about four days we should have most of the food and other necessary supplies moved out of here then I can send two patrols out to South and Midtown Lowes to see what is the situation there." Keven replied.

"Okay, lets step up the community support if we can. We have been expanding our food storage to any garage we can fill. We can now start nonfood items like all of the playing cards, crossword puzzles, coloring books and crayons, Mr. Buddy heaters, work gloves, vitamins, tooth brushes and paste, bath and laundry soap, white bed sheets, dog and cat food and litter box supplies, nuts and chocolate candies, and I hate to say this but alcohol, especially Vodka." Sam said.

Sam's bicycle brigade switched from hauling supplies to their neighborhood to supplying adjoining neighborhoods. They concentrated on the neighborhoods closest to them and spread out towards Arctic Blvd. and 76th. street. Sam felt that they were just prolonging the inevitable but if they could get them to mid-summer, she had enough vegetable seeds for acres of gardens that and the russet potatoes they can use for seed the outlying neighborhoods could last two or more years especially with the salmon runs in Campbell creek. Sam knew she needed a rooster for her hens and put word out where ever she went that she was looking for one and a guard dog.

SEPTEMBER 6

It was bound to happen, the ten days of good weather started to turn and one day it started to rain. But that didn't harm them because they were finished moving the supplies from Costco. They now were breaking all of it down to distribute to the people who helped take the store and protect it and the neighborhood while they moved the supplies.

With the rain, Samantha put out totes, that she wasn't using at the time, to collect the rain water. She knew the tap water was about to end and the animals needed to be watered.

One day Sam got out their gas-powered lawn mower. She took the bagger off of it and opened the side discharge mowing there grass and the neighbors grass, making "windrows of the grass and when it dried she raked it up and stored it to feed the rabbits and chickens in the winter.

When Harry brought home the first pair of rabbits, he soon bought a pellet making machine to make rabbit and chicken feed pellets. They would dry grass clippings, leaf clippings from the vegetables they grew and they would shred carrots and dry that. When everything was dried, they would run it thru the pellet maker. Both the rabbits and chickens loved the pellets. In the summer they had pens for the chickens to free range and they would put their rabbits one at a time in a separate pen to free range on the fresh grass. Harry and Sam would harvest green shoots from their raspberry bushes to also feed the rabbits. They would toss ripened raspberries into the chicken run. They would also pick the slugs from their gardens and throw them into the chicken run. It was hilarious when the chickens saw them coming with Red Solo cup's they knew the slugs were coming.

The days started to turn colder and shorter on daylight. There was another short period where it didn't rain and things dried out. Samantha took this period to make one last batch of rabbit and chicken pellets.

SEPTEMBER 10

She got with Keven and a few others and they made a trek to their garden at another part of town. Sam had several totes of food supplies and cases of water for their tenant living there. She was apprehensive as to what she would find since she wasn't there since the event happened. She was afraid the garden would be over-run with weeds.

The two tailers and four security riders on bikes made quite a show.

John Sullivan downstairs tenant at duplex peeked out of the downstairs bedroom. Recognizing Samantha, he came out of the apartment, his wife stayed inside.

"High Samantha, I'm afraid I won't be able to pay any rent for a while." John said.

"John, don't worry about it just keep the place safe and the garden weeded. I brought you folks some food and other supplies. I'm here to see what the garden has and see if there was anything that can be spared for us." Sam said.

"I'm embarrassed to say but we have been harvesting some of the vegetables in the garden." John replied.

"Don't be, winter's coming and I want to get the potatoes out of the ground. I want enough Yukon Gold and Red potatoes for seed next year and if enough a few to take home. I like Yukon Gold better than Russets. I also want some cabbage to make sauerkraut and pepper cabbage if there is enough there. I'll take a few Parsnips and some Carrots, Turnips, and Snow Apples. I'll leave most of it here for your family. Do you have any firearms?" Sam asked.

"All I have is a nine-millimeter pistol." John replied.

"I thought so, that's why I brought you a select fire M-4 and a semi-automatic magazine fed twelve gage shotgun and enough ammo for them." Sam said.

"How can I thank you." John said with tears in his eyes.

"Just keep the place safe." Sam said.

"Now let's get to work. I wont dig all of the potatoes and Parsnips up. I'll let them in the ground for you to dig latter but before freeze up." Sam said.

With the exception of the cabbages which she took all but ten, harry planted forty plants and they all looked good. Sam gave John a recipe for Pepper Cabbage and pickled carrots. She had the guys dig up about a third of the potatoes and other ground vegetables. Sam told John that Parsnips can be mixed in with potatoes when you mash them and they are good raw.

Although Sam took only about a third, they filled all of the totes Sam brought and they made an area where they could put the cabbages where they wouldn't roll off of the trailer.

There was a water bath canner and a new pressure cooker in with the supplies Sam gave John.

"John, you can wash and peel the potatoes and carrots and then pressure can them. You can put them on the shelves in the arctic entryway and they will last a year. That way they won't start to sprout." Sam said.

They said their good byes and Sam and the group left.

Keven pulled up beside Sam. "That was some garden you have there," he said.

"Yeah, it's a little over two-thousand square feet in size. If properly managed you can get a years-worth of some of the vegetables from it," Sam replied.

As they turned onto Arctic from Tudor Sam looked up Tudor towards the Chugach Mountains she stopped. "Keven, do you see what I see." Sam asked.

"Yeah, this doesn't look good, let's hurry back." He replied.

"We won't get back in time to mount a defense, get on the radio and call the neighborhood and warn them" Sam replied.

"Neighborhood Net, Neighborhood Net, Farmer Sam, Farmer Sam." Keven called on the radio.

"Farmer Sam, Neighborhood Net, do you need assistance?" came the reply.

"Negative, situation alert, large force of approximately one-hundred soles on "C" Street moving South past Tudor now. Destination and equipment unknown at this time. We are expediting travel your location. Notify John." Keven said.

It was discovered that on Tom's house his back sundeck had a straight line visual to Arctic Boulevard. The deck was reinforced and sandbags two wide were placed around it with shooting positions facing North, East, and South. This gave one or more shooters an excellent position for long range sniping of a force before it became too close to the neighborhood. Along with strategically placed hidden force multipliers, Seventy-first street would become a killing zone.

If they came from either side by Rovena Street there were open areas where these snipers could take any attacker under fire.

Couple this with the giant 988H loader and it's large bucket for a last ditch psychological defense, an attacking force with anything short of an RPG wouldn't stand much of a chance against the neighborhood defenses. The neighborhood when they took control of and protected Costco were able to recover several M-4 select fire rifles.

On the way back Keven broke off from the group to surveil the group coming down C Street.

Sam and her group pulled into the neighborhood. They all went to their homes to get geared up incase of an upcoming fight. Sam parked her bike and trailer in the front yard, going into her garage she pulled out several rifles. One was a bolt action Remington 7MM Magnum with an ATN x-sight 4k pro 5-20x pro smart day/night scope mounted on it. Opening an ammo can she stuffed five boxes of twenty Black Talon bullets in one of her pockets. She also brought out a Winchester 30-06 with another ATN x-sight 4k pro 5-20x pro smart day/night scope mounted on it. She wanted the 30-06 because Harry found some light armor piercing bullets for it at a gun show. He bought all ten boxes the vendor had, he said at an inflated price. She pulled a Glock 19 out of the safe and put it into her leg holster along with ten, fifteen-round magazines with expanding nose bullets. She donned a ballistic vest with a ceramic plate. She put ten thirty round AR magazines into the pouches on it. This was incase the fighting got close and faster firepower was needed and slung an M-4 across her back.

She went out her back door since Tom was no longer a problem a pathway to his back yard was cut into the fences that separated them. Sam and Harry had a six foot wooden cedar fence between them but Tom was so chicken shit, he had a chain link fence built on his property.

Climbing the stairs to the shooting position Sam loaded her weapons, using the BAOFENG radio let everyone know overwatch was in place and settled in to wait. She listened as other locations called in their status.

She felt the porch vibrate, turning with the Glock in her hand she saw Malissa Samuels head pop up. Holstering her firearm Sam let out a breath. She didn't know she was holding it.

"Hello Malissa, you got my attention coming up the stairs," Sam said.

"Did I do something wrong?" Malissa asked.

"In the future try to announce yourself as a friendly before you get close. In a firefight you could be shot by accident." Sam replied.

"Come on in and settle down. Do you have any long-range shooting experience?" Sam asked.

"Yes, my dad takes me out to Birchwood, we take our own target frame with a groove cut into the top, with us and set it up at six-hundred yards. We put large area washers about the size of a silver dollar into the groove and see how many shots it takes to remove them." Malissa said.

"Six-hundred yards is just about what it is to Arctic. Did you ever see the old movie, Sargent York?" Sam asked.

"No, what is about?" Malissa asked.

It's about a soldier in World War one who received the Medal of Honor for his actions. In the movie he asks his buddies if they know how to shoot a whole flock of turkeys without scattering the flock. Do you know how to do this?" Sam asked.

"A shotgun," Malissa replied.

"No," Sam said as she lined up some bullets on a sand bag.

"You shoot the one at the back of the flock, removing a bullet, and the others don't know it is missing. That is what we will do. If we have to we will shoot the last one in line and work our way front." Sam instructed.

"We wont worry about killing them, at this range they might not know right away where the bullets are coming from so just aim center mass and if we wound them, their screaming might undermine their courage and they will leave." Sam stated.

Get comfortable it may be a long wait." Sam said.

"Neighborhood Net, OPFOR crossing railroad." The radio squawked.

"What's OPFOR? Malissa asked.

"It stands for Opposition Force. The bad guys," Sam replied.

"Now we wait and see if they go past Raspberry or turn down it." Sam said.

"OPFOR turning on Raspberry, repositioning."

"Okay now we guess which way they will go. Straight or left or right." Sam said.

"Straight," Malissa said.

"They aren't from the neighborhood so unless they have information on the area I'll say left." Sam replied.

"OPFOR turning left onto Arctic. Repositioning."

"Okay, now which way, straight, 70th. 71st. or 72nd." Sam said.

"71st." Malissa said.

"All three streets. Remember the one at the back of the flock." Sam said.

"One group down 70th. Street."

"One group down 71st. Street."

"The rest down 72nd. Street. Get ready folks."

"Mrs. Miller, there a bunch of them." Malissa said.

"Call me Sam. When they get to that Crab Apple tree on the left stop shooting the ones in the back of the pack and start shooting the ones in the front, as fast as you can." Sam said.

"Ready?"

Malissa nodded.

"Let's do this," Sam said and started to shoot. The first shot missed but Sam now had the range and was dropping attackers with every shot. Many were shot in the stomach. In this day and age, a slow painful death. Sam stopped to reload and watched as Malissa, who was shooting jacked rounds had a shot go through one into the person behind him.

"A twofer," Sam called out as she started shooting again but not aiming as slowly as before. She shot as fast as she worked the bolt action and reloaded her rifle.

The crowed reached the Crabapple tree and Sam switched to the M-4.

As fast as Sam pulled the trigger a person fell but they were coming too fast. As they turned left on Rovena the people in a trench that was dug earlier by Peter and the large back-ho came into play. Ten people shooting semi-automatic rifles put down a hail of lead. It was long when the other two break-of groups joined together but they were being whittled down by people on raised sundecks along their route.

Several of them broke free and ran toward the raised decks to take concealment behind a six-foot-high wooden fence. This was their mistake. People on the ground from the neighborhood rushed between the houses and riddled the fence with bullets, half-inch cedar is no match for 30-06, or .300 magnum rifle rounds.

The attackers made it to 71st. Court before they ran into the main force from the neighborhood. The street had a double row of concertina razor wire across it and a small wall of sand bags with twenty shooters behind it. Two of them had select fire M-4s that mowed the balance of the attackers down.

All of the attackers were on the ground. Everyone was commanded to stay in place until further orders.

Malissa asked Sam why they were supposed to stay in place.

"In order for the wounded to bleed out and make it safer to go out and finish what we have to do." Sam said.

"What do we have to do?" Malissa asked.

"In a gun fight there is a saying, when in doubt grey matter out." Sam said.

"If you have to use the sand box go ahead, I'll stay here and watch the street." Sam said.

Sam didn't think Malissa was ready to do what had to be done.

Sam left her post taking her weapons with her to the garage to be cleaned. She went into the safe and retrieved a .22 pistol and a hand full of magazines for it loaded with .22 hollow point ammunition. She wanted to save the larger caliber ammunition for when she really needed it. Thinking two .22 hollow points should do the job and cheaper.

With her M-4 on a sling she walked to the end of the street where she found out that they didn't get away without casualties.

A teenage boy was sprawled on the street his father holding him. He was very dead. Sam quietly asked one of the men what happened.

"We were behind the sand bags shooting when the boy said this was just like being at the arcade and stood up and continued shooting until he was hit by two rounds. No one else here was injured." The man said.

Well, it's time to go out and finish what we started. I'll need someone to come with me to cover me. Are you up to it?" Sam asked.

Sam started walking making sure she put two bullets into the head of every one of the attackers, both visibly dead or still living. The pleading eyes of the living were the hardest but there were no doctors and why should they be concerned with those that were ready to kill them for what they had. Samantha would have nightmares for weeks.

When some of the wounded heard the shots from the .22, they tried to crawl away. Sam had to follow more than one blood trail. She soon heard the heavier caliber guns firing on the other streets; she knew she was not alone with the bloody task.

As she went up 71st. Street she started to come upon those that were shot in the stomach with the Black Talons. The exit wounds were horrific. Many of them knew there was no hope of surviving and accepted their fate. One of the worst ones was the old man who apologized to her for making her do what she was doing and thanked her for what she had to do.

He looked at her and said he was sorry and to do what you have to do. I'm ready.

When Samantha reached Arctic and the last person was shot she went to the steps of one of the houses and sat down and cried.

A man came from the house with two glasses and a bottle of Crown Royal. He poured two fingers in both glasses, handing her one he sat beside her and sipped from his.

"You're the lady that brought us food. Thank you for that. You're a good person, there are no doctors and you had a hard job to do. It will stay with you for the rest of your life but don't let it control you. You are a good person, my wife and I saw that in you when you gave us food and water.

Sam was still crying and had drained her glass when the man gave her two more fingers of Crown Royal.

This is where Keven Peterson found her. The man drained his glass and poured two more fingers into it and handed it to Keven. He took it and sat beside Samantha. The man went into the house and he and his wife each came out with a glass in there hand, Pouring some Crown Royal into each glass they also sat with Samantha sometimes talking and sometimes just being quiet.

The man topped each glass off pouring the last into Samantha's glass. She took a few more sips and then gulped the last of it down. Standing shakenly up and handing the glass to the man she said "Thank You."

He stood up and gulped the last of his drink, and heaved the glass and bottle into the street breaking them. Samantha did the same as did Keven and the man's wife.

"Don't thank us, we should thank all of you for protecting us." The man said. As he turned for the house. The woman went and hugged

Sam, "Honey if you ever want to talk I'll be here for you to listen." The woman said and went into the house.

Keven stood up and holding her arm guided her past the carnage to her home.

SEPTEMBER 11

Samantha woke up with a headache. She stumbled to the kitchen for some aspirin. Pouring herself a cup of cold coffee from the pot on the Coleman propane stove sitting on the electric kitchen stove. She sat at the kitchen table and slowly drank it. It tasted awful cold but Harry always drank it hot or cold with no qualms. He would say hope one day you don't have to drink it cold. Thinking of Harry and the boys just made her cry some more.

"Harry where are you? I need you come home soon." Sam said to the empty house.

She heard the 988H loader working in the street behind her home and knowing what it was doing brought tears once again to her eyes. Sitting there and quietly crying she heard the chickens. Getting up she went o the bathroom and a small trickle of water came from the spigot, she made a face cloth wet and washed her face, going to the bedroom she got dressed. Taking a deep breath, she went outside to tend to the animals and gather the eggs.

Going out her front door the first person she saw was Keven Peterson. Looking up from a clipboard he called out, "Good morning, General, did you have a good night's sleep?"

"I have a splitting headache and I'm no general." She replied.

"Well, the people around here feel you are. You are the one bringing all of these people together." He replied.

"I don't have any military training like you do. You can be our General." Samantha replied.

"Well, if I'm the General then you are the mayor of this area. The people respect and look up to you." Keven replied.

"Whatever, this mayor has to feed the rabbits and chickens and gather the eggs." She said as she went into the back yard.

As Sam took care of the rabbits she though for a minute and started to do the math. It's September eleventh, thirty days would be around October twelfth. Ninety days would be mid-January. Samantha opened a pen and grabbed a Doe and put her in with a buck. Then she went in and took care of the chickens. Walking out with six eggs. *We need a rooster, now that there is no more rule of law, who cares if I have a rooster. Especially if I can give away a few eggs a week.* she thought.

Going into the house she put the eggs on the steps going to the top of the house and went for what she expected to be her last shower for a long time.

Getting out of the shower and toweling off she went into the utility room and turned the gas off to the water heater.

She walked past a pile of dirty laundry. Well, I know what I'll be doing today.

Meanwhile Keven started to inventory the firearms and ammo taken from the raiders killed yesterday. So far there wasn't anything interesting. Just hunting rifles, shotguns, pistols, and a few revolvers.

The clean-up went on all day. A large trench was dug in a grassy area off Raspberry Road. Without the large back-ho it would have taken a week to dig a trench long and deep enough to bury all of the bodies. It was important to get them buried to prevent the spread of disease.

Sam spent the day around the house. She needed more feed to last the winter so getting the lawnmower out she started to mow lawns one last time before winter set in. She felt a change in the air hoping that it didn't rain until all the grass she mowed dried enough to take into her garage to process. When she was finished she pulled a few carrots washing them and taking a peeler she made long slivers to dry in the sun.

Before she went to bed, she put the chickens back into the coop and pulled the Doe from the buck. She felt that there was ample time to get the deed done. She'll put the Doe back with the buck in a few days, if she fights him of then she is pregnant.

She was in luck it was cool and sunny for two days so checking the moisture of the grass that she raked every day she felt she could move it tomorrow into the garage.

SEPTEMBER 14

Samantha spent the day bagging the grass into burlap bags and trans porting them to her garage, She, then went to the raised bed and container garden alongside and behind the house that Harry built in case there was a time that they couldn't get to their main garden. She pulled all of the carrots in one of the raised bed gardens, then she dug through six large totes for potatoes, getting close to a hundred pounds of Yukon Gold potatoes. Going back to the raised beds she harvested close to thirty pounds of Snow Apples. There was a 4 X 10 foot bed planted with Parsnips. She never ate Parsnips before she met Harry. He made mashed potatoes and mashed some Parsnips in with it. It changed the flavor tremendously and she liked it. He also sliced them into thin slices, putting them in a zip lock bag with two table spoons of Olive Oil and some Canning Salt and coat the Parsnips. He would spread them on a lightly greased cookie sheet and bake them at 350 degree for a few minutes. On the holidays, Thanksgiving, Christmas, New Year Day, and Easter Harry would make something he called Mashed Potato Filling. He would sauté a very large diced Onion or two and a few stalks of diced Celery in a frying pan with a stick-and-a-half of butter. He would then toast four slices of bread and cube them and add them and Parsley flakes to the pan to soak up and butter. Then he would add that to the mashed potatoes and Parsnips which he had added milk and two or three eggs to along with powered garlic and blend that all together. Then he would put that into a Corning Ware bowl, put a few pats of butter on top and bake it at 350 degrees for about a half-an-hour or until a brown crust appeared on top. He said it was a Pennsylvania Dutch thing his mother would always make. Sam filled a burlap bag with about forty-pounds of Parsnips leaving half behind because they could stand colder weather and when they got cold they became sweeter. She then picked string beans and Wax (Yellow) String beans. These they used when ever they had a ham. Harry would boil the bone to get all of the ham off of it and add cut up pieces of ham to the water along with cutup potatoes and parsnips and then several jars of green and yellow string beans. There was a 4 X 10 raised bed of cabbage and another one of cauliflower and one with Brussel Sprouts. She left these alone since they could stand cooler weather also.

Samantha spent the rest of the day canning what she thought was the last of the vegetables for the year. She still had the rest of the Parsnips, Snow Apples, and Brassicas to harvest.

She was finishing up cleaning and putting away the canning equipment when she went out the back door onto the sun deck and saw it was starting to snow.

Oh Harry, where are you? You and the Boys be careful I need you here. She thought as a tear ran down her cheek. That's when she saw a male and female Stellers Jays on the porch rail looking at her and bobbing their heads. They flittered over to her and landed on the patio table next to her. She remained still as the male hopped over to her hand and rubbed his head on the top of her hand. The female flittered over and rubbed her head on the back of the Male, then hopped over and started rubbing her head on Samantha's hand also. They both looked at Samantha and chirped a few times Samantha whispered, "Protect Harry and your boys." They then flew off to the North towards Palmer. Sam put her elbows on the table and her face into her hand and started to sob. She raised her head and let out a blood curdling scream ending in a wail.

Keven and Earl were next door at Toms house. When they heard Samantha scream they dropped what they were doing and running over going thru the side gate and up the porch steps with their pistols drawn they saw Sam sobbing into her hands.

"**SAM, are you okay?**" Keven asked.

Sam turned her head and through tear filled blood shot eyes she replied, "yes, my son and daughter-in-law were just here. They went to protect Harry and the Boys."

Holstering their guns Keven said, "Sam you have been working too hard you need some rest."

Looking at them with tears still streaming down her face and a quivering voice she told them what just happened. She saw tears rolling down both of their cheeks.

"Sam, get some rest. We got this." Earl said in almost a whisper. Then he and Keven turned wiping their face and left.

When they got back to Tom's house Earl looked at Keven, "do you believe her story?"

Looking at Earl, Keven said, "lets sit down." And told Earl the story. "Harry is one of us."

Earl cocked his head looking quizzically at Keven.

In a low hollow voice Keven said, "I heard about a Captain Harry Miller when I was with the Teams. He was severely wounded in Vietnam leading an A-team and a platoon of Vietnamese Rangers on an ambush. Intelligence was faulty and they were ambushed by a lead platoon of a company of North Vietnamese regulars. There was a running gun fight where Harry was wounded but he helped carry two of his wounded team mates to a pickup LZ while attack helicopters and the Air Force kept the NVA at bay. He received the Distinguished Service Cross for Gallantry for his actions and was medically discharged after he recovered from his wounds a year later.

He came up here during the Pipeline days and later met Samantha and got married. They only had one son and after his military service came back as a pilot and flew for one of the many small bush airlines we have here. During the Iditarod he and his wife flew supplies out to the villages for the Iditarod in their Cessna 180.

They went missing on one of these flights. After everyone gave up and stopped searching Harry and Sam continued searching in his Cessna 180 but they never found any sign of the wreckage. Their son and daughter-in-law had two young boys that Sam and Harry are raising as their own."

"That's quite a story, and do you think the two Stellers Jays were their son and daughter-in-law?" Earl asked.

Keven looked at Earl and in a very low voice replied, "yes." and turned away.

Well, "I hope to hell he and his grandsons make it." Earl said.

"He will even if he has to carry them." Keven replied.

SEPTEMBER 15

Samantha spent the day shredding cabbage to make sauerkraut and pepper cabbage.
    She had to stay busy to take her mind off of the visit by the two Stellers Jays.

SEPTEMBER 17 PALMER, ALASKA

Harry woke up but was slow to get off of the cot. If it wasn't for his bladder which he felt was about to burst he would have stayed in his sleeping bag longer.
    Coming back from the restroom he saw the others were now stirring. He put a pot of coffee on the propane stove to perk and started to pack his backpack.
    "Let's eat breakfast. It looks like the storm is going to soon break up." Harry said.
    They had finished eating and were washing their dishes when they heard and saw thru the front windows of the service station several snowmachines pull up.
    Officer Baker came in the door followed by five other men taking their helmets, goggles and parkas off. "Are you guys ready to leave?" he asked.
    "As soon as we finish washing our dishes and thank you for the breakfast." Rick replied.
    "These guys managed to get some snowmachines running and found gasoline for them. They have two Akio's and some child plastic toboggans, and snowshoes for you guys. They will take you as far as their fuel will allow. Then you will have to foot it the rest of the way. They feel they can cut two or three days off of your trip."
    "That's fantastic," Mat replied.
    Harry came out of the restroom, looking around and he headed toward one of the men as that man headed toward him.
    "Todd you son-of-a-bitch, you made it." Harry said.

"Captain thanks to you, you asshole," the man said. And they both embraced each other in a tight hug.

Todd turned to the group, "guy's this is Captain Harry Miller, this bastard carried me on his back, even though he was wounded, out of an ambush in Vietnam when I was wounded. He saved my life. How the hell are you, Captain?"

"Hell Todd, you were still shooting the Gooks as I was carrying you. You kept them off of us. All I did was run." Harry replied.

"I'm older and slower Todd. I'm glad you made it." Harry said.

"Welcome home brother. I'm also glad you made it. I was told you didn't and go the Distinguished Service Cross posthumously for it" Todd replied.

"Well, news of my death was premature. Guess who I met on the way down here?"

"There's no telling, who?" Todd asked.

"Joey Bowman, he and his wife and kids live on the other side of Glennallen on the way to Tok close to Chistochina" Harry said.

Tod started laughing, "did he ever meet up with those nudists we stumbled across on that hike?"

"No, but when he was stationed in Germany, he went to the Englisher Garten in Munich and found him one there. He has a great set-up and a nice wife and family." Harry replied.

"If things ever get back to normal, we have to go there and get drunk with him again." Todd said.

All the while Todd and their grandfather reminisced, they sat on their bunks listening. They saw the scars on their grandfather whenever he took off his shirt but never knew the story behind them. They couldn't believe that their grandfather was a real hero. He never said anything about it.

"Are you guys ready to leave?" Todd asked.

"As soon as we finish the dishes and finish getting packed. One question, what about our dogs?" Harry asked.

"We heard about them and have two kennels on the Akio for them to ride in. Where did you get two dogs?" Tod asked.

Harry quickly told them the story as he finished packing.

"Are those bastards behind you? Anyone who leaves a dog like that doesn't deserve to live." Another man said.

"As far as I know they didn't get past Chistochina." Harry said.

As they finished packing the men grabbed some coffee and were off in a corner talking. Harry saw Officer Baker nod his head a few times and leave with a snowmachine.

He soon came back with two more snowmachines pulling Akio's and extra riders.

"Harry, the plan was to take you guys as far as Mirror Lake but plans have changed. Well drop your friends off at their homes and then take you to your home. Officer Barns says you live down by Arctic and Dimond. Is that right?"

"Yes." Harry replied.

"If need be, do your boys know how to use their rifles?" Tod asked.

"They're my Grandsons and yes they can shoot." Harry said.

While this conversation was going on, Rick and Mat were off to the side with a big shit-eating grin on their faces.

"Is everyone ready?" Harry asked.

They loaded up, strapping their pack to the empty Akio and donning helmets and goggles they took off.

Racing down the Glenn there were no tracks in the snow but an occasional moos track. While passing the Palmer Hay Flats they say several moose in the flats eating brows. They slowed and stopped at a checkpoint at the bridge over the Knick River. Todd talked to the men stationed there, shaking hands he came back and off they went again. They saw more moose tracks going across the road and more moose in the swampy area on their right.

As they went past the Eklutna Bridge going back to the native village of Eklutna, Harry saw they also had a checkpoint on the single road to the village.

The snow storm kept people in their houses and no one was outside except the moose.

As they came to the North Exit to Eagle River from the Glenn Todd took the off ramp and stopped short of the road. Taking his helmet off he waved to people on the bridge who waved back. Putting his helmet on they raced down the on ramp and did the same thing at the Highland bridge.

At the Fort Richardson overpass they slowly went up the off ramp where a Stryker was parked. Todd once again got off of his snowmachine and removed his helmet and goggles. It seemed he talked a little longer than at the other checkpoints.

Coming back, he went down the line telling everyone that the Army was slowly pushing thru Anchorage helping people as best as they could with their limited supplies and having a running gun battle with gangs who were foolish enough to challenge a Stryker. The lieutenant in charge radioed their units to allow us to go by without any hassle but we will be getting into what they called uncleared country.

Taking off they went down Muldoon Road to Tudor. At the Tudor curve they again saw moose tracks and two moose eating in the brush close to the road.

It was now around noon and they still didn't see many people. That could be because they were going around fifty miles per hour and by the time, they heard us we were past them.

Harry told his driver to catch up with Todd. Pulling up Harry pointed to the parking lot for the State Police headquarters.

Harry told Todd to turn down MLK drive to Elmore then left onto Dowling Road.

They continued racing down Dowling Road and stopped at C Street. Todd asked, "now where?"

Harry said, "go left and you better let me take the lead, when we get to Raspberry Road."

At the Fish and Game building Todd slowed for Harry and his driver to take the lead.

Harry had his driver go slowly to Arctic. The noise the snowmachines proceeded them and Harry had his driver stay as far left as he could and stopped him just before 70th. street.

Harry took his helmet and goggles off and made a big show of handing his rifle to his driver. Walking down to 70th. street with his arms out, he didn't see any one there. He turned looking down the street and waved his arms over his head. Not seeing any reaction he walked thru ankle deep snow to 71st. street where he waved his arms again. He didn't see any reaction down the street, but a door opened on his right.

"Don't move," a man's voice said. "What do you want here?" he was asked.

"Well I don't want to get shot after my grandsons and I walked all the way from Chicken to get here." Harry replied.

The man was surprised when a male and Female Stellers Jay landed by Harry.

"Do you live around here?" the voice asked quivering. He knew the story of the Stellers Jays.

Earl had told Gary the story of the Stellers Jays and it spread like wildfire throughout the neighbors. When finished with telling the story there wasn't a dry eye to be found.

"Yes, down the street." Harry replied.
"What's your name?" the voice asked.
"Harry Miller," Harry replied.
"Don't move, stay right there, I'll get back to you.
Keven's radio crackled "Eyes on Arctic calling base."
Keven replied, "Base go."
"Are you alone?" the voice on the radio asked.
"No, I'm with Earl and Samantha at Gary's house." Keven replied.
"I need either Earl or you to start to me and I will meet you part way" the voice said.
"What is the level?" Keven asked
"Very green." The voice said.
"I'll be there." Keven said.
"Do you want some company?" Samantha asked.
"No, you guys stay here and continue the inventory. I'll be back as soon as I can." Keven said.
"Harry, have your friends come up here with their machines." The man said.

The man looked down the street and saw Keven walking up it kicking snow.

"Boss man, Eyes here, I'm sending a person down who wants to talk to you. He'll be on a snowmachine."

"Roger that." Keven said.

"Have your driver take you down to Keven." The man said.

Harry waved his driver front and headed down Seventy-first to Keven waiting at the end of the street. The man waved to others front to him.

Before Harry got to Keven, a Male and Female Stellers Jay landed by him. Keven saw them. *I'll me a son-of-a-bitch HE MADE IT.* Keven thought.

Harry got to Keven and took his helmet and goggles off.

"I'll be a son-of-a-bitch, you made it. Samantha will be happy to see you. But I must warn you, we had a rough time a few days ago so be understanding with her.

The garage door was up at Gary's house so Sam, Keven and Earl would have light to inventory the goods in it. Keven and Earl thought it would be best to keep Sam busy doing mundane tasks like inventory to keep her mind off of what she had to do during the attack. Two Stellers Jays landed in the drive way and started to sing. Sam noticed that there was a difference to the tone to their chirping. They then flew off to the East towards the mountains

"I have more friendlies headed your way, Eyes out" the radio crackled.

The man waved the rest of the snow machines down Seventy-First.

Keven was told to get on the back with Harry and they drove to Gary's garage.

Gary and Samantha heard the snowmachine coming towards them, stopping what they were doing and watched as Kenny the driver, stopped a few feet short of the door. Keven hopped off the back as Harry got off.

When Harry took his helmet and goggles of Samantha fainted.

Gary was behind her and was able to grab her and cushion her fall.

Handing his helmet to Kenny, Harry ran to Samantha, sitting on his knees on the floor he held her in his arms. "Sam, SAM, we're safely home." Harry said as he hugged her.

Sam opened her eyes looking at Harry. Her arms went around his neck pulling him down as she buried her face in his shoulder and started to sob uncontrollably. Her shoulders heaved with her sobs. The Stellers

Jays flew into the garage and started chattering and hopping around. Two Magpies flew in and started to chatter, soon more Magpies and Ravens showed up. All of them were singing and chattering in their own voice. The screech of an Eagle was heard as two of them circled the garage landing on the roof of Sam's and Harry's house and continued to call out.

The rest of the snowmachines had to stop because of all of the birds on the drive way and in the street. The cacophony of the birds brought many of the neighbors from their homes to view the spectacle.

Harry helped Sam to her feet tears were flowing down her cheeks. The female Stellers Jay landed on her right shoulder as the male landed on Harrys left shoulder. All the birds stopped their chattering as they walked out of the garage and the Stellers Jays raised their heads and beaks to the heavens and started warbling, all of the birds let force at once with their own songs. The Eagles took off and swooped up and down the street calling out. It was a spectacle no one ever saw before as more birds continued to come.

Michael and Adam got off of the snowmachine they were on, taking off their helmet and goggles the Stellers Jays flew to them singing and landed on their shoulders. This caused the birds to sing in their unique voices even harder as even more showed up. The birds parted so Michael and Adam could join their grandparents. They hugged each other and cried unabashedly as did the people witnessing the event.

Someone opened the dog kennels, Buck and Snoopy went running tails wagging to Harry and the boys rubbing against their legs and Samantha's legs whining with tails wagging. They were also getting excited with the reunion.

Buck raised his head with a howl as did Snoopy and they both howled with the birds.

With one last throaty warble the Stellers Jays took flight as did all of the other birds and silence returned to the street.

Sam got herself under control as did Harry and the boys. Looking at Harry Samantha said, "Where did the dogs come from? what's with the beard and you guys need a bath you stink."

Walking across the street Harry waved the snowmachiner's front as neighbors came to welcome them home.

Keven went and talked to some of the neighbors and soon every snowmachiner had a person showing them where to park inviting them into their homes for the night and a meal.

The next day the all the snowmachines left but one. Todd left his snow machine and an Akio with Harry and rode back with another driver.

Harry, the boys, and Buck and Snoopy were home but they were still in untamed country. What will the winter bring.

Thank You for buying and reading this book
Here is an excerpt from my other book
NOMADS

An excerpt from the book
NOMADS

At the oil pad in Texas

THE ATTACK

Betty hit the large red panic button by the trailer's door sending a signal to the company's reaction guard force. Grabbing the portable boat air horn located on a small shelf next to the panic button she let loose with a loud long blast.

"That isn't going to help you," the Mexican shouted to Betty.

"No, but maybe this will," as she pulled a Mossberg 500 pump shotgun and fired off a round.

Hector Mendoza dove for cover when he saw the shotgun as the rest of his gang of six laughed at him. "What's the matter you afraid of just one Chiquita?" they taunted.

Watching three Pronghorn Antelope in his scope Ken was trying to lay out a route to sneak up closer for an easier shot; fresh meat would be nice for a change he was thinking when the air horn broke the silence.

Wasting no time getting up from where he was at he started at a slow lope back to the trailer where his wife Betty was. Then he heard the gun shot. He immediately dropped his small pack and started to run to the trailer. There was trouble, Betty wouldn't shoot unless she was in danger. Coming to a small hill 100 yards from the trailer and he got down on all four's and crawled to a vantage point where he could see the trailer. What he saw made his blood boil and instincts took over. As he eased his rifle up, he did a quick scan seeing 2 beat up pickup trucks and seven Mexicans that had the trailer under surveillance and calling to Betty to put down the gun. If she did so they would show her

231

a good time. Ken lined the crosshairs of his scoped rifle on the head of the one doing all the talking and waited to get his heart rate down a little more from the run here.

Crack and the Mexicans head exploded, crack, crack two rounds center mass of the farthest Mexican and the others turned their backs to the trailer looking for the shooter, they still didn't know there he was.

Boom, Boom, Boom Betty was unloading her shotgun at them now causing even more confusion. Blam, Blam Ken now was systematically targeting the Mexicans with center mass shots. He had his M1A1 Scout and was using soft point hunting rounds and not 7.62 X 54 steel jacked rounds. The damage they did was psychologically devastating on the remaining bandits they thought that they had an easy target to loot. When finally got over the shock and surprise the remaining ones made a run for their trucks. That's when Betty hit one low in the leg and he fell down.

Ken replaced the empty magazine with a fresh one and fired several more times. Then it was over.

Yelling down to Betty to have her give the signal if she was hurt or all right, he was relieved when the ok sign was given.

Ken waited a few minutes to make sure there would be no surprises when he went down there not knowing that Betty only wounded one. Backing down from the crest of the slight hill he walked wide around the ambush site this way he could get a different view of the area. Stopping he got out his binoculars to look the site over.

That's when he saw the wounded bandit trying to crawl to a truck. Checking the other bandits slowly with his binoculars he verified with the wounds they had and blood in the dirt all but one of the bandits were dead.

Ken slowly got up and circled around him knowing a wounded animal was far more dangerous. Calling out to his wife in the trailer to see if she was ok. Betty, his wife, replied in a very shaky voice that she was unhurt just scared.

"Well, you should be," Ken replied, "but it's almost over."

"What?" she asked.

That's when Ken left her know that all but one of the attackers were dead and he was going to try to interrogate him.

An Excerpt from the book NOMADS

As Ken walked up to the attacker he saw that the attacker was heavily tattooed and was hit hard with his legs shredded from two buck shot blasts.

Ken knew he wouldn't last long. "What were you trying to do by attacking us?" Ken asked. When he got no reply he switched to his limited Spanish. The attacker spit at Ken saying he was a dead man and his friends would rape his wife while he watched and then they will take knives and cut parts off of her while he watched and then they would kill both of them.

Ken laughed at him and said how will this happen when all of your friends were dead and you my friend are soon on a trip to hell.

The Mexican then replied with pride that there were hundreds of them coming across the border and soon they will take back that which was stolen from them by our corrupt government.

As Betty came warily walking up Ken leveled his rifle and sent the attacker to his maker to atone for his sins. Giving Betty a long hug he felt her body shaking with sobs from the incident. After consoling her and getting her to stop shaking and crying he heard the dull beating of helicopter blades.

Taking the Mossberg from his wife's hands he checked to make sure it was loaded and on safe, then putting his arm around her shoulder led her back to the camper.

"It sounds like the cavalry is coming this time better late than never." Ken said.

Getting a green smoke grenade Ken tossed it out, going back into the trailer to hold Betty as she was still shaking and crying.

He watched out a window as the reaction force cautiously approached the trailer. Letting go of Betty he went to the door, opening it he watched as the force went to the ground.

"Hay, it's me.' Ken called out.

"You guys are late to the party. It's all clear the area is Green. Did you guys bring any beer?" Ken teased.

As the reaction force warily got to their feet Ken only recognized two of them, Captain Bartholomew and Sargent Michaels, the rest were strangers.

Captain Bartholomew came toward the trailer as the rest of the squad checked the area and the bodies for any intel they might have.

"Looks like you had visitors, is everyone alright?" Captain Bartholomew asked as he looked at Betty.

"Just a little scared," Betty replied with a quivering voice and asked, "what will happen now?"

"Well, several things, we will clean up this mess and load the bodies into their pickup trucks, then we will drive them way out into the desert and dispose of them. Don't worry about the authorities since you all are un-hurt there are no reports to fill out."

Ken looked at him, "it's getting that bad?" he asked.

"Not yet." Captain Bartholomew replied, "but things are getting real squirrely at the border with Mexico."

"Then what We've been hearing on the ham radios is true?"

"Well I don't know what you are hearing but by the best estimates several hundred maybe as many as a thousand Muslims have crossed into the U. S. and have fanned all over the country. More than the FBI and DHS can watch. Couple these with the ones that grew up here and the ones immigrated here over the years, it's estimated that there are between 3 and 4 thousand jihadists Muslims living in the U. S. Some are suicide bombers but most of them are tasked to destroy the infrastructure and cause mayhem throughout the United States."

"The intelligence analysts feel that there is about 6 months maybe as long as a year before things go south."

"What direction will they take? What will be their targets?" I asked.

"Well, the best the analysts can guess is the Muslims know that they cannot do a direct attack and take over the country, so they must do other things. Our road and rail systems are wide open. Drop a few traffic or railroad bridges across the big rivers like the Mississippi, Missouri, Snake, Columbia and others with barge & ship traffic, that would cripple the economy by stopping shipping of grain and other products by both road, rail and water for months. Most people in the big cities don't have more than a few days' worth of groceries in their home or apartments. So in about a week most of them will have run out of food or will be dangerously low on food and by then it will be too late to buy any food even if you could find some. Food riots will

An Excerpt from the book NOMADS

start then start and if they turn off the electricity, there are three power grids in the continental U S and these are basically unprotected, either by sabotage or computer, this would shut down a lot of services. Many medicines need refrigeration like insulin add to that Kidney Dialysis, people on life support in the hospitals and nursing care facilities not to mention in the summer the air conditioners and lights in the big cities. It's been estimated that a coordinated attack at the right time could over a period of weeks or months kill one quarter to one half of the population of the United States and if it lasts longer, even more people will die and that's without firing a shot. The people themselves will do the job for them. Gangs will at first fight each other for territory control and then they will band together forming large armies to take what they want or need to survive." Captain Bartholomew replied.

"What does this have to do with Betty and Me?" Ken asked.

"Well, the powers to be know about your waterhole, they have all of the waterholes around the desert mapped. They want us to set up an observation/listening post and see who uses it. They feel that your water hole may be one of several in a trail system into the United States so after we clean up your mess here, I'll leave a 3-man team to monitor the water hole. They will be resupplied by you from supplies we leave behind or bring to you. We want a low-key dark-op so we felt that since you know the area and the drill to have you do the resupply and if needed you will be the reactionary force until we can make it there. Before you answer talk it over with your wife because she will be part of the operation also."

"Talk what over?" Betty asked. As she walked up.

Ken was briefing Betty when Captain Bartholomew took over.

"How are you feeling?" he asked Betty,

She looked at him, "I have had a better day. What will become of us?"

"What do you mean?"

"Well, there are a bunch of dead people around here, how do we explain it to the police?"

"What bodies?" the captain asked.

You could see Betty was still shaken by what happened but if she was worried more about the authorities than what happened here this was good.

Captain Bartholomew knew she would come on board with the operation. "Betty you and Ken did really good here are you hurt in any way?"

"No," Betty answered, "just worried about what we will tell the police."

"Well Betty, don't worry about the police, they have bigger issues to worry about than a few illegal Mexicans, did I say illegal I meant to say undocumented Mexican drug runners after all in these times we must be politically correct mustn't we.

What will happen is, we will clean up the mess you and Ken made. We'll take the bodies and trucks out into the desert and they will just disappear. But Betty, I must know how do you feel mentally and emotionally? While what we are about to undertake doesn't have a lot of risk but there is some risk involved. I must know can we rely on you to hold up to the situation?"

'Tell me," Betty asked, "what just happened? Was this a random act or were we intentionally targeted?"

"Well, this is what we want to find out, and is the reason for the surveillance post we want to establish. Three of my guy's will spend some time out in the sand watching the water hole to see just what is happening there. We want to see what traffic there is and if it is being used as a drop site, a meeting site, or just a rest spot to travel further. Besides an observation post it will also be a listening post. We have some interesting hardware with us so we can listen on what, if anything is being said at the water hole. We also have some cameras to photograph the people using the water hole and other things. We want Ken to do the resupplies of my men and if necessary to act as a reaction force until we can get here. Your job in this operation is to stay here and be the guard force here. There may be a scenario where we will be busy at the water hole and you will be alone here but if that happens, we will already be enroot here and will be only minutes away."

"I would feel better if there was another person here, I don't think I could defend this place by myself. It's one thing for you guy's to be Rambo's but I don't have the training or skills you people have." Betty replied.

"That's a good point." Captain Bartholomew said.

"I think one person here and three at the water hole should suffice. Ken, I still want you to be part of a relief force if you feel up to it."

"Yea, but I would feel better if I had some more equipment, like a vest, MOLIE gear and some other toys you guys have."

"No problem, I can get you and Betty geared up and I guess some spares wouldn't hurt.

What we are going to do now is to clean up your mess and we will be back."

BACK IN IDAHO

It was a busy Friday, Sam and Shirley went to the U. S. Bank Branch in Potlatch to set up a checking account and a savings account. Then to the Pullman-Moscow airport.

Sam was driving up US 95 headed back to their trailer after seeing Shirley off at the Pullman-Moscow airport, he was deep in thought mentally checking off all that had to be done in a very short time when he was startled to see a small heard of Elk in the road. He managed to swerve and stop in time avoiding hitting one and doing damage to the pickup truck.

Sam managed to get back to the trailer before nightfall and was settling in for the night. In the morning he was going to move the trailer to the property and start overseeing the construction of their new home. He and Shirley decided to go with insulated poured concrete walls for the shell and a metal roof. When questioned about the construction Sam replied that the house would be almost fireproof if a forest fire came this way. That satisfied the contractor and after all it was his money.

The footprint of the basement was twice the size of the house plans the extra area was to be used as a root cellar or other storage. The roof extended about eight feet past the walls of the house on each side to make a roofed porch area that had a river rock wall thirty-eight inches high down both sides of the house.

AN EXCERPT FROM THE BOOK NOMADS

The floor was poured concrete and underneath was a storage area on each side of the house with a hidden door to enter from the basement.

In winter the porch could be enclosed with glass or plastic visqueen to make a greenhouse to grow vegetables and supplement the heat source for the house.

For decoration, there will be a river rock facade at key points around the house, like under the windows to add extra ballistic security to anyone firing from the window to the outside and with the exception of the furnishings like rugs and furniture the house was virtually fireproof and bullet proof from small arms fire.

Construction seemed to go slowly at first but Sam knew once the foundation forms were set in place and was poured then the rest of the construction would go quite rapidly.

During this period Sam had three wells drilled around the property, one for the house, one for a garden area and one for a barn for the livestock and a work shed.

A septic system was installed twice the size normally needed. Sam explained this as a fear of a septic problem. The contractors humored him after all it was his money.

He stayed in the trailer since they were letting Sally and her child live in the cabin rent free. The only thing that was constant was his calls to Shirley every evening.

During their conversations he discovered that their decision to liquidate all of their real estate holdings was a correct one. During one these phone conversation's Shirley said that she could see a beginning of a control by Liberals and special interests. She told Sam of new firearm regulations being implemented and of the minimum wage increases around Sea-Tac airport.

During Shirley's time as a real estate broker, she always had a buyer or two willing to buy houses, duplexes or fourplexes if the prices were reasonable. When she got to Seattle, she quietly contacted these buyers and offered them all of their holdings not at fire sale prices but at a price they would be willingly to buy. She had movers pack a few cherished items of furniture and all of Sam's tools and had them shipped to their new home in Idaho. Every day while Shirley was in Seattle, she would go to the Ivar's stand at Lake Union for a bowl of their clam chowder. She thought that there was no telling when she would get a chance to get some of their clam chowder again so why not eat it while she could.

Her contacts came through for her and what they couldn't buy they passed on to other buyers that they knew. In two weeks, she had all of her rentals sold as well as their house.

BACK IN TEXAS

Ken was sitting on or in a folding canvas camp chair with Sargent "Willie" Williams. They were drinking sweet mint iced tea after eating a dinner of antelope steak. The radio that one of them always carried was next to them and their conversation stopped. There were three squelch breaks which Sargent Willie replied with two breaks then they herd four squelch breaks and they grabbed their gear beside them and took off. All of this happened before Betty knew what was happening.

As Ken and Willie trotted off Betty went into the trailer and performed her security jobs. She turned off all the lights and filled several buckets and pots with water and put one large pot on the stove to start boiling water so that could sterilize anything that would need sterilization or to throw into the face of anyone who got into the trailer.

Then went and retrieved her Mossberg 500 shotgun and loaded it with 00 Buck Shot and placed bowls of shells around the house. She then went and got her AR rifle and a satchel of magazines for it. Opening the trailer door, she waited.

It wasn't long before she heard the crump of hand grenades and the rapid fire of an M-60 machine gun and the automatic fire of AR rifles. She couldn't tell how the battle was going but all of a sudden everything went quiet.

It was nerve racking not knowing what happened and who was hurt. Betty jumped when the radio in the trailer crackled with the words Green, Green Amber.

Betty looked at the sheet of codes on the wall next to the radio and was both relieved and frightened. Green, Green meant there were no injuries to the men but Amber meant one got away.

Ken and Willie had dug a firing pit at the back corner of the trailer overlooking approach points from the watering hole and the road. Betty got her weapons and hurried there closing the trailer door behind her.

But before she left, she keyed the mike to the radio and said Brown, Brown letting them know she was going to the firing pit. When Betty got into the pit, she pulled the camouflage netting over the pit and opened the ammo box in there. There was a claymore clicker in it along with a diagram of where the claymore mines were. There was also a range card to various landmarks around the trailer and a military style flashlight with a red lens. Betty settled in and waited.

She didn't make any fast movements as she scanned and listened for movements. Her eyes and head were hurting from her scanning the area when she thought she saw something from the corner of her eye. She slowly turned her head and scanned the area when she saw movement. It looked like someone was trying to sneak up to the trailer. Once Betty identified the threat she slowly and cautiously raised her firearm and trained it on the figure crawling toward the trailer when a thought came over her, what if this was a diversion for others to get close to the trailer. She then continued to scan the area while keeping special attention on the stranger. Betty knew the trailer was his intended destination; he didn't waver or change his course. Betty saw that he was about 100 feet from the trailer and he didn't see her position. It looked to Betty like the approaching threat was slowly getting onto its feet and getting ready to rush the trailer. Betty eased her rifle up to her shoulder, getting a good sight picture she pulled the trigger. Nothing then she remembered the safety; she thumbed it off and pulled the trigger again.

The rifle bucked and the person started to thrash around then laid still. Betty stayed in the firing pit and then saw another figure coming as she was moving to take this one under fire, she saw a red light start flashing the friendly signal. It took a moment for her brain to register this and then relief flooded over her. It was Sargent Willie from the listening post by the water hole.

He raised his rifle over his head and cautiously walked toward the person that Betty had just shot he quickly brought the rifle to his shoulder. This got Betty's attention and she quickly brought her rifle to bear on the prone figure. Then she saw another figure coming up on Sargent Willie and she shifted to cover him when he turned and waved at the figure, it was then that she recognized Ken her husband and she was both relieved and furious that she almost shot him.

Betty climbed out of the pit and started towards Sargent Willie and Ken berating Ken for rushing up like that. I could have killed you she screamed don't you know the procedure for approaching here. Ken was puffing out of breath and Sargent Willie was laughing. Betty, you would make a great drill instructor Sargent Willie said. The old man isn't in as good of shape as he thinks he is. Let's see what you bagged he said to Betty.

The figure laid still but they all could see he was playing possum he wasn't wounded very seriously. They cautiously approached from three different directions with their rifles at the ready. The man was dark brown skinned but not a Mexican. Sargent Willie slung his rifle and pulled and cocked his pistol as he cautiously approached. He circled around to the back of the man's head and placed the mussel of his pistol against it.

"If you move, I can send you to hell because there will be no Virgins for you", Sargent Willie said he then quickly grabbed the man's arms and producing a zip tie he secured the man's hands behind him. Sargent Willie then cautiously checked for a hidden booby trap or grenade before rolling him over. While his wound was serious it wasn't life threatening at this point, if proper first aid was administered.

Sargent Willie asked him in English where he was from and received nothing in reply. They heard someone shout "Friendly coming in" and then one of the men from the listening post showed up.

"Oh, good," Sargent Willie said, "it's Sargent Fish our language expert, can you talk to this person?" Sargent Willie asked.

Sargent Fish walked over and first spoke Spanish, then Farsi and finally in English said, "enough of this charade I'm tired and hungry so be a nice person and answer our questions or you will suffer the consequences, we can treat you as a combatant and treat your wound or a foreign spy and invader, the choice is yours."

He then turned to Sargent Willie and said, "ask him your first question."

"Where are you from?" Willie asked. The person just looked at Willie with a sullen look.

The gunshot startled everyone and everyone but Sargent Fish, and they hit the dirt. Sargent Fish stood there with a pistol in his hand and the person on the ground howling in pain. When the howling stopped Sargent Fish said, "You have another foot, 2 hands, knees, elbows. This can be very painful or not it's up to you. Now what is your name?"

"Good," Sargent Fish replied, "and now where are you from?" Sargent Fish made a motion like he was cocking his pistol and was aiming it at the other foot when the man said he was from Iraq.

"Why are you in the United States?" Sargent Fish asked. The man said nothing and Sargent Fish calmly walked around to the man's foot and said, "I won't ask again why are you in The United States?" and kicked him in the foot that was shot.

The man howled in pain and Sargent Fish kicked him again in the foot. It took several more kicks but the story finally came out. He said he was part of a large group of people from Iraq, Iran, Afghanistan, Syria, Libya and a bunch of other Muslim countries from the Sand Box who are infiltrating into the United States. Their job was to scout out locations where explosives could be placed to disrupt commerce in the United States, power lines, large electrical transformers, highway, rail bridges and communication systems. Sargent Fish asked him how many were in his group and at first, we thought all of this was just wishful thinking for a few foreign terrorists until the man bragged that his group was just one of over 100 groups of 20 men and some women who were trained and were in the United States already.

Sargent Fish turned and walked away. "There are over 2,000 operatives here in the states and these are just the ones this guy knows about, Sir."

I turned and saw Captain Bartholomew. When did he get here, I thought I never heard him come?

"That's just his group of cells', I wonder how many different groups are here already?" Captain Bartholomew said.

"Sargent Fish, ask him how many groups are in here."

"No can-do boss, he is finding out how many virgins are waiting for him."

"I have to get this to higher ups asap and I should do it in person."

Sargent Michaels take over clean up this mess and the one at the water hole and then stand by here.

Captain Bartholomew got into a van and took off.

Ken helped where he could in cleaning up after the fight and during this, he saw that Betty seemed relatively calm for what happened.

The special ops guys took the bodies out into the desert and left the scavengers do their job. They then came to the trailer and took up positions around the trailer a couple of hundred feet away. As night came Betty started shaking. I knew what was coming. I went to her and held her close, saying everything is alright the guys will pull security and we can get some sleep. In the morning we will have to decide what we want to do.

There was a light knock on the trailer door and I thought Betty would jump out of her skin. Looking out, I saw two of the special ops men so I opened the door. One came up, "I'm Mitch but they call me doc, is Betty ok." He asked?

"Yes, just a little jumpy." I replied.

"Well, she should be, she isn't trained for this, you and us we have been there but she hasn't. May I see her?" he asked.

"Yes, come in and he went to Betty. Betty," he said, "I'm Mitch, the squad's medic, I would like to check your blood pressure and ask you a few questions will you be ok with this?"

Betty agreed and when Mitch was finished, he made sure Betty took a pill he gave her saying it would help her to sleep.

I asked what about me, Mitch looked at me and said, "take two aspirins and call me in the morning," then he left.

The head-ache came just as I remembered them and I took the aspirins. I saw Betty was getting sleepy eyed so I told her to go to bed and I would clean up the trailer.

I awoke with a start grabbing my rifle, then I remembered where I was and what happened. Looking at the clock, 04:30, crap too early to get up but too late to go back to sleep, so I quietly got out of bed and looked at Betty, she was still out so I went to the kitchen and quietly made a pot of coffee. Filling a thermos, I grabbed some cups then quietly went outside.

I heard a low whistle to my left and went there first it was an operator I didn't know but he was appreciative of the coffee and we sat there in the dark sipping coffee just looking out across the landscape.

It's strange how some people can just sit and not say anything but say everything. I heard two more low whistles and went and gave them cups and coffee also.

The sun was coming up so I went inside the trailer and made another pot of coffee and started making a big breakfast of French Toast, Bacon and Scrambled Eggs. I knew the guys would be hungry and MRE's just are nasty.

Betty came down from the bedroom I looked at her and immediately knew. We have to talk I said but first here is coffee and breakfast eat it will be good for you.

Captain Bartholomew drove very fast, breaking all speed limits and arrived at the team's base of operations. There was a helicopter waiting for him, he quickly secured his gear taking only his sidearm and a clean change of uniforms with him. He was airborne within an hour headed for Ft. Hood. They landed at the Killeen-Ft. Hood Regional airport and there was an Air Force Lear jet waiting for him its engines were started as he walked across the ramp to it.

His bag was stowed and as he took his seat as the airplane started moving. Capt. Bart fell asleep almost immediately. He often said the fastest way to get somewhere when flying is to go to sleep. He woke when the engines were throttled back for landing.

An excerpt from the book NOMADS

He surmised it would be Dulles airport and when the jet landed, he knew he was wrong it was Pope Air Force Base. As the aircraft's engines were shutting down the aircraft passenger door opened and he saw Air Force One sitting on the tarmac.

General Bixby the Army Chief of Staff came walking toward him. Captain Bartholomew saluted the general and was relieved of his bag by the generals aid a Major.

"I must apologize for my appearance," Captain Bartholomew said.

"Don't worry about it, most of us were Captains once." He followed the general and was led to Air Force One.

There was a truck with stairs against the side of it and two men at the bottom. I could see bulges under their jackets. This will be interesting I thought since I was still carrying my sidearm.

As we approached one of them stepped forward and said, "Captain Bartholomew we will hold that for safe keeping and we will return it to you when you leave."

I looked at the General and he gave a slight nod. I handed over my service pistol to one of the secret service agents and followed the general up the stairs. He stepped inside the door and turned right with me following him to a large conference room.

The president was at the head of the table and all the joint chiefs of the different military branches as well as the secretary of defense and state.

The president looked up and motioned Captain Bartholomew to sit which he did so rather stiffly.

"When was the last time you had a meal?" the president asked?

Captain Bartholomew looked at his watch then up, "it's been a little over 36 hours ago sir." he replied.

The president looked at the Secretary of State and said, "go find my chef, ham, eggs, how would you like them, Captain?" "Scrambled would be fine sir," "eggs scrambled, home fries and have him bring in a large pot of coffee and then make more. Then you come back here."

The Secretary of State left and almost immediately and returned.

"Captain if you would please fill us in from the beginning." The president asked.

##

247

APPENDIX

(1) On the morning of September 1, 1859, amateur astronomer Richard Carrington ascended into the private observatory attached to his country estate outside of London. After cranking open the dome's shutter to reveal the clear blue sky, he pointed his brass telescope toward the sun and began to sketch a cluster of enormous dark spots that freckled its surface. Suddenly, Carrington spotted what he described as "two patches of intensely bright and white light" erupting from the sunspots. Five minutes later the fireballs vanished, but within hours their impact would be felt across the globe.

That night, telegraph communications around the world began to fail; there were reports of sparks showering from telegraph machines, shocking operators and setting papers ablaze. All over the planet, colorful auroras illuminated the nighttime skies, glowing so brightly that birds began to chirp and laborers started their daily chores, believing the sun had begun rising. Some thought the end of the world was at hand, but Carrington's naked eyes had spotted the true cause for the bizarre happenings: a massive solar flare with the energy of 10 billion atomic bombs. The flare spewed electrified gas and subatomic particles toward Earth, and the resulting geomagnetic storm—dubbed the "Carrington Event"—was the largest on record to have struck the planet.

Charles Brobst

Bright Flare, Dark Lines

Compared to today's information superhighway, the telegraph system in 1859 may have been a mere dirt road, but the "Victorian Internet" was also a critical means of transmitting news, sending private messages and engaging in commerce. Telegraph operators in the United States had observed local interruptions due to thunderstorms and northern lights before, but they never experienced a global disturbance like the one-two punch they received in the waning days of summer in 1859.

Many telegraph lines across North America were rendered inoperable on the night of August 28 as the first of two successive solar storms struck. E.W. Culgan, a telegraph manager in Pittsburgh, reported that the resulting currents flowing through the wires were so powerful that platinum contacts were in danger of melting and "streams of fire" were pouring forth from the circuits. In Washington, D.C., telegraph operator Frederick W. Royce was severely shocked as his forehead grazed a ground wire. According to a witness, an arc of fire jumped from Royce's head to the telegraphic equipment. Some telegraph stations that used chemicals to mark sheets reported that powerful surges caused telegraph paper to combust.

On the morning of September 2, the magnetic mayhem resulting from the second storm created even more chaos for telegraph operators. When American Telegraph Company employees arrived at their Boston office at 8 a.m., they discovered it was impossible to transmit or receive dispatches. The atmosphere was so charged, however, that operators made an incredible discovery: They could unplug their batteries and still transmit messages to Portland, Maine, at 30- to 90-second intervals using only the auroral current. Messages still couldn't be sent as seamlessly as under normal conditions, but it was a useful workaround. By 10 a.m. the magnetic disturbance abated enough that stations reconnected their batteries, but transmissions were still affected for the rest of the morning.

Sky on Fire

When telegraphs did come back on line, many were filled with vivid accounts of the celestial light show that had been witnessed the night before. Newspapers from France to Australia featured glowing descriptions of brilliant auroras that had turned night into day. One eyewitness account from a woman on Sullivan's Island in South Carolina ran in the Charleston Mercury: "The eastern sky appeared of a blood red color. It seemed brightest exactly in the east, as though the full moon, or rather the sun, were about to rise. It extended almost to the zenith. The whole island was illuminated. The sea reflected the phenomenon, and no one could look at it without thinking of the passage in the Bible which says, 'the sea was turned to blood.' The shells on the beach, reflecting light, resembled coals of fire."

The sky was so crimson that many who saw it believed that neighboring locales were on fire. Americans in the South were particularly startled by the northern lights, which migrated so close to the equator that they were seen in Cuba and Jamaica. Elsewhere, however, there appeared to be genuine confusion. In Abbeville, South Carolina, masons awoke and began to lay bricks at their job site until they realized the hour and returned to bed. In Bealeton, Virginia, larks were stirred from their sleep at 1 a.m. and began to warble. (Unfortunately for them, a conductor on the Orange & Alexandria Railroad was also awake and shot three of them dead.) In cities across America, people stood in the streets and gazed up at the heavenly pyrotechnics. In Boston, some even caught up on their reading, taking advantage of the celestial fire to peruse the local newspapers.

Ice core samples have determined that the Carrington Event was twice as big as any other solar storm in the last 500 years. What would be the impact of a similar storm today? According to a 2008 report from the National Academy of Sciences, it could cause "extensive social and economic disruptions" due to its impact on power grids, satellite communications and GPS systems. The potential price tag? Between $1 trillion and $2 trillion.

(2) U.S. Military Field Phones, by Ken in Michigan
JAMES WESLEY RAWLES APRIL 2, 2021

If you are looking for a secure communication system for your farm, ranch, or retreat, then look into a military phone system. You can create an ideal communication system, any size, from two positions overnight to multiple positions in a large permanent retreat.

Military Field Phones ("MFPs") do not require external power. They are designed to operate in adverse conditions and most importantly, do not emit any electronic signal. MFPs cannot be overheard by radio scanners or radio direction finders. MFPs keep your location undetected by electronic surveillance, unlike today's radio communications that can be overheard and DF-located using today's technology. Radios are also subject to interference, intentional or unintentional, friendly enemy or atmospheric. The only disadvantage in using a MFP is the requirement of the use of hard wire. A two-wire cable is used to connect the phones. This is "old-school," otherwise known as POTS (plain old telephone system).

A little history is needed to fully understand the MFP: The first US MFP system was developed in 1910. In WW1, the EE3 phone was used with good success. In 1932, the MFP was improved and was standardized with the EE8 phone and the BD71 and BD72 switchboards connected using WD-1 wire, which aided in better communication. In the beginning of WW2, the EE8 phones had leather cases. The leather cases were replaced with a hard canvas case in 1944 (the leather did not hold up as well in the South Pacific during the Vietnam War; the canvas just rotted away). In 1967, the hard canvas case was replaced with a nylon case.

During the Vietnam War, the equipment improved with the TA-1 PT, TA-43 PT and TA-312 PT phones. The phones were connected with the SB-22 switchboard and had improved wire (WD-1A).

All of the MFP equipment is interchangeable and compatible. The 1930's equipment can be used with all of the 1960 and 1970's equipment. The plus is the MFP can be used with foreign nations phone equipment as well. I currently have four German phones in my inventory. I cannot personally guarantee that the Russia and Warsaw Pact's will work with our simplex **analog** phone system.

Here are some of the basics of how the phone system works:

- Each phone contains a hand crank generator that produces 90-100 volts AC at approximately 20 Hz (which signals the receiving phone to answer the call). This generator is strictly for signaling and has nothing to do with voice communications.
- Communication is a "push to talk" button, just like any 2-way radio system. The system has a carbon microphone and uses 2 D-Cell batteries (referred to as BA-30 in the manual). The 2 D-Cell batteries give, in series, three volts of DC to amplify the voice communication.

The most basic system would be to connect two phones together. No switchboard necessary and polarity is not a problem. Several phones can be connected this way, but all phones would ring at the same time. It would be possible to work out a code: 1 crank to answer phone #1 and 2 cranks to answer phone #2, etc. There would be a limited number of phones to be connected this way. For most users, we would use a simple wiring system called the Platoon Hot Loop. This puts all the phones in a series, with no switchboard. Simply connect the first phone with the wire, pair one wire on each terminal on both terminals at the 2nd and any other intermediate phone (simply split the cable and only cut one wire). Terminate the two cut ends on the next phone leaving one wire uncut. The last phone is where you connect the two wires to the two terminals for connection, just like the first phone. This places all the phones in a loop in series. Polarity of the connection does not matter using this system. I found this in an article regarding TA-1 phones, but I do not see why it would not work on other field phones.

The next step up is to set up a SB-933/GT switchboard (Manual TM 11-5805-294-12). The switchboard is a small device weighing about 2 lbs. And consists of a terminal strip with moveable lighted plugs to connect to different lines. This system can be used for up to 7 phones and also requires an operator to answer the call and connect the call. The next larger system uses a SB-22 switchboard and weighs approximately 30 lbs. and can handle up to 12 lines. When a remote phone call is received, a buzzer alerts the operator of an incoming call. There is also a black flag on the incoming line that will flip white. The operator then plugs his phone cable into that line to connect with the caller. If the caller needs to communicate with another position, the operator can then connect to the desired phone line. In a common use situation, the switchboard would be in the headquarters requiring someone on duty at all times. The remote phone should be located at an observation post, defense position or sleeping quarters, etc.

The MFP's range is listed at 14 miles in wet conditions and up to 22 miles under ideal conditions. There are various manuals with conflicting tables, so you may have different results. In the technical manual,TM-11-333, page 10 ranges varied from 11 to 100 miles for point-to-point systems, with different wire sizes. Communications can be used up to 360 miles with the use of overhead phone poles with open wires for point-to-point systems. A point-to-point system consists of batteries at each field phone and also at the switchboard. A switchboard-powered system consists of a power supply system at the switchboard and no batteries at the individual field phones. The range of this system is reduced by half the distance of a point-to-point system.

Another table shows range as 230 miles with a pair of #14 copper wires and 520 miles on a part of #12 copper wires. The switchboard power system must have the 3 volt DC for communication and a supply of 90 volt AC for signaling. This would be only be useful for extra large systems or to replace having to use D-cell batteries, at both the phone and switchboard. If you could limit a solar panel to 3 volt DC, that could work. Still use a hand crank for signaling to the phones. Switch the selector switch on the TA43/PT and TA312/PT phones from LB (local battery) to CB (common battery). There are several power supplies to provide this power either from 24 volt DC or 120/240 volt AC. For a 24 volt DC power source, use a PP-990/G power supply. For 120/240 volt AC, use the TA248 or 248A/TT power supplies. (Technical manual TM11-5805-304-14.)

Military phone wire is not a necessity. For the simplex analog phones referenced, they require a two (2) conductor cable. Any two

(2) conductor cable will work as an extension wire, speaker wire or phone cord. It is even possible to use a single conductor with one terminal grounded at each phone. This will greatly reduce the range of communication. The military specification wire would still be best, it is designed for this use, if you can get enough.

JWR Adds: For permanent or semi-permanent installation at or between farms, ranches, or retreats, you can use any sturdy signal wire that is rated for underground (buried) use.

COMMON SIMPLEX ANALOG EQUIPMENT:

- EE-8 phone (used from 1932 to the 1980's); 2 D-cell batteries required; total weight approximately 10 lbs. Technical Manual TM-11-333
- TA-43/PT a much more compact phone with a canvas case and hand set; buzzer volume control; 2 D-cell batteries required; total weight approximately 9 lbs. Technical Manual TM-11-5805-256-13
- TA-312/PT almost the same as the TA-43/pt but now has a receptacle to accept a H-144 headset instead of a handset; 2 D-cell batteries required and total weight approximately 9 lbs. Technical Manual TM-11-5805-201-13
- Additional manuals:
  TM11-5805-201-23P (Parts Manual) TM11-5805-201-12 (Operator Manual) TM11-5805-201-35 (Maintenance Manual)
- TA-1PT a compact phone, totally within the handset. It has a buzzer control volume that can be turned off when needed and has a black and white spinning disc to notify of incoming calls. No batteries required, but range is reduced from 3-4 miles. Comes with a hard plastic holster and canvas bag to be worn on your belt or carried in your pocket. Technical Manual TM11-5805-243-13, approximately 3.5 lbs.

*Additional manual: TM11-5805-243-23P (parts).

Optional Amplifier: TA-287/G. This will add 24 miles to the range of any single phone.

Switchboards:

- SB-993/GT is a simple mini switchboard that can handle 7 lines, no batteries required.
- BD71, WW2 and Korea era. It is a wooded case with folding legs, handles 6 lines and requires batteries.
- BD72, WW2 and Korea era. This is the same as the BD71, but handles 12 lines.
- SB-22/PT Vietnam era. This is a 12 line switchboard with an aluminum case and is more compact and durable than the earlier wooden cased switchboard systems. This switchboard weighs 30 lbs. And two can be stacked together to create a total capacity of 29 lines, when assembled with an accessory cord pack.

  Technical Manual TM11-5805-262-12 (Operational Manual) Technical ManualTM-5805-262-35 (Field and Maintenance Manual)
- SB-86/P is a 30 line, expandable to 60 lines, 180 lb switchboard with a watertight case. This system is beyond most of our needs. This is used at brigade level to communicate with battalions.

While I have been listing manuals, one good one for the larger system is FM24-20, Field Wire and Cable Techniques. This manual covers running phone wires and splicing. It also lists other equipment to put larger systems together. This manual makes it easier to understand how systems work together.

Wire (most commonly used): Early wire was a twisted pair of 22 gauge copper wire with rubber and cotton insulation. The most common wire we see today is WD-1A/TT, which consists of 2 conductors of 20 gauge wire. Four of the seven strands are copper and the remaining three strands are steel. This gives the wire a 200 lb pound tensile strength with a black nylon extruded jacket. This weighs 48 lbs. per mile. A second common surplus wire is WF 16/U, consisting of a red/green twisted pair of wires. This weighs 62 lbs. per mile.

Wire Reels:

- The most common (and handiest) wire reel is the DR-8 (9" diameter x 8 1/4" wide). It holds 1/4 mile (1,320 ft) of WD-1/TT wire and weighs 12 lbs. It has a 2 post terminal strip (M-221 connector) with the inner end of the wire connected to it. It will hold more of the thinner WD-1A/TT wire and up to a mile (5,280 ft) of WD-36/TT wire that comes in canvas donuts. The purpose of the terminal strip on the reel allows you to unreel only the amount of wire needed without cutting wire off. Connect the phone to the terminal strip and re-reel wire when done. There is a hand cranked dispenser and can be unreeled with one hand or can be mounted on a backpack frame or shoulder straps to rewind. This is a RL-39.
- The next larger reel is the RL-159 (19 1/4" diameter x 7" wide) that holds two kilometers (6,562 ft) of WD-1A/TT wire. This reel has a square 1" hole to mount on a hand or machine-driven reel machine. The largest reel (for our use) is a DR-5 (19 1/4" diameter x 18" wide) that holds 2 1/2 miles of WD-1A/TT wire (120 lbs of wire). This goes on a vehicle. You will need a braking system to stop or slow its spin. If you allow a reel to over-spin, you are going to have a big mess. Imagine a giant fishing reel full of backlash (or a birds nest).
- The one wire we haven't talked much about is the WD-36TT (assault wire), a 2 conductor 22 gauge aluminum wire cable (9 lbs per mile, tensile 25 lbs). Black nylon jacket that comes in canvas donuts (cannot be put back in donut). Original Vietnam era canvas donut MX-306A/G, 1/2 mile of WD-1/TT (2,640 ft) weighing 23 lbs, 13" diameter x 6 1/2 deep (obsolete by 1967).
- The same MX-306A/G (1/2 mile) was upgraded to the WD-1A/TT and was produced until about 1995. More current and available are the MX-6895/TT (2 1/4 lbs for 1/4 mile) and the MX-6894/TT (4 1/4 lbs for 1/2 mile).

General rule for Donut Wire: Do not prewire — use only when needed. One person can carry four 1/4 mile donuts, dispense while walking, splice together as needed (9 lbs per one mile). When done with this wire, roll it up on an empty DR8 reel.

Reel Winding Tools:

- We mentioned the RL-39 for the smallest reel, DR-8. For the RL-159 reel use a RL-31E. Basically, a folding sawhorse that can handle (2) RL-195 or (1) DR-5. This has a crank handle and a manual brake.
- A power reel machine for RL-159 reel mounts on a Jeep or other vehicle and is run by a 24V DC motor. It's A RL-172, weighing 100 lbs (TM11-3895-207-14). The reel machine for the DR-5 reel is gas engine driven, it is a RL-207 (weight 500 lbs) [a pipe across a stepladder will work too!].

All of the simplex analog equipment mentioned above will work with each other from WW1, WW2, Korea and Vietnam. The more modern military phone equipment goes digital and is requiring a 4 wire cable. This allows direct dial from phone-to-phone and eliminates the need for a switchboard operator. The most common digital phone system I have seen available is the TA-838/TT and SB-4170/TT switchboard. There is a tone signaling adapter to put on the SB22/PT switchboard to connect to some digital phones. I have not worked on digital phone systems, so I will leave that to someone else. I hope that what I wrote will allow others to understand the MPF systems.

(3) An Ahkio sled or scow sled is designed for people to pull heavy cargo over snow. It's perfect for hauling a tent, food, and other supplies to a hunting site or other remote snow-covered locations. It can also be used as a deer sled or for evacuating someone who is injured or ill.

The heavy canvas tarp protects supplies from weather. The rope and hook system ties down the tarp over the contents so everything stays securely in the sled. Towing the sled is facilitated with a system of U-bolts. The bottom of the sled has rounded sides and three heavy-duty runners so you can easily maneuver your haul over the snow.

Ahkio Sled Specifications

(2) Dimensions: 88" x 24" x 8"
(3) Capacity: 200 lbs
(4) Color: White
(5) Sled Material: Rigid Plastic
(6) Cover Material: Heavy cotton canvas tarp
(7) Sled Weight: 38 lbs

www.ingramcontent.com/pod-product-compliance
Lightning Source LLC
LaVergne TN
LVHW041911070526
838199LV00051BA/2581